CULTISTS

CULTISTS

ELYSIUM'S MULTIVERSE | BOOK 3

Ranyhin1

Podium

Podium

CULTISTS

CHAPTER 1

Justin's gigantic body roiled and churned, warping into something greater as dark metal tore through the air around him and through him like a cyclone of the profane. He was a walking apocalypse, a titan of a man, born from the Unholy powers of this universe to pass judgment on those weaker than himself.

And he would not be undone by this nobody.

The cobblestone street beneath him shattered, and Justin launched himself like a rocket from hell, swinging his enormous, spiked mace with a thunderclap of power, a cloud of shrapnel tearing through space around him.

The shrouded rogue he was fighting, another participant in the Chalgathi trials, dove left in a blur of shadow that sent wraithlike daggers whipping out from his trajectory in a torrent of shadow mana. The man easily avoided the first colossal swing, flipping onto a nearby thatched roof and then shifting through space twenty meters away. Whipping around and pulling out a crossbow laden with putrefying bolts, the rogue used an ability to rapid-fire replicas of the enchanted bolts in a hail of projectiles.

Despite the enormous amount of incoming missiles, Justin's cloud of whirling shrapnel was fiercer, and the majority of the bolts were easily blocked. Those that did land either bounced off his thick metal armor entirely or only lodged partway. Unfortunately for the rogue, though, this was not nearly enough. The putrefaction did not take hold, because what kind of poison could affect a body created from Unholy metal?

Justin's muscles flexed, and with a roar, he swept his enormous mace in the rogue's direction that sent shock waves of kinetic energy ripping through the town structures and blasting the rogue skyward in a scrambling and uncontrolled flight.

"Forsake the heavens and bring me fury!" Justin finished the miracle's incantation with a sweeping gesture of his arms into the sky. In an instant, demonic hieroglyphs lit up in the center of a flaming pentagram high above.

CRASH

The sky above the rogue exploded, and the clawed, flaming hand of some untold behemoth ripped out from the infernal pits of hell to smash down into the screaming man. The rogue was flattened from above in a fiery explosion that leveled entire streets, dissipating into a tornado of infernal flames that continued to billow into his enemy, and Justin's whirling cloud of black metal soared higher as he yet again blasted forward to cover the distance.

But just when he was about to reach the site of impact, his danger sense screamed at him to dodge left.

Unquestioningly, he pivoted and rolled, narrowly avoiding a black laser beam that left remnant holes in the fabric of space itself for seconds afterward. Justin's eyes narrowed, looking at the burned figure of his opponent, who was stumbling out of an alley, spitting blood.

Justin glanced back to the still-raging tornado of flames, then to the rogue again. He picked himself up and leveled his mace, easily weighing over a thousand pounds, with just one arm at the Agility user. "How did you get out of it? That miracle is supposed to keep you locked in place."

The smoking man let out a raspy, gasping fit of laughter, then fell to one knee and dropped his crossbow. His eyes slowly lifted, part of his face still burning while he sneered. "Fuck you, Justin . . . You fucking prick . . . *GASP* . . . When the others find out what you've done, they'll hunt you down . . . Just like . . . *GASP* . . . You did to me . . ."

Justin couldn't help but let out a low chuckle, and he shook his head in disgust. "Daniel. You don't understand . . . The cult was only a means to an end in the beginning. That end was to reach Chalgathi, and we accomplished that."

Justin held up both hands to either side, turning around and gesturing at the ruined town where family members sobbed over loved ones and the injured cried out for help. "All of this world, Daniel, is for the taking . . . but there can only be one king. Outside of ideologies, the cult is no more now that its purpose is solved. The goal is the same—it always has been for men like you and me, but we were never friends. We were allies of circumstance alone, and after the trials were completed . . . I had no more use of you. Just like the others have no more use of me. No doubt they will hunt me down, but I am hunting them. So are we all hunting one another in order to acquire the artifacts needed to breach the resting place of destiny."

He turned back around and began walking toward the other man with his mace resting on one shoulder. "There can only be one to lay claim to the prize, Daniel. There can only be one king. I am sorry. Well, not really, but I need your Chalgathi artifact . . . and we both know you'd come after me if I let you live after taking it."

Justin approached with a malicious smile from underneath his layers of fused armor, and his cloud of shrapnel began tearing the smaller man apart—ripping pieces of his body off in a gore-laden spray. Daniel didn't scream but merely glared while he was violently torn asunder.

The cloud of shrapnel receded soon after Daniel died, pulling back into Justin's body. He smiled wickedly and knelt down, picking up the items he had come for. They were completely undamaged from his assault on the prior wearer, and he could feel the mana-bond that kept them a single unit despite being physically separate.

They were gauntlets, and each was a masterpiece. A testament of Unholy might. When the rogue had worn them, they were made of red leather, with small knives protruding from each knuckle and green runes adorning them. However, when Justin picked them up, the gauntlets changed into a solid, iron-like substance, still adorned with the same flickering, Unholy green runes and casting an ominous aura of malice just by looking at them.

[Chalgathi Cultist Claws: ???]

He frowned, but not for long. No doubt he'd have to go back to that trashy identifier again to get a read. Still, he'd acquired what he'd come for. It was one more piece to the set; he had two of the five now, including his breastplate, and the quest line hadn't even propagated fully yet.

He was way ahead of the curve.

When he put the gauntlets on, his metal body fused over each of them and incorporated the pieces into his shell. Feeling a pulse of power and a chilling sensation overcome him, Justin let his mind frolic in the feeling of success and let out a long sigh of contentment.

"THERE HE IS! HE'S OVER HERE! CALL THE—"

CRASH

The soldier's body splattered across the cobblestone street, leaving a bloody trail behind his corpse. Justin blinked, snorted, and slowly turned away from the burning town to make his way south. He still had an agenda to keep, and although he was way ahead of where he thought he'd be at this point in time— that didn't mean he could get lazy.

It was time to set up the ritual again. It was time to find more targets.

[System Quest Eradicate the Greenskins has been disbanded due to failure to hold up your end of the bargain with the high elves of Greenstalk village.]

[Hidden System Quest Backstabbing Pointy-Eared Racist Bastards has been successfully completed by defeating the elves who tried to trick and kill you.]

System Regional Quest Crusade Against the Undead has been defeated after killing Benjamin, otherwise known as Prophet.

You have angered the minor Holy god Petori due to your actions. You have pleased the apocalypse beast Chalgathi due to your actions. Your B-ranked prize previously promised through the failed quest Eradicate the Greenskins has been upgraded into an A-ranked prize due to your actions:

- **Your Elysium altar (currently in rod form) has been given the Unholy orientation with terraforming abilities and strengthens those of the Unholy foundational pillar as long as they are within its area of effect on terraformed land. Your Elysium altar will now increase your ability to cultivate all Unholy foundational pillar and associated subpillar Daos within its area of effect. Terraforming landscape is permanent when chosen, gives different unique bonuses depending on which type of Unholy landscape is chosen, and may be selected between randomly rolled options of Haunted Forest, Hellscape, and Shadowlands. Additional options are available for purchase if you wish to pay the appropriate fee. Your Elysium altar now has the ability to forcibly orient <u>willing</u> participants toward the Unholy foundational pillar for an appropriate fee, rewriting their original orientations completely but with similar affinity percentages.]**

The army of goblins, orcs, and undead marched on either side of the lines of shackled elves making their way north toward Brightsville. Not only had the greenskins brought their fighting force, but they'd brought their entire civilian population, which took up the rear end of the columns. Simultaneously the greenskins had small groups of escorts protect them from local monsters. The humans following Prophet had all been butchered mercilessly, while the majority of the elf village had been successfully subdued without much resistance given their loss of manpower over the last weeks.

Looking out from underneath his hood, Riven's glowing red eyes gazed impassively across their ranks from atop a hill in the light of midday. Allie's distant tower could be seen from here, shimmering even in the daylight with teal and black power while her bone garden continued to terraform the structure.

How fast that would speed up after he planted the Elysium altar's rod was only speculation at this point.

Sniffling and the rattling of chains to his left caused Riven's head to turn, and beside him the elf Genua—mother to Ethel—was wiping away more tears while glaring bloodshot eyes his way. Her usually silky blond hair was frazzled and caked with mud, and her occasional glance toward the group of elf children being gently herded by skeletal undead caused her brows to furrow in worry.

He stared at her, undisturbed by her source of mourning. Her scantily clad body, which he'd once upon a time found attractive, just like her daughter Ethel's, now did nothing but disgust him. She, her husband, Farrod, her eldest daughter, Ethel, and the entirety of their village had tricked him and tried to kill him. For what? For helping them and saving their lives? They'd played themselves off as victims when they'd started the war with the greenskin village in the first place, and then they'd tried to murder him simply because of what he was even though he'd shown them nothing but kindness.

Well, his kindness was gone now. It was long, long gone.

"Will you eat her?" Genua's voice cracked with emotional pain, head bobbing toward the large group of children who'd been separated from their parents. "Will you kill Len like you killed my husband and my other daughter?"

Riven snorted with derision, hands shoved into the pockets of his cloak while his staff, Vampire's Escort, hovered in the air at his side. "Please. You all had this coming, and your punishment is more than generous after what you tried. Do not act like the victim here. As for Len, no. I absolutely will not kill her. I intend to re-educate all the elf children so they can grow up into adults with futures in our community. We can't have you racist fucks raising a bunch of future enemies that'll try to rise up against us. My sister, Allie, wanted those kids immediately killed, but I refused. This was the compromise."

Genua's knees shook, her cracked lips trembled, and she fell to her knees with a single audible sob. She'd long since cried any tears she had left and was becoming dehydrated. "Will I ever get to speak to her again? To my darling daughter Len?"

Riven raised an eyebrow, then followed her gaze to where the spunky little blonde girl in a reed dress, whom he'd become so fond of, was marching with scared glances up the hill toward their position. He didn't know what to think of Len, honestly. She'd only done what her family had told her to do; perhaps she was too young to really understand the meaning and consequences behind her actions. Could he expect anything less of a child, even though she'd lied to him as well?

He let out a long, drawn-out sigh. "Yes, you'll be able to see her. But only under certain circumstances."

"Which are?" Genua pressed with a shaking voice.

"You'll either be chaperoned each visit, or you'll allow yourself to be made into a thrall. Stay a slave with supervision on regular visitation periods or become a thrall and allow your mind to be warped so you don't hold us in a negative light. I hear it isn't so bad, and some people even actively pursue such a route for power. Or so I'm told." Riven gestured toward the hundreds of enslaved elves marching between the military columns. "The same goes for all of them. The adults of your village won't be forced into backbreaking labor, but they'll still be forced to work and will be allowed to live simple but happy lives if you choose to make it that way. I can make that promise because you're all my charge now; you're my cattle, my personal slaves, or, to think better of it, you are all slaves of the new government of the Thane Necropolis.

"That government is split down the middle between Allie and me, and Allie wants nothing to do with you. She thinks your bodies would be better used as more willing, undead participants rather than with your souls inside you. But it was my decision to keep you alive. The people of your village that can't work because they're too old and weak will be made into cattle for the vampires as we create a coven within this necropolis we've built, but you'll all be treated fairly enough. For those of you who wish it, becoming a thrall will be an option if you manage to persuade one of the vampires or future vampires here to do so."

Genua took her eyes off the column and gave him a scathing glare again. Her fists trembled in rage, and he could tell that she was holding the venom back from her words. "You want to turn us into monsters like you."

Riven shrugged. "Think about it however you want. I don't give a shit. This is your life now, the consequences of your actions. We could not just leave a fanatic group of racist elves and holy warriors wandering the wilds nearby our newly established faction, so pucker up and deal with it."

He blinked her way and waved back to Fay when the Succubus flew overhead, gliding over the columns and circling back around toward the mountains. Then he turned his head to look at her one more time. "You know, Genua, I had hoped this would turn out very differently. But it didn't go as either of us hoped, and now we're here. You'll get to see Len regularly, regardless of whether or not you choose to become my thrall, but if you want unrestricted access, that's the only way to go about it. Either way I'm going to feed on you weekly, or daily, or whatever suits my needs—because I don't care anymore, because I need blood to survive, and because I want to make you remember who it was that you fucked with at the end of every day before you go to bed. The others are dead—all the other elves I knew are now dead. Gone. You and Len are the only ones remaining, and call it petty if you want, but I want to rub it in your face every time you see me succeed. I want you to know that I could have been your friend, an ally to your family, but instead you and yours chose this. You tried to murder me for nothing but my good will, and now you pay the consequences."

He gestured to Azmoth, who was standing behind them and listening curiously. "Come on, Azmoth, pull her along. We've still got a long march ahead of us, and we have to make it to the meeting with that rat man Snagger. No need to dilly-dally."

Azmoth grunted in acknowledgment and yanked on Genua's chain, following Riven down the hill, dragging the elf along by her shackles until she managed to get her feet under her again and stumble to a walk.

For the captured villagers of Greenstalk, it was going to be a very long trip.

CHAPTER 2

Marching their army through the ruined southern reaches of Brightsville toward downtown was quite a novel experience. It appeared there were a lot more undead than before, a LOT more, and a crowd of them was waiting at the city's edge when they arrived to wave them in and cheer on their success.

"Scouts were sent ahead to let them know Prophet was killed," Allie stated with a nod in the direction of the cheering populace on either side of the road. "Makes you feel good, doesn't it?"

Riven just took it all in, not knowing what to say in reply. Most of the undead populace that weren't mindless minions were the skeletal humanoids called skresh or the fleshy humanoids called ghouls. They were a step up from zombies or skeletons, which by default were mindless or only involved soul shards instead of true souls. However, there were more than a handful of large, brutal-looking golems, both flesh and bone varieties. There were three bone giants, each the size of a three-story building, and a couple ethereal ghosts flew above the crowd, shimmering with dim gray or blue light.

There were even a couple of unique undead that the system called undead abominations, which essentially didn't fit the make or mold of anything else. They were each completely unique, no one abomination matching the next.

And all these creatures were cheering Allie's name.

"Allie! Allie! Allie! Allie!"

"Long live the queen!"

"Long stand the Thane Necropolis!"

Allie held up a hand for silence, and the column stopped. The crowds on either side of the street quickly went silent, completely obedient to the woman who'd kept them protected over the past months, and watched as she drew a severed, shredded head from a bag on her hip. She held it up for all to see just as four skeleton minions came up from behind to lift her over their shoulders, and Allie yelled out while gesturing to Riven, "Many of you have just been born into this world for the very first time! Others come by happenstance through our bone garden, coming from other worlds where our kind is persecuted just because of what we are! You arrived here, hoping for a chance to find happiness and peace, only to be hunted down as in so many other places across the cosmos! BUT THAT ENDS NOW! THIS IS OUR CITY NOW! MY BROTHER HAS KILLED PROPHET! BEHOLD, THE HEAD OF THE MAN WHO TRIED TO PURGE US FROM THESE LANDS!"

In a fraction of an instant, the crowd went berserk, and many of Allie's new citizens rushed forward to try and touch or embrace the two vampires at the front of the army with screams for a job well done, sobs of pent-up relief, or outright calls for a holiday in their name.

Allie laughed and reached out to touch many of the crowd, letting herself be swooped away to crowd-surf the wave of undead. Riven, with a shrug at Azmoth, quickly joined her before being tugged away amid the chanting of Allie's name.

Night was now upon them, and the celebrations were still going on back at the tower downtown. Riven frankly couldn't believe that the sentient undead here were so . . . humanlike in their emotions. That thought made him quickly realize that he wasn't human any longer, either, yet he still felt human, so to judge these undead creatures—no, undead *people*—otherwise was wrong. They had feelings, emotions, hopes, and dreams just like any of the friends he knew growing up.

It was weird to think about. Mara or the more humanlike undead were easy to associate with, but some of the abominations really threw Riven off. He'd have to work on that. Not that they scared him or repulsed him, but he had a hard time identifying with them even though they were self-aware creatures with thoughts and feelings just like himself.

The garden was peaceful under the pale moonlight and starry sky, a quiet place on the southern edge of the city. A large willow tree stood in the center, gently swaying in the gentle night breeze. Its long, slender branches arched outward and down, providing a canopy that sheltered the tombstone underneath it. The crumbling remains of the old stone cathedral behind them would have added weight to the fact that this place had not been used in quite some time.

And yet . . . the flowers of the garden were all well cared for and organized. This was likely due to the single skeletal gardener who'd been posted there, a minion of Allie's who stood motionless in the shadows of the old cathedral, stoically watching the two vampires.

The tombstone was aged, probably over a century old, chipped and weathered by time and the elements. The inscriptions that had once been there had been smoothed out and replaced before Allie had moved it, with new lettering adorning the front that read, *Here lies Jose, a loving friend never forgotten. May you find peace and rest.*

Allie and Riven had both placed bouquets of flowers on the headstone, a testament to this man's life, and Riven was laughing and simultaneously crying as they retold stories of their old friend. The man they'd grown up with, a brother to both of them when their parents had vanished one after the other. Jose hadn't had any real family of his own, either—not any that he'd want to openly claim, anyway—and they'd all leaned on each other for emotional support over the years.

Sniffling but maintaining a smile at the thought of the last time Jose had tried to make cheese pancakes for the Thane siblings, Riven rubbed a hand over the tombstone and nodded to the ground beneath. "Wherever your soul is now, old friend, I hope beyond measure that you've finally learned how to cook."

Allie let out a sputtering, sobbing laugh, and the two of them hugged. "Who knows . . . his soul might awaken in some far-off part of the cosmos one day. Maybe he'll be cast adrift into a mindless sleep, forever, like so many others . . . but maybe not."

"If that day ever comes, I'll have him cook those damnable cheesy pancakes for us again so he can make up for the last failure." Riven sniffed, wiping away a tear with his hand and letting go of Allie. "Wow. That hit harder than I thought it would. I'd thought I'd been able to cope, but we're both a mess."

He cleared his throat, then looked out over the rolling fields on Brightsville's southern side just where the city ended. The forests to the southwest and west climbed up the mountainsides, and the changing colors of their leaves promised a shift in the seasons coming soon.

"So how'd you do it?" Allie asked hesitantly, standing beside him and looking over the countryside. "I'm still curious."

Riven continued staring ahead, hands shoved into his pockets. "You're talking about what happened with the elves and Prophet?"

Allie nodded. "Yes."

He paused, noticing Athela on the sidelines, giving them a wide space for privacy, then smiled and waved at her. The demoness gave him a brilliant grin, a heartfelt wave of her own, then disappeared into the shadows with Fay. "Well, there were a couple things."

Riven held up a finger, then started counting his fingers one by one as he mentally checked off the list. "First, the orc chieftain's words of warning caught me off guard. I'd just found out they hadn't been the aggressors and the elves were still adamant that the orcs leave without being willing to compromise—at least that's how Senna's father, Ren, put it. It rubbed me the wrong way and shed a different light on the elves than the one I'd garnered from fantasy novels as a kid. I realized I was just desperate for acceptance from people like me, but at the same time, I realized that the elves weren't anything like me anymore. The way they looked at me when I walked through their village was only barely polite, if that, and thinking about it made me wary. That's when you mentioned in one of our communications that Prophet got away from your forces and was looping southwest, according to your scouts, but you didn't know where his destination was and they were traveling fast. After that I sent Fay to scout it out from above, confirmed Prophet's trajectory as a straight shot for Greenstalk, with a single elf leading the way. I sent Fay back to negotiate with the orcs after that, and according to Gurth'Rok—their chieftain; many orc tribes change leaders through military domination or duels. He considered my battle at Greenstalk symbolic of my victory over him and pledged to me if we took his people under my wing. Then, lastly, was Ren, Senna's father. I baited him into admitting a couple things—I asked him if Ethel had told Ren about your recent battle with Prophet. Again, it was bait; I never told Ethel anything about that battle, but Ren confirmed he'd been told—so there was a good chance he was either lying or he'd been told by someone else. Coincidence, when Prophet's forces were headed directly for the elves and being led by an elf? I thought not."

Riven gestured up to the stone church where Fay and Athela were now sitting cross-legged, having a soft chat that the vampires could barely make out. "When I bonded with Fay, she gave me a trait called Silvertongue. Well, it's actually a spell now, because my physiology won't consider it a trait, but it does the same thing, just at a higher mana cost."

"Fay is the Succubus, right?"

"Right. Athela is the other one. You haven't been introduced, have you?"

"No, just in passing."

"We'll change that soon. I'm sure you'll love them. Azmoth, too. Anyways, Silvertongue is an Unholy ability that allows me to infuse words with Unholy mana. It allows me to capture the minds of lesser beings, those with lower Willpower than myself, but even people who have a lower Willpower stat can resist it if they try hard enough. Let's just say Ren's mind wasn't very resistant . . . and it was easy to make him talk."

He pulled up the status page for his Silvertongue ability and shifted the screen over to Allie so she could get a look.

[Silvertongue (Unholy): Soak your words with Unholy mana to briefly capture the minds of lesser beings, allowing only those with less Willpower than you to be affected and enabling you to persuade them more easily. This spell scales with both Willpower and negative Charisma, as well as the amount of mana you put into it. This spell may be developed into a better version of itself by acquiring the Depravity subpillar. Extremely high mana cost, low cooldown.]

Allie's eyes lifted. "Whoa. That's really useful, especially given our negative Charisma."

Riven nodded. "Yeah. My ability is all right, but it's only a shadow of Fay's—hers is even better because it is inherent to her species and she also has the correct subpillar. Whereas I was able to hold Ren's mind captive for a very short time, maybe thirty seconds, Fay can do it for minutes at a time. After Ren realized what I'd done in forcing him to admit the situation, he tried to run—but we tied him down in Athela's webbing and contacted you for a meetup. Azmoth volunteered to bring in barrels supplied by the orcs, using them as a trojan horse for the bombs I made, and Ren was dressed up in Fay's hallucinations to be sent down in my place when meeting the elves. The rest is history."

Allie shot the blue-skinned Succubus a wary look. "Those are some pretty formidable powers she has."

"Formidable if used right. She's more utility than anything else. Even though she does damage, it isn't as direct as what Athela or Azmoth can produce. She also has a trait that gives her bonuses while using curses, and although curses cause her pain when used, she's gotten accustomed to the backlash. Eventually she wants to pick up a curse-related class, and I've also been trying to teach her one of my own utility spells. It's called Wretched Snare. But she doesn't learn as fast as we do. It appears you and I, Allie, have rather unusual affinities and abilities than other people or creatures do."

Allie flippantly tossed her hair to the side. "I learn death magic at an extraordinary rate, apparently. The others I pick up on somewhat, but the Death subpillar is what I focus on, because I'm able to gain insights and learn those kinds of abilities thrice as fast as anything else."

"That's how I feel about my Blood subpillar. What's your affinity for Death?"

"One hundred percent."

"Ah. My Blood subpillar is 100 percent, which is probably why I oriented to it so fast. My Death subpillar is 95 percent, and I haven't learned a single spell related to death yet."

Allie grinned. "I can teach you! But your soul fractals are almost halfway used up in terms of space."

There was a long pause, and Riven's gaze slowly focused on his smaller sister. "Say what? What the hell are soul fractals?"

Allie raised her eyebrows in surprise and began to laugh. "You really didn't know?! Riven, you're telling me that you've come all this way only to learn about soul fractals just now?! What the heck were you doing that entire time in hell?!"

"Surviving," Riven muttered with a scowl, only getting another and louder laugh from Allie.

She held up a hand when he was about to protest. "Sorry! Sorry, I just think it's hilarious that you're so strong and have no idea. Have you at least seen your internal soul structure yet?"

Riven flatly stared, but nodded. "Yeah, I can see my soul complex rather easily. Whenever I want to, actually."

"Good. Now focus on your core, the one that your pillars are attached to. And . . . Wait, what the hell is that?!"

Riven inwardly directed his thoughts toward his soul complex. Allie's exclamation was no doubt directed toward the other orbiting black core that the shard of Gluttony was forming in his periphery. "That's Gluttony. Remember I told you about it last week?"

Allie gawked at the rotating ball of sinister soul energy and nodded slowly. She blinked, rubbing her eyes and redirecting her focus onto Riven's main core again with a shake of her head. "With necromancy I am able to see most soul structures . . . and I've never seen anything that malevolent. Riven, be very careful when interacting with Gluttony after it finally forms. Whatever it is, it's very sick and twisted . . . even for us."

Riven frowned at her comment. Gluttony had saved his life once, and it'd never felt sick or twisted to him. It felt right at home, so he disregarded her comment and moved on. That wasn't important right now. "So tell me about these soul fractals already."

Allie huffed. "All right, take a look at your pillars. See how your Blood subpillar has tiny etchings inscribed into the surface?"

Riven paused, then nodded. "Yeah, I see them."

"Okay, good. Well, whenever you utilize a spell, the system recognizes that spell and your pure energy erupts from your soul and into the pillar. These fractals orient the spells you create and are why only parts of your pillar can freeze up at a time, directly correlating with cooldowns when they happen. But do you see how the Blood subpillar you have in particular has far more etchings or patterns than the rest of your pillars? After that, your Unholy foundational pillar has the second most. To be exact, your Blood subpillar has four fractal patterns, two of which are larger than the others, which correlate with your Tier-2 and Tier-3 spells. Then your Unholy foundational pillar has three fractal patterns to correlate with your three Unholy spells. You have three Unholy spells, I assume?"

"Correct."

"Yeah, as I thought. After that you have one fractal pattern in your Infernal pillar and one in your Shadow pillar. Each fractal pattern takes up space along their individual pillars, but soon they start to spill out into your main core. If you look closely, your Blood and Unholy pillars have their fractals starting to trickle into the white center of your soul space, but though they can go into your core, they can't traverse into other pillars. This means that you and I and everyone else only have limited amounts of space to create spells that we can command. More pillars means more space as well, lower-tiered spells mean they take up less space, and every spell or ability is different in how much space it takes up. Even though

I am wary of your Gluttony core, it also means that you'll likely be able to create more spells on the separate core, too—allowing you to learn more abilities than what is normal."

Huh.

Riven rubbed his chin thoughtfully, then shook his head and ruffled Allie's hair with one hand despite her grunt of discontentment when she swatted at him. He smiled her way. "I think I'll take you up on that, but I only want to learn enough that can be kept within the Death subpillar itself. I'll be saving all my core space for blood. Is it possible to erase old spells to make room for new fractals?"

"Yes, yes, it is certainly possible—NOW STOP MESSING UP MY HAIR!"

CHAPTER 3

"Fine!" Riven laughed and held up both his hands in surrender when Allie whipped out her wand and started jabbing him in the side. "I'll stop fucking with your hair, okay! Jesus! OW!"

He snickered at her expression, then took a look at the fields of grass and wildflowers immediately adjacent to their position. "This should be a LOT more than three square miles. Are you ready?"

"As ready as I'll ever be. We barely have an idea of what to expect, so let's get it over with." Allie snorted and waved over Mara, Vin, and Nin, the three undead necromancers who Allie had befriended in her own trials. They'd been waiting dozens of yards away to give Riven and Allie some privacy before planting the Elysium altar's rod.

The three necromancers walked forward along with a host of undead minions. Riven's demons were all present, too, with Azmoth coming out of the ruined chapel to stand beside his master and the scarred orc chieftain Gurth'Rok followed the undead with a couple of his elites.

Azmoth presented Riven with the red box holding the rod, and the vampire warlock pulled out the item a moment later. It was mostly as he remembered it, but the colors had changed since acquiring an Unholy orientation. It still had golden trimmings along the shaft, but the shaft had turned from porcelain white to a deep gray color. The previously white jewel fitted in the top had turned from white to black.

[Elysium Altar Planting Rod (Unholy Orientation): Plant this rod into the ground to begin creating an Elysium altar. An altar requires at least three square miles of space in all dimensions in order to place it.]

Riven looked back at the others, then signaled Fay over to him. "Take me over."

The Succubus smiled, spread her wings, and her tail whipped about as she launched herself into the night sky while holding Riven by the waist.

She picked up speed, wind whistling by them as they traversed the grass-laden fields for only a minute before landing about four miles out. Riven intended to place his guild hall near Jose's grave, and he didn't want the altar immediately on his doorstep—rather, he wanted it just comfortably close by. Putting a mile or two in between his to-be home and the altar would mean he had to deal with less foot traffic but also would make it convenient to visit.

The Succubus gently brushed Riven's hair with slender blue fingers after the wind had tossed it about, stepping back with a slight bow and letting Riven find a spot. He wasn't too specific on any exact spot, so it only took him a couple of seconds before he slammed the rod like a spear into the earth beneath his feet.

[Do you wish to activate Elysium Altar Planting Rod (Unholy Orientation)? Doing so will lay claim to the Elysium Altar that forms, allowing you to choose a terraforming option from the presented list. You will also be able to select who can and cannot use the altar functions if you wish to exclude others. Killing you will change ownership of this altar to the one who has slain you. This Elysium Altar will take up approximately three square miles of land and is approximately twelve hundred feet tall at its highest point. After planting the rod, you will have opportunities to buy from the system store, or you may allow foreign entities across the multiverse to set up shop within your altar's structure if you and the trading partner meet the right requirements. This Unholy orientation also allows willing participants to change their affinities to those of the Unholy foundational pillar. Other Elysium Altar functions are available but locked until bought with the appropriate fee cost.]

Twelve hundred feet tall? That was almost the height of the World Trade Centers before September 11. This thing would be utterly huge.

Riven scratched the back of his neck with raised eyebrows, turning when he heard Fay cough to get his attention. "Yes?"

The Succubus met his gaze, then shuffled awkwardly and hummed. Clasping her hands behind her back, her tail went rigid and she set her posture straight with determination. "Um, my brother . . . He was wondering if he could join us after you set up your guild hall tonight?"

There was a long pause.

"Your . . . brother?" Riven asked curiously, one eyebrow raised in amusement. "Interesting. Why bring this up now?"

"Because you're probably going to hire a bunch of mercenaries to protect the guild hall and fill up the slots with other contracts soon. I wanted to get ahead and reserve him a spot . . ." She gave Riven a sheepish but hopeful smile. "He's honestly not that great at fighting, though . . . Honestly it's more that I'm asking a favor. In fact, the rest of my family thinks he's something of a failure. He doesn't like violence at all—not very . . . demonic. Even less so than me. He likes petting animals and exploring nature . . . that kind of thing. But I—"

A snorting laugh from Riven cut her off, and she immediately frowned. But he waved his hand in apology and bade her continue.

"It's not funny!" Fay stated, angrily puffing her cheeks and stamping her foot with clenched fists. "He's a terrible incubus and he gets bullied all the time! Can we at least talk about it later?! Before you decide?! I think this would be a good opportunity to get him out of a bad situation. Please?"

"You do realize I live a very violent life, right?"

"Yes, but binding to the guild hall isn't the same as binding to you with a minion contract!"

Riven's grin didn't fade, but his eyes softened slightly and he nodded. "Yeah, that's a conversation for later, though. We'll need to talk before I choose who or what can bind to the guild hall. It's also been a while, so I'll have to review the rules on binding. Anyways . . ."

He put his hand back on the planting rod and selected the option for claiming it as his own.

Overhead a clap of thunder roared, electrified clouds rapidly gathered in the sky, and a beam of sickly green light tore through the heavens to blast the rod and the entire area around it. Riven was shocked and fell backward, but it didn't hurt—the magic merely swirled around him and his Succubus like a gentle ocean wave.

And before his very eyes, the structure began to take form out of thin air.

Smooth beams of black metal rapidly rushed out of the ground, coated in jagged spikes that lifted skyward to form a circle that would be the perimeter of the altar. Obsidian plates covered the ground—some of them lifting into the air and condensing to interlock with one another, creating four enormous, separate platforms that hovered above the earth and encircled a huge towerlike spire that soared toward the heavens. The central black spire held no entrance in or out, it had no windows, and it was completely smooth—but a myriad of layered neon-green runes adorned its surface. A huge halo of green flames encircled the very top of the spire, casting the surrounding landscape in a dull green light until the fires dimmed to a more reasonable level.

After that, veiled walls of semitranslucent glass light started dropping down from the peripheries of the four platforms. They each flashed briefly when the walls touched down onto the dark plates along the ground spreading out from the base of the pillar to the periphery where the black spikes stood, and more of the multilayered green runes appeared on the veils of the four platforms, too.

Each of the four platforms and their shrouding walls of glass was easily the size of a stadium—huge structures in their own right. The central spire was half the size of them in width, but in height it absolutely dwarfed all of them and could no doubt be seen for miles out. Given that it had a glowing halo of green fire, Riven didn't doubt at all that it would draw the attention of other people in the surrounding lands.

Which could be very good or very bad.

[Your Elysium Altar has been created. Do you wish to name your Elysium Altar at this time?]

Name it? No. He'd talk to Allie about that first; if it was going to show up in any kind of display for himself or others he'd want it to reflect the city they were in. And Brightsville was certainly not a name they were going to keep for this city after cleaning the rest of the scum out of that prison or subduing the gang wars in the suburbs.

[You have declined to name your Elysium Altar. You can change this at any time through your status page. Options for terraforming have been randomly selected from potentials. Please select the kind of terraforming you'd like to see with this Elysium Altar's Unholy orientation:
- **Haunted Forest**
- **Hellscape**
- **Shadowlands**

Other options are available. To see this list in further detail and to expand your options, please pay three hundred million coins to the Elysium Altar.]

Riven nearly gagged at the price tag for the other options. There was no way that was going to happen; last he checked, after all the killing and looting they'd done, he and Allie had had a combined total of around 976,000. She'd entrusted him with the choice of terraforming based on traits they'd give and had even refused to come check with him, stating that it was his prize and no matter what it'd help their sect. So he was on his own to choose. When he selected each one for further details, it expanded and gave him an idea of what each terraforming option did.

[Haunted Forest: This terraforming option slowly turns surround-ing terrain into a thriving and heavy mix of Unholy-attuned life

and undeath. Local animals and plant life will evolve and multiply accordingly, with a vast boost to Unholy-related alchemy ingredients being made available. System-randomized monster spawns related to the Unholy foundational pillar and Death subpillar will increase by significant numbers. These pillars will also have increased bonuses to cultivation and more frequent Dao insights. Creatures associated with these pillars will experience a 4% buff to all stats while remaining in these lands and a 2% XP increase, as well as minor amounts of passive regeneration.]

[Hellscape: This terraforming option slowly turns surrounding terrain into a barren wasteland of fire and pain. Local animals and plant life will quickly wither away into extinction, but in their place, minor demon spawn will begin to emerge. This terraforming option also changes mineral composition, allowing one to find highly sought-after ores of varying types that are usually only found in the lower tiers of hell. This terraforming option focuses on the Unholy foundational pillar and Infernal subpillar. These pillars will also have increased bonuses to cultivation and more frequent Dao insights. Creatures associated with these pillars will experience a 7% buff to all stats while remaining in these lands. All demons gain an additional 10% buff to all stats while remaining in these lands, regardless of pillar orientation. Creatures associated with the Holy foundational pillar will experience passive amounts of damage and pain while remaining here.]

[Shadowlands: This terraforming option slowly turns surrounding terrain into cold, darkened badlands that normal light cannot penetrate. Species of plants and animals native to the shadow realms will slowly begin to seep in from the outer shadow realms and the void, either devouring or possessing local species to create new ones. Liquid Shadow, a very expensive material often used in stealth-related enchantments or Shadow-related Dao rituals, will be found in minor amounts here as a natural resource. This terraforming option focuses on the Unholy foundational pillar and Shadow subpillar. These pillars will also have increased bonuses to cultivation and more frequent Dao insights. Creatures associated with these pillars will experience a 20% buff to attempts at stealth or possession while remaining in these lands and will be able to draw in passive Shadow energy for quicker resource-pool regeneration.]

Well. There wasn't much of a choice here. Sure, Hellscape would increase the power of his demons, but he was really the only one living here who'd benefit. He was thinking of the society rather than just himself, and most of Allie's people were undead. Only one of the options had Death-attuned bonuses, and besides that, he really didn't like the idea of barren landscapes that Hellscape or Shadowlands seemed to provide. Would orcs and goblins flourish in a haunted forest? Probably; the abundance of Unholy life and undeath—plants and animals alike—would mean more food, and they'd been starving until now. Would the greenskins flourish in a hellscape devoid of anything to hunt or scavenge for food or in a realm where they couldn't see anything? Absolutely not. Haunted Forest would also supply their faction with alchemy-related resources, which he wasn't necessarily interested in, but he could see the crafters in their new faction finding it useful, and more monster spawns meant more monster drops when they were killed. This in turn meant more levels and more money, and the small XP boost wasn't anything to scoff at, either.

On top of that, there wasn't a landscape for the Blood subpillar specifically. It was a shame, but he wasn't sure he'd have chosen it even if it was offered, due to the lack of other Blood-oriented creatures in his populace.

Maybe the blood elves he'd heard about were blood oriented? He could only assume so, and that made him want to meet them even more. Perhaps they had insights that he'd not grasped yet—it'd be pretty damn cool to see in the future, should he ever meet any.

"I select Haunted Forest."

[**Haunted Forest has been selected**. **Immediate landscape affected: a radius of fifty miles from this position. All plant and animal life within this radius that are not considered intelligent enough to be participants by Elysium will be forcibly evolved immediately. Terraforming rate has been set to: minimal. Upgrade this altar's functions by paying the appropriate price of Elysium coins in order to increase terraforming rate. Unholy foundational pillar and Death subpillar associated creatures will experience 4% buffs to all stats, 2% XP increases, minor amounts of passive regeneration, increased bonuses to related cultivation, and higher chances for related Dao visions while remaining within these terraformed lands.**]

WWHHHOOOOOMMMMMMMMM

The spire at the altar's center radiated with Unholy green and black light before radiating out in all directions when the halo surrounding the top of the structure blew apart. A shock wave rippled through Riven's body, not affecting him much at all but giving him a little bit of a tingling sensation. However, when he turned around, his eyes widened as he saw the landscape the shock wave passed over abruptly change.

First was the grass. Swaths of it across the fields, along with wildflowers, all abruptly mutated from vibrant green spotted with flecks of yellow. Now the grass turned a silver-gray, though it didn't look unhealthy. It just looked . . . different. As for the flowers, the majority of them turned into plants with silver stalks, black petals, and neon-teal bulbs that literally radiated death mana in small amounts. Scattered among them were other wildflowers that'd become a bright neon green, with Unholy power that looked ominous but also beautiful.

The forest beyond changed similarly—the bark of trees went from brown to shades of gray or black. About a third of the trees withered and appeared to die, but many of them actually grew in size, which made Riven question whether or not they'd just become some kind of death-oriented plant species? The ones that didn't lose their leaves varied in color between black, silver, and neon teal, with rare smatterings of neon green.

And every once in a while, unique-looking, bright-red vines could be seen growing up the black bark of what had once been oaks.

Fay gasped aloud and covered her mouth with her hands, jumping up and down on the balls of her feet. "It's so pretty!"

Riven tried to ignore the bouncing Succubus for two obvious reasons and stared out at the scenery, quite flabbergasted himself. "This . . . this is not what I expected. You're right—I didn't expect it to be so nice to look at. It's like . . . an evil paradise? It's like the forest became sinister, but with an artistic stroke of genius to it."

Fay snickered and glanced his way, nudging him with a hand. "Come on! You can't keep correlating the Unholy with evil. That isn't how it works."

"That's not what Athela told me. She said that in order to get the Unholy affiliation without being born into it, evil acts helped quite a bit."

"That's because Athela only has a basic understanding of the pillars." Fay crossed her arms and smirked confidently. "I'll have to re-educate her."

"Her and me both, then."

Now that the altar had completely organized itself and the ring of green fire had re-formed, Riven's group of allies had started making their way over to the huge structure. Technically he was standing *in* the altar, even though it was open to the air, because the dark stones underneath his feet were all part of it.

But as Allie, her undead, his other two demons, and the orcs neared the newly founded Elysium altar, another notification sprang into space.

[You have gained access to the Elysium general store. You may restrict who can and cannot use this altar by thought, be it generalized or specific, and Elysium will comply. You may sell wares to the

general store at any time for Elysium coins at a marked-down price. The most basic forms of amenities in many categories can usually be found here at marked-up prices. These prices are always compared to average prices across your sector of the multiverse and may be prone to fluctuations. Elysium buys low and sells high, which in turn gives you incentive to trade with others.

The platforms arrayed around your Elysium Altar are called trading ports. Each port may be given to another faction, as long as they have their own port to sync with at another Elysium Altar. Factions that have chosen to sync with your own will be able to send representative merchants to this altar for trading purposes, with all interactions being taxed by the Elysium administrator at a 1% fee. If trading partners are off-world, their merchants will not be allowed to leave the vicinity of the altar's boundaries unless they travel back through their link to the homeworld they came from. If your trading partners are on-world, they may leave at any time but will be warped back to the altar after twenty-four hours of absence. Destruction of any altar or transfer of ownership will disband all merchants and send them back to their original home-bound location.

Due to your world being in an integration phase, all off-world trading partners have a maximum merchant level of 90.
You currently have zero requests for trading partners.]

[Update available. Update available. You currently have two requests for trading partners. These factions each wish to set up a trading commune designated in the space enclosed by one of your altar's platform barriers. Please decline or accept the following faction offers:
• Negrada, Minor Hellscape Dungeon
• The Blood Moon Requiem]

Riven nearly laughed out loud. "Negrada wants to say hello?! Wow. Didn't see that one coming . . . but who or what the hell is this Blood Moon Requiem? Any ideas, Fay?"

He turned to the Succubus, who was staring at his notification with a paling face.

She looked up at him with genuine concern, then back to Allie, and then back to him. If she'd had cat ears, he was sure they'd be laid back against her head by the stare she was giving him. "Oh, fucking roach tits . . . Um . . . That may be an iffy subject for me? I'm not entirely sure it's my place to say. Perhaps you should ask Athela . . . she'd be able to explain things in more detail."

CHAPTER 4

Hakim quickly swung his huge axe down onto the monster's head with a Lacerate martial art skill that would make any of his fellow barbarian-class counterparts green with envy, and the lizard spasmed while many more of its blue-scaled kin rushed his way. Their large talons scraped against the stone hallway and their hissing sounds were accompanied by sizzling, a by-product of the acid they could launch out of their mouths that now ate away at their surroundings and Hakim's armor. His flesh had already been burned off or melted to fuse with his fur armor in various places, causing him extreme pain and decreasing his mobility significantly, but despite his dire circumstances, he had to remain strong for the front line to hold. He was the primary tank of their group, their newly formed guild that had been created even before official introductions of the guild system, and if he went down, the others behind him would quickly follow.

And their three other front liners were already lying dead farther down the hallway. That didn't even include the assassin they'd lost to a pit trap—he'd been the guild leader.

"Goddamn it, they're closing in!" A fire mage by the name of Chad called out with a snarl, launching two more fireballs that exploded down the large passage to the shrieks of the incoming swarm. "I can't kill them fast enough!"

Caleb finally reloaded with shaky hands and started firing his semiautomatic rifle again, trying to stutter out words over the spray of bullets and cursing the creatures. "My regular bullets aren't penetrating! They just bounce right off their scales, and I'm out of enchanted ones! I don't want to die here!"

Julie hit Hakim with another healing spell and started cursing frantically while generating another Holy barrier to try and slow down the wave as her younger brother, Tim, was trying desperately to open the door at their backs. The young man was by far the best thief they had and had financed their group by stealing from more successful fighters after they cleaned up monsters in the wilderness or ventured into dungeons that were popping up nearby to spawn monsters. Yet even he was having difficulty with this lock, and the solid wood of the door before them was enchanted somehow—not allowing Hakim or any of the others to break it down.

Tanya was going to kill Hakim if he let anything happen to her two children, and their mother was no slouch in how frequently she'd let Hakim know her thoughts on their exploits.

"Why do you three always have to go out and put yourselves in danger when others can do it for you?"

"How many times are you going to get yourselves into life-and-death situations? The town is just fine with the other fighters keeping the dungeon monsters away—no need to get yourselves hurt!"

"Come help me with my clothes-making craft instead—people need clothes after the fall of Earth, and there's no shame in an honest day's work!"

And now they were stuck in a newly formed dungeon, the entrance closing behind them to unexpectedly trap them inside. It'd been unexplored when they'd entered, and the original plan had been just to scout out the top floor, but after the door had shut, the only way out was completion—and although it wasn't nearly as big as their tutorial dungeon had been, it was large enough that they'd gotten lost in its tunnels numerous times.

BAM

Hakim shoulder charged another of the lizards and unleashed a crescent swipe—sending out an arcing line of kinetic energy that sliced through another of the monsters before crying out as another latched onto his leg with acidic venom.

"DAMN IT!" He was beginning to panic slightly but activated his *War Cry* martial art with a booming shout. His skin immediately thickened, his bravery skyrocketed, the pain of the acid and ripping teeth lessened, his muscles visibly expanded, and he smashed his fist into the eye of the giant blue lizard to get it to let go.

CRUNCH

Hakim bellowed and spun, a whirlwind of mana from the Harmony foundational pillar blowing apart enemies to give his allies time. He was the last man standing between the monsters and the squishier members of their party, and Julie was starting to cry as barrier after barrier of her Holy mana shattered when set upon by waves of bodies barreling toward them. She just didn't have enough mana to keep them solid.

"GOT IT!" Tim screamed over the ruckus, flinging the door open just as blue-scaled lizard men, wearing brass armbands alongside feather headdresses and wielding primitive weapons, turned the corner of their tunnel.

The monstrous humanoids hissed and screeched, raising their spears and dashing alongside their quadruped cousins. Their tails whipped out behind them with bloodlust, and Hakim turned to run.

He fumbled for his bag, leaving bodies behind him to chase after the others and looking for the treasure he'd received in the tutorial dungeon that he still kept as a trump card. He'd been holding on to it for an emergency, and now seemed like a perfect match for that scenario.

Otherwise, he and the others would likely be dead very soon.

Riven was letting Allie and the others explore the altar or run over the details of the terraforming, getting a lot of praise from Vin, who cackled gleefully at the opportunity presented to them, while simultaneously talking to Athela.

"The Blood Moon Requiem is a very powerful and ancient vampiric civilization," Athela stated with a shrug, glancing over to Fay, who continued to fidget with her hands. "And your parents may have been from there."

Riven's eyes widened in shock, and Allie's head snapped left from where she was evaluating the terraforming details to stare at the demoness.

"Did I just hear that right?" Riven said in a low voice while his sister pushed others out of the way to move in close. "My parents may be from this place? How is that even possible? And how do you know of my parents?"

"I don't know your parents at all," Athela said with hands raised. "However . . . call it a hunch."

"That's a pretty bold statement for a hunch."

Athela grinned and set her hands on her hips with a swish of her black hair. "All right, then let's put the pieces together. Do you remember that notification you received in hell when you first activated Malignant Prophecy?"

"You have that ability too?!" Allie asked in shock, her feet planted out to either side of her with her arms crossed. "Why didn't you tell me?!"

Riven scowled. "You didn't tell me you had that ability, either—"

"That doesn't matter." Athela cut them both off with a wave of her hand. "You both have it. But do you remember what that notification said when you first used it?"

Riven's brows furrowed, and he stared at the ground, shoving his hands into his pockets and not thinking too long before remembering the details as clear as day.

[Malignant Prophecy has activated; previously unrecognized heir has been found. Qualifications have been met, link established, royal lineage recognized despite tampering and suppression measures. Imperial system has officially recognized Riven Thane as a prince of the empire, thirty-seventh in line for the throne. All citizens, nobility, clergy, and leadership of the empire have been informed.]

"It said I was a prince of the empire, thirty-seventh in line for the throne. Allie, did it say something similar to you?"

"It said I was thirty-eighth in line."

"Ha!" Riven pointed a finger her way. "That means I'm obviously superior in all ways—bow before me, plebian!"

"What's about to happen is you're about to get my foot up your ass."

"That's just plain rude. Anyways, Athela, back to the matter at hand . . . You're saying our parents, the ones who disappeared years ago, were from this place?"

Athela shrugged again and swept her foot out along the dark stone of the altar. "Perhaps it's because that bloodline you have and the Malignant Prophecy you can utilize has only ever been found in their royals?"

Riven blinked. "Why haven't you told me about this sooner?"

"Do you think this is where our parents went?!" Allie asked curiously, but she immediately sagged when Athela shot her hopes down.

"You never asked, and it wasn't important until now. As for Allie's question—absolutely not. Whatever happened to your parents, it was on Earth. Why your parents left is a mystery to me, though. If you exit Elysium's boundaries, Elysium brands you a heretic and will send its enforcers to hunt you, and doing so takes tremendous effort and monumental resources."

Riven's blood ran cold. "Wait . . . you're saying if my parents are out there somewhere, the system of Elysium itself has marked them for death?"

"Yeah, people will get a super-big prize if they kill your mom and dad now, and that's if they aren't already dead. Who KNOWS why they left you two? I mean, neither of you has any idea, right? Maybe a bounty hunter found them and they left you behind to spare you."

The shocked looks on both siblings' faces were more than enough for the Succubus to step in. Fay let out a long drawn-out sigh. "Athela, try to be a little bit more sensitive."

"What?! I'm not trying to be mean, that's just how it is. Anyways, they've obviously somehow found you, and Elysium altars are one of the only ways established factions outside your world can interact with integrating planets before restrictions lift. To see that they so quickly offered you a trading post means they've been watching you—how long or for what reasons is anyone's guess. But you two are royals. It's likely they want you back home to raise you properly."

Riven exchanged uneasy looks with Allie, neither of them knowing how to take the news.

"That is . . . unexpected," Riven stated flatly, scratching the back of his head with a frown. "I . . . don't even know how to react to that. Are you saying the Blood Moon Requiem is able to get us off-world?"

"No, they absolutely cannot do that until the system restrictions end, but they can eventually. They're probably just trying to establish contact in the meantime." Athela gave him a large smile and a pat on the shoulder. "Look at you, prince boy! A fitting warlock partner for a princess like me!"

Fay snorted and got a death glare from the other demoness.

"They could always pull him through as a merchant, but he'd be restricted to the altar zone on the other side," Fay threw out. "Consider that for a moment."

"Uh . . . actually, that is true." Athela gave herself a thoughtful chin rub. "Hmm. Doesn't really matter, though—it's very likely a good thing rather than a bad one. Unexpected that they'd find you so quickly, but then again, they are one of the greatest vampiric empires in the cosmos. Of all the major vampiric factions, there are a couple dozen that are dangerous enough to warrant attention, nine of which are considered S-grade factions. The Blood Moon Requiem ranks eighth on the vampiric power scale according to common knowledge. That is no small feat. They own over twelve hundred worlds, I'm told, and have a few vassal states under their wing as well that they essentially lord over. Right, Fay? Or am I remembering incorrectly?"

To Allie's left, Fay nodded in silence, a soft smile on her lips.

And then, to everyone's confusion, a glowing orb of multicolored light appeared in front of Riven's face.

"What's that?" Allie asked, pointing. "Looks weird . . . I can't get a mana read on it, either. Is that an illusion of some kind?"

Fay looked around, obviously puzzled. "I think so . . . But where it's coming from I cannot tell. It should be harmless, but . . ."

Her words trailed off when a notification accompanied the glowing orb.

[Hakim Bluebush has activated a two-time-use system artifact: Heroic Intervention. One of two charges has been used. Heroic Intervention has selected the five most powerful people Hakim has interacted with since Earth's integration, and you—Riven Thane—are one of them. Hakim Bluebush is currently in need of your help and has placed a live-stream feature in the orb before you that will connect momentarily. You will be able to speak to him briefly as he explains his current situation before deciding whether to aid him. You can choose to assist or refuse his request. All or none of the selected participants may go or stay without penalty. If you choose to aid him and risk yourself, you will be teleported to his location until his plight is over. Then you will be teleported back to your current location after a short rest period. Please hold for connection.]

All eyes centered on Riven, and Athela gasped in surprise when she read the notification herself.

"Hakim from our tutorial! I was wondering what happened to him!" Athela laughed loudly and slapped her hands onto her hips. "Wow! That's a really interesting artifact to have. Very neat, actually."

"Sounds like he's in trouble, too . . ." Riven muttered, grasping his staff of flesh and wood to tap his fingers along its shaft. "Huh. Wonder what he got himself into."

Riven didn't wait long to find out.

They were cornered.

"HOLD IT DOWN!" Hakim screamed at the other, panicking people, encouraging them to keep pushing amid the crash of bodies that kept jarring the thick iron door leading into the circular, dimly lit treasury they now found themselves in. Torches flickered along the walls in three different places. Piles of coins, treasures, and items of power littered the ground, but none of it was any help to them now without an identifier. "HELP WILL COME SOON!"

Caleb was sweating profusely, his rifle hanging at his side while he braced his back against the entrance to keep the lizard men out. "I'm out of bullets!"

"Hakim, I'm scared!" Julie yelled shakily over the battering of the door. Her red hair was covered in the even brighter red of her brother's blood, and Tim sat, pale-faced, in a state of mute shock while examining his missing leg. They'd bandaged the stump before his sister had sealed the wound shut.

Flashes of multicolored light illuminated the ground nearby, and Hakim's statue of a tiny knight brandishing a sword, his artifact Heroic Intervention, began to pulse.

Five illusionary baubles appeared overhead, displaying the faces of men and women. Each represented one of the five people the system deemed the most powerful characters Hakim had encountered in Elysium's multiverse thus far.

Hakim's heart lifted with a slim sliver of hope, only to be brutally dashed as one of the five immediately declined and winked out. He'd been a guild leader, a man Hakim had respected until just a moment ago, and now that man hadn't even given him the time of day for a single sentence to plead his case.

"I . . . I need your help!" Hakim shouted out over the banging of the door—wide-eyed, with dents, creaks, and groans from the metal becoming ever more abundant. "Please! We're going to die down here!"

"Many people die every day since the system was introduced. Why should I help you? What's your situation? I barely met you for less than a minute. You are not entitled to freebies," a blonde woman by the name of Zerfi asked. She was a storm mage in the next city over, wearing a long blue silk dress and brushing her hair out at a desk as sunlight filtered in through a window. "Do explain quickly.

I am already late to a social event, and if I come I'll need guarantees that this will be fast."

Her words stung Hakim's pride, but he bit back his irritation and swallowed. "We're in a newly spawned dungeon on the southern side of Pelmonth. The dungeon locked us in, and lizard men warriors have cornered us in the treasury alongside their giant lizard pets. Help us, and you can take whatever you can carry back!"

Zerfi glanced through the globe, inspecting the treasury, then snorted and went back to brushing her hair while the other three figures in their own baubles remained silent. "Anything related to the Storm subpillar?"

"WE HAVE NO IDEA. DOES IT LOOK LIKE WE'VE HAD TIME TO EXPLORE THESE THINGS?!" Julie screamed at the other woman, her face wet with tears as she snarled. "Please, just help us!"

Zerfi let out a long, drawn-out, and exaggerated sigh, then put the hairbrush down and smoothed out her silk dress. She turned fully in their direction just as a spear managed to puncture a weakened, repeatedly battered dent in the top section of the doorway. They could hear the roars and chanting screams becoming ever louder.

The blonde woman frowned. "I'll come only if you get two others to come as well. I may be strong, but I'm usually backed up by a competent team of A-rankers . . . not riffraff like yourself. I do a lot of damage, but I am poor on defense and need to have people peel enemies off me so I can appropriately strike out—and I will not throw my life away for people who are barely more than strangers."

Again, the words stung Hakim's pride, but his hope began to climb. She'd come as long as the others also said yes, so he turned his gaze to the next portrait. "James! Remember me from the sparring bouts we had a while back when you were giving me pointers? I'll be in your debt forever, just—"

James held up a hand to stop Hakim midsentence. He was African American and wore the kind of camo getup you'd see on military types back on Earth, which was appropriate, considering he was a retired special-ops sniper and ex-SEAL. He carried two large knives on either side of his belt, a pistol, a couple packs of ammo, and a large sniper rifle in his hands. "I cannot. It sounds like you're holding an entire army back behind that door, and I can see from the vision's angle that there are many hundreds of creatures just on the other side. That door is about to break at any second, and though I'd like to help, you must realize I am a single-target-oriented assassin. I would be of little help to you in a battle like this and would likely just die alongside you. I am sorry, Hakim, and I truly wish you the best of luck."

With that, James closed his communication down, and the bauble winked out.

Hakim's heart dropped, and he felt like the world was falling out from under him. He'd thought James was a friend, but he'd simply abandoned him. Abandoned *them*. James had known Julie in passing, too, along with her brother, Tim, and he'd just . . .

A ball began to form in Hakim's throat at the thought of what was about to happen, and his back took another jarring hit when the metal behind him bent forward. He grunted, wide-eyed, and charged the door to ram it back into place after dust started flowing down from the cracks along its top.

"Hakim." A familiar voice sounded out, and he looked up toward the other two visions he hadn't addressed yet.

One was of a bald, bored-looking, middle-aged knight-type warrior, heavily armored and sipping an ale at a bar as others crowded around him to happily take bets on what would happen. The other vision was where the voice had come from. Unlike the others, this man was shrouded in darkness instead of daylight with a dim green glow coming from overhead. The man's eyes were a bright crimson, and Hakim couldn't say that he recognized this person at all due to the runic mask of softly glowing sigils he wore. And for the life of him, Hakim couldn't place that voice—even though he knew he'd heard it before.

"Yes? Who are you, and will you help us?" Hakim's voice cracked, getting a laugh from the people at the pub in the middle vision while a sympathetic frown adorned Zerfi's features.

The unknown man chuckled, then nodded from underneath his hood. "Yes, Hakim, I selected the option to assist you, and I'm already on my way. See you soon, bud."

A howling roar unlike anything Hakim had ever heard before vibrated throughout the halls, and the pounding on the door stopped. Croaks, snarls, and commands in a language he didn't understand started reverberating off the other side of the metal barrier in between him, his guild, and a quick death—and the ground started to shake as something enormous started to approach.

"H-Hakim!" Julie cried out from where she'd backed up, trembling, her wooden staff clutched in slender hands. She was obviously terrified, but she had the right idea—they needed to get away from that door before whatever was coming crushed it.

A feeling of utter hopelessness overwhelmed him in that instant. Hakim had never felt so disillusioned about other people in this world, nor had he felt such despair. He'd thought that his relic would help them, that it would save them in a tight spot, and yet . . . these people didn't care about him at all.

He was trash to them.

One had declined immediately, one had told him it was just too dangerous, and yet another was outright watching the proceedings like a TV show while his friends wagered money on who would die first.

Zerfi had conditionally volunteered if she got additional help, which was far more than those other three had done—but even she wasn't coming now that only the masked and hooded man had stated he'd assist. She was likely the most powerful one in this group, too, and for her not to help meant Hakim had a much smaller chance of surviving this.

As for the one person who'd said yes, his bauble was quickly dissipating and turning into thin mist like the others who'd declined—and for a moment Hakim began to panic even more. A thread of hope was still left, but only barely, and for a second even that thread disappeared when he thought he'd been lied to by the stranger. Perhaps the stranger had simply said yes, then declined?

But then a portal of multicolored light formed that was far larger than the similarly constructed bauble, and out stepped a man.

He was hooded and cloaked, about six feet tall, with an athletic build and bright-red eyes. The creepy staff made from black wood and flesh had streams of blood running up and down or into its length, with spikes of Crimson Ice and a long, wicked dagger at the top end. His very presence caused the room to abruptly grow cold, and the mana fluctuated around his body in twists of crimson energy unlike anything that Hakim had ever sensed before. He'd met a handful of very powerful people in his time, watched their auras switch on or off in a way normal classers just couldn't replicate, but Hakim had never felt anything like this.

This aura was on another level.

Hakim was so caught up in the man's palpable mana signature that he failed to realize the thudding footsteps outside the door had stopped—until the metal barrier was smashed in with a booming thud. Dust was flung into the air, and the screech of tearing iron caused Hakim to wince and take a knee. His eyes settled in horror on the massive, clawed hand of what could only be a drake. Blue scales and a large yellow eye stared in at him from outside the treasury—iris dilating to half the size of the doorway—and the monster drew its lips back in a wicked smile, exposing rows of teeth each the size of Hakim's arm.

Immediately but calmly, the spellcaster to Hakim's right made an incredibly quick set of motions, his hands blurring in intricate patterns while he drew in the crimson lights that drifted in the pool his aura produced.

And what Hakim saw next had him shook.

"Nefajia crecus Blood Nova."

CHAPTER 5

WARNING
WARNING
WARNING
DUNGEON BOSS FIGHT BLUE DRAKE HAS BEEN INITIATED.
DUNGEON CAPTIUS HAS SEALED OFF YOUR POINTS OF EXIT
UNTIL THE BATTLE IS COMPLETE.
BEGINNING BATTLE IN
5 . . .
4 . . .
3 . . .
2 . . .
1 . . .

The ground shattered, trembled, and split. A massive shock wave directed forward was followed by an enormous globe of swirling blood mana, vaporizing the ground underneath and directly in front of Riven and blasting the entire front wall into smithereens before colliding with the drake's large yellow eye.

KABOOM

The eye was decimated and the drake's huge head flung backward in a spray of debris. The enormous multiton creature went torpedoing head over heels, roaring, thrashing about in agony with wings and claws as it smashed into a crowd of its lesser cousins, which were immediately crushed under the drake's weight.

The monster's body came to an abrupt stop when it slammed violently into the far wall of a much larger underground chamber, an octagonal room extending many hundreds of yards in all directions with a skylight reaching miles high and numerous statues of draconic figures spaced out between ruined stone buildings.

Julia and Tim both took in deep gasps, Hakim just gawked with incomprehension, and Caleb began to laugh like a madman after seeing the huge drake blown backward like a speeding bullet.

Riven's red eyes shifted right, not seeing the horde through the debris in the air but hearing hundreds of heartbeats close by. When he raised a hand, dozens of spinning red blades smoldered into being around his position. Pulling on the blood of the fallen bodies that'd just been crushed in the drake's wake, spiraling wisps of red were ripped out and quickly condensed into over a hundred more.

"Get fucked."

Riven's fingers extended, and a swarm of spinning blades tore through the rubble still falling through the air, blindly carpet-bombing the crowds of enemies nearby with each disc exploding seconds after impact. Explosion after explosion rocked the underground ruin, to the screams and cries of lizard men and other reptiles, leaving a field of ruined bodies and rubble when the dust finally cleared.

The drake picked itself up from the other side of the enormous room and screeched in anger, sending out a fireball twice Riven's size that sped toward him and crashed into his body. The impact was enough to blow him back a couple feet, but he remained standing, and when the dust cleared again, his skin was covered in black metal plates and he continued to writhe in the flames of hellfire.

The drake's one remaining eye narrowed upon seeing Riven take no damage, and it started to flap its wings—chanting in a low, serpentine voice to cast a spell while wind started roiling about it in a tornado of power. The small stone buildings around the large beasts ripped apart, adding their rubble to the swirling vortex of silver mana.

In turn, Riven drew on his own reserves and the newly decimated bodies of the lizards nearby. More blood tore out of the corpses and swirled about him, dancing in a howling, raging storm of crimson might. It began to freeze, then liquefy, freeze and liquefy, over and over again while fluidly churning around him in a spiraling storm to match the drake's own.

The drake snarled, Riven's aura pulsed, and the two energies launched across the room in a maddening howl of power.

Hakim watched the raging battle take place before him with utter shock. He'd never seen anything like it; the sheer amount of energy being unleashed between the combatants was unlike any fight he'd even *heard* about.

The drake and caster darted through the air, the drake flapping its wings and imbuing them with air magic of some kind to maneuver and dodge incoming projectiles that shot out faster than Hakim could even keep up with. They were just red blurs, splitting the sound barrier and being launched by black nets that would create festering wounds in the drake's body whenever the red-tipped spears penetrated. Sometimes they'd miss due to the amazing dexterity of the great beast, but the man sparking with red lightning was just as fast—and whenever he found himself in a tight spot, he'd create a rift through space to teleport away and send a barrage from behind the monster pursuing him.

Black lightning bolts cracked the air, fireballs and blades of solidified wind tore and blew through buildings, and spires of crystallized blood whipped through the air like living things as they sought out the drake to crash and splinter against its hide.

"Who . . . is that?" Julie asked with awe, raising both eyebrows and covering her open mouth with one hand when a red snowstorm billowed out around the caster in midair to blind the drake.

The monster snapped its jaws, creating a shock wave to blow the bloody snowflakes away, only to have another bolt of black lightning crash into its face. The drake screamed in pain and slammed into the ground but pulsed with a shimmering gray light seconds later and exploded outward in all directions—destroying the landscape around it and launching the caster backward to skip like a stone on a lake across the ruined ground.

Hakim's heart sank and he began to panic when he saw the man's neck bent back at an unnatural angle, and Tim screamed out for their ally to get up. Julie held her breath and Caleb gripped his hands together so hard his knuckles turned white.

But to their relief and sheer amazement, the man picked himself up like nothing had even happened.

The drake's remaining eye went wide, and it snorted in disbelief when the caster's neck violently snapped back into place. Manually cracking his neck again with both hands and stretching a bit, he shook himself and looked as good as new.

"He should be dead!" Caleb wheezed, trembling violently. "How is he not dead? His neck was obviously broken!"

The drake seemed to agree, and it charged furiously toward the man in a pincer attack as two dozen of the lizard men rushed out from the shadows at his back.

"Athela, Azmoth, Fay."

Three portals ripped open in the air around the man. One was void black, another rimmed in hellfire, and the third was shrouded in purple miasma. Each of them produced a different creature—a different demon. One was a stunningly beautiful Succubus with sky-blue skin, white hair, black wings—and she wore a wide smile of perfect white teeth. Another was a titanic, four-armed brute lacking skin—instead, he was adorned in thick black metal plates between patches of red muscle, while his flaming body also sported a tail and two additional sets of eel-like maws from behind. The last was another menacing woman with black skin, six scythe-like blades spreading out of her back, and a long, bladelike tongue that dripped necrotic venom. These newfound allies took to the battle immediately without exchanging a single word.

The man abruptly vanished, turning invisible and splitting into three versions of himself that sprinted in different directions. The Succubus launched herself skyward, with green runes lighting up in the drake's path, while the arachnoid woman blurred toward the nearest group of lizard men and began rapidly decapitating them or removing limbs in a flurry of blades.

The huge, flaming monster that was twice the size of any man Hakim had ever seen slammed his numerous fists together and grinned at the oncoming drake, which was barreling through buildings at high speed. He looked left only long enough to open up the two eel-like appendages over his shoulders, producing two torrents of flame that bathed another group of blue-scaled lizards and cooked more than ten of them instantly.

The drake had changed targets now that it had lost track of the caster, and its maw opened up with another roar. Crackling sparks started accumulating from its innards, traveling up the inside of its neck and condensing into a ball of lightning that flashed forward and collided with the taunting, flaming, four-armed demon in front of it.

Fire and lightning clashed, and the drake was only fifty yards away when it hit the Succubus's invisible minefield.

Unholy runes lit up with green light and detonated, blowing small holes in the huge monster and causing it to stumble. But momentum kept it going forward, even as rune after rune continued to blast into the monster, another series of sonic booms rippling forward from across the room.

Red and black magic tore through the air and collided with the drake's neck and shoulder, again piercing its thick scales and creating festering wounds under the netlike black ends of the sharp projectiles that ate away at the draconic monster's flesh.

Enraged now, the drake whipped its head around to fire another lightning strike in the caster's direction—only to have its head yanked down by the lower jaw when the large flaming demon leaped up to grab a tooth.

"AZMOTH CLIMB INTO THROAT AND BASH BASH BASH!!!"

Breathing flames and ignoring the cascade of lightning despite pieces of his armor being torn off, the demon started biting, tearing, and ripping into the drake's insides with gleeful, insidious cackles. But what really did massive amounts of damage was when the demon slammed his foot down and set a shock wave of kinetic energy through the drake's throat—ripping apart layers of flesh and bone alike.

The drake immediately began to thrash, panicking now and rolling around on the ground frantically while trying to create more and more lightning inside its throat to get the monster now inside its body out again. Its body sparked and rippled with electricity, but still the demon raged inside.

Hakim was so caught up in the battle before him that he didn't hear the scraping of claws nearby until it was too late.

CLANG

Hakim and everyone in his group startled, and he nearly tripped over his own feet, stumbling back when the flash of a sword was stopped by another blade only an inch from his face.

Right in front of him, a lizard man gagged and gurgled—blood trickling out of its toothy mouth while it stared wide-eyed into the sinister smile of the woman with pitch-black skin and six blade limbs protruding from her back. In one clawed hand she held the lizard man's heart, one of her blades was holding back the lizard man's sword that would have no doubt killed Hakim had it fallen, and two more blades pierced the monster's stomach and neck.

The demoness slowly extended her long, black tongue, licking blood from one of the lizard man's wounds before ripping out all her blades at once and letting the body drop to the ground. Tossing the monster's heart to the side flippantly, she calmly turned and focused her red eyes on Julie, then Tim, then Hakim.

She completely ignored Caleb.

"Well, well, well, what do we have here . . ." a familiar voice asked with a chittering laugh, and the smile she gave them was rather genuine. "You've got to be more careful, you know. We won't always be here to save you."

BOOM

The room exploded when another of the Succubus's minefields blew apart a group of lizard monsters that'd been tricked into pursuing another hallucination, and flashes of red light illuminated the room overhead when more of the caster's projectiles flashed forward to puncture the hide of the huge, flailing drake that now had smoke billowing out of holes in its neck.

The demonic woman with black skin shifted her gaze to the right, where another eight lizard men were rushing through a corridor and toward the treasure room's wrecked wall, and she let out a loud belch. "Be right back!"

A blur of blades and shadow collided with the group of reptilian warriors before they even knew what hit them. The woman's delighted laughter was mixed with the peppering thuds of red needles being launched from her arachnoid limbs and the sounds of body parts being chopped off. Meanwhile, the lizard men could only scramble away for their lives and scream.

CHAPTER 6

Riven's staff channeled sparks of dark lightning up the fleshy, whiplike tendril attached to its embedded blade. The large monster spasmed and twitched—and eventually settled down into death when Azmoth ripped a large hole and stepped out of its smoking throat.

"Nice job, big guy!" Riven gave the demon a fist bump and withdrew the fleshy tendril, the sinister blade of his sorcerer's staff snapping back into place. "You did some real work there, even if you were a crazy motherfucker climbing inside that thing."

**CONGRATULATIONS
CONGRATULATIONS
CONGRATULATIONS
YOU HAVE DEFEATED THE DUNGEON'S PRIMARY BOSS,
BLUE DRAKE. DUNGEON CAPTIUS HAS LOST, AND
AS PRIMARY CONTRIBUTING PARTICIPANT IN THIS
DUNGEON RAID, YOU—RIVEN THANE—ARE THE ONE
WHO DECIDES WHAT HAPPENS NEXT.**

[Now that Dungeon Captius has been defeated, you may choose to either take the dungeon's bribe—or to destroy its core. Taking the dungeon's bribe allows it to offer you treasures otherwise hidden inside its realm. Taking the bribe allows the dungeon to either relocate entirely or to enter a hibernation mode where the Elysium administrator guarantees its protection and gives it time to rebuild. Choosing to destroy the core will kill the dungeon permanently, preventing future monster spawns, but you must find the core first to do so.]

[You have one hour to collect your winnings before Heroic Intervention sends you back home. If you wish to leave earlier, just inform Elysium of your will to leave and it shall be so.]

[You have gained three levels. Congratulations!]
[Additional bonus levels have been given based on performance.]
[Your minions have received their XP and level-ups as well. Congratulations!]
[You have acquired a new title. Please see your status page for more information.]

"Hmm. This is a lot different from when I beat Negrada's miniboss." Riven scratched his chin and smiled at Fay when the Succubus landed beside him to rest an elbow on his shoulder, looking down at his notification with interest. "What are your thoughts?"

Fay shrugged, then motioned to where stone was beginning to form a figure of a lizard man only a few feet away from their position. "Depends on what Dungeon Captius has to offer. By the way, did you ever assign those points from the last time you leveled up?"

"When I killed the elves back at Greenstalk? Yeah."

"All right! Just making sure." Fay gave him a playful nudge and adjusted her crop top. "You are quite forgetful, you know."

Riven furrowed his brows and opened his mouth for a rebuttal, somewhat confused, but slowly closed it as the Succubus winked his way and walked off with an obviously intentional sway to her hips. He wasn't sure if she was using her charm ability on him just to fuck around or not, but he doubted she even could—as that would be a breach of contract. He wouldn't have been surprised otherwise, though, because goddamn, did she look good. He'd always had a thing for athletic-looking women, and Fay had all the right curves.

"Bad, bad, bad," Azmoth said with a sour growl. He put a clawed hand on Riven's shoulder and avidly shook Riven's smaller body back and forth. "Succubus evil, Riven. Don't look. Don't be simp, boy!"

"Oh, knock it off!" Riven said with a laugh and a slight blush, pushing his large demon away—but he swiped another quick glance when Azmoth turned around. "Jesus."

"Mama didn't raise simp, Riven. That what said."

"I KNOW, I know . . . I know what I said, Azmoth."

"Just make sure."

"I KNOW! I'm a straight, single, lonely young man, okay?! Give me a break! I was only looking—I promised myself I wouldn't go down that road."

Riven grumbled to himself and Azmoth gave a sage nod before the vampire turned his head to address the creature he'd identified as Dungeon Captius.

[Avatar of Dungeon Captius]

It was about half his height, a miniature lizard man, with no weapons whatsoever. It looked up at him with an expression of fear mixed with irritation and slowly began to rise up as a stone platform underneath let it hover in place.

"Greetings, Vampire . . ." Dungeon Captius said with a hesitant bow. "I am hoping to beg for my life . . . as dictated by the rules of Elysium. You have slain the primary guardian of my realm, and my fate lies in your hands. May I present the bribe I have prepared for you?"

Riven nodded slowly, looking around at the rubble of the ruined underground complex. "Yeah, I would like to see the bribe you've prepared . . . I'd hate to have to go looking for that core of yours just to shatter it. Then again, killing you would keep the local people out of harm's way, wouldn't it . . ."

Riven put on a savage smile, taking off his mask and exposing his fangs to the avatar. "And there is a treasury room not far off. I have no doubt I'll get something out of this either way."

If Dungeon Captius could have paled, it would have. It gave a hesitant nod. "I assure you there are more treasury rooms than just the one you've found, and they're all hidden—as is my core. It is in both of our best interests to exchange the bribe, as you will likely not find all my treasures otherwise—and I do not want to risk dying should you actually find the core now that my greatest defenders are gone."

"Well, go ahead and convince me, then. And is there any way you could package this stuff for me? I have to leave soon."

"Package . . . ?"

"Like, in chests or some kind of spatial holding thing. If you have those. Lastly, I'll be claiming that treasury room anyways—this bribe has to be stuff you don't already have there. If it isn't good enough, I'll obviously be declining. Capisce?"

The avatar's shoulders slumped in relief, realizing that Riven was more likely to take the bribe than he'd thought. "Oh . . . yes, I can come up with something. Here, take a look at the bribe and tell me what you think."

Riven strutted across the last stretch of the rubble and jumped off a building, landing beside Azmoth to do a superhero pose before straightening and wiping the dust off his newly acquired bling.

He wore a large golden crown adorned with jewels and mithril etchings, one that radiated some kind of unfamiliar magic. He sported a gold-trimmed robe that had diamonds sewn into the back to create the image of a rose—an item that was far too flamboyant for anybody who wasn't out of their mind. In his off hand, he carried a purple satin sack of extremely good quality, and underneath his right armpit he held a flamboyant royal scepter also made of gold and jewels that had a single large rune flickering inside the fist-size diamond on the scepter's head.

Beyond that, Riven also wore a pair of very fluffy green slippers, a couple of enchanted amulets of gaudy design, a pair of poofy yellow silk pants, and a massive two-handed bone sword way too big for him to use that radiated neon-teal death mana and had numerous spikes along the serrated blade.

The bone sword along his back dragged, scraping on the floor to make his approach very noticeable to the small crowd—Riven's two female demons, as well as Julie, Hakim, Tim, and the man Riven didn't know yet.

Athela was in spider form, originally shifting to prove it was her, and was animatedly talking to Julie, who was laugh-crying now; she, Tim, and Hakim, having survived, were all in incredibly good spirits. Athela was telling them of her adventures with Riven since they'd last parted, while Caleb was just trying to take all this in—and the two floating orbs containing the other strong people Hakim had met were still watching what'd just happened in a state of mute shock.

Hakim turned, a huge smile on his face, wiping away tears from laughing at Athela's stories. His eyebrows raised at Riven's gaudy attire, and now that the mask was gone, he could clearly see it was his friend from the tutorial after all. "Riven?! It really is you! I hear you're a vampire now."

Fay glanced backward, along with some of the others and immediately began to laugh, while Riven stopped dead and struck a pose with Azmoth at his back. "No, good sir, I have evolved into Pimp Riven, and that is how I shall be addressed. Have you met my three hos yet? Their names are Athela, Azmoth, and Fay."

"Me no ho, I am Azmoth!" The titanic demon folded his arms with a disapproving shake of his head.

"Fine! Just them, then." Riven gestured to two female demons, both of them quickly scowling as Athela screeched and launched herself at her master before Riven swatted her out of the air with the large satin sack he carried. "DOWN, FOUL WENCH!"

"I am a PRINCESS, you bloodsucking buffoon!" Athela quipped, bouncing off the stone floor, only to be pinned by Riven's foot at the base of her neck. She glowered up at him, but it was obvious neither he nor she was actually putting true effort into the scuffle. "Humph! This is NOT how I should be treated! How horribly insulting!"

Fay rolled her eyes at the two of them as Riven kept Athela pinned, and she folded her wings behind her while simultaneously crossing her arms. "You better watch yourself, Riven. You're rather cute sometimes, but don't push your luck. You wouldn't want to get on my bad side."

The Succubus grinned at him to make sure he knew she was kidding, and he let out a laugh—letting Athela go as she morphed into her humanoid variant.

"Who's the big guy?" Hakim asked, staring the smoldering, muscular form of Azmoth down with an impressed nod of approval. "They're all your demons? You've really come a long way since we last met . . . You're incredibly powerful now, even if you do wear fuzzy slippers and your fashion is lacking."

"Very lacking!" Julie snorted a laugh and covered up her smile. She was supporting Tim, who'd lost a leg in the dungeon earlier that day, but both siblings couldn't be happier just to be alive.

Riven pointed a finger in mock warning at the three of them, waggling it back and forth as his crown slipped over one eye—it was slightly too big for his head. "Don't you judge my fashion sense! I'll have you know these slippers are enchanted with a speed enhancement that gives me three hundred points to Agility!"

Tim gawked. "Seriously?"

"No, I am absolutely lying. I just thought they looked funny, so I had them included in the bribe deal."

Riven grinned to match the others and then head nodded over to where Caleb was staring blankly his way. "Who's the new guy?"

"Caleb!" The brunet man in jeans with the empty rifle slung across his back warily reached out a hand, obviously nervous and sweating slightly, but when he looked over to the others of his guild, he got nods of assurance and straightened his posture. "Thanks so much for saving us. We'd be dead without you. I . . . Um, you're very intimidating. Even being around you while just standing here feels dangerous somehow."

"Probably my negative Charisma at play again." Riven rolled his glowing crimson eyes and shook his head. Then he jingled the satin bag in his hand and tossed it to Athela. "Yo, take a look at that shit. It's a bag of holding and we hit it big, but we have to leave soon or we'll be teleported out. That goes for everyone."

Athela caught the bag, inspecting it as a notification of its contents popped up, and she gawked with a high-pitched squeal of laughter. "OH MUR GAWD, RIVEN! Can I have that tiara? It'd fit my princess status perfectly!"

"Only if you earn it."

"WHAT DO YOU MEAN, ONLY IF I EARN IT?!"

Riven booped Athela's forehead with his royal scepter and scowled. "Don't talk back to your pimp that way, or you shall feel my Unholy wrath of—OW—OOF—HEY!!!!"

Athela jabbed him in the rib cage and Fay swatted the back of his head, the two women viciously attacking his weak spots as he fell to the ground in surrender.

"I'll be taking this!" Athela announced proudly, pulling out a shimmering tiara made from ebony metal and inlaid with rubies. When she placed it on her head, the demoness shuddered and her red eyes went wide. "Oh . . . Oh, that's very nice. Is this enchanted?"

Riven took Azmoth's helping hand but was pushed back down by Fay's foot and then sat on.

He looked up at the smirking Succubus, raised an eyebrow when he glanced down where her tail was slowly wagging back and forth, and then looked over to Athela. "Yes. Did you look at the status info yet?"

"No, I just saw it was a tiara."

"Well, it was made specifically for you. In fact, part of the deal was that each of my summons got a unique item handcrafted by the dungeon to fit your needs, and that's yours."

Athela slowly turned to him, jaw dropping and hands cupping her mouth as he smiled up at her. "You seriously had them custom made?! That's so nice!"

"Wait, what are ours, then?" Fay asked curiously, turning over from a sitting position to lie completely on top of him while kicking her legs out and grinning deviously.

"NO, NO, NO! BAD, BAD, BAD!" Azmoth grabbed the startled Succubus by her hair and without warning launched her across the room, sending the screaming woman soaring into the distance.

The large demon dusted his hands off and humphed with approval. "Riven needs chastity belt. Too easy for evil Succubus to trick."

Athela gawked as her friend soared across the vast chasm, and Riven cackled while finally taking another helping hand from the large demon to pull himself up.

"God, these slippers are ridiculous. Anyways, we'll get to reading off the statuses of all your personal items later when we're sent back. We have other things to deal with right now."

Riven turned around to where a new arrival was digging through the piles of money and treasures not far off. He was bald and middle-aged, wearing armor and piling as much of the stuff as he could into a bag of holding very similar to the one Riven had just acquired. What he put in disappeared, and Riven stalked over to the man in silence while the others watched.

"AHEM!"

The man casually turned around, showing himself to be the same man who'd watched with his friends and taken bets on who was going to die first when Heroic Intervention had initially activated. He snapped his bag shut to address the slightly smaller caster who'd approached.

"What is it?" the armored knight asked, tilting his head to look at the demons and other members of Hakim's party. "Can I help you?"

"Can you help me?" Riven repeated, his voice dropping to a flat, cold tone, the playfulness now utterly gone. The scepter underneath his arm clattered to the floor, and he stepped out of his fuzzy slippers and tossed the crown haphazardly to the side with a clatter of metal on stone.

The knight took a step back when Riven entered his personal space, and he put a hand on the large sword at his side, sizing Riven up. "I wouldn't take another step if I were you. Back off."

Riven paused, then smiled widely with fangs extended and began to laugh in the man's face. His laugh was genuine but also malicious, climbing higher and higher until he clutched his sides. The mood grew dark, and Hakim backpedaled and motioned for the others to do the same—while the one remaining orb of multicolored light showing the blonde storm mage still hovered there as she too watched the scene unfold.

Riven calmed down, and the man remained unmoving with one hand on his sword in a defensive stance. The vampire's features brightened, and red flickers of blood mana started creeping up his right arm. "Fucking unreal! You stay back, watching in amusement while thinking Hakim is going to die, until you realize that he's NOT going to die and you come to claim the treasure? At the very last moment, when Hakim's artifact is about to expire the event? Get fucked. Drop that sack before I start cutting off your skin to wear it like a cape."

Riven's eyes flared, and trickles of bright red started crawling across his face along his veins from his eyes. His aura exploded into a dense, writhing, palpable force of will that crashed down onto the entire area around them. The air shimmered in red hues. Crimson frost started collecting on everything—the walls, the ceiling, the floor, and even the treasure and people's clothes. Bloody snowflakes popped into existence one by one and started drifting in the air.

The man hesitated, the first sign of nervousness crossing his features and sweat starting to collect along his forehead despite the temperature drop. "We were both among the top-five most powerful Hakim has met. I am no pushover. Do you want to take that risk with your life? There is more than enough treasure to go around and no way for you to collect all this before you leave. Why not share?"

"I have more than enough space to take all this back," Riven lied. His spatial sack was already full to the brim—he'd made sure of that when the bribe had come through—but he wasn't about to let this ass clown take the treasure back home after he'd decided to let Hakim die and make a sporting event out of it. "And don't even think of comparing yourself to me, you pathetic, weak insect of a man. I am *leagues* above you; I can feel it in your very presence, in the way your heartbeat is racing as we speak. You are afraid, we both know it, and I'm playing nice by even giving you the opportunity to give up and head home like the scared little bitch you are. Be true to your nature and run, little piggy . . . You have five seconds to drop it, otherwise I follow through with my promise to cut off your skin—and I'll even use you as my next meal."

Riven's staff lit up with arcs of crackling black electricity, his aura pulsed to even greater heights, and the blood mana condensing along his arm flared over the right side of his body to enormous proportions of silky red that dwarfed his entire body three times over. The amount of unleashed mana was so palpable that Hakim and his three guildmates had to backpedal in order to void passive damage, and his growing smile of sinister intent spread beyond what a human could do with regular facial muscles.

Red frost began collecting along the man's skin while he stared down the fangs bared his way. His eyes shifted to the three demons closing in around him, and then to Hakim, who watched nervously from behind.

"Two seconds," Riven said, neither man moving.

A portal similar to the one Riven had arrived in abruptly flared open behind the knight, and he jumped backward, trying to make an escape with the loot he'd already obtained—only to be ripped back from the portal with a scream when a Wretched Snare latched onto his armor.

Riven's arm, shrouded in a dense cloud of flickering blood mana, slammed into and through the heavy iron armor and pierced out the other side—sending the man into a horrified wail of pain.

The man thrashed for a moment, skills and defensive rings along his fingers lighting up—only to be shattered when they came into contact with Riven's own power. The convulsing, greed-stricken man belched blood, and then his upper body abruptly exploded upward onto the ceiling when Riven discharged the energy he'd been storing.

"Pathetic."

The thick aura abruptly faded, and the frost accumulated around the room began to recede. Riven glanced up at the plastered remains stuck to the ceiling, then casually shook his hand to get the remnants of the lower body off. To his left, the other orb showing the storm mage Zerfi displayed her shocked expression, before she covered her mouth with both hands and just continued to look.

"Wanna try?" Riven asked the blonde woman, who only stared back. "Good. Pimp Riven has been known to smack a ho on occasion. Case in point: this asshole on the ceiling."

He snorted, put his fuzzy green slippers back on, slapped his crown onto his head at an awkward angle, picked up the large gaudy scepter he'd found, and aimed a toothy grin at Julie, Tim, Caleb, and Hakim. "These were really the best you've met so far? Jesus. What a bunch of fucking wimps. Anyways, now that problem is sorted out, so let's get on to business. See all this shit here?"

He gestured back at the piles of treasure as the four guildmates nodded. "This is all for you. Whatever you can take, anyways. Maybe take that asswipe's spatial bag to carry a lot of this stuff, but we've got a time limit before the system closes this dungeon off. Whatever you can't carry, I'll get my demons to try and bring with me back home."

Riven picked up the dead knight's spatial bag and inspected it before frowning. "Well, there's no way we'll get it all, but we can at least try. This thing is a lot smaller than mine."

He tossed the bag over to Hakim, who caught it and looked down at the bloody fabric.

"Riven . . ." Hakim said awkwardly, sharing glances with his guildmates while Julie stared open-mouthed, simultaneously supporting her brother. "This . . . is a lot to take in. You've changed a lot . . ."

Riven raised an eyebrow. "In a bad way?"

Hakim considered the question, then evaluated the man plastered to the ceiling, and shook his head. "Well, I hope you really don't eat people, but other than that? No, not necessarily . . . you're just pretty brutal, man. But then again, when we first met, you did kill all those people who were attacking Julie and her family . . . So maybe not so much. I just didn't expect you to murder him."

"He would have left you to die," Riven stated simply, uncaringly, and he smiled when he got nods of approval from Athela. He didn't answer the part about eating people, not wanting to address it after having accidentally killed that poor sod in Negrada. "Tough shit. If he wanted the treasure, he should have come to help. What he shouldn't have done is try to steal from me afterward. Fuck that guy."

"Agreed," Athela added proudly, ruffling Riven's hair from underneath his hood and crown and glancing at the large, shimmering bone sword on his back. "You're growing up! I'm so happy for you!"

"Shut it."

"I'm being serious!"

Riven rolled his eyes and then started walking up the piles of money to where other enchanted items were halfway buried. "Anyways, there shouldn't be any Unholy-related stuff, as I already took it all from the dungeon coffers—but a lot of this stuff should help you guys out. There's an enchanted axe, some healing scrolls over there, an imbue enchantment card for projectiles . . . and I made sure it was all pre-identified by the dungeon avatar so you know what you're looking at. Hurry it up! We don't have all day!"

CHAPTER 7

"NO! THESE ARE MY SHINIES!" Athela, in her spider form, screeched, wearing a small empty treasure chest on her head while simultaneously waist-deep in the pile of gold and platinum. She angrily swatted at the coins to make her hill of wealth shake, reminding Riven of a toddler when they didn't get their ice cream. "MY SHINIES! MY SHINIES! MY SHINIES!"

Riven couldn't say he'd ever seen a spiderlike creature wearing a treasure chest swimming in a pool of golden coins before, but he also couldn't say it wasn't hilarious. "Come on, Athela, you can't move it all, and we need to go. Time's up."

"NO!" Athela screamed, swatting her little legs faster and faster in a full-blown nuclear temper tantrum. "MINE MINE MINE!"

"Azmoth, get her out of there."

Riven face-palmed as Azmoth hunched down over the ridiculous spider to grab her with a large claw.

"Argh!"

"Athela, are you biting Azmoth?"

"ARGH!"

"You do realize your mandibles aren't penetrating his hand armor, right?"

Athela released her hold on Azmoth's claws and pointed a quivering foot Riven's way. "SHUT IT, TWERP!"

"Well, it's good to see Athela hasn't changed much!" Julie said with a wide, laughing smile. She walked over from where she was sitting with her brother, put down the chest of gold she'd collected, and gave Riven an unexpected but purely friendly hug. "Thanks, Riven. I appreciate what you did for us, once again."

Riven hugged her back a bit awkwardly and gave her a polite smile. "Not a problem at all. Try not to use that last charge with Heroic Intervention any time soon, but just in case you need me, I'll be there. Oh, and say hi to y'all's mom, since she wasn't here this time!"

"Riven." Tim gave him a firm nod from where he lay. He was taking the loss of a leg rather well, but then again, his sister was also a healer, and with magic in the picture it was highly likely he'd get that leg back one day.

Hakim came over and clasped hands with Riven, evaluating his fuzzy green slippers one more time with a chuckle and shake of the head. "It is good to see you again, my friend. Where is it that you're staying now?"

Riven and the bigger man let go. "Brightsville, or that's what we called it originally. I believe we can use the cortex to communicate with one another, should we ever visit the same spot, but even better would be if your community found an Elysium altar. We just got one, and we could set up a trading outpost in each other's communities, system shenanigans and whatnot."

Hakim nodded with a grunt, hoisting his bag of loot over his shoulder and sporting the new rune-laden battle-axe at his hip. "I look forward to it. We don't have access to an Elysium altar at all, unfortunately—never even seen one yet—but I have heard that one of the factions founded by the former Vietnamese government has a few high levelers that acquired one up north from us. Do you think we'd be able to travel to your city to see it for ourselves? Your sister and the undead-greenskin thing you've got going on is rather interesting . . ."

"Probably not by foot. It's daytime here, right?"

"Yeah."

"It's nighttime where I'm from, we're probably on the other side of the world somewhere."

"Shit."

"I know. Well, not much we can do about it, but if the opportunity ever comes up, we've named ourselves the Thane Necropolis. Look us up when we're rich and famous."

Hakim snorted a laugh and gave another nod, glancing over at the redheaded young man who was missing his leg. "Ugh . . . his mother is going to have my head."

"Nuh-uh! Not after I tell her about your heroics to save us!" Julie got up on her toes and gave Hakim a kiss on the cheek, then skipped back over to her brother.

Riven exchanged a look with an obviously embarrassed Hakim and raised both eyebrows with a widening grin. He hiked a thumb Julie's way. "You and her, huh?!"

". . . Yeah . . ."

"How long?! Don't be embarrassed—she's very pretty!"

"Um . . . about a month now." Hakim smiled shyly and scratched the back of his head while looking to the ground. "Her mom doesn't know yet. Do you think she'll care?"

Riven gawked. "Hakim. What's not to like? You're a gigachad if I've ever seen one and a nice guy to boot."

"What is a gigachad?"

"You obviously haven't kept up with pop culture, mate. Just accept it, take your riches, and move on."

Portals flared to life with a notification stating the dungeon would close in less than a minute and that forced teleportation would commence soon.

"Hah. Okay, then. I'll see you next time, Riven, and thanks again for saving us. We owe you our lives."

"What're friends for, right? Stay alive."

"You, too. Stay safe—keep Athela safe, too. She's kinda scary, but I love that ridiculous spider girl!"

Riven smiled warmly and stepped away with a wave. "As do I."

The portal back home collapsed, and Riven found himself back under a night sky. Only an hour and a half had passed. Allie and the others were all waiting for their return, and it took a little bit of time to fill them all in.

Especially given the massive amount of stuff Riven dumped out of the chests they carried. Then, on top of that, there were all the things in his spatial bag, which amounted to a three-meter-high and six-meter-wide pile of coins, jewelry, trinkets, weapons, and a couple of spell scrolls. Most of it was Unholy related to boot, but there were a lot of items related to the Fae foundational pillar that the orcs could use, too. In particular, there was a Storm spell tome and a Storm martial arts manual, which were probably some of the most valuable things in this entire pile. Only a couple of abilities were described in each, but those abilities would be more than enough to take the average orc warrior to a new level should they learn it. Hell, even the goblins could probably learn it if they had high enough affinities—though most of the goblins were rather stupid.

Funny, now that Riven thought of it, that the greenskins were oriented toward the Fae foundational pillar, considering they had negative Charisma like he did. They had the option of switching to the Unholy foundational pillar, too, now, by using his altar, but it wasn't necessarily a requirement, and he was sure many of the shamans would want to keep their already-practiced spells instead of starting over. Plus, it'd be nice to have some variety inside their city—at the very least, it couldn't hurt, and the orcs had already expressed to Allie (after some very recent experimentation) that the haunted forest would do their Forest subpillars well with training despite the Death aspect to it.

It was looking like Riven had made a very good decision picking that terraforming option.

"These treasures are . . . quite valuable," Gurth'Rok muttered while inspecting a gnarled root that was twisted into patterns that looked something like a dreamcatcher. "Do you mind if I take this? I can happily pay you for the item, though we are somewhat poor."

"What does it do?"

"It halves the resource cost of any Storm or Forest pillar abilities as long as they're Tier 1."

Riven's eyebrows rose. "Holy shit, that's really good. Yeah, take it as a sign of goodwill. For free."

The orc chieftain took off his wooden mask, showing a genuine look of surprise—though it was somewhat hard to tell due to his missing upper lip and the scars adorning his face. "That is unexpected. Thank you, Riven. It will be remembered."

Allie, on the other hand, was inspecting the gigantic, spiked, death-attuned bone sword Riven had brought back. The sword was way too big for her or any of the normal death knights, but one of the large, muscular flesh golems could wield it easily enough and was taking swings with it at Allie's request. Every time it was swung, the air crackled with neon-teal energy, and it had the ability to rip life out of an opponent with soul damage just by being in close proximity rather than doing only physical damage.

It was a rather dangerous weapon.

"I'm not sure I want to give this out to just anyone . . ." Allie said, gesturing for the flesh golem to put it back in the pile. "I appreciate the gift, but I certainly can't use it. I don't have the Strength stat, not anywhere close, and it's not my combat style, either. Perhaps I'll wait to hand it out if we have a notable champion arise in our ranks . . . It will be good incentive for the recruits to strive for greater things. Perhaps even an orc could wield this if they changed pillars at this altar."

Riven shrugged, looking up at the green halo of flames encircling the rune-lit black spire far overhead. "Whatever. Figured I'd give you a gift—if you hate it, that's fine. I get it. I'll just cry myself to sleep tonight—no big deal."

Allie smirked and gave an exaggerated eye roll. "Oh, do shut up. It looks like your minions are also enjoying their own new toys. I can see Athela, in particular, is loving hers by the way she shows it to everyone."

And indeed, she was showing it to everyone. Athela was prancing around having a grand old time telling the orcs, the goblins, the undead, the other demons, and even Dr. Brass how her new tiara was a symbolic gesture from Elysium itself indicating how she was a true-blue princess.

She had quite the obsession. Not only because it looked the part of a princess and the black metal with ruby gemstones fit her colors well, but it gave her a very overpowered effect, in Riven's opinion. Not that he was complaining.

[Tiara of Silent Killing (Blood/Shadow trinket): After successfully killing a target without being noticed by anyone else, gain a charge

of critical strike. Your next unseen attack has a 100% chance to be a 2x–8x critical hit, with multiplied damage coming in the form of kinetic burst energy from the strike site. Requires a 26% or higher Blood _or_ Shadow pillar affinity to wield, and the wearer must be female.]

"I'm just happy she's happy," Riven said, chuckling. "Apparently the dungeon was scared shitless of me, because it spent a load of stuff to get me out of there. And the other demons seem to like theirs as well. This whole dungeon-diving thing was *incredibly* profitable, Allie. I think that we should start looking for more of them in the immediate area. If Hakim's town has multiple nearby, I'm sure we could find some here."

Azmoth's handcrafted item was an infernal maul of dark-gray stone, three times the size of Riven's entire body, with streaks of lava flowing along the surface. It was utterly huge, pretty simple in design, did passive burn damage on hit, and had a physical base damage that—unsurprisingly—tripled Riven's own staff. Being hit with that thing would terminate any human instantly—it was the perfect weapon for Azmoth, because it wasn't a weapon made with skill in mind. He'd just whack things with it as hard as he could. Even Azmoth, as strong as he was, needed two of his arms to wield the damn thing effectively, but it still left his other two arms available for normal grappling. The huge demon had been utterly excited to get the maul and had been smashing boulders or scattered trees with it since they got back. Even now, Riven could feel the ground shake slightly from the magma explosions in nearby fields.

[Hell-forged Maul (Infernal/Volcanic Weapon): 319 average physical damage on strike, two-handed for full effect, with each strike dealing additional burn damage on hit and over time. 10% bonus to stun chance. Requires 532 Strength stat with the Infernal or Volcano subpillar to use.

• **Magma Strike: Activate this ability to increase the damage dealt by 40% in the form of an additional magma-based explosion. Mandatory five-minute cooldown.**]

Fay had been given a set of fur-lined, rather feminine-looking, brown-scaled boots with a dozen orange-red feathers coming out each of the lateral ankle areas. The boots came up to her knees, and they'd fit perfectly. She'd blushed furiously when being handed the gift and had awkwardly accepted before running off to put them on. Ever since, she'd been looking down at her feet with a rather broad grin. These boots had an enchantment that could be used by anyone, which was called a generic enchantment, according to Athela—even though it was technically a Storm subpillar enchantment due to using air magic for the effect. This was unlike the other two items he'd given his demons, but they still did her a serious solid for her flying abilities.

[Boots of Feather Step (Light Armor) (Enchanted Boots): 36 average defense. Increases any kind of flight speed by 23%. While flying, gain an additional +50 Agility and +81 Sturdiness.]

"If I get loot like this every time I go dungeon diving, I'll be fucking rich," Riven added with a nod at Fay, who smiled shyly and walked off toward Mara and Athela on the sidelines.

Allie furrowed her brows and folded her arms. "I haven't known Fay very long, but isn't she acting a bit odd?"

"Her last summoner was a real jackass, apparently. This is the first time she was ever given any kind of gift. That's what she told me, anyways."

"Oh? What a lady-killer."

"Let's not go down that road again." Riven ruffled Allie's hair, knowing she'd hate it, and he got a quick jab to the ribs again when she huffed loudly. "Anyways, let me apply my points real quick. Hold that thought and we'll discuss the altar's trading posts."

[Riven Thane's Status Page:
- **Level 44**
- **Pillar Orientations: Unholy Foundation, Blood Specialty, Infernal, Shadow**
- **Core of Original Sin—Gluttony: (Under Construction) (???)**
- **Traits: Race: Pure-Blooded Vampire (Extreme Darkness Regeneration) (Sunlight Decay) (Extreme weakness to silver weapons, Sun pillar, and Light pillar attacks), Class: Warlock Adept, Adrenaline Junkie (Blood) (+15% to Agility)**
- **Abilities: Blessing of the Crow (Unholy), Wretched Snare (Unholy), Silvertongue (Unholy), Bloody Razors (Blood), Crimson Ice (Blood), Blood Lance (Blood) (Tier 2), Blood Nova (Blood) (Tier 3), Hell's Armor (Infernal), Riftwalk (Shadow)**
- **Stats: 74 Strength, 159 Sturdiness, 404 Intelligence, 194 Agility, 10 Luck, -380 Charisma, 188 Vampiric Perception, 124 Willpower, 9 Faith**
- **Free Stat Points: 24**
- **Minions: Athela, Level 34 Arshakai [36 Willpower Requirement]. Azmoth, Level 38 Hellscape Brutalisk [44 Willpower Requirement]. Fay, Level 27 Succubus [29 Willpower Requirement]**

- **Equipped Items: Crude Cultist's Robes (1 def), Vampire's Escort (104 dmg, 102% mana regen, Shadow and Blood dmg +22%, Black Lightning, Scorpion's Sting), Chalgathi Cultist Amulet (???), Leather Boots (1 def), Backpack of Supplies (Guild Hall: Stone Manor), Witch's Ring of Grand Casting (+26 Intelligence), Breath of Valgeshia (48 def, +13 dmg & +9% mana output dmg for blood dmg, 6% mana regen)**
- **TWO PENDING NOTIFICATIONS]**

Riven tapped his foot, thinking about where he wanted to apply his twenty-four free stat points. He'd been applying some to Sturdiness or Willpower on occasion, most of them into Intelligence, and little else. Strength was nice to have, but he didn't like to engage in close combat if he could help it. His Faith stat was utterly useless to him because he never intended to go the miracle route and therefore wouldn't ever convert his pure soul energy into divinity (nor did he even know how miracles worked), and his Luck stat? He didn't know how Luck worked, either, but he'd heard from both Athela and Fay that having a high Luck stat was generally correlated with surviving to the highest levels across the cosmos.

So, figuring it couldn't hurt to have a statistical advantage, he slammed all twenty-four points into Luck.

Or at least he tried to.

[You have maxed out your Luck stat at ten with your current qualifications. In order to increase your Luck stat beyond ten, you must meet further unspecified requirements.]

"Well, FUCK YOU, TOO!" Riven raised both hands and flipped off the sky in a gesture toward Elysium, then slumped his shoulders when his sister saw the notification.

"Tough luck," Allie mused. "What are those two pending notifications? Have you checked?"

Riven glared, then split the twenty-four points down the middle into Sturdiness and Intelligence with a frustrated wave of his hand. "What bullshit. And no, I haven't checked yet, but I'm willing to bet one of them is the trait I'm getting for defeating that dungeon boss. Let's go ahead and see."

When he clicked on the line of text, two different screens appeared. One was relating to Azmoth, one was relating to a new trait, and both had two different options to choose from. "Oh. Oh boy. Hey, Azmoth! Get over here—we need to chat!"

[Your minion Azmoth has been judged by the system to have met requirements for two different classes, based on actions and fighting style. Please select from the following starter class titles if you wish to do so:

- Legion Berserker Initiate (Class Title)—A physically demanding class that supplies this class holder with a new resource pool: Rage. This class rewards the participant with an influx of HP (health points), SP (stamina points), and RP (rage points) every time he or she makes a kill. The higher the rage points get, the more damage output the participant has, and the more the participant loses his or her ability to think properly. Gives bonuses to two-handed weapons and heavy armor. +2 Strength, +1 Sturdiness, +1 free stat point per level. (Comes with the knowledge of the Unholy martial art Wretched Cleaving) (Increases Willpower requirement by 6)
- Infernal Crusader Initiate (Class Title)—A fire-attuned physical class path that focuses on tanking through martial arts. This class increases defensive capabilities with inherent bonuses, the amount of Sturdiness gained per level, and abilities granted by the system at regular intervals. +1 Strength, +4 Sturdiness, +1 free stat point per level. Gives bonuses to heavy armor and fire-attuned abilities. (Comes with the knowledge of the Infernal martial art Dome of Flames) (Increases Willpower requirement by 5)]

[You have been granted the choice of two new accomplishment titles. You may only have one accomplishment title active at any time, and changing titles is permanent. Accomplishment titles are granted based on actions that are out of the ordinary and deemed worthy of note by the system. Please choose between the following:

- Dragon's Bane 1: Any draconic enemies you fight now receive a generalized debuff to all stats at a flat baseline of -60. (Received for solo killing a greater drake of higher level in less than thirty minutes.)
- Bloodthirsty 1: Corpses around you supply you with 5% increased Blood mana, and Blood magic does an additional 1% damage to enemies. (Received for utilizing environmental blood resources on a grand scale numerous times against overwhelming odds.)]

The option for his accomplishment title was an obvious one—he didn't even have to think about it before selecting Bloodthirsty 1. Though he did note that the Dragon's Bane title talked about how he'd solo killed that dungeon boss, and his thoughts went back to the time Athela told him the system considered all summons as part of him. How true that was, because he certainly hadn't killed the drake without the help of his minionsh.

Not that it mattered too much, because he wasn't selecting it anyways.

As Riven looked up from his screens and closed one of them, Azmoth came bounding over, his enormous maul in one hand. Though the demon couldn't maneuver the weapon as effectively in battle without two, carrying it with only one was still possible given Azmoth's massive strength.

"Riven call me?" Azmoth asked, taking a knee and bowing in an unusual display of allegiance.

Riven pooched his lips but didn't comment on it, and he gestured to the weapon. "Having fun with the new toy?"

Azmoth grinned and avidly nodded. "Yes, I love new toy!"

"Great to hear, man. Question for you, though—did you know you had a class choice up for grabs?"

Azmoth tilted his head, then nodded. "Yes, yes. I not know which pick. Was going to ask, but you busy. What you think?"

Riven exchanged a glance with Allie. "Um . . . Honestly, I don't know. I'm kind of torn. On one hand, the berserker class would make you an absolute menace offensively, and killing things would regenerate you even more than that Hell's Amor you have going on, while on the other hand, you get two more stat points per level and a focus on defensive abilities with the crusader class. I'm sure you're already aware of this, and I know I'm stating the obvious, but I just wanted to make sure you knew. I think it's best if you follow your heart and choose for yourself, though, because to me, there isn't an obvious winner here. Either one would be great."

Azmoth grunted his acknowledgment, then stood up. "I think on this. I let know."

Riven smirked in turn. "All right, buddy, just tell me when you decide. It's exciting either way, so congratulations on the achievement!"

CHAPTER 8

Riven side-eyed his sister with a growing grin as Azmoth walked over to play with his new hammer, and he nudged her to get her attention under the dim glow of starlight and the flaming green halo overhead. "Hey, I do have one other thing for you before we move on."

Allie evaluated his smug posturing and took a wary step back. "You better not fucking tickle me or something stupid like that. I'll fight back."

"No!" Riven let out a long laugh and shook his head, then reached into his spatial bag and pulled out a small flashing bauble. It was orange in color and semitranslucent and had a small picture in it that changed based on the way you looked at it—though Allie couldn't tell what it was by any angle.

"Um . . . What's this?" Allie asked curiously, inspecting it and getting only question marks popping up for her identification information.

Riven smiled fondly. "Well, first I have a question for you. Do your minions level up?"

". . . Why?"

"And what kind of minions can you make?"

". . . Those are very odd questions, but fine, I'll play ball. My minions can level up, yes. It's why some of my skeletons are simply skeletons while others I've outfitted to be death knights, though they're technically not REALLY death knights YET. The ones I've been calling death knights are really just leveled-up skeletons I'm preparing for the actual class of death knight." She waved a hand at where some of her more heavily outfitted and armored skeletons stood silently. "The problem is that mindless undead minions can't have classes. They retain the abilities their old bodies had, or Unholy versions of the abilities they had, but their classes and associated perks disappear. In order to have a class, they need to have a true soul, but these only have soul fragments. It's been a pain to deal with, but I know I can eventually figure out how to imbue true souls without the bone garden's intervention."

"Why not just use the bone garden, then?"

"Because then they wouldn't be my minions. They'd be self-aware undead that serve themselves rather than me."

"Hmm. I see. But they can still level up?"

"Yes, they can. They also start at half the level they were when they were raised from the dead. So if they started out at level 20, they come back as a level-10 skeleton. Concerning your other question, I'm a swarm necromancer and have a heavy focus on bone. I have two hundred basic undead minion slots and two captain undead minion slots that control my other minions. They're supposed to be intelligent, but again, I can't seem to figure out how to create them without the bone garden, and the bone garden doesn't add them to my minion slots. My class allows me to specialize between bone, soul, and flesh, and bone is my specialization. So most of my creatures lose their flesh pretty fast, but I can also modify them to build them up with bone from other creatures or even grow new bone to fill in gaps when needed or for extra protection."

"Can the captain undead minion slots be used on any creature when you figure it out?"

Allie suspiciously grinned, then eyed the bauble. "What exactly is that, Riven? Why are you asking me all these questions?"

Riven touched one hand to his heart and took a step back as if accused of something horrible. "Well, I just figured that since most of my sack was filled with the body of the dungeon's drake boss that I'd ask if you could—you know . . . use it."

Allie's jaw dropped. Her eyes landed on the orange bauble in her hand, then she looked back up to Riven. "You're kidding me."

"Not kidding you," Riven stated cheerily with a finger uplifted. "That's a compression device because we couldn't fit it into the bag's opening, but it still took up a lot of space. The dungeon was more than happy to get rid of it instead of filling up the entire damn thing with more of its loot. The body would have gone to waste otherwise. So . . . if you ever figure out how to use it, there's your pet drake. It's pretty big! Careful where you break that bauble, because if it shatters the body comes crashing down."

". . . Well, thank you, Riven. You've always been very thoughtful, even while we were growing up." His sister gave him the childish, excited grin she used to get whenever he gave her Christmas presents back on Earth when they were young. She palmed the bauble, then shoved it into a pocket and patted it down. "It won't be usable for quite some time, and it'll probably take up quite a few minion slots, from what Mara told me about the relative strength of minions to necromantic master, but it is certainly appreciated. Perhaps in a few months I'll have figured it out. You're the best, as always."

[You currently have two requesting trading partners, zero claimed trading ports, and four open trading ports. These factions each wish to set up a trading commune designated in the space enclosed by one of your altar's platform barriers. Please decline or accept the following faction offers:
- **Negrada, Minor Hellscape Dungeon**
- **The Blood Moon Requiem**]

Riven touched the screen and mentally selected which port he'd like to utilize. "I accept Negrada's trade request."

To his left, one of the stadium-size platforms came to life with a myriad of lights illuminating the night sky.

[The faction Negrada, Minor Hellscape Dungeon, is transferring its trading commune now. Trading commune is set to Tier 1, and you may now set up your own commune on the opposite end of this connection. Setting up your own trading commune is not a necessity, but those recognized by the altar owner as merchants representing your faction are allowed to cross over via portal access in the trading port. Tier 2 can be purchased by either trading partner after one year's time. Tier 3 will be unavailable until the integration phase is over and the world quests have been completed. Please hold.]

POP

And just like that, a large red tent appeared, a sizable portal beside it.

The portal itself was wreathed in flames, and shifting images revealed what Riven could only assume was the hellscape, with demonic figures roaming about on the other side in more organized a fashion than he was used to—but no sounds came through it whatsoever. The tent itself was rather large and spanned a space not nearly as large as the area given to the faction to build on, but was more about forty yards wide and eighty yards long. The depiction of a black, flaming-eye symbol was engraved onto the front of the tent, and the large tent flaps at the front were parted to reveal a couple dozen Jabob demons in purple robes, a dozen or so scantily clad and collared succubi of varying skin tones, a very tall incubus with orange skin and black hair who held leashes attached to the succubi, and a handful of heavily armored purple gargoyles with yellow eyes that each were the size of a rhinoceros.

Fay immediately hissed in irritation and took a step back, quickly hiding behind Riven to make herself look small when the incubus settled his gaze on her, and the demon smirked at her reaction before leaving the leashes he had with a gargoyle to follow one of the older, bearded Jabob demons, who walked with a cane.

"What's wrong?" Riven asked, feeling Fay's forehead and her small horns push up against his back to hide her face. "You okay?"

Fay uttered a growl, and Athela began to laugh while walking over and adjusting her tiara.

"You have a lot to learn about demonic culture, Riven." Athela patted him on the shoulder and watched the two demons from Negrada approach. "A lot to learn."

Riven frowned but let Fay hide in his shadow until the old Jabob demon with the twisted, knotted beard came to a stop before them—evaluating Riven in particular with three bright-green eyes that were unlike most Jabob demons Riven was familiar with. Beside the red-skinned, apelike old demon, the incubus calmly stepped into place with eyes firmly glued to him as well.

"You can tell your Succubus that I have no intention of trying to claim her," the extraordinarily handsome orange man said. So much so that Allie audibly inhaled a sharp hiss of air. He had a very strong jawline, was toned but not huge, had his black hair in a ponytail that hung down to his back, and wore a white shirt with brown pants and boots. His wings were similar to Fay's but larger, and the tail was a lot thicker at the base, while his horns were far larger than Fay's and curled at the tips. Out of thin air, he produced a stone tablet very similar to a clipboard and summoned a glowing pen made of red light. "I would not dare anger my master Negrada by attempting to take something that is yours, Riven Thane. Even if I wanted to, I cannot, because my mercantile license through the system does not permit me to attack you on altar grounds unless I was stolen from or attacked first. Not only that, but bonded succubi familiars are much harder to capture than free-roaming ones anyways. Though I must admit . . . I would thoroughly enjoy having a blue."

A blue? Was he referring to Fay's skin color? Riven glanced back over to the other scantily clad succubi and noted how there were green, orange, bright white, brown, and purple succubi present—each with slightly different demonic features.

Fay's grip relaxed, and she peeked out warily from under Riven's arm where he held Vampire's Escort with the butt planted onto the ground.

Still, she did not move from behind him.

Riven remained silent, blinking with one hand on his staff and the other shoved into a pocket, and he shifted his gaze when the old Jabob demon began to laugh.

"My name is Fred, and I'm the leader of this trading commune as a representative for my master, Dungeon Negrada. It is a pleasure, boy." The gnarled hand stretched out for Riven to shake. "This incubus is Zelmontar Shushvar Trok, but you can call him Zelmont."

Riven stared down at the shorter demon, then accepted the handshake firmly with a polite nod. "I assume your name isn't truly Fred, either."

"No, it is not, but it's an easy enough name to remember and was picked from the knowledge we have of your world. My actual name is Forskar Mentunivini Chubrakwanton. But you can just call me Fred."

Riven chuckled and released Fred's grip, gesturing to Athela—who was glaring daggers at the incubus as if daring him to do something—and then Azmoth. "These are my minions, Athela, Azmoth, and Fay. This is my sister, Allie, as well as her advisers Mara, Nin, and Vin. And this is Gurth'Rok. I've got to admit, I'm rather curious as to what you can offer us and what we can offer you at such an early stage in the integration process. I appreciate the gesture from Negrada—he didn't seem like too bad a guy there at the end of my stay—but it is nevertheless confusing to see him wanting to establish trade connections. We barely have a civilization set up to begin with and don't have much in the way of production or goods yet. Do you mind explaining why he chose to come?"

The apelike red demon stroked his beard thoughtfully and then examined the surrounding landscape, eyes settling on the partially terraformed tower in the distance. Though plant and animal life had changed thoroughly for miles due to the altar's work, the altar hadn't changed the buildings of Brightsville. "Truthfully, I'm slightly confused myself. I was hoping you'd know, but it is not my place to question the master. If I had to guess, it is that he sees a lot of potential in you and your newly growing civilization. It is a rarity for him to invest in such younglings like this; most of our trading partners are other dungeons or established factions in the hells, but truthfully, the curiosity of it all makes me quite keen on being here. I'm excited to see things unfold, as no doubt time will tell us both why we were sent. This is your first time experiencing an altar's trading system, yes?"

Riven nodded, as did Allie and the others.

"All right, I'll start with the basics. First and foremost, the system store is accessed by putting a hand on the central spire there—the one with the halo of green fire surrounding its top. It generally has marked-up prices, and you should only buy from there if you're desperate. Trading communes are the primary way civilizations trade off-world. With larger negotiations, there are some who trade via other means to avoid the 1 percent system tax on their Elysium coins that comes with any trade deal, but that usually isn't worth the effort unless the quantities are huge or the item tiers are vastly greater than the world tier. It's pretty simple otherwise: we take goods from the dungeon and present them here, with Tier-1 communes like this one being limited in size as well as the scope of what we can bring. Communes are also limited for what they can bring over by the tier of worlds, and because this is what the system considers a F-class world, we get taxed much more for even attempting to bring over any higher-tier goods."

"This is the first time I've heard of world tiers," Allie stated with a raised hand to interrupt the two. "Is F-class bad?"

"F-class is what all worlds usually start out at when they integrate. It isn't anything to be ashamed of." Fred the Jabob shrugged, supporting his weight more heavily on his gnarled cane. "It just means that if we bring over SSS-, SS-, S-, A-, B-, C-, D-, or E-class items, we'll be taxed exponentially for even the transfer of goods. It works like this: if Negrada sends over supplies that are labeled F-class to this F-class world, we only get taxed 1 percent on transactions for anything we sell. If we give you F-class items for free in an F-class world, then we get taxed by another base percentage of 1,000 percent of the item's average worth, which will certainly not happen from Negrada's standpoint, I can tell you right now. And free stuff is even outlawed by Elysium in newly integrating worlds to stop unfair advantages from happening until the world has been entirely claimed by one native entity or an invasion force with a token. E-class items we supply to you will be taxed at 100 percent the normal value on top of the sale price. D-class items we supply an F-class world with will be taxed at 1,000 percent the average cosmic price. C-class items we supply an F-class world with will be taxed 10,000 percent the average cosmic price. This goes on, adding zeros for each tier above the world tier until you get to SSS tier, which nobody in their right mind would ever sell, even if they managed to get such an item. But theoretically, if we brought over an SSS-class item to an F-class world, the tax on what the system considers the average price to be would amount to a 10 billion percent markup."

The demon huffed as Riven did the numbers in his head.

"If the items are labeled elite, within their item tier it also increases the value with another zero. If it is labeled legendary by the system within their item tier, like that soul-woven set you have there, girl"—the Jabob poked at Allie's bone armor and then her wand—"that status will elevate the price by two zeros on top of whatever the normal tax would be. These percentages are between all altars, even those within the same faction. And that, my friends, was all meant to explain why we have only brought F-class items with us to this commune!"

The incubus Zelmont chuckled and shook his head, scribbling down notes with his magical red-light pen while evaluating their surroundings as well as the three other unoccupied commune trade ports on the altar's three-square-mile platform. "That was rather long-winded. I have a question for the master of this altar—" He gestured to the other trade ports. "Do you have any others that you're going to be setting up shop with sometime soon?"

Fred frowned and scoffed up at the other, taller demon. "How in Negrada's name would a place like this get another trading agreement moments after establishing an altar? You do realize this is a newly integrated world, right? You're being rude."

Zelmont rolled his eyes and tapped his pen on the stone tablet he carried. "I am only being practical, *Fred*. I don't expect them to have other off-worlders of note here, but it is still certainly possible that they have other on-world trading ports with other Panu-based altars."

"Why does it matter?" Riven asked curiously.

The two demon men turned his way.

"Well, we can trade with anyone inside the altar's boundaries," Zelmont stated with a polite smile. "So if you are able to get more factions established within your altar, we are able to trade with them through this connection. It's more profitable for everyone present if you have all four trading ports filled. Taxes go up even more if communes trade with one another, but we won't bore you with those details like Fred did earlier, and it won't affect your own trading prospects at all."

Fred scowled up at the incubus, who played dumb to the glare, and Riven smirked at the interaction.

"I see. Well, there is one other faction that I have yet to accept. I was wanting to talk to you first."

"Oh?!" Fred perked up, and he rubbed his knotted hands together with a vigorous smile while Zelmont pulled some kind of drink out of a spatial bag at his side and began to sip. "That is splendid news! We also appreciate the gesture of good faith in speaking to us ahead of the other. I assume you've made an on-world ally?"

Riven and Allie exchanged looks.

"No," Riven said, pulling his altar's functions screen out of his own status page to view the notice. "It's something called the Blood Moon Requiem. Ever heard of it?"

Zelmont immediately choked on his drink and spat it out all over the ground, eyes going wide as Fred froze in shock. The incubus blinked and wiped the liquid from his chin, then scowled in disbelief. "I may have heard wrong, and excuse my rudeness, but could you repeat what you just said?"

CHAPTER 9

Trumpets sounded and drums reverberated across the broad street between towering marble buildings of monumental architecture.

Kathrine Vonsilla Crushada the Ninth, eldest daughter of the duke and duchess of House of Crushada, 107th in line for the vampiric throne, was nervously waving to the crowds of vampires while they roared with thunderous applause.

Red flower petals poured down from the balconies and airships far overhead as an orange dawn broke the horizon and cast the beautiful hues of sunrise on the capital of their world. The prophecy concerning Riven and Allie Thane had been spot-on, marking the exact time and date that their altar would come into being and connect their world with the homeland they'd fallen so far from.

The return of a prince and princess was a big deal. To the Senate, to the noble houses, to the High Queen Nephridi, and even to the masses. Even more so, it was a big deal to the enemies of their empire. It marked both the beginning of political discontent among the power players of their civilization, and the Blood Moon Requiem as an increasing threat to the surrounding systems of their controlled sects of space, but it was also symbolic in nature to their empire's citizens. The queen's favorite granddaughter was still missing, but her granddaughter's children had been found, and of all the citizens of their empire, the royal family had always produced the best and brightest of the Blood Moon Requiem. It symbolized potential for the rise of a new chapter in their great dynasty, and it added yet another powerful cog to the network of prophetic potential that the royals represented. The royal bloodline was one of extreme power, and having not one but TWO more of them capable of Malignant Prophecy would only further ensure the security of their people. After all, though Malignant Prophecy was found only within the royal lineage of their empire, just twenty of their number had ever been able to use this gift, and it often skipped generations despite aggressive or selective breeding practices.

Well, now that number was twenty-two.

Kathrine continued to glide down the paved streets toward the brilliantly lit palace, and despite the sunlight, she was not bothered by the glare. It had long been the case that their homeworld was granted a great boon by the queen, allowing all vampires in their homeland to walk in the light as daywalkers would. And for that, Kathrine was truly appreciative. Some things could only have their beauty appreciated in the light.

Her long, straight, perfectly combed brown hair only barely shifted with each step she took at the front of the small column. The floor-length, beautifully made black dress with embroidered red flowers that matched her glowing eyes flowed out behind her. Handpicked apprentices to elite military branches, all at the maximum level the system would allow in the integrating world—ninety—marched behind her, wearing black, gray, and red plate armor of intricate designs, huge pauldrons, plumed, visored helms, and metal boots. Each handpicked soldier wore elegantly crafted swords at their sides that were a cross between a scimitar and a long sword, runes etched into their blades, with flag-adorned halberds and tower shields displaying a black background behind a red crescent moon.

Ahead of her, up a wide flight of steps, positioned on the raised platform above the roaring crowds in front of the palace gates, was High Queen Nephridi in all her elegance. The long-lived matriarch of their empire was the undisputed powerhouse of this sector of the galaxy, a true terror to their enemies and beloved by the people she lorded over—those who were not the lesser beings enslaved as livestock. Beside High Queen Nephridi were Kathrine's parents, the duke and duchess of House Crushada, given a place of honor in this ceremony after Kathrine was chosen to be the voice of their empire on Panu. They'd even been placed in front of the high queen's own children and Prince Jalel, the man who'd found the two new royals. Kathrine was still very young, just slightly older than Riven and Allie, actually, and met the low level requirements to enter the temporarily quarantined frontier world. She was the only member of the royal bloodline who met this qualification, and she had been the youngest of their lineup until the discovery of the new prince and princess.

Her parents had obviously been thrilled, but this in turn had caused friction between House Crushada and the other royal branch families, who were jealous of the sudden favor bestowed upon them. It was written upon the faces of their rivals even now as the noble houses looked down on her approach from the platform above with thinly veiled contempt.

Most normal citizens would not recognize it for what it was, but after being raised as aristocracy, it was easily noticeable to her. It was evident in the way their eyes narrowed by the barest fraction, by the way they shifted slightly in their stance as if ready to pounce, or co in the way their lips twitched at the corners while they watched her move forward.

She started up the marble steps, bloodred flower petals continuing to shower her in a drifting cloud of elegance while flags above shifted in the warm breeze. Keeping her posture perfect and eyes on the steps in front of her, she tried to contain the pounding of her heart.

Until she finally arrived.

She found herself kneeling at the edge of the platform, and a large portal behind the nobility and directed to their chosen altar ripped through space to show the rest of the trading commune awaiting her arrival on the other side.

"Kathrine Vonsilla Crushada the Ninth . . ." High Queen Nephridi said softly, the palpable power of her words echoing out above the trumpets and drums to silence them immediately along with the applause of the crowd. "I welcome you, child, and congratulate you on your selection."

The queen's own dark-brown hair was decorated with red flowers over a plain, formfitting white dress, and the usual ruby amulet around her neck sparkled in the sunlight. Her youthful, extraordinarily beautiful features smiled warmly down at her distant niece, and a light touch ushered Kathrine to stand and meet her gaze.

"Thank you, Majesty," Kathrine stated with hands clasped in front of her, not daring to look over at her parents for emotional support despite how much she wanted to. This was without doubt the most important event of her life thus far, and she was deathly afraid of messing up.

Queen Nephridi gave an amused hum of contentment, red eyes looking her younger relative up and down approvingly, and she reached a hand out to fix Kathrine's collar where it'd been ruffled by wind.

Kathrine blushed in embarrassment, keeping her eyes on the queen's chest, but she didn't move.

"I hope you realize the importance of what you are doing," Queen Nephridi said softly, her words still easily heard over the vast expanse of the long main street leading through the capital where hundreds of thousands or even millions of people were now gathered. "Despite my power, I am unable to intervene directly with the events on this new planet. Panu, I believe it to be called. You will be my eyes and ears, a more direct line of communication, and will be responsible for guiding them back home. Despite the trainers, advisers, teachers, and resources we supply, it is a very real possibility that both the prince and princess will die in the coming years. I know you never experienced one for yourself, being born in an already established world, but integration trials are not easy. Above all else, the invading armies of other kingdoms will no doubt soon be aware of their existence, and be it murder or a hostage situation for political gain, they will seek to harm both Riven and Allie. And you. Their world is far from our own borders, and we cannot spare our legions on a crusade so far from our lands. That means that, aside from the trade access and benefits thereof, we will be unable to send aid. Their altar could be attacked at any moment, assassins could come for you or them, and you must be aware of the risks. Do you still willingly accept this position as the mouth of the empire in my stead?"

There was a palpable silence as Kathrine Vonsilla Crushada, eldest daughter of the duke and duchess of House Crushada, took in a breath. "I humbly and willingly accept this position of honor, Your Majesty."

Kathrine bowed, and the crowds roared with approval.

"Good." The queen smiled, glancing over to Kathrine's beaming parents with a nod. "Prepare yourself, Kathrine. The portal is ready, and the prince has just accepted our trade agreement as prophesied. It is time you leave. If you ever need anything—you know where to find me."

Kathrine stepped onto a platform of black metal plates underneath a star-filled night sky. Overhead a black spire familiar to her as an Unholy-oriented altar displayed a green halo of flames, and a chill night breeze rustled her black and red dress.

Standing behind her were the advisers, trainers, merchants, and other important people of the empire that the Blood Moon Requiem had sent over to Panu. Behind them still were two columns of heavily armored soldiers, all level 90, all elites for their level and grade. Their tower shields and halberds waving with the black flag of the red crescent moon blew in the wind just as Kathrine's brown hair did, and her glowing eyes settled on two sets of similar gazes not far off.

She glanced briefly behind her, looking up at the small stone keep with towers and battlements that'd been sent over as their version of the trade commune, and she nervously took in another deep breath before solidifying her resolve and walking forward. To know that the eyes of the entire empire were on her right now through scrying abilities crossing the portal was . . . intimidating, to say the least.

Two of her thrall servants, both older human men in nicely fitted satin robes with cleanly cut beards, followed her mutely. Each carried a small, intricately carved box made from ebony and platinum, with the royal crest of the blood moon depicted on the lid.

Holding her head high in front of the rather shoddy-looking bunch of characters, Kathrine came to a stop only ten feet away. It was an odd bunch: demons, orcs, various undead, and even a human who was no thrall in the background, all stared at her silently. She looked right to the other trading commune that'd been set up. It was, to her knowledge, from a small and insignificant dungeon from the hellscapes that'd been part of Riven's tutorial process, and she was rather uninterested in the lot as they stared her way.

Refocusing on her primary objectives, she smiled politely and briefly curtsied. "My name is Kathrine Vonsilla Crushada the Ninth, eldest daughter of the duke and duchess of House Crushada, 107th in line for the vampiric throne. I believe we are distant cousins, Riven and Allie Thane, and it is a pleasure to make your acquaintance."

There was a pause as Allie and Riven exchanged looks.

"Um . . . Well, this is unexpected, and I'm not quite sure how to react," Riven, the newly found prince, said while scratching the back of his head. "It's nice to meet you, but . . . you're really related to my mom and dad, then?"

"Told you!" Athela crowed from the background with a laugh while the Jabob demon and incubus nearby just gawked mutely.

Before Kathrine could reply, the new princess butted in.

"Do you know if my mother is in your world?" Allie asked with a concerned furrow of her brows. "Do you know anything about her disappearance?"

Kathrine opened her mouth to speak, unsure of how to reply, then hesitantly shook her head. "We are not sure where Princess Sheline is, I am sorry. High Queen Nephridi hopes to find her, though, and she asked me to tell you both that efforts to find her granddaughter and her granddaughter's husband are ongoing."

Allie's face fell in dismay, but she nodded in acceptance.

Riven's disappointment was apparent, too, and he held out a hand to take his sister's. Gently squeezing it, he gave her whispered words of encouragement—which was something of a shock to Kathrine. Growing up in an aristocratic family, public displays of affection like this were often frowned upon and considered signs of weakness. However, the prince and princess did it so openly, so blatantly, that it temporarily stunned Kathrine into silence.

She had to remind herself that her own upbringing was far different from those of these two newfound royals, and she internally considered what it would mean and how much she'd have to teach them about court life and the proper way to conduct oneself in the public eye.

"Riven and Allie Thane, or, better said, Riven and Allie of House Wraithtide, we have much to speak about." Kathrine gestured toward the immaculate keep where their commune had set up. "Would it be all right if we speak in private? There are many sensitive topics I'd like to discuss, and I'm sure you have lots of questions."

But before Riven or Allie could reply, the thrall servant next to Kathrine let out an abrupt scream. He dropped the present from the queen while falling to his knees, clutched at his bulging gut, and his body exploded in a hail of blood and silver shrapnel imbued with white fire that raced toward all three of the royals like homing missiles.

Kathrine had little time to register the assassination attempt in her confusion before hot, searing antivampire metals and enchantments ripped through her abdomen and soared straight for Allie's head.

CHAPTER 10

Blood and viscera tore through Kathrine's abdomen, and white sparks of high-speed shrapnel blasted toward Allie's face with a high-pitched screeching sound that dulled the senses. Allie's eyes went wide, Kathrine let out a horrified scream, the heavily armed guards jolted forward with shouts of alarm, and more of the flaring metals continued to blast out of the exploding thrall to head toward the three royals.

THUMP

THUMP

THUMP

The world turned to shades of gray, black, and red, slowing momentarily and then speeding back up in the course of a few seconds.

The metals whipped forward and shredded Allie's face, neck, and brain—sending gray matter peeling out the back of her skull and letting her body slump to the floor. Riven saw himself scream and rush toward her only to get blasted himself, ripped apart a thousand times over by a swarm of burning metals that eviscerated his body and tore the head cleanly off Kathrine's riddled body.

They were all so close to the thrall that'd ruptured and there'd been so little time to react . . . It was inevitable. The guards hadn't been able to take more than two steps forward despite their superhuman speed before all three of the vampiric nobility were utterly torn apart in a storm of white fire, glowing metal, and body parts that refused to heal. The nearest guard to them stumbled to a stuttering stop, gawking and dropping his halberd in utter dismay at the carnage. Athela screamed, Azmoth looked on in shock, and Fay put her hands up over her mouth in horror right before all three demons were ripped from this plane of existence and vanished into portals leading into the nether realms.

And thus, Riven watched himself die over and over again—the image replaying in front of him.

Riven's eyes dilated, and the world around him abruptly calmed on the fifth replay, slowing down just when three shimmering fragments of metal were within an inch of Allie's face. The land around them was still tinged in shades of black, red, and gray, and the familiar out-of-body experience halted space all around him as cold, resonating energy rippled across his skin.

His ethereal body, a replica of his own but without physical representation, stood staring at the scene— red eyes blinking down at a hand created from gray wisps of mist.

[Malignant Prophecy has activated.
Desired Action: High-Tier Manipulation. Current Willpower stat: 124. Sufficient Willpower to perform desired action. Performing this act will put your Malignant Prophecy on cooldown for significant amounts of time. Do you wish to proceed?]

THUMP
THUMP
"Yes."

[Desired action: Save yourself, Allie, and Kathrine from impending death. Malignant Prophecy's two options are as follows:
- **Option 1: Create an exact replica of miniature rifts in space to match incoming projectiles. At least 137 individual miniature rifts must be properly timed and created to divert all vital strikes. Up to 320 individual miniature rifts can be created at short distances and at enough of a narrow space-time before your mana runs out. Chance for success: High.**
- **Option 2: You must force Core of Original Sin—Gluttony to awaken early. This will empower you enough to survive and devour incoming projectiles, but it will greatly damage your soul's Blood subpillar to the point of nonuse. Chance for success: High.]**

[Desired action has been selected—Option 1.]

Immediately, time unfroze and the colors of the world went back to more normal hues.

Blood and viscera tore through Kathrine's abdomen, and white sparks of high-speed shrapnel blasted toward Allie's face with a high-pitched screeching sound that dulled the senses. Allie's eyes went wide, Kathrine let out a horrified scream, the heavily armed guards jolted forward with shouts of alarm, and more of the flaring metals continued to blast out of the exploding thrall to head toward the three royals.

A half second later, the flaming, white-hot shrapnel was within a centimeter of Allie's head, and less than a millisecond after that, a small black rift opened up between her and the missile that would mark her death.

Riven's hand shot forward, and dozens upon dozens of small rifts blew holes in space open around them, each one only an inch in diameter with a cost far less than a normal Riftwalk. His red eyes quivered and shot back and forth at insurmountable speeds while following the patterns Malignant Prophecy drew out in his mind, and his Shadow subpillar flared to life.

Missiles intended for himself, Allie, and Kathrine were all simultaneously swallowed in the blink of an eye and were launched elsewhere into the landscape around them. Explosions of hot-white flames dotted the black floor of the altar, and the sound of metal scraping on metal could be heard when many of the projectiles came to a grinding, sparking halt.

Riven's heart pounded in his chest, and blood leaked from his nose as his body shuddered. He dropped to one knee, vision going in and out while shouts from his allies and the vampires rushing over to help Kathrine up quickly started healing her and making sure he was okay.

He heard Allie's enraged screams and moments later felt Azmoth's strong armored claws pick his sagging body up, and then his mind faded into darkness as he passed out from the strain on his body.

[Your manipulation of fate has gained you three Malignancy Points. Current total Malignancy Points: 4]

Jalel ran a hand up through his short silver hair. He watched, awestruck, as the queen's fury was unleashed on the idiot who'd tried to circumvent Elysium's bylaws to kill the three younglings on the integrating world. If the man had only tried to kill Kathrine, that'd be one thing. He'd have succeeded, without any trace of what he'd done. But despite being many millennia old and being well over level 1,000, this moron had still failed to cover his tracks well enough to subvert the wrath of Elysium's administrator.

Within mere seconds of the assassination attempt being orchestrated, curses of magnitudes far greater than Jalel had ever seen visibly washed over the greater noble while his body began to rot and wither.

It took mere seconds for Queen Nephridi to realize what her distant cousin had tried to do to her nieces and nephew, and she'd acted to save him so that she might exact vengeance herself.

And she was certainly making an example of the man.

The prince, once the head of a great house of their empire, was stripped of clothes and titles before being nailed to a cross right there on the platform in front of the entire empire. She'd flayed his skin from his body, torn scars through his very soul, eviscerated him over a hundred times, broken all his bones dozens of times over, and was slowly pulling his brain out of his skull just fast enough to keep him alive while he regenerated it bit by bit inside his head.

All the while, the queen wore a cold expression of contempt as the cousin and his family begged for his life while he let out inhuman screams of pain. And all the while, the crowd jeered and cheered to keep it going while chanting for his death.

Jalel understood why his relative would have tried it. The situation represented a great opportunity, one he could capitalize on to kill other competitors in the aristocracy. Kathrine, in particular, was of a house that this man had conflicting interests with off-world concerning competing trading companies and slave harvesting along the border of their empire, but Kathrine was where the man should have stopped. He'd gotten greedy, foolishly thinking his use of a thrall would not tag him as the perpetrator of the crime. Perhaps the man had used multiple lines, multiple people beneath him, one after the other to pass the traitorous message along so that he wouldn't seem immediately responsible for the act. Perhaps the man had not thought Riven or Allie would have a full grasp of their Malignant Prophecy's powers yet.

But he should have known better, and Jalel could only shake his head at the absolute idiocy of it all.

"Quite the bold move," another man on Jalel's left said, and his red eyes shifted to where another aristocrat, another prince by the name of Blusoth, calmly watched the torturous execution with an unwavering gaze. "What an amateur. He deserves to die simply for the inability to properly carry out a plan, and even more so for poor judgment of time and place. He should have left it at Kathrine and the system wouldn't have intervened."

Blusoth adjusted his ornate, platinum-trimmed silver robes and smoothed back his blond hair. His lips quirked into a predatory grin, and his sideways glance at Jalel was met with stoicism. "Oh, don't be like that, dear cousin. I'm just voicing my thoughts, is all. I had been wondering if you were going to be the one to try it—unfortunate that that wasn't the case. It appears you have more of a brain on your shoulders than I'd anticipated."

"I fail to see why you'd think I'd attempt to assassinate the newly found royals," Jalel stated flatly, hands clenched in the pockets of his well-made black robe-suit and fingernails digging into his skin as he tried to subdue his rage. His red eyes narrowed. "Do enlighten me."

Blusoth smiled widely, exposing his fangs as red flower petals continued to shower the crowds from above them, the screams of the tortured man not far off echoing out above the shouts for his death. "My dear cousin, I just find it humorous that you tried to hide what you found there, deep in the heart of hell."

Jalel's blood ran cold, and he stiffened despite an act of Willpower to not do so. His pale face got paler, and the reaction was all Blusoth needed to start laughing. "I'm not sure what you mean by that, Blusoth. Stop speaking in riddles."

"Oh, come now," Blusoth teased, nudging past Jalel to step away with a backward glance. "I wonder what the queen would think if she noticed you failed to mention the shard in Riven's soul. Perhaps, if you pamper me enough with bribes, the money may make me forget that little . . . oversight. However, should you fail to do so, it may very well be that I accidentally let it slip. Who knows. Anyways, have a jolly time with the show! I'll see you around, cousin!"

Blusoth sneered and continued walking away and across the platform to where some of his concubines awaited his return, and Jalel's heartbeat raced as he silently pondered what to do. Did he kill Blusoth to try and silence him? If so, how would he do it? Could he even do it if he wanted to? And if not, how much money was Blusoth going to milk out of him before Jalel was a broken beggar of a man?

And what was even worse was that Blusoth—and possibly other nobles of the court—now had knowledge of Riven's shard. Of his building core of Gluttony. How had they found out?! That piece of Gluttony was his, NOT Blusoth's! Jalel had been the one to find it, and he'd be the one to claim it! A vein on Jalel's forehead popped as internal rage boiled up to the surface, and he silently swore to himself as he concocted a new plan to get him out of this mess.

Two days had passed, and the meeting with the rat man Snagger was coming up very soon. Gurth'Rok and the greenskins had been placed as overseers of the enslaved adult elves, and areas of land for farming had been designated in the fields adjacent to the Elysium altar, with the elves being particularly good at growing crops due to their affinities and plant-based magic. The elf children had been sent to the tower at the center of Brightsville, where they were enrolled in re-education programs under the thumb of their new undead teachers. Their entire force had been fed easily enough with various foodstuffs from the altar's central spire, from the general system store, or from Negrada. They'd used half of Riven's accumulated money, but this also allowed them to stock up on enough food to last their entire small nation—slaves included—for at least half a year.

The Yellow Skull Tribe as well as the adult elves had been placed under direct supervision by Riven while Allie maintained control of the undead part of their faction. Allie was assimilating smaller groups of humans in the northern reaches of the city either by force or by coercion, and the Thane Necropolis now controlled the entire eastern, northeastern, southern, and central grounds of the city, with only the northwestern and western reaches being controlled by other, smaller groups. The western reach was now controlled by the convicts from the prison, who'd enslaved most other small groups in the area and were living like kings while abusing their lessers, and the northwest part of the city was still being battled over by numerous suburban gangs that refused to bow to anyone or anything. They were high on the newfound power their classes gave them, obsessed with the inhuman new powers the system brought, and were determined to remain free of others despite Allie's declaring Brightsville as under the control of the Thane Necropolis in the cortex forums.

Meanwhile, meetings with the Blood Moon Requiem had indefinitely been put on hold, and Riven was half tempted to banish them from the face of their planet despite pleas and apologies offered by Kathrine or her subordinates. He didn't necessarily blame Kathrine, and he also wanted to know more about his parents, which were both reasons why he hadn't outright dismissed their trading commune from the altar, but nevertheless he and Allie had almost been killed that night.

And his malignancy points, which he still didn't know the true value of, had built because of it. Whatever it was, his body had ached and occasionally spasmed for more than a day after what he'd done to avoid death. Allie had theorized this was in large part because of how he'd split his Riftwalk spell into numerous, very small versions of itself—the overdrive of power had likely damaged his mana channels—but he wasn't entirely convinced that was the case.

But now that he was finally recovered and standing outside the chapel next to Jose's tombstone in the late hours of dusk, Riven was about to conjure his guild hall.

[Guild Hall: Stone Manor
***Plant this at a chosen location to create your premade guild hall.**
This is a packaged, onetime-use item*
- **Homeward Teleportation: Very long channel time**
- **Fifteen attendant spots available. Six hundred Elysium coins per month per active attendant are taxed by the system administrator**
- **Three-mile exploration radius for attendants before forced retrieval back to guild hall**
- **Core Sturdiness: Moderate**
- **Defensive wards: None**
- **Other features: Library, kitchen, dungeon, cellar, armory]**

His demons were obviously there. Azmoth was stoically standing by, playing with his magma-imbued hammer but being very careful not to damage anything in the area under strict orders from Riven. Fay was somehow telepathically talking to her brother in the outer realms, letting him know that they'd contact him soon for a guild hall contract. Dr. Brass, Gurth'Rok, and Genua were all present. Dr. Brass was excitedly shifting back and forth, knowing full well that his impending transformation into a vampire was going to be done tonight, and talking animatedly to Athela about it on the sidelines. Genua wore a heavy iron collar and shackles, was chained to a nearby tree, and was glaring up at the others with ill-hidden rage. Gurth'Rok was merely here to talk to Riven about how integrating the greenskins into the city was going, but he'd told Riven he'd wait until the manor was summoned and explored before going into any details, as they weren't urgent.

"Hurry it up!" Athela called from the back. "Dr. Brass is talking my ear off! It's torturous!"

Riven chuckled and looked over his shoulder to see the old man scowling Athela's way. "All right! All right, hold on."

The rod in his hands was quite similar in design but different in color to the altar rod he'd used to create the enormous structure not far from their current location. Only a few miles away through the silver, death-attuned fields to the south, over the hundreds of tents and small wooden houses being built by the orcs and goblins, over the pens and farmland occupied by the enslaved wood-land elves, the Unholy altar and its halo of green flames were easily seen in the distance. This rod was blue and gray, with a simple power stone in the pommel and a sharp, pointed end to jab into the ground.

Which he promptly did, and a notification screen appeared soon thereafter.

[Do you wish to activate the item Guild Hall: Stone Manor? Doing so will lay claim to the guild hall that forms, allowing you to access the guild hall functions, enlist attendants through contract, and assign it to a guild. This guild hall will take up approximately seven thousand square feet of land and is approximately sixty feet tall at its highest point.]

Pictures and visions of the guild hall displayed next. It was a rather luxu-rious-looking stone mansion, three stories high, very similar to Victorian-style architecture with a rectangular build. It had a wide tower climbing up over the front entrance, stone gargoyles holding up the balconies, and a wide metal gate around the front courtyard with gardens in the back. Inside, red carpets lined hallways with empty picture frames on the walls. There was an indoor pool with a skylight, a large dining room and kitchen, dozens of empty rooms for living in or storage areas, a library at the top of the central tower, and a large area for social gatherings in the front that wasn't necessarily a ballroom but had the same feel.

Visualizing where he wanted the guild hall in his mind, Riven made sure that the willow tree over Jose's grave—now changed into an Unholy-oriented tree species that stood up straighter with slightly glowing, neon-teal leaves—was placed in the center of the garden out back, and he incorporated the chapel's garden into it while building the manor adjacent to the old chapel so they'd be able to touch up the ruined building and make it an extension of their guild hall later on.

[Activating Guild Hall: Stone Manor. Please hold.]

CHAPTER 11

Flashes of multicolored light erupted from the planting rod, and over the course of minutes Riven's guild hall came to fruition.

When he moved around to the front of the building, he saw it was just like the pictures. A large central tower loomed over the main entrance, which had very thick, wooden double doors with an enormous ringed knocker. The third level had balconies, each with a stone gargoyle underneath. Metal-barred fences of expensive design began encircling not only the garden of beautiful Unholy-attuned flowers and the chapel in the back with Jose's tree, but also the sides and the front of the property, too. The front contained a courtyard with a gate and a cobblestone road leading out to it, with a lot of empty space in between.

"Shall we?" Riven asked with a backward glance at the others.

Fay picked up Genua's chain and tugged the collared elf to her feet, winking Riven's way. "After you, Master!"

Riven blatantly ignored the Succubus, walked up to the double doors, and pushed. They opened with a slight creak at first, then silently glided to a stop.

Lanterns, lit not by flame but instead by yellow baubles of light, adorned a rather short main hallway leading into the much bigger greeting room, with a ceiling at least thirty feet high. On either side of the large, square, mostly empty room extended large hallways with red carpets on top of wooden floors. A large spiral staircase with a guardrail was placed in the back-left corner of the greeting room, two large brown leather couches sat facing one another in the middle of the room, and tall glass windows halfway up the wall let in light in addition to the lanterns' magical glow.

Riven clapped his hands and gave a nod of approval. "Not too shabby. Spread out and explore, everyone—and meet back in twenty minutes! While you're at it, pick out a room if you're living here. Fay and Athela—I think there's a dungeon here somewhere. Find it and lock Genua up for me."

"Yes, sir!" The Succubus saluted and bounced on the balls of her feet excitedly, tail flipping merrily around before she dragged the elf away in search of a staircase leading downward.

Genua struggled vainly, getting smacked hard in the back of the head by Athela and stumbling while becoming outwardly enraged. "You're just going to dump me underground?!"

"Yup! At least for now, anyways. You might be given a chance to redeem yourself later," Riven said with a salute and a wave, just as Fay and Athela tugged her out of sight and into an adjacent hallway. "Now . . . let's see what this place has to offer."

The hallway to the right was shorter than the one on the left. Each room they passed was outfitted with very basic feather bedding, a small mirror, a nightstand, a closet, a glass window that had thick, locking wooden shutters, and a dresser for clothes. There was a communal toilet in the hall as well, likely to be in every hall by the looks of the layout, which had small power stones with Stormpillar affinities that powered the toilets and sinks.

"Pretty neat," Riven said while turning the water on and off again and flushing the toilet. The toilets were a little different from the ones back home—they didn't have tanks. Rather they were just round, wooden bowls with piping that led elsewhere. "Any idea where the waste goes?"

Dr. Brass shrugged and adjusted his glasses while peering down into the bowl. "Maybe it dumps it all outside or has a portal of some sort?"

"That's as good a guess as I could think of. Maybe you're right. When are you going to ditch the white coat?"

"Hmm?" The old man looked down at his doctor's uniform, then laughed. "Oh, this old thing? I think I'll keep it. Maybe even repair it. The coat reminds me of back home before the world fell apart."

Riven returned the doctor's sad smile with a nod. "I get it. You doing okay?"

Dr. Brass slowly held up his hands to either side. "As well as one can in a situation like this. I think I'll be more okay whenever you turn me tonight. I've been looking forward to it for a while. But . . . have you thought about my need for blood as well?"

Riven straightened with a confused expression and walked out into the hall with the doctor in tow, stepping out of the way of Azmoth, who was checking out a large supply closet with Gurth'Rok. "What do you mean?"

The two men started down the hall again, this time toward the larger door at the very end that was different from all the others—likely leading to something that caused this hallway to be shorter than the opposite one.

"I mean, you have Genua to feed on, but what about me?" Dr. Brass eventually said, stopping in the hallway and turning to meet Riven's gaze. "I'm going to need someone to feed on regularly, too."

"Oh. That." Riven gestured out a window in the direction of the fields. "You can go ask around to see if anyone wants to be a thrall. If they don't, just talk to me and we'll pick someone for you. It'd be better if they volunteered, but one way or the other, we'll get it done."

"All right. By the way . . . I think you should consider talking to the Blood Moon Requiem again."

Riven paused just as he was about to open the large door at the end of the hall. "What makes you say that?"

Dr. Brass sighed, then came to lean against the wall with his hands in the pockets of his white coat. "Look, son. I realize you are angry about what happened—"

"Yeah, I'm fucking angry." Riven glared back at the doctor with an edge to his voice. "We were almost assassinated just two days ago, man! Why would I feel any other way?"

"Because you're putting yourself in danger by not doing it," Dr. Brass said flatly, unflinching as he met the gaze of the much stronger and younger man next to him.

There was a long, drawn-out silence as the two men stared at one another, and Riven took his hand off the door to match the doctor—putting his hands in his pockets while his staff floated next to him. "Allie told you about the malignancy points, didn't she?"

Dr. Brass nodded hesitantly. "Yes."

"She wasn't supposed to do that."

"She wanted my opinion, and I think it's incredibly foolish not to ask." Dr. Brass lowered his glasses and peered over the rims with a knowing gaze. "Just because you're upset doesn't mean you should pursue the path of the fool, Riven. After what Athela has said about your bloodline being solely found in the royals of the Blood Moon Requiem, it's almost a certainty that they'd know more about these malignancy points. The very name *malignancy* does not give off good vibes, and accumulating more of them without knowing what they do is sheer stupidity. You may be angry to hear it, but you know it's true. As indebted as I'll be after you turn me, changing me and giving me the gift of eternal life when I'm on the precipice of ending this one, I feel like it is my duty to advise you against stupid, irrational ideas guided by emotions. Kathrine wasn't even the one who tried to kill you and she was nearly offed as well, so drop the grudge. You don't have to be friendly with them, but at least use them to make sure whatever is happening isn't going to harm you."

Riven simply glared.

"Please," Dr. Brass stated flatly, keeping their eye contact steady.

Eventually Riven's shoulders slumped, and he gave a grudging grunt of affirmation. "Fine. But not yet. I want to make them wait at least another day. I want them to squirm, thinking I'm not coming back or that I'll banish them."

"Out of spite?"

"Definitely out of spite."

"Fine, but don't let it last too long. This could be seriously detrimental to your health."

Riven rolled his eyes, then laughed at Dr. Brass's smug expression. "Is that the look you give patients when you finally convince them to stop smoking cigarettes?"

"Hardly. Anyways, are you going to open that door?"

Riven shifted. "Sure thing, boss man."

Gripping the handle of the abnormally large door, Riven tugged—and the hallway opened up into an indoor pool. The pictures of hadn't done it justice—it was a lot bigger, with additions that hadn't been included in the preview package. Not only that, but it was connected to another portion of the house that Riven hadn't expected to be here.

The central pool was rectangular, with slowly flowing water that was powered by yet another Storm-affinity stone water at one corner. It was crystal clear, warm to the touch, and felt absolutely great when he dunked his hand. A few racks holding rolled-up fluffy towels sat to one side, and a skylight reaching far above them up to the height of three stories let the rays of dusk trickle in from orange-streaked clouds. But the part that surprised him most, which he hadn't expected, was the elevated platform just beyond the pool where the dining room was set up.

Instead of the dining room being separate, it was actually only separated by five steps leading up to an elevated platform at the back of the room. There, two long wooden tables with steel cutlery, wooden plates, and iron goblets were all lined up. Each table had twenty chairs, making a total of forty spots for diners, and a kitchen with a fireplace, grill, oven, and storage units was placed behind an open counter.

One of the storage units, upon closer inspection, was a fridge, charged by another power stone with the Glacial affinity, which created frost. The oven had a gemstone with a fire-type affinity, meaning it was Sun, Infernal, or Volcano, but Riven couldn't tell which. He could turn the fire on and off with a knob from which magical engineers had connected rune-laden power lines to the stone, and it very much reminded him of technology back on Earth in many ways.

"This will definitely be an area I visit often . . ." Riven said, staring out the glass windows from the elevated platform to look down on the courtyard, and then glancing over his shoulder to where the pool was still slowly rippling and churning. "This is really nice."

"Maybe we can sneak peeks whenever Fay or Athela are around," Dr. Brass stated with a kidding smile, then held up his hands defensively when Riven cocked an eyebrow. "What?!"

"You're quite the old pervert, aren't you? You do know that Athela walks around naked all the time, right?"

"Not really."

"What do you mean, *not really?*"

"She wears a chitinous protective layer on top of her skin, which is why she looks the way she does. It's just rather formfitting, but she doesn't walk around naked. Ask her about it."

"And how would you know that?"

"She told me."

Riven's lips pooched in surprise, and he put his hands on his hips. "Wow. All right, I will. That's kinda interesting. But I wouldn't go spying on them even if that's true. Athela will kill your ass, and I won't stop her."

Dr. Brass huffed. "I was only kidding!"

"Uh-huh."

"I was! But between you and me, in all seriousness, if I ever get my own Succubus . . ." Dr. Brass's voice trailed off, and he wiggled his eyebrows and nudged Riven's side with an elbow. "Maybe you can teach me how to take a warlock class! Eh?! Eh?!"

Riven's eyelids drooped. "Old. Pervert."

"Calling people names is rude."

The rest of the manor was a little less exciting, but it was still nice to get a feel for the place. Leaving the eastern wing, or the wing with the dining room, kitchen, and pool, they crossed back over to the western wing and found the living quarters. There was a stairway leading down into the basement where it split off into a cellar filled with storage racks, an armory that had mannequins and display cases, and then the dungeon—complete with five different holding cells.

One of which was occupied by Genua, who sat curled up on a pile of hay with her head tucked between her knees—and the chain connecting her shackles and collar was now latched onto the cell bars with a heavy padlock.

Genua didn't look up or even acknowledge them as they passed by.

The second and third floors in either wing were strictly living quarters, with only the first wing leading to the pool and dining room. There were three stairwells, the central spiral staircase and two more—one at the end of each wing. But the tower, which could be accessed through the central stairwell, led up to a large room at the top that had lots of windows and empty bookcases. There were also a few armchairs, a single couch, and some tables as well.

It was supposed to be the library, no doubt, given all the bookcases, but without any books, it was just another empty room.

He'd have to fill it up sometime. It'd be a shame to let it go to waste.

"Bleed them."

Athela's claw superficially slit Genua's wrist—not enough to do true damage, but the elf woman cried out in pain. Azmoth held the shackled blonde woman down as crimson liquid flowed into one of the iron goblets they'd brought from the kitchen.

The other elves that'd been brought in as a recommendation by Gurth'Rok, eight of the newcomers in total, were there because of their absolute unwillingness to work over the past two days. Two of them had been too old, an elderly couple with graying hair, thin skin and fading eyes, while the six others had been young or middle-aged adults who'd refused anything until they got to see their children again.

Riven wasn't against reuniting them with their children in time, but only after re-education or if the parents allowed themselves to be turned into thralls. None of them wanted the second option.

So they'd become his food supply for the foreseeable future and were added to the guild hall's dungeon as its new inhabitants.

One by one the scantily clad men and women of Greenstalk were held down, terrified yelps or screams erupting from their lips, only to be let up again and have their arms sewn shut by Athela's red threads. It was painful for each of them, but it also stopped the blood loss completely.

His demons collected the blood person by person until they had enough that Riven felt comfortable proceeding with their current agenda: turning Dr. Brass. They'd do it here, in the dungeon, where the captives were behind locked bars and it'd be hard for Dr. Brass to escape if he went into a crazed rage like Riven had done.

"It's a bit dark down here," Dr. Brass said, squinting in the dim light of the one lantern that cast shadows along the wall. "Can't we do it upstairs?"

Riven's smile slowly spread, and he shook his head no. "Easier to contain you here. In fact, Athela, tie him down just in case. And don't worry, Dr. Brass, it won't be dark down here for much longer."

The change would no doubt take care of that.

"EEEEYOOOOO!!!" Allie's voice echoed down the stairwell, and her feet smacking against the stone steps gave Riven pause. Looking left, he saw her slender form hop, skip, and jump to the bottom, where she whirled on him with a wide smile. "Hey! You weren't going to begin without me, I hope!"

"Not a chance. Did you already move your stuff in?"

"Yup! Well, no, not really, but my servants are taking care of it now." She pointed up at the ceiling, where the clambering of feet could be heard, and she grinned widely.

Mara, the female ghoul necromancer, and Vin—one of the skeletal skresh necromancers—followed close behind.

Vin pointed over his shoulder and up the stairway from where he'd just come, shifting in his black robes to gaze his pale, glowing orbs into Riven's red ones. "My lord, the lady dictated we take up residence on the bottom floor. Does this sit well with you?"

"Take whatever rooms you want, just make sure your undead aren't trampling the garden outside or breaking any furniture when moving stuff around. We don't have much as it is. And Allie asked about a lab of some sort? Just move the stuff out of an adjacent room and you can set up your alchemy equipment— or use a storage closet." Riven turned to Allie. "Do you need me to bring in more elves to harvest? Or are you going to be good?"

She shook her head, the smile fading slightly and a look of embarrassment overcoming her as she blushed. "Uh . . . no, I'm good!"

"She has two thralls," Mara stated blandly with a yawn, covering her mouth and stretching to expose three wands tucked into a sash at her waist. "Mmm. She won't be needing any elves; you'll see for yourself soon enough."

Ah. Yes. Riven had almost forgotten when this had been mentioned before. His curious gaze drifted back from Mara to Allie, and his sister gave him a guilty smile while pulling the hood over her eyes.

He gave her a skeptical look, crossing his arms as Azmoth set the goblets of blood on a nearby table that a skeleton had brought down and Athela began tying Dr. Brass up with her threads. "Allie . . . why do you look so guilty?"

"Heh . . . heh . . ." She gave him a sheepish laugh. "No reason!"

Mara sighed and pulled back her hood, letting her raven hair flow around her with a shake of her head. "You'll see them and immediately understand."

"Understand what? Wait, I thought thralls took a while to create? Don't they?"

"I was going to KILL them otherwise!" Allie protested with a growl, ignoring Riven's question and glaring in Mara's direction with a hiss. "They were crusaders from Prophet's forces! You can't blame me!"

"Oh, I certainly don't blame you, my lady. I very much understand," Mara replied flatly.

Riven blinked in confusion, then his eyebrows lifted when he saw a hulking, handsome, muscular, shirtless bald beast of a man step down the stairs.

His features were normal. He looked every bit human. But his smell . . . his smell was off the charts good, and it somehow reminded him of the two men who'd been following Kathrine before one of them had exploded.

"My queen," the husky man said, bowing onto one knee and taking Allie's hand before kissing it gently. His pale-blue eyes looked up at her with admiration, his chiseled features set in an adoring expression, and a perfect white smile escaped his lips while his rippling abdomen caught the light. "I have taken your bed from the tower and placed it in one of the larger rooms on the third floor so that we may enjoy ourselves at your leisure. Kraig is already awaiting us there."

Huh?

Riven's jaw dropped, the goblet in his grip burst as his fist subconsciously tightened, and he nearly spat blood.

Oh, hell no.

CHAPTER 12

"It's not that big of a deal!" Allie protested in hushed tones, embarrassed that she was getting chewed out by her older brother in front of the people she led, even though they'd gone into the adjacent cellar to have some privacy. "Keep your voice down!"

Both of them ignored the mindless skeletons bringing in crates or sacks of stored food, which they'd bought in mass quantities from the Elysium altar.

"It's a little bit of a big deal," Riven stated sourly. "Allie, goddamn it, why is it that I have to . . . You know what? We'll talk about this later. I'm tired of fighting with you."

"Oh, no, no, no . . . You don't get to do that," Allie said, barring his way and pushing Riven back with one hand. "You've literally enslaved an entire elf village so you can feed—you don't get to play the moral high ground here!"

"That's completely different from what you're doing."

"Is it? How? Because you took your enemies to feed on and I took mine to have sex with—it's different? Oh, and they HAPPILY follow me now, by the way, unlike the prisoners YOU keep." She jabbed a finger into his chest, not backing down. "Or would you rather I killed them?"

"That's exactly what I think."

"So killing them is ethically correct while giving them a happy life of pleasure isn't?"

"You essentially warped their minds, Allie. It's sick."

"WE'RE FUCKING VAMPIRES, RIVEN! We literally have it built INTO OUR DNA to create thralls so that we don't have to go and do what you just did today!" Allie waved at the adjacent room beyond the basement hallway. "Those elves over there? They're terrified of us. They hate their lives and no doubt curse us by the hour for what we did to them. Even if it WAS them that started this mess and it WAS THEM that betrayed you. They deserve every second of what they get, and I genuinely think that you're being too nice to those pointy-eared, murderous bastards. Yet, when you compare what their lives are like to the lives of the two men I 'mind-warped'—let me ask you this: Who do you think is happier? You saw the look on Alexander's face—he adores me!"

Riven's lips twisted in disgust. "Alexander?"

"Alexander is the bald, muscular one that you just saw. If you see a bearded, skinny pretty boy, that's Kraig."

Riven violently face-palmed and began rubbing his forehead vigorously, taking a deep breath to calm himself down. "If I didn't love you and you weren't my sister, I swear to god I'd throw you through a wall. Whatever, fine, keep your sex slaves, but just know I think it's disgusting, gross, and morally repugnant."

"YOU have an enslaved SUCCUBUS, RIVEN!"

"I don't sleep with my Succubus. And she's not a slave."

"Does she do whatever you tell her to do?"

Riven aggressively rolled his eyes and scoffed, throwing his hands out to either side and pacing back and forth while his shorter younger sister glared up at him with her hands on her hips. "All right, I can see this is going nowhere. How about, before we say something we'll regret, we just take a step back and cool down. We'll talk about this later, okay?"

"Only if you promise to be nicer about it next time," Allie demanded, folding her arms.

Riven felt a vein pop out on his forehead, and he ground his teeth with a rigid jaw. He took in another deep breath and let it out slow. "Fine. I'll be . . . nicer, when talking to you about this next time."

Allie hesitantly nodded, then stepped forward to put her arms around his waist. Drawing Riven close, she buried her head in his chest and groaned. "I hate fighting with you. Please don't be mad at me."

Riven's rigid body relaxed slightly at her words, but he was still internally fuming. Embracing her back despite his anger, he shook his head and muttered to himself under his breath, "Yeah. Me, too."

"Want to go change Dr. Brass into a vampire?"

There was a pause.

"Yeah. Let's go do that, but this conversation will be continued later."

Allie humphed. "Yeah, I know."

Riven's fangs sank into the trapezius of the old man lying underneath him on the floor, and Dr. Brass shuddered. He was bound with Athela's webbing after both Allie and Riven had shared their similar transformation experiences—clarifying that it would likely be a very violent or ravenous change when Dr. Brass actually turned.

Though Allie had made two thralls so far, she'd never made another vampire before. Not only that, but the way she'd made those two thralls was outside the norm—she'd acquired an item from a quest that allowed her to speed up the process.

So without much of a guide on how to do it and not wanting to talk to the Blood Moon Requiem unless he had to—just to make them squirm a bit more—Riven tried it on his own. At first nothing happened but a stiffening of Dr. Brass's muscles and a pained wince, and Riven felt the man's blood flowing down his tongue into his throat. But as with many things in Elysium's system, once he focused on the act that he wanted to perform while having the necessary credentials, a notification appeared.

[Do you wish to turn this target into a vampire? Doing so will inject a piece of your vampiric essence into the target. You may currently create new vampires at a thirty-day cooldown period without risk to yourself. How much they inherit from your gift is partially dependent on them and partially randomized.]

Riven thought, "Yes."

[Proceeding with vampiric change. Target has been injected with vampiric essence.]

In an instant, pulsing red veins started lacing their way out from where Riven was biting Dr. Brass. The old man stiffened and let out a scream, writhing on the floor as the rapidly spreading blood or essence or whatever it was tore through his body and sent him into spasms. His hands, feet, face, and even his eyes pulsed with throbbing red veins in a display that was very much different from Riven's own change, but nevertheless Riven proceeded as planned.

Meanwhile, the others of Riven's group and the elf slaves imprisoned here watched in silence.

The old man grunted and twitched, and his bloodshot eyes rolled back into his head as fangs sprouted from his mouth. His musculature changed—toning and expanding slightly from the wiry old frame to a more steadfast and tougher body. His wrinkled skin ripped in dozens of places to adjust to the new bulk, only to sew itself shut seconds later, and came back as a younger, smoother, much paler version of the skin he'd once had. His face narrowed and then filled out again, bones snapping and rearranging to become more attractive and symmetrical—and his graying hair turned a stark silver while filling in all the patches that'd previously been thinning.

And finally, minutes later, as his eyes rolled back into his head, a deep and dull red color had replaced the brown eyes Dr. Brass had once had. However, they weren't the brilliant crimson glow of Riven's and Allie's.

[As creator, you are now granted insight into the stats you have granted this newly born vampire:

Greater Vampire (Blood/Shadow/Death)—Changed by a rare pure-blooded vampire, a chosen descendant of the blood god, you have acquired better-than-average affinities and bonuses when compared to your vampiric peers across the multiverse. However, though your heritage empowers you with many bonuses, it also comes at a steep price. Please review the following changes.

Negatives:

- You suffer 400% additional damage from any silver-based weapons.
- You suffer 300% additional damage from any Light and Sun pillar abilities.
- You may not be healed or have active buffs applied to you by any Light or Sun pillar abilities.
- Your mana and stamina slowly drain while your skin is exposed to direct sunlight. If exposed to sunlight when they start to run low, your health will also deteriorate.
- You are required to feed on the blood of mortals on a regular basis. You will lose your sanity and go into a rage if underfed.
- Your heritage bestows a baseline -150 Charisma. -1 Charisma per level.

Positives:

- 51% affinity to the Blood subpillar, 36% affinity to the Shadow subpillar, and 45% affinity to the Death subpillar. These pillars now take less resource consumption to use abilities with, control is increased, and potency is increased.
- Your heritage also bestows upon you a baseline +30 Strength, +50 Sturdiness, +50 Intelligence, +80 Perception, and +40 Agility.
- Perception has been upgraded to Vampiric Perception and has extra emphasis per stat point applied for heartbeats, dark vision, and smell.
- Your race change to Greater Vampire upgrades the number of stat points per level to +1 Strength, +1 Sturdiness, +1 Intelligence, +1 Agility, +1 Perception, and +4 free stat points.
- You gain passive regeneration while in dark places.
- You are immune to most diseases.
- You will not die of old age.
- You may currently create new vampires at a ninety-day cooldown period without risk to yourself; how much they inherit from your gift is partially dependent on them and partially randomized.]

The changes were very similar to Riven's own but had some major differences. The negative Charisma gained was less, and the pillar affinities—though high—were nowhere near Riven's own. The Strength, Sturdiness, Intelligence, Perception, and Agility immediately gained were also a good amount less, and the gains per level were significantly less, too. Other than that, instead of extreme regeneration in the dark, Dr. Brass as a greater vampire got passive regeneration, which was probably just a lesser version of what Riven had. There was also a difference in how fast Dr. Brass could create vampires.

Dr. Brass blinked rapidly behind his glasses as Riven evaluated his screen, then screamed in a primal rage with fangs extended while trying to bite Riven's hand. Thankfully Athela's webbing was enough to keep him down and subdued amid his struggles, and Riven took one of the cups they'd brought down from the kitchen before putting the blood to the old man's lips.

Or perhaps not old anymore. At least not by the looks of it. Dr. Brass now looked like he was in his late twenties or early thirties, and the stark change was a little unnerving.

The newly created vampire quickly chugged the cup, ravenously draining it before gasping like a dehydrated man in a desert who'd just found water. Cup after cup, taken from the elves, was poured down Dr. Brass's throat—and after some time, the man began to calm down. Shuddering and rapidly blinking again, Dr. Brass eventually fell into a deep sleep—passing out right there on the floor without saying another word.

"Well, that went well!" Fay said, clapping her sky-blue hands together excitedly and extending her bat-like wings while Riven gave Azmoth the order to carry Dr. Brass upstairs to a bed. "Now that he's not starved of blood, mind if we go get my brother from the nether realms? I'm so excited to see him!"

Athela, who was perched on the ceiling in her spider form, let herself down along a single red thread and landed atop the Succubus's head. "ONWARD! To the core!!!"

Riven couldn't help but smile at the two as they skipped up the stairs and out of sight, then gave Vin, Nin, and Mara a polite smile before ruffling Allie's hair. "Are you coming to breakfast tomorrow like we planned?"

His little sister beamed. "Wouldn't miss it! I'm making pancakes. I even got the ingredients from a local grocery store!"

"Oh ho?! Exciting. Well, love you, sis. See you soon."

Riven waved for Gurth'Rok to follow, and the large orc chieftain gave Allie a polite bow before using his carved-wood cobra staff as a walking stick to follow his liege up the steps onto the first floor.

Nin and Vin shared a glance with one another, the skeletal brothers not saying a word but staying put with their hands in the pockets of their black robes, while Mara gave Allie a suspicious side-eye. "You and Riven okay?"

Allie huffed, briefly glaring at the blonde elf woman Genua at the back of her cell, then put her hands on her hips and gave all her undead friends a reassuring grin. "Yeah. We used to fight like this all the time, so we'll move on from this soon enough. But anyways, let's go! We need to set up your rooms, and I still need to meet the boys upstairs for a little relaxation time before bed. Kraig gives really good massages."

The guild hall's core could be moved at will and was essentially a large, blue crystal ball that floated wherever it was placed by the owner and controlled the guild hall's functions—but it couldn't leave the manor itself. For a basic guild hall like this one that didn't have any functions beyond the few presented here, it wasn't a hard concept to grasp.

> **[Guild Hall: Stone Manor (Unnamed)**
> - **Assigned Guild: Unassigned. Owned by Riven Thane.**
> - **Homeward Teleportation: Very long channel time. Only hired attendants or guild members can utilize this teleportation function. Currently there is no guild assigned to this guild hall, and there are no attendants, so the teleportation function is limited to Riven Thane.**
> - **Fifteen attendant spots available. Six hundred Elysium coins per month per active attendant are taxed by the system administrator. You may either mentally link this guild hall to the nearest friendly Elysium Altar that you have access to in order to hire attendants from the general store, or you may hire attendants from associated factions at that altar.**
> - **Three-mile exploration radius for attendants before forced retrieval back to guild hall.**
> - **Core Sturdiness: Moderate**
> - **Defensive wards: None**
> - **Change Guild Hall Location: one year of channeling needed.]**

Riven was currently holding the guild hall's core while sitting on his feather bed, having just dismissed Gurth'Rok back to the greenskin camp south of here to oversee building. Progress was apparently going very smoothly, with only a few scuffles between the elves and orcs, but a few goblins had had to be put down after attacking the slaves against orders. Apparently the goblins hated the high elves even more than the orcs did, but most of their efforts were being put toward building a new town in between the edge of Brightsville, where Riven's manor sat on the city's edge, and the fields leading to the altar farther south.

Meanwhile Riven was very much enjoying his new room after sleeping in the dirt and grime so often; his was one of five rooms on the third floor's western wing that were larger than all the others and took up the entire wing due to their combined size. There were two on the northern end, two on the southern end, and one on the far western end. As one of the master bedrooms, his was positioned adjacent to the spiral staircase facing south toward their courtyard (the front side of the guild hall) in the middle of the manor, while Allie's was two doors down at the very end of the hallway. Each master bedroom had a balcony, glass windows, a lot more furniture than the other rooms, including the comfy quilted feather bed he now sat on—king size—a personal bathroom, unlike the public ones for the rest of the hall, and a writing desk with two shelves inside a closet. The walls on the interior were made of white plaster with wooden frame trimmings, and the magically infused lamps lighting up his room could be turned on and off with a button.

"This is super nice!" Athela said, her dog-size spider body bouncing happily up and down on the bed. She raised one of her arachnid limbs. "I'll be staying here, too."

Riven raised an eyebrow, taking his eyes off the hall's display notification and the bowling ball–size blue orb in his hands, and silently stared Athela's way.

The large spider stopped bouncing and shot him a death glare. "What?! Don't you dare send me across the hall or to my own room! I'm sleeping here!"

"No, you ain't."

"Yes, I is!"

"Nope."

"Yus!" Athela clambered over Riven's legs and stared him in the eye, mandibles clicking twice, then she jabbed him in the stomach with a foot. "It's not up for debate!"

"You snore, Athela. I can't have my beauty sleep disturbed by—"

"I DO NOT SNORE!"

Riven grinned. "Okay, maybe not. But wouldn't you want your own room? Fay and her brother are taking the master bedroom directly across the hall."

He gestured to the beautiful Succubus, who was standing anxiously at the bedside, hands clasped in front of her while her black tail swished back and forth in impatience. "And Azmoth is going to stay in that old chapel outside because it gives him more space. You could even have the room next to mine if you want it."

"Who's the last master bedroom going to?" Athela asked curiously, motioning to the door.

Riven shrugged. "Probably Mara, if I had to guess."

"The ghoul lady?"

"Yeah."

"Ahem!" Fay cleared her throat rather loudly, stopping the conversation in its tracks before Athela derailed it too far. "Master, may I suggest we proceed? My brother is awaiting the contact message now."

Riven huffed, then put his right hand on the blue orb again with a nod. "All right. One moment."

Fay immediately beamed with a brilliant white smile. "Thank you, Riven! I won't forget this! He's been having a hard time in the nether realms, and he nearly got killed on his last trip into the hells . . . He's not in a good place. Mother and Father have disowned him, so I owe you for this one."

Riven gave his minion a warm smile. "Not a problem. Just a second."

CHAPTER 13

[Fifteen attendant spots available. Six hundred Elysium coins per month per active attendant are taxed by the system administrator. You may either mentally link this guild hall to the nearest friendly Elysium Altar that you have access to in order to hire attendants from the general store, or you may hire attendants from associated factions at that altar.]

The screen flared, and mentally linking his guild core to the altar he actually owned himself, he quickly saw a new set of messages along with a very long list and a search option. There were also category checkmarks, with numerous options such as Utility, Tank, Damage, Subterfuge, Crafting, Scouting, Magic-Based, Martial-Based, Miracle-Based, Long Range, Melee, Level, Guild Association, Corporation Association, Faction Association, Group Contracts, Individual Contracts, and others. There were even categories divided up into what type of pillar the attendants were associated with, and the lists could be divided up by hiring price from lowest to highest or vice versa. Each of these categories had subcategories of its own, and the vast majority of listed groups were from the General Elysium Store, while fewer than a twentieth of them were from Negrada or the Blood Moon Requiem.

[You are now accessing attendant listings from the following: General Elysium Store, the Blood Moon Requiem, Hellscape Dungeon Negrada. You may organize choices based on category to narrow down the search function.]

"All right, what do I put into the search?" Riven asked, looking up when Fay came over to sit on the bed next to him.

The Succubus narrowed her eyes, then started pointing out category tags. "He'll be from the general store, so click that one."

All the Blood Moon Requiem and Negrada groups disappeared.

"Um . . . Click 'demon' for race, and type in 'Sojavi clan' for faction association."

Riven did as asked, and the list narrowed significantly from many tens of thousands of pages to only a handful, each with having a couple dozen options. "What's the point of hiring off the Blood Moon Requiem or Negrada here when I could just look up their factions?"

Fay smirked, then patted him on the head. "Silly man. It's because doing it through the general store is much more expensive. You get a large discount by hiring through associated friendly channels at the altar."

"But isn't it only six hundred coins per month? That's what my guild hall status page said."

"Yes, but that's only for maintenance. That doesn't include the up-front fee to hire, and it doesn't include the personal fee that the person you're hiring requires, either. The personal monthly fee that you're paying them to be here isn't taxed, because you're paying a maintenance fee to the system to keep that person attached to the guild hall, but the up-front cost is always doubled as a tax for using the Elysium general store. If you hired the same group or individual from, let's say, Negrada, you could either do it through your altar's channel and disregard the fee entirely, or hire that same group or individual through the general store and pay the doubled up-front cost. And then there's also the distance tax, too, with longer distances costing more. I have no doubt that both Negrada and the Blood Moon Requiem had to pay quite a bit of money just to send their trade communes and all their people here under the same principle, as neither one is in this vicinity of the multiverse. We're talking a LOT of money."

Riven scratched his head. "I see. Interesting. All right, what's next?"

They selected a few other options after that, and the list became smaller and smaller. First they selected Fay's homeland from the nether realms, then they cycled out group contracts and made them individual contracts only. After that, the race was further narrowed from demon to incubus, and then they picked "crafting" as yet another category.

"What kind of craft does he do?" Riven pondered curiously while scrolling.

The Succubus kept her eyes on the screen, scanning the names. "Well . . . not any one thing in particular. He's . . . trying to figure out who he is as a person, but he doesn't have any combat classes or even a class at all. However, I did tell him to list himself as a cook or scribe . . . Aha! Got him!"

She punched a name on the list, and an image appeared on screen. Just like Fay, this man had sky-blue skin, black eyes, black wings, small black horns, and white hair past his shoulders. He was far broader and taller than Fay, obviously handsome, and had a thicker tail than his sister did.

[Tupper. Level-2 Incubus Demon. Classless. Crafts listed by participant: cooking. Combat abilities listed by participant: Not available. Affiliations: Not available.]

THUD

Riven startled slightly when a huge, saddled bird with golden feathers and a hooked beak landed outside on his balcony. Not getting up but turning his head with an expression of bewilderment, he and his two nearby demons watched in confusion as a human knight in heavily decorated, gold-trimmed plate armor stepped off the gigantic bird with the chink of metal plates. The visored, white-plumed helm shifted, aimed straight at Riven, before the knight gave him an odd salute and bowed respectfully.

The voice that came from that helm was deep and masculine, but not confident.

"Forgive my rudeness! My name is Veswuad Morandium, and I am a messenger representing the kingdom of Dawn not far from here. I was told that this is the place to find Riven or Allie Thane? Is that correct?" The man waited expectantly, and Riven hesitantly stood up to walk over to the wide-open balcony doors.

Looking up into the darkening sky to make sure there weren't any other monstrous birds flying about with fully armored knights on their backs, he was surprised to spot two others. Both were circling the mansion overhead, but they didn't appear to be hostile and kept a distance. Most likely they were just trying to make sure this man came back safe.

He identified the bird cleaning its feathers nearby.

[Great Golden Roc]

Hmm. The identification information called the massive, elephant-size bird a roc, something he'd read about in fantasy books as a kid, and it made Riven wonder just how much of his childhood readings were based in myth versus reality after these odd coincidences kept happening. Someone from the outer multiverse—other than his parents—must have visited Earth in the past to spread these legends in the first place.

Riven looked down at the bowing man with an unamused expression, shielding his eyes from the last rays of the sun as it began dipping below the horizon. "Yeah, I'm Riven Thane."

His expression became all the more irritated when the bird spewed a white stream all over the balcony floor, and he let out a long, audible, exasperated sigh that caused the knight to wince slightly. "Who are you and why did you come here? Other than to let your bird shit all over my stuff? I don't like having strangers land their gigantic pets on my stuff—you're lucky I didn't think you were an enemy. I could have accidentally killed you."

"Uh—my most sincere apologies!" The fancy armored knight straightened and chastised the bird with a tsk, to which he got a squawk and ruffled feathers. The knight shook his head and grumbled to himself, then pulled a letter from a satchel at his waist. "I was just in a rush . . . you see, I am in need of assistance. More accurately, my country is in need of assistance, and from scouting reports, it appears that your faction is one of the few in the area that could help us. Others are dealing with their own problems and cannot assist, unfortunately."

Riven took the paper envelope and examined the wax seal, which was the image of a bird very similar to the one this man was riding. Riven's glowing red eyes glanced up to the bird, then back to the knight, and he ripped the letter open a moment later. "I'm surprised you're not either afraid of me or trying to kill me. That's what I get from most humans and elves here."

The knight cleared his throat, drawing Riven's attention. "Truthfully, it is very off-putting to be in your presence, yes. But our agents told us that although you've had your conflicts with some of the locals, you also are allowing humans to become fully fledged citizens of your newly growing faction. It was enough to persuade my king to ask a favor of you, and as neighbors we hope that you and yours will oblige to solidify a relationship. Of course, terms of payment can also be discussed."

Without looking down at the parchment, Riven continued to evaluate the man more thoroughly. A long sword was at his waist, a very long lance was attached to the side of the roc's saddle, along with a couple of large round canisters, and Riven could feel trickles of mana from the man fluctuate every couple seconds—though this was the case for all the casters Riven had met, and it likely only meant this knight could use some sort of magic.

"I'll be frank," Riven said, waving the letter in the air. "I haven't read this yet, but I can already tell you that after our experiences with the other 'enlightened' races in this area, I'm already wary of some kind of trap."

The knight hesitated, considering. "Understandable. However, you must consider that my colleagues up above—as well as myself—could have dropped bombs on your manor from the clouds without you ever having known we were here. To present myself to you is a sign of trust, and I am hoping you take it at face value."

The letter sat unfolded on his desk a half hour later, the black ink illuminated by the yellow light of the mana lantern attached to his wall, and Riven tapped his fingers along the wooden surface, while pondering what to do next. He'd no doubt have to talk to Allie about this change of pace, and he was more than a little unnerved by the idea that these knights from Dawn could have bombed his guild hall into oblivion without even the slightest warning. He'd have to correct that somehow, and sometime soon, but it appeared they weren't hostile and genuinely did need his help.

That would be a discussion for tomorrow morning, before he set out to meet the rat man Snagger at the designated spot in the underdark.

At his right, Athela, in her humanoid form, was curled up under the blankets of his bed—yawning comfortably now that night had fallen and she'd claimed the bed for her own while declaring that he sleep on the floor.

He snorted in amusement, remembering, and said he'd just go to another room before she'd denied him and physically stopped him from doing so by dragging him back into the room by his legs.

"Master?"

Fay's voice brought him out of his thoughts.

He gave her an apologetic wave of the hand and reached out to grasp the guild core again. "Sorry, let's resume things."

"Thank you!"

[Tupper. Level-2 Incubus Demon. Classless. Crafts listed by participant: Cooking. Combat abilities listed by participant: Not available. Affiliations: Not available.]

Her brother's information populated the screen again, and the image of the blue-skinned incubus came on screen. He selected the option, and another notification appeared.

[This attendant will cost you one Elysium coin up front, with a matching tax of one Elysium coin and a distance tax of 78,924 Elysium coins. Maintenance fees for this guild hall are set at six hundred Elysium coins per month per active attendant, with zero of fifteen attendant spots already being filled. Do you wish to hire this attendant?]

Riven slowly shifted his gaze to the large pile of coins Azmoth had brought up to his closet, then to Fay, who was giving him a sheepish smile. "Seventy-eight thousand, nine hundred and twenty-four? Really?"

Fay lowered her eyes apologetically. "Sorry. Is that too much? I wasn't sure what the distance fee would be—the nether realms shift positions relative to physical realms all the time, so if you need to wait, it might reduce the price. Or it might increase the price . . ."

Her voice trailed off in disappointment, and she looked sideways at the wall, embarrassed.

"What are the odds it'll decrease versus increase?" Riven asked, knowing full well he could afford it but also knowing that was still a lot for an attendant based on other prices he'd seen.

"Um . . . It'll probably increase in the immediate future, but if you wait a year or two, it may decrease. The nether realms are huge."

Riven could see she was obviously disappointed. Whatever was going on with her brother, it was affecting her as well. "Then let's just get it over with."

He selected the "yes" in relation to the prompt for hiring an attendant, and a final notification popped up right before a portal appeared in the middle of the room—and a large chunk of money vanished off the top of his nearby closet stash.

[Tupper, Level-2 Incubus Demon, has been added as an attendant to this guild hall; 78,926 Elysium coins have been taken from your belongings. One of fifteen attendant slots filled. Current monthly cost for all attendants: six hundred Elysium coins. Tupper has been imbued with permanence as long as the guild hall core remains intact. Upon death, Tupper will be resurrected as long as guild hall core remains intact. Tupper has been restricted to a three-mile exploration radius surrounding the guild hall before forced retrieval back to guild hall. Tupper can now utilize the ability Homeward Teleportation to teleport back to this guild hall after a channel time based on distance.]

CHAPTER 14

What stepped out of the portal was very far from the handsome figure of Fay's brother. Riven could make out distinguishing features that told him it was the same man, the same incubus, but he looked haggard and beaten to an extreme.

Tupper's right leg was necrotic and bent at an awkward angle, and the rest of his body looked starved. His face was half burned, skin flayed off the side of his skull as he limped forward, and one of his wings had been torn off completely. Tears streamed silently down his face, and one eye was glazed over with a sickly green ichor running out of it. He staggered and fell to the ground only two steps out, letting out a whimper of pain through cracked lips and getting an audible gasp from his sister, who rushed over to him, trembling slightly while she whispered comforting words into his ears.

Riven just gawked, not knowing what to say, do, or even think. Were demons able to be tortured in the nether realms? Or had Tupper not been in the nether realms?

On the other side of the portal from where Tupper had come was another blue-skinned incubus, snarling and obviously screaming at Tupper with an enraged flush to his skin before the portal winked out. The only signs that the portal had ever opened were both the mutilated, grotesque version of an incubus on the floor and the wisps of purple miasma that were remnants of the dimensional passageway that'd just shut down.

"Riven . . . could you help me lift him up?" Fay asked without looking back from her kneeling position on the floor, voice quivering. "I need to carry him to my room."

"Might makes right. It's the way things are in demonic culture, and when you're a weak, tree-hugging, animal-cuddling hippie wuss like that guy, it only makes sense that you'd be persecuted. At least that's how Fay portrayed him, even if she did so lovingly." Athela shrugged indifferently and bit into an apple, her long, pitch-black legs up on the table while she enjoyed the warmth of the morning sunshine on her skin through a window in the dining hall. "Don't tell Fay I said that, though. I'm sure she's already heard it all. Poor sod looked like he'd been stomped—like how I used to stomp babies."

Riven grunted his acknowledgment. Not a lot he could do about it, and what he could do he'd already done by giving Tupper a way out of whatever hellish home life he'd had before. "Figured as much."

Allie dumped some more scrambled eggs on his plate, kissed him on the forehead, and happily went back to making pancakes with Mara and the two thralls she'd outfitted in aprons while telling them what to mix and how to cook the bacon.

Bacon.

He had fucking bacon. All that money he'd spent at the altar was more than worth it now.

Riven lifted the pancake-bacon-egg-pancake sandwich to his mouth, drooling, and only managed to sneer briefly at Allie's muscular dream-boy fucker across the dining room before snarfing down another bite. Chewing and letting the taste sink into his taste buds, his shoulders slumped and he relaxed into a blissful state again. He knew full well that Allie was doing this on purpose as a bribe to go easy on her, but it'd been so goddamn long since he'd had a good meal.

"I'm surprised this food all tastes the same as it did back then . . ." Dr. Brass commented from beside him, and Athela gave the newly formed vampire an eye roll while he continued to check his new body out in a small mirror he'd taken from his room. "And damn, do I look good. *Goodbye*, bald spots!"

Riven snorted and kept eating, putting the meal down when he'd finished half his sandwich and Allie came by to discuss the events of last night.

"Ah, now that breakfast is ready for everyone—let's talk." She straightened her hoodie out and ruffled her jeans, both of which were typical of what she used to wear before the integration happened.

He cleared his throat with a fist to his mouth, jerking in surprise when Athela's foot poked him in the stomach from under the table. He smacked her leg aside and shared a grin with the demoness, then addressed the situation by putting the letter he'd received from that roc-riding knight on the table. Then he began reciting the words aloud. "Ahem. All right, here goes."

To Allie and Riven Thane of the Thane Necropolis: your reputation precedes you.

My name is Theodore Munchamp, court wizard to the king of the kingdom of Dawn and practicing scholar of the sun arts. It has come to the kingdom's attention that you have claimed most of the city known as Brightsville to our northwest and are mere weeks away from having it completely under your control. We know you've raised an army numbering thousands of undead, as well as a lesser number of orcs and goblins. We know you've opened up an Elysium altar, the first we have yet to see anywhere. We know you've enslaved a group of high elves that tried to assassinate your leadership, and we have video evidence of the tremendous power you two each individually wield.

That in turn opens the door for us to begin diplomacy, as equals.

Our kingdom was once a bastion of civilization in the world of Zazir, and in many aspects what remains still is. Though we are but a mere fraction of the kingdom we once were due to our country being split apart, the capital city and three other large towns belonging to Dawn arrived together on Panu, and we are in dire need of assistance.

We were hoping for your help.

To your southeast and into the plains you'll find our civilization besieged on all sides. One of our towns has already fallen, and the citizens we could evacuate safely have left for the capital, though the situation still remains uncertain. The majority of our armies, save the single legion stationed in the capital upon integration, were lost when the system arrived. We do not have the forces necessary to guard the capital city of Mandon, the town of Bradshire, and the town of Belmington all at the same time. We are stretched too thin, and many of the other civilizations we find ourselves bordering are either too fragmented, too caught up with internal struggles for power, or too involved with their own external problems to help us.

Truthfully, we could consolidate our forces into one area and evacuate the towns, but this would lead to a massive refugee crisis. That in turn would lead to food shortages, and simply abandoning the settlements would set our civilization back decades.

We will be up front about our intentions, and in turn we hope to make a deal that can be struck in both of our favors—simultaneously empowering both the kingdom of Dawn and the Thane Necropolis. There are five things that we wish to negotiate with you.

The first is access to your Elysium altar.

The second is local trade routes between our factions.

The third is protection for our northernmost town, Bradshire, which borders your territory.

The fourth point of negotiation is support for the war we are involved in.

And lastly, the fifth topic to discuss is that we wish you to cease terraforming land when you reach our borders. Though it is a slow spread, the Unholy taint your altar is creating has already been noted and will likely reach our lands in the months or years to come. This would be very bad for our crops and agriculture and would lead us into starvation if we did not act.

I am sure you're asking yourself why you'd allow us access to your system stores, trade, and protection. I'm also sure you want to know why I think you'd join our cause, or why you'd stop terraforming areas of land to better suit you. The answer is simple: we have common enemies, and we can help each other grow. We could provide you with information on the surrounding areas, information on two world quests, pay you for your services, and, once the war is over, ensure that you have a faithful ally to protect your southern border.

As you've already experienced in your own isolated exchange with the high elves of these lands, they are arrogant and selfish in their desires to thrive. We too have had our own share of conflict with their peoples and are currently engaging in guerrilla warfare with a host of warriors many thousands strong that matches our own in strength. They burn our crops to try and starve us, butcher our people and caravans, and have even gone so far as to ally with a nearby dungeon to attack us on two fronts.

We also know that if our kingdom falls, your people will be targeted next. What will the elves do when they find out that their most hated enemies, both the undead and the greenskins, have banded together and enslaved a group of their own kin?

Thus, my king and I have proposed a meeting. I am willing to meet you at any time and any place of your choosing to show myself in good faith, and I can promise you both riches and new bodies to use in building up your forces with if you choose to help us. If you decide to accept my invitation to discuss terms, infuse mana into the sigil of the roc at the bottom of this letter and a communication link will open so we can discuss these things at an in-person meeting place.

I hope to hear from you soon.

Sincerely,
Theodore Munchamp

Riven folded the letter and pushed it over to Allie so she could read it again. "I'll be keeping the greenskins out of this one. As I'm responsible for them, I'll be first to say that they are far too worn-down to help. I butchered most of their remaining fighters at Greenstalk, and before that they'd already been set upon by numerous enemies. So they only have elites, the old, the young, and some goblins. I told Gurth'Rok they needed to focus on rebuilding. What you choose to do with your undead is up to you."

Allie's red eyes flickered over the parchment as she stuffed a pancake into her mouth. Taking a goblet of elf blood and sipping it to wash the pancake down, she let out a hiccup and folded the parchment again. "They want altar access, trade routes, protection for their northernmost town, an alliance against a dungeon and the elves attacking them that apparently number in the many thousands, and they thought they could just expect us to help? Us? Vampires and undead helping humans?"

Riven held up both hands, then swatted Athela's leg away before yanking her under the table when she tried to poke him a third time. Grinning at the screech he got from the Arshakai demon, he put a boot on her stomach and kept her pinned while she growled up at him. "Who knows? They sound desperate, and when you get desperate, you do a lot of things you normally wouldn't do. So what do you think? Are you going to use that sigil on the paper or are you going to shred it? Wouldn't hurt to have some allies in the area, but I'm not sure we can trust them, either."

Allie hummed in agreement. "Yes. And we've already had poor experiences with the elves of Greenstalk; if their entire culture is like that . . . perhaps it'd be wise to aid them after all. The enemy of my enemy is my friend, and until proven otherwise, I will assume the elves of these lands will treat us the same way they treated you earlier. Then again, the humans of Brightsville were little different . . . Hmm. Mara."

"Yes, Mistress?" Mara asked, coming to stand beside Allie and putting some syrup they'd stolen from a local grocery store on the table before bowing low in her black robe. "What can I assist you with?"

"Send some of your raven familiars into the southlands and find out what you can about the ongoing political events there. Confirm whatever you can about this letter, and make it fast."

"Yes, Mistress."

From where they'd been perched on a window above, two ravens flickering with Shadow mana took flight and tore into the darkening sky above. A clap of thunder rolled across the city, echoing from the mountains to the north and west, and the sunlight began to fade while black clouds hovered on the horizon.

"Storm's coming," Riven noted casually, getting up from the table and pushing his chair in. He nodded to Dr. Brass. "Hey, old man, get some training on curse magic from Fay when you can, since she's already here taking care of her brother. You need to acquire your Unholy pillar so you can get some actual abilities instead of just staring at yourself in the mirror all day."

Allie snickered and Dr. Brass dropped to scowl at the younger man.

Riven smirked, helped Athela up to her feet, and then thanked his sister for the meal. "I'm off to the underdark. Are you still raiding the prison today?"

Allie's tapping fingers came to a stop on the table, and a sinister smile played across her lips while she waggled her eyebrows. "Oh yes. Vin and Nin have already begun preparations for the assault. Those inmates won't know what hit them before they're all dragged out as corpses to add to our empire."

"Just be sure to spare the ones they've enslaved."

"How hypocritical."

"Damn it, Allie, we've had this conversation—"

"I know! I'm just kidding." Allie waved off Riven's glare. "It's just fun to poke you there, because I know it bothers you. What are siblings for, right? Seriously, though, you're always WAAAAYYYYY too on edge. Chill a bit, live a little, and stop being so rigid. Anyways, have fun, be safe, and for fuck's sake, you better run if there's anything actually dangerous down there. We have that deal in place, remember? If there's a real threat, we throw our minions at whatever it is, hightail it, and meet up to face it together later. Okay?"

"Yup, I know. Same goes to you." Riven waved at his sister, then to Mara, and Athela followed him out into the eastern wing of the manor, bypassing a few armored skeleton soldiers stationed in the hallway. "Time to go meet that big rat again."

"He probably wouldn't appreciate it if he knew you called him a *rat*. He's a rat *man*, not a rat," Athela stated simply, skipping to catch up to him and leaning against his shoulder with narrowed eyes looking upward. "So . . . You gonna tell me what happened with Fay last night or not?"

"I already told you, she's staying here while we're gone to take care of her brother."

"That doesn't explain much."

"He came out of the portal all fucked-up, and she was upset. That's literally all I know. If you want to know more, then ask her yourself."

Athela sighed. "Fine! I'll ask her later. But as her master, you can always just force her to tell you."

Riven shot Athela a glare.

"Might makes right, remember?!" Athela said with a wide, brilliant smile. "Make her do what you want! Plus, she owes you! Big-time, if you ask me. I can't believe you actually let that useless twat into the guild hall—and paid so much money to do it! That's insane to me! Truly, you're not a normal warlock, Riven. Or a normal vampire. And wait, aren't we going to go talk to that Princess Kathrine first? The Blood Moon Requiem should know about your malignancy points after all, and they're no doubt dying to talk with you after what happened."

Riven shook his head, drawing his hood down over his eyes to protect himself from the sunlight and stuffing his hands into his pockets to avoid more of the rays. Then he headed toward the chapel, where Azmoth was doing god knows what in the old building he'd claimed as a room to pick his other demon up for the trip to the destroyed hospital. "No. We don't have time; we'll talk to Kathrine later. The meeting with Snagger is only a couple hours away."

CHAPTER 15

[Azmoth has selected the class Infernal Crusader Initiate. Due to genetic makeup, class title benefits have integrated with species traits
- **Infernal Crusader Initiate (Class Title)**—A fire-attuned physical class path that focuses on tanking through martial arts. This class increases defensive capabilities with inherent bonuses, the amount of Sturdiness gained per level, and abilities granted by the system at regular intervals. +1 Strength, +4 Sturdiness, +1 free stat point per level. Gives bonuses to heavy armor and fire-attuned abilities. (Comes with the knowledge of the Infernal martial art Dome of Flames) (Increases Willpower requirement by 5)]

Riven stumbled and nearly fell over while walking through the garden at the back side of the manor before quickly balancing himself. The neon-teal leaves of the tree overhead shuddered and quaked, and he found himself needing to catch himself yet again on Jose's tombstone when a pulsing wave of heat rippled across the black, red, and silver flowers that decorated the walkways.

And then all went still again, and Riven shared a curious glance with Athela before hurriedly walking over to where the heat wave had come from.

The old stone chapel that Azmoth now was making his own home was only a couple dozen yards away, across the garden and behind the manor where Riven now lived. It was a far bigger room than the smaller ones in the manor could offer such a large demon, and Azmoth had volunteered to stay there after scoping out potential places to call his own.

Coming around the side of the ruined old building and entering through a wide, doorless archway, Riven froze when he saw Azmoth inspecting one of his arms.

Azmoth had undergone a significant change.

His body was generally the same shape and composed of the same materials, but he was slightly bigger and meaner-looking. Just previous to selecting the class, before the class title integrated with Azmoth's species traits, the thick black iron plates covering his body had had large gaps between them, exposing sinewy red muscle uncovered by skin. Here, however, those gaps had significantly decreased and had mostly been replaced with more of the black metal. More spikes had been added along the ridge of his neck and head to boot.

The effect made Azmoth look like a titanic, demonic black knight of sorts—with a tail, four arms, no eyes, and two eel-like maws made of black metal that gnashed their teeth and flickered with cinders. Only small slits of muscular red flesh could now be seen between the plates—Azmoth's body had become something of a living set of armor.

His movements were still fluid, however, and he turned his sightless gaze upon Riven with a grin to expose the usual rows of obsidian teeth while picking up his gigantic stone maul. Resting it on a shoulder, he waved with his two free hands. "Class count body as armor and give more bonus. We go now?"

Riven looked the large demon and his metallic exoskeleton up and down with newfound appreciation. "You really look the part of a doomsday knight, my friend. Congratulations on picking a class! And yes, we're going. Fay's staying behind with her brother unless I need her. Anyways, have you had a chance to try out your new ability yet?"

"Dome of Flames?" Azmoth muttered, looking down to a notification that appeared before his face—and he shook his head. "Try later. I burn down house if stay here. Let go."

Walking down the cement road toward the remnants of the half-destroyed hospital, Riven saw a couple of decaying human bodies that hadn't been here last time. Some of them were being fed upon by birds like roadkill, but they all had obvious gunshot wounds—indicating that they'd been killed by other humans instead of by monsters, goblins, or anything else.

He avoided the remnants of the men and women who'd been killed by the nightmare creature, too, frowning at the memory of these creatures rampaging through the crowds.

He kicked open the hole they'd patched in the floor leading to the hospital's basement, shoved aside some rubble and remnants of Athela's webbing that were still there, and dropped down into the dark.

The stench hit his nostrils immediately, and he nearly gagged at the putrefaction that the clown-like dream creature was undergoing at this very moment. He stood in a puddle of the necrotic ooze leaking out from the massive beast, along with some of the other dream creatures' smaller bodies, and he kicked the clown monster's corpse for good measure while walking by in a spiteful act of retribution for the headache it'd given him. There were no signs of anyone having

returned after the mass exodus when the creature had attacked, the hospital basement being completely devoid of any life, and he, alongside his two minions,
found the sewer entrance in the back room without incident.

He dropped down yet again, feet landing on the hard stone of the sewer's
walkway while his eyes immediately adjusted to the deep black of the tunnels
beneath Brightsville.

"Which way?" Azmoth asked after his huge body slammed against the floor
with a thudding boom. The newly formed black armor was so fucking sick, and
Riven could only shake his head with a large smile of approval while looking at
his Unholy paladin, who randomly flickered with smoldering flames. The huge
stone maul Azmoth wielded was very similar—it too simmered with heat.

Athela waved away the dust that Azmoth had kicked up, giving the bigger
demon a grimace, and pointed left. "That way."

Riven nodded in affirmation, holding out his staff to confirm Athela's gesture, and stepped ahead. "Let's go."

The tunnels were devoid of any heartbeats other than those of the small
rodents and amphibians that somehow lived down here in the muck without getting herpe-gonnorrh-syphil-AIDS, but that wasn't reason to be without caution.
The armored wyrm creatures that'd attacked him last time down here had come
as a swarm; they were ambush predators, and Riven hadn't picked up any heartbeats from them last time, either. The battle between Riven, Athela, Snagger,
and the swarm of wyrms had left huge numbers of the creatures dead—but that
didn't mean there weren't more.

The tunnels turned and twisted a couple times and then led farther down
into the ground where they connected with a large cave system that spanned
many hundreds of yards out in any direction; no doubt the system had attached
it on purpose when fusing the three worlds together. It had many stalagmites and
stalactites, a couple pools of water that looked far cleaner than the sewage pockets from up above, and several patches of bioluminescent moss. This was the real
entrance into the underdark, where Riven had been instructed to meet Snagger.

Riven was not disappointed.

Already standing in the middle of the cave was Snagger, accompanied by
three more rat men each quite a bit smaller than Snagger. He looked the same—a
scarred, brown-furred, muscular rat man who stood up on two legs like a human,
a little taller than Riven. He wore the same spiked knuckle pieces he'd used to
bash the wyrms with when Riven'd first met him and had the same worn leather
chest piece across his front as well.

Unlike Snagger, who looked like he'd eaten roids for breakfast for the past
nine years, the three other scrawny rat men each stood somewhere between four
and five feet tall. Two of them were colored gray, while the other had white fur,
but all of them had long, bare tails and large ears like Snagger. Riven couldn't tell

if any of them were male or female from the rags and cloaks they wore, but one of the gray-colored rats carried a caster's staff and the other two carried daggers and slings. They all perked up upon Riven's entrance, chittering in hushed tones to one another while Snagger stepped forward and came to greet the vampire himself.

"It is happy-good that you-we meet here!" Snagger chittered in the same raspy voice Riven remembered. "We-I am excited to show-introduce you to my nest-brood. Come-come, I will show-tell the name-signs of my kin-brood!"

The rat man was obviously excited, and Riven couldn't help but feel the same way. Despite everything else that was going on in the world, he was here meeting creatures akin to aliens and likely going where no man from Earth had ever gone before—into the underdark. This was the kind of stuff books were written about.

"Good to see you, too, Snagger. I'd love to meet your friends. By the way, this is Azmoth—I know he wasn't there with us last time, but he's another of my demonic servants."

The rat men were already evaluating Azmoth with wary eyes, or at least the newcomers were. Azmoth's foot was enough to crush them to dust, and the huge demon's formfitting obsidian plates were a testament to the enormous strength underneath.

"A strong minion-demon-slave, yes-yes. You are certainly-truly powerful-strong!"

Snagger nodded enthusiastically and raced over to the other rat men on all fours, moving slightly faster than he would have been on two legs, and showing Riven that he and his species likely could run or walk either way depending on what suited them at a given moment.

Snagger motioned to the white-furred rat first. "This is Mesha-kin, my cousin-kin."

He then motioned to the gray-furred rat with the staff, and the other gray-furred rat with the twin daggers. "Cheshish-kin and Bort-kin. They help-fight with me-me and Mesha-kin. We take jobs-fights for the brood-nest and mother-queen; we explore the surface-city and upper-higher underdark, try-find helpers and ally-friends."

Mesha, the white rat and apparently Snagger's cousin, bowed low and offered her two daggers out hilt-first toward Riven. Her voice was far squeakier and higher-pitched than Snagger's, and she kept her eyes low upon her own introduction. "I-we heard-listened to story-tales about you, great vampire mageling. I thought you summoned-kept only one demon slave-servant, but you acquired-have two? Much impressed-awe, not an easy-flimsy thing-item to do."

"I actually have three. One of them is on personal business." Riven silently snickered at the way Athela was giving the rat people a dirty look at the mention of "slaves" when referencing his two demonic minions, but he kept his humor underneath his mask. "All righty, then. I believe you were going to show me around your nest? Is it like a city, or . . . What should I be expecting here? Either way, I'm rather excited to find out. I've never been to a settlement created by your people before."

"You-you have not?" Cheshish, the gray-furred caster rat, asked curiously, adjusting the leathers he wore so that they weren't too tightly bound.

It was a conversation he'd already had with Snagger, but he was patient. Riven shook his head. "Nope. On my world, Earth, your people don't even exist. Or they didn't—Earth isn't around anymore, as it was incorporated into Panu."

Mesha cut into the conversation with wide eyes, stepping over to evaluate him in more detail. "Interesting-fascinating. Maybe why your eyes are red-bright, and not red-dull like other bat-vampire friends we-we have. We come-travel from Zazir world-planet, but we will show-see you to our nest-city. It is very akin to other nest-cities in the underdark, and you will be welcome-friended there! Travel-follow me-me!"

"Zazir, huh? I don't think I've met anyone from the third planet. Everyone I've seen so far is either from Earth or Zazir . . ."

And that was when Riven heard it—rapidly increasing heartbeats from farther down the tunnel. His eyes narrowed, and he peered farther ahead until he focused in on what looked like a helmet . . .

Yup. That was definitely a helmet, a set of eyes, and a long brown beard on a face peering out at him from around a ledge farther back. He could vaguely hear the clicking of bolts being loaded into crossbows, and then a shout-squeak of alarm went up from Snagger as a flurry of incoming missiles was launched through the tunnel toward their position.

CHAPTER 16

WHOOSH

Azmoth immediately tore forward and slammed a foot down in the direction of the oncoming projectiles, not wasting any time and sending a shock wave of kinetic energy through the air. Stone shrapnel from the cave floor was thrown up, creating a temporary cloud of dust, and the vast majority of the projectiles shattered or were thrown aside by the shock wave.

But three made it through.

Mesha squealed in pain and hit the ground, a crossbow bolt protruding from her back, and a second bolt clipped Snagger's shoulder, making him grunt. Simultaneously the other rogue, Bort, took a similar bolt to the eye. The small rat man dropped to the ground instantaneously, his weapons clattering to the stone floor while he slapped face down beside them hard and lifelessly.

"KILL THE BEASTS!!! KILL THEM ALL!!!" a deep, bellowing voice roared out, and in an instant a party of at least over thirty stout, bearded men came tearing through the tunnels leading farther into the underdark.

[Dwarf Warrior]
[Dwarf Warrior]
[Dwarf Warrior]
[Dwarf Sharpshooter]

The dwarves and rat men alike were able to see in the deep tunnels of the planet, just like Riven could—that much was made very clear by their coordinated movements even in the absence of actual light. The only thing a normal human would have seen was Riven's glowing red eyes or the flames beginning to billow around Azmoth's fused black plate armor and the maul he carried.

The stout men bore heavy metal crossbows on their backs and large stone axes in their hands; some of them had thick round shields, and all of them wore incredibly heavy-looking stone-plate armor. The warriors were all rather thick, muscular, and about four to five feet tall apiece.

Azmoth responded with a roar and tore through the black depths to meet them head-on, blowing up into an inferno and swinging his hell-forged maul overhead. The weapon glowed a bright orange intermixed with yellows and reds, the magma along its stone body coming to life, and with a thunderous downward stroke, Azmoth smashed the first two dwarves.

The room reverberated under the impact, and an explosion of magma tore from Azmoth's position to shower more of the short, stout men like the eruption of a volcano. Thick, molten, flaming metal splashed in a wave in front of the demon's position, and a number of the dwarves ahead of him screamed in shock. Simultaneously, Azmoth's armored, eel-like maws extended from his back over his shoulders to breathe more flames onto the incoming enemies, baking many of them alive and bringing the brunt of their attack to an abrupt, stupefied halt.

Two Blood Lances whizzed past like streaks of crimson through the dark. The unfortunate dwarves in the front that met those Blood Lances were each sent backflipping when their heads and helmets exploded. More crimson mana began to stream out of the charred corpses on the ground like silky ribbons, flowing to collect into a red orb in front of Riven as a power reservoir, and Athela jumped up to the cave ceiling to begin flanking the enemy.

Snagger rushed over to Mesha, who was still writhing on the ground and clutching at the bolt in her back. The large rat man inspected her briefly and then screamed in rage before he leaped toward one of the armored enemies that'd managed to make it around the demon's flames.

Not wanting to hurt Snagger with friendly fire, Riven decided not to send in a barrage of exploding discs—rather, he began to collect more Blood Lances and started attaching Wretched Snares for the slingshot effect. Even more dwarves were rushing in, and most had put away their crossbows in favor of close-combat weapons.

Axes slashed, cut, and bounced off Azmoth's enormous body while the large demon snapped necks with his claws, crushed bodies with his maul, and ripped off plate mail to better expose his enemies, breathing fire and cackling all the while.

CRASH

Riven's crackling beam of Black Lightning ripped across seven of the dwarves simultaneously, killing two outright just as an orb of purple energy rocketed out from Cheshish, the rat man caster, burying itself in the gut of one of the oncoming enemies and exploding in a cloud of shrapnel made of stone and body parts.

Unfortunately, two more dwarves dressed in brown robes had stayed in the back line and returned fire with spells of their own. From beneath Cheshish a large stone hand ripped from the cave floor and grasped the rat, squeezing him as he squealed until his body exploded from the force.

Riven had to dodge a similarly targeted spell, but he was far faster than Cheshish and knew Athela was already on the lookout for any potential back-line casters or sharpshooters. The enemy mages would be dealt with soon enough; he trusted Athela's judgment.

His body lit up with red electricity when yet another stone hand ripped out of the cave floor and he riftwalked past the enemy spell—landing right in the fray amid Azmoth and Snagger when the tear in space expelled his body.

WHAM

Riven's staff sent a shock wave of Shadow magic as its spikes near the top blade collided with one of the dwarves from the side. The dwarf only had time to blink in shock at Riven's abrupt appearance before his body was launched into the opposite cave wall, crashing to the ground in a limp heap atop his weapon.

The dwarves were still very surprised by the resistance, but they were trying to rally and redoubled their efforts while screaming out crazed war cries and banging their weapons on thick metal shields. "TOGETHER, MEN!!! BRING THE DEMON DOWN!!!"

Snagger's spiked gauntlets crashed into enemies one after the other with quick blurring motions, dancing back and forth between axe swings and taking an occasional clip here or there. Azmoth took on seven at once, tossing dwarves overhead and punting the smaller enemies across the cave while shrugging off most of the blows aimed at him.

A pang of hunger washed through Riven's body.

"COME HERE, LITTLE DWARF RUNTLING!" Azmoth cackled and batted aside another swing from a sturdy dwarf just ahead of him. His clawed hand grasped the short man by his beard and yanked him up, screaming, to meet Azmoth's eyeless grin with rows of obsidian teeth. "GOODBYE!!!"

Azmoth's mouth exploded with a beam of flames that cooked the screaming dwarf alive, still in his armor, like a boiling Hot Pocket.

Meanwhile, Riven had his own problems to deal with. He blocked an incoming strike powered by some kind of martial art that made the dwarf's axe glow orange. Riven turned his shoulder at just the right moment, redirecting the brunt of the attack, and the axe slid off Riven's angled staff to crash into the stone—sending cave-floor shrapnel up into the air.

Riven counterattacked, his hand launching forward and getting a firm hold on the dwarf's neck. His fingers exploded with Crimson Ice, turning his entire right arm into a crimson spike trap that skewered through the dwarf's neck and out the opposite side in a spray of blood.

Sneering, Riven retracted his ice back into his body and flung the corpse aside before being tackled to the ground by another dwarf—but Riven used the momentum to roll and fling the dwarf off. Holding up his hand, he sent Blood Lances at this new enemy.

Black and red tore forward from the spot where he'd been only twenty seconds before, breaking the sound barrier and splitting the man in three places while piercing his armor like a knife through butter. Blood and brain sprayed out in fountains of gore, and the dwarf's corpse was flung backward over a dozen feet, a trail of blood splattering along the ground.

BOOM

An explosion behind them confirmed that Athela was fighting her own battle against the two mages who'd attacked Riven with the stone hand and killed Cheshish. Briefly evaluating her situation, Riven could see that Athela had already assassinated one of the dwarf mages and strung him up—headless—by his feet from a stalactite. The other mage was putting up quite the fight, though, hurling rocks that he ripped out of the cave walls, ceiling, and floor, desperately sending a storm of stone at Athela from all directions as the demoness ducked and wove with an extreme display of agility.

Another pang of hunger swept through Riven's soul.

Riven came back to his own fight only a moment after that and spun his staff around to block an attack directed at Snagger. The weapons clashed, Riven could feel the hot breath of the panting dwarf warrior directly in front of him, and the staff in his hands quivered with an odd sensation of pleasure when he felt his flesh temporarily meld with Vampire's Escort.

The staff's crimson spikes surrounding the main blade spun, twisting along the weapon, and then two of them blurred forward—extending well over three feet and tearing into the dwarf's weaker chain mail at the armpit.

Riven didn't have time to be surprised; he just drew back his weapon while the warrior swore and staggered back, holding his limp left arm with a grimace before he turned to run.

CRUNCH

Azmoth's maul smashed through the dwarf's body and flattened him like a pancake, armor and all, the flaming demon chuckling to himself before leaping away again toward a new victim.

Nearby an axe swung in an uppercut and lodged itself in Snagger's rib cage. Snagger let out a howl of pain, staggering back, and then took a gauntlet to the face. The dwarf warrior ripped his axe out and bellowed a battle cry—jumping forward to end the rat man.

Another Blood Lance ripped apart the warrior's side and the armor covering him—plastering his guts along the far wall.

WHOOSH

A bolt from a handheld crossbow Mesha produced in the back line flew within inches of Riven's face, passing straight by and slamming into a dwarf who'd managed to get behind Riven. The dwarf swore and stumbled, clutching at the bolt lodged in a weak spot between two plates of armor, and then screamed when Riven's next lance tore through his armored head.

Riven kicked off to the left, blasted another man in a spray of Bloody Razors that he charged with mana and exploded before they made impact. He dodged right underneath another axe swing and smashed the man in the back of the knees.

The man fell in a cry of agony, but Riven didn't have time to finish him off. With Bort and Cheshish dead and Snagger out of the fight, it'd come down to Riven and his two demons at the front line while Mesha hid behind a boulder and fired occasional bolts, grimacing, the projectile still sticking out of her lower back.

But if Riven had to be honest, he wasn't exerting himself much. Not that he hadn't wanted to, but he'd been unable to do so with Snagger getting in the way. Friendly fire had been a very real possibility, but now that Snagger had retreated from the front line of the fight, Riven could go all out.

The sound barrier broke and the lines of incoming enemies were eviscerated as another six prepared Blood Lances slingshot their way forward through the dwarves' ranks. Another explosion of magma lit up the cave, and black nets alongside spiked walls of red ice sprang up between Riven's position on the high ground and the crowd near Azmoth below.

KABOOM

CRUNCH

SMASH

"AAAAAHHHHHH!!!"

BOOM

SNAP

"BY GROM'S BEARD, WILL THIS CREATURE NOT JUST DIE ALREADY?!"

"AZMOTH DOES NOT FEAR DWARFLINGS!!! AZMOTH WISHES TO PLAY!!!"

CRACK

THUD

It was like watching kittens trying to kill an adult rhinoceros. Azmoth had come into a habit of batting them across the cave as hard as he could with his maul or tail; seeing them crunch or splat against the stone cave, he let out comical, demonic grunts of amusement. The warriors were just too weak to bring him down, their weapons only scratching his obsidian plates.

RIP-RIP-RIP-RIP-RIP

Stones of all shapes and sizes rapidly tore out of the ceiling overhead, centered on Azmoth's position, and after they started to glow with an unnatural brown light, they rocketed downward with the fury of a torpedo. Azmoth only had a brief moment to look up before he slammed one hand down onto the ground in an explosion of flame.

Abruptly, a dome barrier of Infernal mana bloomed out around the demon, evaporating two nearby enemies with a pulse of hellfire far stronger than his normal fire breath, and the very ground beneath the demon's feet began to melt. The temperature was so extreme, in fact, that Riven's eyes hurt just from looking that way, but it only lasted for a few seconds.

The incoming enemy spell ripped downward and collided with the flaming barrier, the mana-infused stones disintegrating upon contact and turning into ash that floated away on the dull current of wind. Azmoth looked up from where he now knelt in a pool of lava, grinning at the awestruck mage in the background and the stunned warriors nearby—just as the mage's head was severed from his body in a lightning-fast strike from behind via one of Athela's blades. Chaos erupted in the back lines a second later, and Azmoth began to cackle when his flaming dome dissipated.

There was no doubt in Riven's mind: ever since he'd acquired Azmoth as a familiar, the Hellscape Brutalisk had drastically increased his defensive prowess and ability to take hits. He'd been a tank since stepping out of the nether realms on that very first day back in the Dungeon Negrada, but now that stat points and evaluations had been stacked so much over the course of leveling up . . . it was just unfair. It made Riven curious: Just what level WERE these dwarves at?

He needed to get an identifier in the party.

Riven teleported left, his body vanishing through another rift. He exploded into the air again, materializing right behind another of the dwarves who thought they'd take care of Mesha and Snagger in the back line.

"Not today, motherfucker!"

CRUNCH

Riven's staff extended its blade like a whip, and it lit up with crimson light when the weapon ability Scorpion's Sting activated. The blade shifted and blasted through the air like a ribbon of death, cleaving through the necks of the two enemies in less than a second before rapidly snapping back onto the head of the staff with a thunk.

He turned slowly, staring down two more warriors who eyed him warily amid the sprawled corpses of their allies.

Riven's aura exploded upon their attempt at assassinating his newfound rat-oriented friends. The energy his aura released was a violent mixture of raw anger and visible crimson power that caused the cave to start freezing around him. Stone protrusions started accumulating frost, the air around him started to simmer, and his red eyes grew even brighter, lines of power spiderwebbing across his face.

Hunger raced through him yet again.

The power spiked and the cave shook when he fed even more of his mana into the aura. His cloak billowed out around him in the storm he'd created, and the dwarf assassins quickly stepped back with wide eyes. Stone shrapnel ripped off the walls and joined the churning waves of mana, and the vampire lifted one hand—palm up and body engulfed with roaring energy—to beckon them with his fingers.

"Come."

The smaller, thicker, armored men took one look at each other in stunned silence. Then their grimacing faces became stony, they gave each other a nod, and they charged.

It was brave, Riven had to give them that, but it was also very stupid. As soon as they hit the cyclone his aura produced, their bodies began to rip apart like paper through a shredder. Riven just watched silently and unmoving as the two warriors tried to push through. Watched as one of them had the flesh stripped off his face and the stone plates carved off his body before he was completely torn asunder. Watched as the other dwarf managed to barely make it through the torrent of wailing crimson winds, only to take a single step beyond it and fall over dead—bleeding out on the ground, his body ravaged.

Well, that'd been easy enough. Test run complete.

The remaining dwarves who'd been fighting Azmoth began to retreat with fearful shouts of despair, sprinting back toward the tunnel, where Athela was finishing off four more mages at the dead end of the enemy column. Piles of debris and stone littered the ground around her where her most recent target lay bleeding out on the floor and impaled by one of her arachnid legs. She saw them coming and quickly began spinning a web to slow them down—dashing back into the tunnels where she knew they'd go and blurring up and down, side to side, with dozens of threads attaching from wall to wall or floor to ceiling every few seconds.

Azmoth tossed his latest victim's ripped corpse to the floor and let out a roar reminiscent of a T. rex from those *Jurassic Park* movies Riven had seen growing up. The monstrous demon lunged ahead to chase them down, his tail sweeping out behind him; he was far slower than Athela but about as fast as the dwarves. With Athela slowing them down, tangling them up in her crimson webs, and Riven firing off blasts of Black Lightning and Blood Lances over Azmoth's shoulders, the dwarves quickly succumbed one after another. The attack lasted only half a minute, the dwarf warriors pleading, begging for mercy, and screaming curses at them until the final one died under Azmoth's clawed foot.

Riven didn't waste any time, quickly stripping off his mask to begin feeding on the dead.

CHAPTER 17

Gurth'Rok looked at the reflection in the mirror and put his hand against the glass to try and wipe away the disfigured features he saw. He'd worn the wooden mask to his left for many years now, a reminder of his failures. The scars he bore and the upper lip that'd been ripped off, giving him his ever-present snarl, still radiated remnant magics of a long-forgotten curse that'd been resistant to his attempts at healing. He'd finally and grudgingly accepted his disfigurement.

Until now.

Dr. Brass stood behind him at the door leading into the hallway, the previously old man now showing abundant signs of vigor and youth. His shriveled frame was now slim and athletic, his features pristine and refined. Graying, thinning hair had turned into a thicker, silky silver—and all the previous health problems ailing him had disappeared entirely.

Beside Dr. Brass, Allie Thane smiled widely—displaying her fangs excitedly when Gurth'Rok stood up. The large orc turned around, bowed to Allie, and straightened again with a clenched jaw. Two of his orc elites were there to witness the transformation, and goblets of blood had already been drained from the elves again, the bindings prepared.

"Are you ready?" Allie asked curiously, gesturing to the chains and shackles two of her skeletal minions held on either side of where she stood.

The orc chieftain glanced over to one of his childhood friends, now an elite guard of the Yellow Skull Tribe, and firmed his resolve when his friend gave him a reassuring nod. "I am. Bind me."

The two skeletons stepped forward and started applying the shackles, and Allie's smile only widened to unnatural proportions when she stepped past Dr. Brass and into Gurth'Rok's personal space. She slid one hand up the orc's neck, feeling his sinewy musculature retract on reflex to her cold touch, and then she motioned for him to lie down. "It may hurt."

"It'll definitely hurt," Dr. Brass affirmed. "But it's worth it. You'll feel . . . different, but in a very good way."

Gurth'Rok took in a deep, wavering breath. This was what he needed to do, not only to heal himself, but to maintain a place of power in the new order. Becoming one of them would guarantee that he would not be thrown aside when the coven's might grew, and he knew it was only a matter of time. If one could not beat them, join them, and he'd seen little reason to do anything else but obey so far. Joining the Thane Necropolis had supplied his people with security, a new home, and new lands with plentiful game to hunt—even if the animals were strangely afflicted with Unholy magics or undeath. Even if the animals didn't supply meat, his warriors were quickly gaining levels and acquiring Elysium coins to use at the altar in exchange for food that way—and their situation had changed from one of starvation and exclusion to one of inclusion and plenty in mere days.

Joining the Thane Necropolis had been one of the best decisions of his life, and he had little doubt that it'd saved his people from obliteration. It was time to turn the page in the book detailing his life; he was finally ready to move on and embrace change, finally letting go of the haunting failings of his past.

Gurth'Rok lay back on the floor, chains secured and neck exposed. He nodded and felt his heartbeat pick up when Allie's sinister figure took steps forward to loom overhead. "I am ready. Please begin."

The world was changing.

CRACK

BOOM

And Riven was at the epicenter of at least one large piece of that change.

Riven's eyes shifted upward, not startled at all like the others nearby—but instead incredibly irritable now that the sudden burst of power ahead of him had been caused by nothing but a rather fancy notification. This one was etched in golden flames, far different from the teal blue–colored notifications he usually got, and he put down the dwarf corpse he was feeding on to evaluate the new set of information.

He squinted, red eyes flickering over the words while Athela started clawing her way over the dead to read it, too.

Then his interest began to rise.

**[World Quest 2, The Apocalypse Beasts: Chalgathi (Updated x1)
The death of this world approaches. Nekra, the Skeletal Devourer, churns in his sandy tomb amid a sea of the unliving. Chalgathi, the Plague Dragon, awaits those that would free him from its skyward prison above the clouds. Chubin, the Glass Kraken, seeks an escape from the abyss beneath the ocean. The cults of the end times gather**

their strength and resources to try and find the lairs of their chosen apocalypse beasts. Should they succeed, your world is doomed.

As one of the three apocalypse beasts born for this cycle of ascension, Chalgathi is destined for carnage. It is a creature of nightmarish power, a beast born of hate and malice. Five years after the beginning of this integration, a wave of destruction will spread across all the world on wings of decay. Empires will fall, billions will die, and the very ground you tread upon will rot and wither—for the plague dragon has finally awakened.

However, there is an alternative to this fate: stop the cultists from raising the plague dragon to his adult form, find Chalgathi's incubation chamber, and destroy or claim his egg for yourself before the five-year period is done. You, Riven Thane, are one of his chosen ones. You have acquired one of his artifacts, the Chalgathi Cultist Amulet, and have started down the path of saving this doomed world. It falls on you to act.

There were fifty chosen ones to leave Chalgathi's Trials, all of whom have Unholy bloodlines of great power. There are now forty-eight originals remaining, with two newly chosen having been assigned upon recent deaths. The chosen ones are divided into two categories: cultists and those who are not cultists, the significance of which will be revealed upon quest updates, and you are all competing against one another regardless of what category you fall into. Depending on which of the chosen reaches Chalgathi's lair to successfully claim his egg, each outcome could have drastically different consequences with the salvation or damnation of Panu. Each surviving chosen one came out of Chalgathi's starter quest with one piece of a five-piece set called the Chalgathi's Inheritance Set. There are a total of ten complete and identical sets, with set pieces being able to shift form slightly based on the build of their wearer. Chalgathi's Inheritance includes the following: Chalgathi Cultist Amulet, Chalgathi Cultist Claws, Chalgathi Cultist Mask, Chalgathi Cultist Pauldrons, and Chalgathi Cultist Breastplate.

▶You must find and collect one of each of these five items to complete the item set, at which point you will gain the locations and access to Chalgathi's altars. You will be required to visit all four altar sites and activate the shrines before acquiring knowledge of the location of Chalgathi's temple, where Chalgathi's incubation chamber has been hidden.

▶You must kill or rob other chosen that have necessary pieces to create the full set. You may find them by utilizing a Ping Chalgathi Artifacts ability provided to you that tracks others of Chalgathi's chosen across the planet of Panu. Ping Chalgathi Artifacts will do exactly as it says in the name and give you a generalized feel for the direction in which you can find these other needed pieces.

▶Acquiring more than one of the same type of artifact will result in banishment of extra same-type artifacts before administering them to a newly picked chosen one, or the system will readminister the duplicate artifacts to chosen ones who are still alive but lost their artifacts. Each time a chosen one dies, their spot in the quest line will be given to someone within the general populace, and they will be given the skill Ping Chalgathi Artifacts. There will always be fifty chosen ones with Chalgathi's subset of the Apocalypse Beasts quest line. If chosen ones die, they will be replaced with new chosen ones at Chalgathi's discretion.

▶Only once all set pieces have been fully equipped to a chosen one will Chalgathi's subquest of The Apocalypse Beasts update to the next stage.

Summary:
▶There will always be fifty chosen ones with the ability to ping Chalgathi's artifacts, having replacements fill in for those who died along the way. Those who are not Chalgathi's chosen ones may not enter the temple.
▶Acquire the amulet, claws, mask, pauldrons, and breastplate by any means, but it is very likely you'll have to kill the other chosen ones to do so.
▶Once the item set is completed, you will have a quest update.

Number of chosen ones holding five artifacts: 0
Number of chosen ones holding four artifacts: 0
Number of chosen ones holding three artifacts: 1
Number of chosen ones holding two artifacts: 0
Number of chosen ones holding one artifact: 47
Number of chosen ones holding zero artifacts: 2]

[You have been gifted the unique ability Ping Chalgathi Artifacts. This ability pings the locations of other Chalgathi Inheritance Set artifacts, only identifying pieces you do not already have after the very first utilization of this ability (the very first activation will set sights on all artifacts), and may be used at any time without any mana requirement. This ability only locates artifacts that you are missing from the set.]

He'd need to talk to Allie about this, and soon.

Riven's eyes slowly drifted down to the medallion that'd been tucked into his shirt. Suddenly he felt a very real need to get this thing identified—fast. Up until now he'd not been able to find an identifier, but now that he had identifiers at the trading communes at his altar, it was very likely he'd be able to swing an easy deal.

That would have to be a very high priority for him, starting now.

He pulled up his status page moments later, noting the level-up he'd acquired but also seeing the new ability he'd been gifted—and he started to apply points. He must not have noticed the notifications proclaiming his level-ups while being so encompassed with feeding on the dwarf, but he'd certainly not scoff at another level.

[Riven Thane's Status Page:
- Level 45
- Pillar Orientations: Unholy Foundation, Blood Specialty, Infernal, Shadow
- Core of Original Sin—Gluttony: (Under Construction) (???)
- Traits: Race: Pure-Blooded Vampire (Extreme Darkness Regeneration) (Sunlight Decay) (Extreme weakness to silver weapons, Sun pillar, and Light pillar attacks), Class: Warlock Adept, Adrenaline Junkie (Blood) (+15% to Agility), Accomplishment Title: Bloodthirsty 1 (+5% increased blood mana from corpses, +1% dmg for blood magic)
- Abilities: Blessing of the Crow (Unholy), Wretched Snare (Unholy), Silvertongue (Unholy), Bloody Razors (Blood), Crimson Ice (Blood), Blood Lance (Blood) (Tier 2), Blood Nova (Blood) (Tier 3), Hell's Armor (Infernal), Riftwalk (Shadow), Ping Chalgathi Artifacts (Unique)
- Stats: 75 Strength, 173 Sturdiness, 420 Intelligence, 198 Agility, 10 Luck, -383 Charisma, 189 Vampiric Perception, 126 Willpower, 9 Faith
- Free Stat Points: 7
- Minions: Athela, Level 37 Arshakai [36 Willpower Requirement]. Azmoth, Level 40 Hellscape Brutalisk (Infernal Crusader Initiate) [49 Willpower Requirement]. Fay, Level 27 Succubus [29 Willpower Requirement]
- Equipped Items: Basic Cloak (1 def), Vampire's Escort (104

dmg, 102% mana regen, Shadow and Blood dmg +22%, Black Lightning, Scorpion's Sting), Chalgathi Cultist Amulet (???), Leather Boots (1 def), Witch's Ring of Grand Casting (+26 Intelligence), Breath of Valgeshia (48 def, +13 dmg & +9% mana output dmg for Blood dmg, 6% mana regen), Satin Bag of Holding]

Normally Riven placed most of his free stat points into Intelligence, some into Sturdiness, and some into Willpower. But now with Fay added to the list and Azmoth's recent evolutions, he was cutting it close for Willpower requirements and didn't want to hold his demons up if they ever needed more for new power-ups. So he placed all seven points into Willpower, bringing it from 126 to 133.

Then, activating his new ability, he found that he got approximate locations via direction and a vague feeling of distance from forty-six other people. It was more of a sixth sense than anything else. One of these other chosen ones was no doubt Allie, who was rather close, with the closest other figure a little over eighty miles away. All the others were much, much farther than that . . . Meaning that although this new turn of events was concerning, it wasn't likely an immediate concern.

However, having other people track him based on his item was something he'd have to consider. Perhaps keeping it in a guarded location rather than wearing it would be wise, as that painted a target on his back.

But he'd make that decision after he actually knew what the fuck this stupid thing did. Perhaps leaving it on was a great boon, and he'd just not had the time or resources to figure it out until now.

Athela and Riven exchanged hushed words before activities resumed.

Mesha and Snagger watched in somber silence as Riven and Azmoth went back to gorging themselves on the bodies of the fallen dwarves—with both ratkin giving each other questioning looks when the golden notification winked out. It'd been too far away for either of them to read it, and they'd been tending their wounds, not wanting to intrude. Athela had patched them up with her meager ability to stitch injuries, though they were still hurt. They just weren't bleeding out anymore.

The spider demon, on the other hand, was going through the inventory of their defeated enemies, occasionally putting a ring, pouch, or trinket into a purple-and-gold spatial sack similar to the one Riven had taken from the dungeon; she'd found the item on one of the dwarf mages. The spatial sack itself was the greatest prize, as it could hold items far beyond what a normal bag of its size should be able to do. It had a storage system in it that could keep items in an alternate pocket dimension linked directly to the bag, and she'd already found a bunch of good stuff in there even before she'd started looting the others. There'd been potions, two books, three rings, some clothes, a bunch of money, some assortments of ores—which she didn't know the value— seven dark elf ears, which had apparently been taken as some sort of sick trophies, and foodstuffs. That list was only adding up as she went, and she still had another dozen bodies to check over.

Mesha absent-mindedly pawed at her white fur, grimacing when she moved in the wrong way to adjust her sitting position against the boulder they leaned back on. She leaned over to whisper to her cousin, "Your friend-allies are strong-mighty."

Snagger didn't bother replying, rather, he lowered his eyes and let out a mournful squeak. Cheshish and Bort had been his friends for years, and losing them to a dwarven patrol this far from the battlegrounds hadn't been something he'd ever expected. The dwarves had been encroaching on the nest's territory since the integration, and the brood was becoming desperate. If something wasn't done about the dwarves and their genocidal slaughter of Snagger's people, the rat men might very well have to pack up and leave. The problem was that the underdark was a very dangerous place, and finding a new safe haven would be very hard to do and doubtless a big risk in itself. Then there was the question of whether a location would have access to enough resources to support the remaining brood, or if moving would mean they'd all starve. The nest had put decades of time and effort into cultivating their underground farms, and if they left, they'd be abandoning those farms to the dwarves. That alone would mean many thousands more of his people would die of hunger.

That was why Snagger and groups like his were constantly being sent out by the queen, searching for potential allies to fight alongside them against the dwarves. Peace talks and envoys had all fallen short, their diplomats' heads put on spikes in the major tunnels where traffic led toward the nest, and crude messages or threats written in the blood of Snagger's people as a response. It was very clear to everyone involved that the dwarves wanted nothing more than to rout the entire rat-kin population and claim this area for their own kingdom. And thus far, the dwarves were winning the war.

"Do you think-imagine the vampire glowing-eyes has more-many of his people to help us?" Mesha eventually pushed again after getting no response from her earlier open-ended statement. "The queen-mother will reward the bright-eyes greatly-much if he has-does."

Snagger grunted and placed a clawed hand on his wounded armpit, still not entirely able to move that particular side even now. It was likely that tendons and ligaments had been torn right through, but he was lucky he'd kept the arm at all. Wounds like this would eventually heal, or he could get a healer back in the nest to seal it over and repair the injury. If he'd lost the arm entirely, that may or may not be the case. "He did not tell-show me-me. I was to ask-inquire of this now-here, when we invite him-him to the nest-city. He may-might be alone but can show-tell of valuable information-facts even if he is one-alone and does not have many-lots of blood-eater vampire-kin with him. We-we do not know-see of the world-planet yet. Nest-kin must know-see of Panu now that world-planets have merged."

CHAPTER 18

"All right, we'll come up with a name for our new city after you cull the opposition. Remember not to just butcher anything in sight, I mean that, and catch you later." The call with Allie ended, and he deposited the black communication bauble in his bag of holding. Riven thumbed through the pages of one of the large books he'd taken off the dwarves, walking behind Snagger down the underdark tunnels with a gleeful grin, and gave Athela a loving pat on the head. "You play fetch nicely! Who's da good dawg!"

SMACK

"OW!"

"I'm NOT a dog! I'm a princess. Humph!"

Riven imbued a command: "Bark for me."

"WOOF! Hey!"

"Sucker."

Athela pouted and folded her arms over her chest. "Not fair!"

"What's not?"

"Don't use my contract like that! I feel violated."

"You signed up for it, girlfriend!"

Riven gave her a wide, teasing grin and then stuck his tongue out while pulling his cheeks apart, crossing his eyes and making a stupid face. She tried to hide her amusement under an eye roll and a quick twist of her hips, walking farther ahead with her long black hair swaying behind her while she pretended to act disgusted.

"Ugh. You humans are immature."

"Vampire, not human." Riven cackled to himself and went back to looking over the notes scribbled into the text. It was one of many items Athela had scrounged up, and it wasn't anything magical, but it was a condensed list of valuable ores and where to find them, with instructions and maps drawn out on the parchment. It contained all the information the dwarves had accumulated so far in their scouting missions—it looked like they'd spent weeks at a minimum jotting it all down. They even had Snagger's nest listed as a potential zone for "extermination."

Mesha, the white-furred rat-kin rogue, was a little farther down the tunnels, occasionally giving the book Riven was holding inquisitive stares, but she'd always turn away when she saw Riven's eyes dart over to her. He caught on pretty fast, though, and intentionally caught her midstare a few minutes later while hopping over a small cave pool.

"Interested in the contents?"

Riven snapped the book shut and casually tossed it over to the rat-kin female, smiling to himself as she hastily nodded with a light squeak of appreciation and then began to flip through the pages herself.

The footsteps of their party—namely Azmoth—echoed off the stone walls as the path narrowed and split off into four directions at a crossroads. Snagger took them left, and they began to descend deeper into the underdark after a spiral loop. These were likely once huge lava tunnels, no doubt, a vast and intricate network of them. That they were intricate only became more apparent the farther they walked, and they soon found themselves on one of the most curious trips Riven had ever been on.

Some of the caverns they passed through were many miles high and even many more miles wide, housing large ecosystems of cave-dwelling creatures—various species of bats, huge black or purple snakes, glowing green mushrooms the size of trees, and moss clumps that created literal hills. Neon-teal grass, fungi, and molds were seen in abundance, creating forests that were rampant with tiny rodents, brilliantly colored salamanders, ants the size of small dogs, and other insects of various types. In pools of crystal-clear water, bioluminescent or pale-white shrimp could be seen feeding on plant algae, with larger, blind, squid-like creatures even farther in the darker recesses of the lakes or basking on the shores underneath the canopy of glowing mushrooms. They were attacked twice, once by a large spiderlike creature that Athela actually spoke to and sent away without anything more than an initial scuffle—much to Riven's amazement—and then by a small group of chitinous giant centipedes. The orange-armored centipedes each weighed a couple hundred pounds, but Riven annihilated them easily enough with a few spells. He didn't even break a sweat. Otherwise Snagger and his cousin Mesha did a good job of keeping everyone out of the dangerous areas and away from conflict.

"It's very pretty," Riven muttered under his breath while they marched along the outer edge of one of these caverns, looking down at where a flock of brilliant pink cave birds were bathing in a central lake.

Snagger smiled back at him approvingly, still gingerly clutching the armpit that'd been stitched back together with one gauntleted hand. "We are close-near to the brood! Wait-stop until you see-view our nest-city! It is much-very nice-pretty as well-well!"

Snagger was telling the truth.

It took nearly an hour after that to get there, and it'd been nearly an entire day of traveling through the underdark, stopping once for a short exchange of naps and standing guard, but they finally arrived at an overwatching point through a small tunnel entrance.

The nesting cavern was absolutely massive, unlike anything Riven would have thought possible. It spanned at least a couple dozen miles, maybe even a hundred miles directly in front of him, but due to the twists and turns in the distance, it was hard to tell just how vast this cavern system was. Thousands of bioluminescent vines hung down from the ceiling, some in clusters that hung dozens of feet and others that were not as long by themselves, giving light to the otherwise dark interior of the cavern. Pools of glistening water rippled with underground waterfalls that came down from the ceiling above, rivers snaking their way through an absolute clusterfuck of activity with no rhyme or reason to it. There was barely any organization—most of the structures were made of hardened clay, a dark-brown wood-like substance, or stone.

The vast majority of these structures were divided up into large mounds or hills anywhere from the size of a large house to the size of a football stadium that held dozens or even hundreds of small caves or tunnels apiece. These mounds were truly the only glimpse of organization in the entire city, but many of them also had beams made of a strange dark-brown substance similar to wood with a very rough texture; together they created a network of roadways above the mounds leading to various points. The beams themselves looked very similar to what construction workers would use back on Earth to set up support platforms while building large buildings or towers downtown, but this was on an entirely different level. Taking in the ragtag fiesta of nonsense construction here in Snagger's nest made Riven's head hurt—some of the wood-like beams even led to nowhere at all, just hovering above the city as if they'd been left half completed.

Hundreds of thousands of rat-kin, most of them a lot smaller than Snagger, about Mesha's size, scurried back and forth over these hundreds of mounds or beams above, diving in or out of the holes leading into the mound interiors. The hills of clay and stone had not only been created on floor level but had also been built up the sides of the cave at forty-five-degree angles and somewhat steep drops down. Most of the rat-kin could easily climb back and forth across these structures.

Riven himself probably would be able to climb up and down those inclines, but he'd personally be worried about falling, as it seemed just a bit unsafe. He'd definitely be avoiding the beams as well, if at all possible.

Aside from the tunneled hills, the beams, and the scurrying bodies of the congregations of rat-kin drinking from the lakes, there were also a couple of what Riven assumed to be shops topside that were more exposed than whatever infrastructure lived inside the hills of caves and holes. He saw an open, glowing forge with green plumes of smoke wafting into the air atop one of the mounds, busy with activity and paying customers. He saw another mound nearby displaying a large collection of jewelry that was no doubt enchanted, judging from the remnant mana Riven could sense even at this distance, with display cases of glass under guard by the shopkeeper's employees. Yet another vendor at the base of another mound was selling leather and chitin goods they'd no doubt made from dead animals found in the underdark.

KABLAM

The nearby forge exploded with red light, sending a couple dozen rat-kin screaming through the air and to their deaths, still aflame, until they landed with crunches and crashes.

"That nest-family is-is experimenting with fire-chemicals—insane-crazy they are!" Mesha cackled, pointing a small, clawed finger at where dozens of other rat-kin had begun coming out of the mound beneath the forge to start cleanup or help the survivors of whatever had been going on there. "They make-create weapon-gadgets and are very rich-wealthy!"

"Come-walk, we must go talk-speak to another!" Snagger said, waving for Riven and his minions to follow and perking his large rat ears up at the sounds of the nest-city below. "Follow me-me!"

The surrounding rat-kin noticed Riven's presence immediately upon their approach. But seeing that Riven was walking alongside Snagger and Mesha put many of the rat-kin at ease—they then gave Riven and his demons only curious glances before returning to whatever work they'd been up to.

The farther Riven walked, the more he realized that this city was truly a ragtag sprawl of various buildings on the insides of these hill-like mounds, which were more unique than he'd originally thought. Passing through the crowds of curious onlookers that shuffled about him, he was able to see inside a lot of the mounds and get a better idea of how these rat-kin lived their lives.

There were family residences, more shops, areas for crafters, storage areas full of mushrooms and grains or equipment, and there was even a colosseum, where Riven paused to watch two large rat-kin—even bigger than Snagger—battle it out in a brutal match to the death. The crowds roared their approval and swapped bets before the final blow smashed the other rat-kin's skull in, and a couple squabbles broke out just after that with knives and claws flashing in the dark—likely because one side didn't want to pay the other when their bets fell through. More died in those scuffles, goods changed hands, and the dead bodies were promptly disposed or ignored, and all the while society just kept on going like nothing had ever happened.

"Is it normal that people just get murdered out in the open like that?" Riven asked, glancing over to where another small rat-kin had been stabbed in the throat and tossed out of one of the tunnels—only for his body to be dragged away by a random passerby.

Snagger glanced over, then shrugged. "The nest-brood has high-many births; we multiple-produce our kind fast-rapidly! When you are mark-branded by the kin leaders, you-you gain protection from rules-laws. Before mark-brands, you are not-not protected-saved by rules-laws."

The larger rat-kin pulled down his vest to display a large triangular marking that'd been burned into his skin. Mesha did the same, showing her own mark, and Riven's eyebrows raised.

"How do people know if you have the mark?" Riven asked curiously, folding his arms and watching yet another scuffle break out to his right. "And the others—they're not protected by your laws at all? Is this like a caste system?"

Snagger paused, trading a look with his smaller cousin. "What is caste-system?"

"It's a social hierarchy where one group of people is considered better than the others. It dictates who you can marry, who you can socialize with or what you can do for work—that kind of thing."

Mesha nodded vigorously. "Yes-yes! Like-similar to that. The mark-brands are given to us and magic identifies-signals us to other clan-nest kin as high-mighty citizen-kin. Rat-kin are high-citizen or low-citizen kin, with low-citizen kin not-unable to be protected by rules-laws. Must earn-collect mark-brand from queen or brood-nest mothers to earn-acquire one. So kill-fighting low-kin is not rule bound-enforced—can kill-fight them without punishment. If a kin kill-fights us-we, as high-kin, guards, and other citizen-rat-kin enforce rules-laws to defend us. It is known."

"So I could just go over and murder a 'low-kin' person and not have anything happen to me?"

"Only if you are-be high-kin. You are not rat-kin, so does-is not applied to you-you. If I-we want to fight-kill low-kin, we can attempt-try, but they can fight-kill us back and take-obtain our mark-brand."

"Kinda fucked-up." Riven frowned disapprovingly, crossing his arms.

Mesha snorted in amusement, sidestepping a larger rat-kin carrying a steel pole into one of the tunnels nearby. "We overpopulate-breed fast; it makes us-we strong-fit for survivors. But with beard-men dwarf-fighters attacking-warring us, queen-kin has told us-we to try and hold off customs-traditions to save our numbers-kin for war."

Riven felt a tap on his shoulder and turned to see Snagger looking down at him rather hesitantly.

"Is it all right–okay if we take-show you to the broodmother? Want to know many thing-happenings of top-surface, of new world ally-friends and fighter-enemies."

Riven's eyebrows raised. "Like, the queen of your city?"

The larger rat man rolled his shoulders and cracked his neck with a toothy grin that looked a little weird coming from a humanoid rat, but nevertheless it was obviously friendly. "No! We take-show information on world-planet to broodmother, Mesha and I's broodmother, head of family-nest—not city-nest. It is our brood-nest. Queen-mother look-seeks for new friend-allies and information, but not important enough for us-we to get audience. That why we take-show to brood-nest instead of city-nest."

There was a long pause as he considered this.

"Huh. Sure thing, that's fine with me. Not sure if I'll be any real help, but I'll answer what I can."

That was more than enough for Snagger, and he and Mesha led the way while beckoning Riven and his two demonic familiars to follow.

Mesha and Snagger eventually led them to a checkpoint along the city's inner perimeter, where the crowds started to thin and things became more organized. A wall had been erected here, encircling one of many larger compounds that sometimes had two or three mounds apiece. This particular mound was singular but nevertheless was heavily guarded and much larger than many of the other mounds in the area.

Guards outfitted in leathers similar to Snagger's own, looking down from a stone tower, called back and forth to the duo, holding crossbows and asking about Riven and the demonic servants, but neither the guards nor any of the other rat-kin passing them by seemed to mind that Riven was a vampire. Nor did they seem to care that he had demons with him, either. The most that happened were a few curious glances, but none of them were hostile, and Riven even got a few open smiles. This only confirmed what Snagger had originally told him about the underdark, that rat-kin here were used to vampires from their old world—and it was rather encouraging after the looks of absolute horror or hate from elves and humans on the surface.

After they'd passed the checkpoint and Snagger told the guards of the dwarven scouting party that'd attacked them, he proceeded to explain he was bringing in outsiders to see their broodmother. The guards let them pass without much issue, and their group entered the compound into the mound with minimal incident.

However, one of the guards hopped down a ladder and rushed off to tell the military of the dwarves' presence. According to Mesha, the dwarves had been encroaching on their territories but had never ventured that close to the city yet.

"The dwarves grow fierce-aggressive," Mesha commented when they entered the mound through a large cave entrance, entering a bustling rat-made cave network of merchants, food carts, and ramshackle buildings. "They kill-butcher us-we, take our goods-things, want our city-spawn."

Riven had overheard Snagger and Mesha talk about the dwarves in brief snippets along their travels but still had little to go on and wanted to clarify a few things. "So why are your people at war with this group of dwarves?"

Mesha nodded and squeaked loudly at a bunch of young whippersnappers who chittered and laughed while playfully racing underneath Snagger's legs. "Yes-yes, the dwarf-wretches kill us, attack us-we, take our shiny things because they want-need our land-things. They hunt-kill us and leave message-threats telling us-we to leave. The queen-mother and many broodmothers have led battles against dwarf-wretches; we win-attack and lose-attack both. We try to make peace-sign with dwarf-wretches, but they say no-refuse."

Huh.

Riven didn't know Mesha or Snagger very well, but based solely on how the dwarves had ambushed them, he couldn't help but be a little biased against the dwarves now. He shook his head. To think he'd dwarves, elves, orcs, demons, and even rat-kin since leaving Earth only about two months ago? It was all very surreal. That being said, he was very excited to explore this underground sanctuary of civilization and was pretty sure he was the first person from Earth to get a good look at any rat-kin city since the worlds had merged.

To boldly go where no one has gone before!

CHAPTER 19

The trees had begun to turn from vibrant green to a dark gray and black, many of them losing their leaves entirely or illuminating deathly teal light. The grass had gone from healthy to a gray-silver, and an unnerving fog blocked their sight even though it was midday. The accumulation of dark clouds in the sky that seemed to settle in evermore without signs of leaving anytime soon didn't help their vision problems, either—and it'd been this way for the past ten miles.

Despite the sightings of skeletal undead wolves or pitch-black deer with ghostly outlines that'd mutated into Unholy versions of their previous selves, the very small trade caravan traveling northward through the last stretch of forest was in hopeful spirits. The guard unit at the front was hacking and slashing away, creating pathways through the underbrush for the other men and women—mostly merchants, who were using mules for carrying luggage.

Cade was one of these merchants. As a younger and more adventurous man, he'd been far more excited than most about the prospect of the worlds merging. He saw it as an opportunity for growth rather than something to be feared, and he'd been among the first to volunteer for his uncle's quest to depart westward from the town of Bradshire, across the plains, to seek out trading partners with the undead of this Brightsville rumors talked of. Some people called his uncle stupid for even attempting it, fearful that he and his caravan would be turned into corpses and used as fodder to create even more of the unliving, but these were desperate times and the war with the elves was cutting food back drastically. If they didn't get more of it, their people would starve—and his uncle had a bleeding heart. Both Cade and his uncle felt that this was not only an opportunity to become rich but also a civic duty to keep their people fed.

So they'd begun their journey with whatever goods they'd had. They'd carried various textiles, pottery, basic weapons and armor, as well as some minor totems. They'd even brought along carts of corpses from the war effort, courtesy of a captain in the army who'd urged them to keep the bodies as a gift to increase chances of success. Now that all the kingdom of Dawn had been mixed and matched across the new landscape—or at least what was left of their kingdom after half of the cities and towns had likely been sent to the opposite side of their new world Panu—new pathways had to be carved out and mapped. Not only that, but the natural resources supplied by each of the settlements left in Dawn were now vastly different from before, other kingdoms that had been trading partners were now long gone, and the people of Dawn had monster problems to deal with.

Not to mention these blasphemous world quests the system had endangered everyone with.

Regardless, Cade was excited and smiled while brushing his hands through his short black hair. With his other hand he kept his donkey Horus close by, making sure to lead it on by giving the grumpy animal occasional carrots so it wouldn't just refuse to keep moving. The reason Cade was excited was news from a runner who'd caught up to their caravan not even an hour ago.

More specifically, it was news that Allie Thane of the Thane Necropolis had sent word: she was going to meet with Theodore Munchamp, court wizard to the king, for official negotiations. This was a huge deal, not only for their kingdom, but it also meant their little voyage northward was a lot more likely to be met with positive interactions than outright hostility. The risk had just dropped.

Contact had been made with the Thane Necropolis north of the forest and adjacent plains just days ago, or so said some of the hunters from Maringrad. The future negotiations were now being celebrated as a potential victory across their remnant kingdom, and the feeling had been a warm and welcome one. No doubt the nobles and the king himself were pushing it as a measure to keep morale high, but it was a much-needed thing. Perhaps, just maybe, the kingdom of Dawn wouldn't be so isolated anymore. Even help from the undead was a very welcome thing—they could use the help from anybody at this point.

He sighed, thinking silently to himself about how his relationship with Alexa hadn't worked out. That cheating bitch had gone behind his back and slept with his best friend—or the man he used to call a best friend, anyways. It was one of the reasons he'd come on this venture, aside from the money—to get his mind off things—and if Cade could get rich while doing it, then great. Better yet, if he could find himself a hot undead girlfriend . . . that'd make Alexa jealous beyond Cade's wildest dreams.

He snickered at the very thought of it. How sweet a vengeance that would be.

Twigs cracked underfoot and sweat dripped down his chin, splattering against his linen shirt. The voice of his uncle called out at the front of the column, "HALT!"

The caravan came to a dead stop, donkeys braying and the men in the back trying to look over the shoulders of those ahead to see what was going on.

The donkey Cade was leading nipped at his ass and the young man swore, swatting Horus's nose and causing it to headbutt him into a nearby tree, the other merchants snickering at him as he picked himself up.

"Gods damned unappreciative animal . . ." Cade muttered, clutching his bleeding nose and trying to nurse his wounded pride without giving the other men the satisfaction of recognizing their laughter. He swatted an insect that landed on his brown linen shirt and grumbled to himself, trying to get a better look ahead, but then the caravan started moving forward again.

This time the pace was much slower, though, and Cade heard whispers from farther up the line as he trudged through the fog. "What's the deal? Why have we slowed?"

He wasn't answered, but he got the answer himself when he came into the clearing where his uncle and all the others were lining up in a row. They were facing another group of people not far off, and Cade's heart froze in terror when he saw a dead man hanging from the branch of a tree in the dark forest ahead.

The man had once been a high elf, no doubt about it—he wore thick, luxurious plate armor with silver and gold trimmings along green metal. A long green cape flapped out behind him when a gust of wind struck his position. He had dead, sapphire eyes and a handsome complexion and a willow longbow with inlaid mithril was draped around his neck along with the noose. His body was just hanging there, silently staring at them with cold, unblinking eyes—blond hair flowing out behind him, his face frozen in a confident expression.

The warrior was just as physically perfect as Cade remembered their kind to be, but not in the typical scanty outfits their woodland counterparts wore. This elf had no doubt been a city dweller.

But what scared Cade the most was the other bodies farther to the left and right—more and more elves hanging from other trees until the fog made it impossible to see into the beyond.

Crows made from shadow flew overhead, landing on a nearby branch and calling out with a squawking sound that made the people of their caravan jump. Then the sound of crunching leaves and twigs started to echo through the forest. At first it was only a couple—then it was dozens—and then it became hundreds.

Cade watched, partially in horror and partially awestruck, legs quivering to run back to his donkey to keep the animal from running away. He held the reins, not sure if they should flee or stay put, while his comrades stood, just as dumbfounded as he was.

That was when they made their appearance from beyond the mists.

Hundreds of shambling skeletons, ghouls with milky-white eyes, enormous, muscular flesh golems devoid of skin, and black-robed back-line casters came into view through the fog.

A pair of red eyes stared at their caravan curiously from a woman at the front. Those eyes continued to approach them, and it was apparent by the way the other undead oriented themselves to her position and the quality of her gear that this person was their commander.

And when she took off her bone mask, Cade's breath caught in his throat. She was medium height, a young woman in her early twenties, with long, silky brown hair and perfectly set features without a single blemish. She had high cheekbones and a well-defined, feminine nose, along with moderately curved hips and breasts. Though looking at her compelled him with a sense of urgent fear to run, her extreme beauty made him want to stay. She was perfectly symmetrical, pale-white skin glistening in the shimmering mist while neon and black magics lit up across her fingertips—and she wore a devilish smile while slowly approaching their caravan's head.

Despite all that Cade knew of vampires and the undead, he kept reminding himself that this was exactly what they'd come for. They wanted to build trade relationships with their neighbors, and they'd even just been saved by these people, so there was no reason to panic.

There was no . . . no reason to panic . . .

His uncle obviously felt the same way, because when he spoke and began to stroke his mustache, Cade could tell that the man was both nervous and eager. His uncle never stroked his mustache unless he was optimistic or in good spirits, but the way his knees almost buckled gave away just how on edge he was, too.

"Hello there!" Cade's uncle, a dark-haired man by the name of Gibry, called out with a wave and a smile. He stepped forward and bowed, letting his baggy red velvet shirt flap in the light breeze. "We . . . we weren't expecting to find you this far south yet . . ."

The woman narrowed her eyes, then gestured to the elf corpse hanging from a branch above her. "Yes, well, if we hadn't been here, you'd all be dead. They were waiting in ambush."

There was a long, awkward silence as her words registered with the men of the trading caravan, who shifted uneasily while muttering to each other.

Cade's uncle cleared his throat nervously. "Ahem. I see . . . We were being hunted? We are merchants from Bradshire and came looking for your people after tales from the capital started circulating. Are you a captain or some ranking officer of the Thane Necropolis, by chance?"

The woman started walking forward again, stopping in front of the man. She glanced around, keeping eye contact with Cade and winking at him briefly, causing him to blush—before turning back to Cade's uncle Gibry. "Ranking officer . . . I suppose you could call me that."

She smiled, giving off a perfect white gleam with fangs that gave Cade mixed emotions of both attraction and terror. "I suppose I should give you my name as well. I am Allie Thane, coleader of the Thane Necropolis, and I have come to offer my protection to your town, at the request of your kingdom."

Gibry straightened up in surprise and brushed his fingers across his mustache again, gesturing to the guards and merchants who still held their two dozen donkeys still and quiet aside from the occasional bray. Then he abruptly realized whom he was talking to, paled, and slammed to the ground in a prostrate position. Many of the others quickly did the same when they realized that she was essentially the queen of this undead faction. "My lady! I—I was not aware that you'd already agreed to terms! You've decided to help us?"

"Perhaps. What does it look like to you?" Allie asked, gesturing over to where her soldiers and minions were ripping bodies apart. She stepped forward, past Gibry, and continued on to where Cade was kneeling with his head bowed. She leaned down, all eyes on her, and used one slender finger to bring Cade's chin up along with the rest of his face. She grinned and gave an amused grunt, letting her fingers trace along his left cheek and causing him to shudder. "I have not come to terms with your kingdom's court wizard just yet . . . but that doesn't mean I will allow these pointy-eared fairies to trespass on my lands. Especially when it involves caravans that I'd very much like to trade with; trade, after all, is the lifeblood of civilizations. But can I trust you? That is the question I must ask myself. Will allowing you into our borders benefit us, or will it endanger my citizens?"

She straightened and put on her mask again, turning from the surprised young man and walking back to the front of the column.

Gibry blinked rapidly, suppressing his growing smile and trying to figure out what was going on. He cleared his throat nervously while exchanging a glance with his nephew. "We are no threat! We merely seek fortune for both our sides! My lady, if I may ask . . . have you heard news of our passage? Were you tracking us? Is that why you are here?"

Allie took her time to answer that.

Cade's heart pounded in his chest, and it was all he could do not to stare at the beautiful woman who'd just grazed his cheek. He did manage a few quick glances, though, but his excited smile turned into somewhat of a frown as the demeanor of the undead behind Allie stayed stoic. He was getting an odd vibe from them, a feeling of pressure or ominous foreboding, like he wanted to walk away just because he was near them. He couldn't see any of their eyes from underneath the dark hoods they wore, and they stood a little farther back from the other armored skeletons up front.

The caravan guards became wary at the awkward silence between the two groups, nervously shuffling and palming the hilts of their short swords, maces, and buckler shields as they eyed the silently staring ghouls, abominations, flesh golems, and skeletons on the other side, who were silently evaluating the trading company in return.

"What is your name?" the vampiric woman eventually asked.

Cade's uncle stuttered. "G-Gibry is the name!"

She slowly tapped her bone-made boot on the forest floor.

"Gibry it is, then. Yes, I have been tracking your caravan for some time now." The woman paused, then twirled a small wand in one hand, mana flaring along its body again. "You see, Gibry, I am at somewhat of a crossroads concerning whether or not to let your people into the necropolis. We have had many problems with others in the area trying to come in and kill, enslave, or steal from us. Recently, many of those people have been of your own race."

"We would never!" Gibry stated, aghast at the very idea of violence. He had never been a violent man to begin with and truly was a merchant through and through. That's why he started kissing ass. "Gaining early access to your great necropolis would be a boon far beyond anything that could be gained by attacking you! The idea that we, a weak and humble group of humans, could win out or succeed in attacks against your kind is foolishness. I would not attack you merely because of past grudges between our races—the idea is absurd! Meanwhile, my family grows rich if I establish trade routes with your city before others of my kingdom can jump on the opportunity, so it would be madness to do anything but remain in your good graces!"

Gibry's unashamed greed was showing through, and this in turn caused others in the caravan to wince—but it got an amused chuckle from the female vampire.

Her eyes glowed a bright crimson when she turned, staring back out at them with a calculating gaze that settled on Gibry, then eventually drifted back to Cade. "Hmm . . . And what price, I wonder, are you willing to pay . . . if I do let you in?"

CHAPTER 20

Riven stood beside his two minions in an audience chamber, with Mesha and her cousin Snagger beside them. The room was adorned with multicolored crystals and illuminated by glowing, kaleidoscopic gemstones set into the walls. Two rows of elevated platforms came down from the sides of the room like the stands of a stadium, with higher-ranking members of Snagger's rat-kin brood filing in for what was apparently the very first meeting on today's schedule at the home court. They all wore fancier clothes than many of the other rat-kin—very well-made silks or stitched shirts with bioluminescent properties similar to the plants Riven had seen through the cave systems. He even saw one of the rat-kin wearing a monocle, of all things.

He was deep inside the mound-fortress Snagger's personal family unit, or his brood, kept. They were awaiting an audience with the family matriarch, per Snagger's request, but she'd been caught up with something else and had sent a messenger to tell them she'd be there shortly. Rat-kin guards about Snagger's size, carrying large halberds and wearing heavy, studded leather armor, stood at intervals along either side of the large room, and tapestries depicting battles, giant lizards, wyrms, drow, and other scenes or creatures from the underdark hung from the ceiling.

It was certainly not what Riven had been expecting after seeing the rest of these creatures' civilization, but then again, each mound had been hard to peer into. He'd expected something dirty, grimy—but although the city up above was somewhat disorganized and violent, it wasn't too outlandish.

Especially when entering the mound.

On their way to this particular audience hall and in Snagger's brood mound, he'd seen smiths, libraries, unique pipeline sewage systems, and even an alchemist in his own little cove of the tunnels—so it was truly a civilization in its own right, and the forums of the cortex here had been extremely active. Snagger had told Riven that he wasn't sure exactly how many of them lived here, but he guessed it was well over three hundred thousand, the vast majority of them noncombat civilians. With that number of people all living in one place, it meant that there'd been subforums of the city created for jobs and quests, barter systems, advertisements, discussions on the war with the dwarves, and many more topics that updated in real time. The city forum itself correlated with the city's name, Deepnest. Not very original for the name of a rat-kin nest-city deep underground, but it was what it was.

"The broodmother of us-we makes her grand appearance-show!" a rather cute, three-foot-tall rat-kin girl with red fur and wearing a white robe yelled out above the muffled whispers of the wealthier brood members in the stands. The rat-kin along the sidelines immediately became quiet, and they all stood to show respect, staying that way as a rather large rat-kin woman entered the throne room from a hallway to the left.

She was slightly taller than Riven, akin to Snagger's seven-foot height, and a platinum necklace hung down over her chest. She was thinner, though, with brown fur, and was dressed in a formfitting white robe similar to the girl who'd just announced her presence. Her long, bare tail, clawed hands and feet, and mouselike ears and face were a stark contrast to any women Riven had ever known—but he could still tell she was feminine for a rat person.

The broodmother waved at the audience and moved gracefully to the large stone throne, sitting down with a courteous smile toward the group beyond the slightly elevated platform the throne stood on. "Mesha-kin! Snagger-kin! You have brought-found a new friend-thing to us? Do tell-show how you've been!"

Mesha comfortably waved back, but Snagger straightened and motioned for the others to stand up before turning around with a large smile. "Broodmother! It is good-fond to see you! I have been well-good. Mesha-kin and I have explored-sought through the tunnels, and it uses-takes much time. It is a travel-adventure though! Sadly, Bort-kin and Cheshish-kin died-passed to the dwarves on way-trek here."

Snagger's face fell at this last bit of information, as did the broodmother's. "They died honor-proud, taking many dwarf-devils with them."

Murmurs of sadness at how they'd passed and approval that they'd taken dwarves with them crossed through the gathered rat-kin in the stands on either side of the vast room. Riven was a little confused at how everyone here seemed to know who these people were, or how Snagger was so familiar with the broodmother in such a large compound, but Athela couldn't help but snicker slightly under her breath.

"Dwarves don't have anything on devils," Athela whispered to Riven on the side. "To even compare the two is an insult to all demonkind."

The broodmother took Snagger's words to heart, though, and her frown was very evident when she lifted a clawed hand and rubbed her forehead. "That is sad-sorrow to hear. Did you show-tell the guards of where the battle-fight happened?"

"Yes-yes, Broodmother, I did show-tell."

"Good. This war is bad-poor to us all, and us-we have lost many family-kin to them already." The broodmother's eyes turned to Azmoth next, then to Athela, and then to Riven. She leaned forward on her throne and steepled her fingers, the jingling of her platinum necklace audible even from a few yards away. "Are you their summoner-owner?"

Riven couldn't help but smile with amusement at the comment, giving Athela a sideways glance when he noticed her glare. "Why, yes. Very much so. I use the big one as a pack mule and the sassy girl here to make me sandwiches. It's been quite the investment."

Both demons looked his way at that one as he tried to not laugh at their unamused stares. The tall broodmother took it in stride, though, and didn't seem to notice the joke at all. "Sandwich-foods? Hmm . . . Well, it isn't-not my place to ask about your preference-tastes. I am Rashtalia, broodmother of Brood-Tarrow in Deepnest-city. What is your name-flag?"

"Riven Thane. It's very nice to meet you."

Rashtalia's smile widened. "Your manners are not forgotten-unnoticed. Many-much of your kind could be taught-learned lessons by you. How-when did my nephew-niece Snagger-kin and Mesha-kin meet-find you?"

Riven cocked an eyebrow at that one, glancing over at the two rat-kin next to him and clasping his hands behind his back. Nephew and niece of the brood-mother, huh? "I met Snagger a few weeks ago in the tunnels under Brightsville. Sewers, actually. It's a city from my own planet, Earth, on the surface."

"So you are-is not from Zazir?"

"No, I didn't even know of Zazir until the integration."

Murmurs of curiosity started spreading among the gathered rat-kin in the stands, and the broodmother nodded slowly, deep in thought. "Curious-interesting that is. So there are vampire–bat-kin on this . . . Earth, too?"

Riven hesitated, then shrugged. "I honestly don't know. I assume so, but I can't be entirely certain. It's a bit of a weird situation—I was originally human and my bloodline was locked until integration happened. We had stories about vampires back on Earth, though, so probably. Other than that, the planet was run by humans. There weren't any of the other races there, aside from legends or stories."

Rashtalia remained silent for a time, unsteepling her fingers and leaning back against her stone chair. She motioned for a nearby servant and was approached with a plate of food, then picked off some kind of berry and stuffed it into her mouth to chew while keeping eye contact with Riven the entire time. "Perhaps that is why you-you have bright-eyes and not dull-eyes. I have not seen bright-eyes of the bat-kin before now-here."

"Ahem!"

The broodmother was interrupted by an older gray rat man who had several trinkets dangling around his neck and along his arms. He wore violet robes decorated with sigils Riven didn't recognize, and he scurried over and whispered something in Rashtalia's ear.

The broodmother's eyebrows raised in turn when the older rat man left to stand a little ways off to her side on the platform again, and she drummed her fingers along the right-hand side armrest. "No-no, that is not right-correct. You are pure-pure-blooded vampire, like what bat-kin have been looking-searching for in the deep-depths."

The room immediately became silent, and all eyes locked onto Riven's form as he stood there, unmoving.

His brows furrowed in confusion, and he exchanged glances with Snagger and his demons—who all had no clue what the broodmother was talking about. He straightened a little, put his hands on his hips, and cocked his head to the side with a curious stare. "Yes . . . I am pure-blooded. But what are you talking about, exactly? Someone is looking for me?"

Rashtalia tapped her clawed fingers on the stone throne a couple times, then leaned forward and nodded while steepling her fingers again. "Other bat-kin."

"Vampires?"

She nodded in confirmation. "They come-run to seek-find purebloods. They want-need help for world quest."

"World quest? Now I'm completely at a loss."

Rashtalia put up both hands to either side. "I not know-perceive why. But vampire bat-kin come-seek you-others of pure blood for world-quest. Perhaps go find-seek them yourself to ask-question them? They come-travel two weeks ago, live in darker-depths of underdark."

"Do you know exactly where? Could you lead me to them?"

Rashtalia shook her head. "Strangers. Not know."

Riven felt himself deflate slightly. Just great, another group of people seeking him out that lived somewhere deep in the underdark of his new planet Panu. This time it was the local vampires instead of the intergalactic ones. Why, though? He didn't have any ties to any vampires back on Earth, and it seemed like they were just looking for purebloods in general rather than Riven specifically. But if it had to do with a world quest, he probably needed to figure it out eventually.

His shoulders slumped slightly, but he didn't take his eyes off the broodmother. The man who spoke to Rashtalia may have even been an identifier. In fact, that was very likely, as when Athela identified him he only came off as [Vampire Warlock]. It didn't even give his full class title of "adept" to people without an advanced identifying class.

Regardless, he was getting off track. Pulling up the old notification that was stashed in his status page, he reviewed the world quests and quickly identified which of them these vampires were likely pursuing him for. However, why that was the case—he still didn't know.

[**World Quests (six of six remaining). You have five years to complete these quests as a worldwide team effort. Further details on each of these quests will be presented to you individually when you come into direct contact with the given quest. Only the basics are initially handed out otherwise. Current threat level is an indication of threat concerning the world at large and not a direct representation of how it may or may not affect you individually. The World Quests are as follows:**

World Quest 1, The Lich King's Plague: In the far reaches of the northern Chaos Wastelands, an ancient lich begins to stir. Advanced details are locked until you come into contact with this quest.

World Quest 2, The Apocalypse Beasts: ***ADVANCED DETAILS HAVE BEEN UNLOCKED* Ah, this is one of my personal favorites. I present to you the apocalypse beasts! Your world has been cursed with three tyrannical creatures of astronomical power that are currently being incubated and grown into their adult forms. Each of these absolute monstrosities is able to turn the world on its head, demolishing countries in its path and tearing the very fabric of reality apart. Know that if these creatures are allowed to awaken, you will likely not live much longer than the five years' limit. Each of these monsters has cultist worshippers from your own planet, given knowledge of these creatures before the integration even began. They will try to awaken the monsters' adult forms to destroy your world entirely, leading to astronomical amounts of power as a reward for the cultists in their success for when they leave the smoldering wreckage of Panu. Your goal is to stop and kill their cult worshippers and find out where these creatures are being incubated so that you will have a world to live on when the five years of time runs out. Current threat level: Extremely high; death toll in the billions. Catastrophe upon failure of completion when five years has passed: Nekra, the Skeletal Devourer, will be unleashed onto Panu. Chalgathi, the Plague Dragon, will be unleashed onto Panu. Chubin, the Glass Kraken, will be unleashed onto Panu. Click for updated details.**

World Quest 3, Invaders From Beyond: Other galactic civilizations greedily watch your fledgling world, wanting these lands for

their own. Invasion tokens have been distributed. Advanced details are locked until you come into contact with this quest.

World Quest 4, Blood of the Fallen God: An unnamed vampiric elder god has fallen from grace after having sinned against the Elysium administrator. The elder god has been trapped within a hidden, guarded labyrinth in the deepest levels of the underdark, and you must stop him from awakening. Advanced details are locked until you come into contact with this quest.

World Quest 5, Realm of the Snow Giants: In the southern reaches of the glacial islands in the Numenor Sea, on the opposite end of the world from where the Lich King lies in wait, an ambitious king of the snow giants has united the warring tribes. Advanced details are locked until you come into contact with this quest.

World Quest 6, Drums in the Deep: The merpeople and naga of this world have been given a choice . . . Advanced details are locked until you come into contact with this quest.]

Yup. World Quest 4, Blood of the Fallen God—that was probably the one.

Sighing, he closed the notification. He already was involved with one world quest, and he had five years to deal with it, so he'd probably push it off for now . . . He'd located another holder of Chalgathi's artifacts only eighty miles from Brightsville and would need to take care of that first. Not only that, but he also had an impending war with another elf faction.

He and Allie were rather busy at the moment and didn't have time to worry about some fallen vampiric god on top of it all.

Riven face-palmed, knowing he couldn't just *NOT* figure this out. What if it was important?

His internal struggles came to a standstill, and he rubbed his forehead with two fingers while letting out a groan. "Rashtalia, do you have any idea where I should start? Even a small clue to point me in the right direction?"

The broodmother blinked, cleared her throat, and motioned to the gray rat man who'd spoken to her earlier. She nodded a couple times as he whispered in her ear, and then she dismissed him with a wave of her hand. "Yes-yes. But not exact location-spot and not much-good clues. Only direction. Bat-kin come to city-nest and ask-query, then leave-run next day. Very fast when realize rat-kin and dwarf-devils at war, not wanting to fight-involve with us. If want, I can tell-show direction later."

Riven smiled, nodded, and nudged Athela. "Hey. How comfortable are you with exploring the underdark by yourself for a little while?"

Athela's face widened into a gleeful smile. "Sounds exciting! Are you going to send me to find the vampire she's talking about?"

"Exactly. I'm hoping the quest will update when you do find and talk to them; perhaps they already have the quest details active and can pass it along. Then, when that's done, we can decide whether that's an important avenue to pursue versus the other things we have on our plate."

Rashtalia followed the exchange, then shrugged. "I hope-plea that you succeed-win in finding the bat-kin. If any of we-us find them, we-we shall tell—otherwise we show-point in direction they came. Now, show-tell me of surface-world and what you know-found. I am very curious-eager to hear news-tidings of beyond the nest."

The broodmother didn't bring up the world quest again. The rest of Riven's meeting was very enlightening for both sides, and by the end of it, he could even say that he honestly liked Rashtalia quite a bit. She made jokes from time to time and she wasn't stuck-up in any way, shape, or form. Rather, she was quite down-to-earth and treated to Riven as an equal rather than acting as the matriarch of Snagger's brood.

Riven told her of how his own experience had gone with his starter events, though he left out the part about Chalgathi. He told her about the hellscape dungeon he had to enter and learned that a few of the rat-kin in Deepnest had undergone unique trials of their own, but it was rather random and a rarity at that. He told her of the surface world and of what he'd seen so far, with lots of information about his old planet and the city of Brightsville above them. There was talk about the elves, the purging of the holy crusaders, and the faction his sister had created. He gave a brief description of the geography topside and mentioned there was another war raging between the human kingdom of Dawn and another high-elf empire he hadn't encountered just yet, but he intended to get more details later.

In turn he learned about the ongoing events here in the underdark. Deepnest had been a cave-city of their small rat-kin kingdom on Zazir, surrounded by friendly communities with only a few hostile forces to deal with in the form of drow or dark elves. The meshing of worlds had shifted Deepnest's location so that none of their satellite settlements were around anymore, nor were their allies, reducing their trade and resources significantly. She told him of the encroaching dwarves and the war she and her people had been unwillingly thrust into, losing many thousands of civilians and military personnel since the conflict had started. The dwarves had also taken over numerous mines full of valuable minerals and areas suitable for farming since the integration, and they had been extremely brutal in their attacks and lack of empathy concerning the rat-kin. The dwarves obviously thought themselves as a superior race and looked at Rashtalia, the other broodmothers, and the queen-mother or their people as beasts to be purged rather than equal sentient beings.

Overall, the knowledge swap was a very positive experience, and by the end the exchange had become rather friendly.

CHAPTER 21

Salazar glared daggers at the departing vampire from atop a ledge above the audience hall. He fidgeted with the hoop earring on his right side, chittering to himself while considering whether he should take the shot at his longtime rival now.

The plan to lead the dwarves over to Snagger's position had been fumbled, utterly fumbled, and he'd been left humiliated while losing out on a huge amount of profit the dwarves had lain out for him and his crew. Now, in all likelihood, the dwarves thought Salazar had betrayed them for his own people.

Ironic, considering he'd done quite the opposite, only to be interfered with by this new vampire oddity. Salazar could only watch helplessly while the dwarven attack squad he'd led to Snagger's position had been demolished and eaten—and this man's sheer power had left him utterly dumbstruck.

How could someone be this powerful? Salazar had spent quite a lot of time thieving, sneaking around, assassinating people, and plotting—putting himself in a position to kill numerous others while they slept for meager XP points. It'd awarded him a grand total of seventeen levels flat. He'd even say he was on the higher end of many of the rat-kin, or dwarves, and yet this Riven had shown up out of nowhere to blast his plans to smithereens.

It irked him. Oh, how it irked him.

"We kill-shoot Snagger, yes-yes?" Salazar's companion, another wretch with brown hair and buck teeth by the name of Brutis, asked with a cocked crossbow.

Salazar snarled Brutis's way, pulling the bow out from sight of those below and slapping his bare tail against the ledge's top. "Idiot-fool! Do you not think-care that broodmother is here-now? She is powerful-strong, favors-coddles Snagger, and Mesha-kin, too. She find-seek us out, kill-strangle us in cold-evil ways."

Brutis frowned in return but stepped back from the ledge with a nod. "Fine-fine. I want dead-kill soon, though. Snagger-kin needs to be dead-gone. Should queen-mother see Snagger helping Deepnest kin-city again-now, he will take spot-place of you-us in the ranks-files of fighter-guards. And where is Lisish? Lisish-kin not here-be where supposed to."

"Not know-see. Find Lisish-kin now. Go-come."

The two turned, heading back into the tunnel from whence they'd come to watch the proceedings below and plotting together about their schemes. The tunnels turned a corner, where over two dozen of their closer coconspirators waited for them, and a shadow they did not notice trailed behind them with a shimmer of magic in the air as they passed.

"Wonder if Lisish think sly-cunning for Snagger-kin to reach fake ally-friends. Need assassinate-kill Snagger now before broodmother tells-hails queen-mother. Can also murder-kill vampire bat-kin, too?" Brutis asked, pulling a silver bolt from a jacket pocket and glowering evilly at his compatriot while his little pawed feet scuttled along the hardened stone and clay floor. A dozen others in their band of cutthroats cackled or snickered at the thought of what they were going to do to their broodmother's favorite nephew, and if the vampire was collateral damage—so be it. Riven certainly wouldn't be the first vampire they'd killed after such a long history of sharing the underdark with their blood-attuned brethren. "If bat-kin red-eyes is dead-gone, Snagger cannot get credit-value from queen-mother or broodmother. Deepnest not need ally-friends from surface— we can win-kill dwarf-devils by ourselves. Yes-yes!"

Another rat-kin with white fur and a pair of goggles behind them raised two daggers high overhead. "Agreed-yes! Kill red-eyes bat-kin and—"

A flash of green light illuminated the tunnel in front of them, stopping them midconversation. It'd only been there an instant, but it was literally a beacon in the dark for that brief moment of visualization. It'd been some sort of sigil, and it'd glowed an eerie neon green before winking out into nothingness once more.

"What that-that?" Salazar said in a hushed whisper, drawing two obsidian blades from the sides of his belt. Others quickly followed suit, drawing their own cutlasses, slings, and pikes moments later.

Then Salazar lurched to one side when another green sigil appeared behind them on the opposite side of the first, and his eyes went wide with confusion and fear. "What that?!"

Then they startled again and again, ears up tall and hearts beating rapidly as sigil after sigil briefly flashed in the air on either side of the tunnel, until all went deathly silent.

A faint feminine laugh echoed through the lonesome, empty corridor—and the two dozen rat-kin went into a full panic. They screeched and bolted toward the exit, skittish and afraid of the unknown, only to slap face-first into an invisible trap sigil they'd not realized was still there.

The blast of Unholy energy triggered other sigils nearby, and the tunnel erupted in an explosion of shrapnel and stone. Blood and body parts flew in all directions before being crushed under parts of the tunnel collapsing, but the violence was short-lived, and soon only dust remained.

At the end of the corridor, beyond the blast zone, Riven stood looking with a slight smile on his lips while slowly clapping at Fay's performance. She let down the illusions, bowing and winking his way while he surveyed the destruction.

"Good job," Riven stated with an unblinking stare, focusing on a limp hand protruding from the rubble; he absent-mindedly smeared blood from his mouth across the rest of his face. "How hard was it to track them through the underdark?"

"Didn't have a problem once you identified them, Master. When we got to Deepnest, it was slightly harder . . . but only a few of the mages here noticed me, and they all attributed my presence to you. Which was accurate, but it wasn't any of their business, and your other demons were already out in the open." Fay perked up, wings spread out, and beamed with a brilliant smile that'd melt any man's heart. "You were the one who noticed they were following you after the dwarves were killed. I should be congratulating you on being so observant."

Riven's cold gaze turned, settling on the one these rat-kin conspirators had called Lisish. She was an older rat-kin mage based in some kind of Earth magics, though Riven could not tell what pillar she oriented toward exactly. A broken wand lay on the ground at her feet, and two other rat-kin who'd been with her lay headless and bleeding out on the stone floor.

The rat woman stood, quivering, eyes wide and a long, bloody claw mark along one cheek. Hesitantly, she looked up to meet his gaze where the blood of her comrades still dripped off his chin. She visibly gulped with an almost comically frightened expression.

"May I go-leave now?" Lisish asked, terror dripping from her words as she patted her blood-splattered brown robes absent-mindedly, fidgeting nervously. "I did as you-you asked-told . . ."

Riven's crimson eyes flared and narrowed, and he reached down—picking up the terrified rat-kin by the scruff of her neck with one hand to bring the shorter creature to eye level. "You did as you were told because I forced you to do so with a spell, you weak-willed little shit. Too bad for you: I don't want to leave any loose strings that could harm my newfound friends . . . and you're not needed anymore."

In a blur of motion, Riven slammed the three-foot-tall rat-kin into the stone wall with a violent thrust of his arm.

CRACK

Blood splattered all along the floor, Lisish's neck snapped loudly, and he let her body drop to the ground like a limp rag doll. Then he stepped back, fangs exposed in a predatory snarl, and turned his head to grin at Athela. The demoness was leaning against the wall, evaluating him with raised eyebrows and crossed arms.

"I think we can safely assume that's all of them," Riven stated, licking his lips and stepping over the new corpse. "Burn them to cinders."

Athela nodded slowly, watching the blood pooling on the floor coagulate before Azmoth stepped forward and began to clean up what remained of the murders. She glanced left, sharing a look with Fay—who just shrugged with a wide and proud smile, no doubt happy to be valued by the master and dwelling on the compliments he'd given her.

Though Athela wasn't so sure this was something to be happy about. What had happened to the cute, virgin-like little man who'd been so easy to mess with and mean-mug back in the hellscapes? She'd noticed a subtle change in Riven ever since the elves had been dealt with, but this was a few steps beyond what she expected for him—even since his lack of trust in others had developed.

Sure, his trust issues had pushed him to investigate the group of ingrates that'd decided to try and kill Snagger or involve Riven in the process—but it was borderline paranoia now, even if he didn't show it outwardly. Not everyone was out to get him, but she could see that Riven was of a different mind-set. He'd put off going to see the Blood Moon Requiem because he didn't trust the intergalactic space vampires. He'd stopped the greenskins from participating in the war to help the kingdom of Dawn because he didn't trust the newfound humans. He'd summoned Fay to follow shadows in the dark because he didn't trust Snagger or the rest of his kin at first, and even now he still didn't.

It was an unhealthy mind-set to have, in her opinion. But after all he'd been through, she didn't blame him.

Sighing to herself and pushing off the stone wall, she came over to where Riven was flipping through a notebook one of the rat-kin had been carrying that detailed their plans to assassinate Snagger. It had something to do with an honored position in the queen-mother's elite guard and was of little importance to Riven or his minions—other than it'd almost swept them up in a murder plot.

Nevertheless, Riven was going through it again and again to make sure he didn't miss any detail, and no doubt he would give it to Snagger on their way out of Deepnest.

"Riven?"

Riven shifted his gaze up to Athela, who'd come to stand with her hands folded in front of her. The casual arrogance she usually showed was gone, and in its place was . . . something different. It made him stand up straighter, taking her more seriously. "What's wrong? Why are you giving me that look?"

Athela's soft gaze let on a timid smile, and she let out a breath she hadn't realized she'd been holding. Stepping forward and pushing herself into Riven's personal space, she let her hands gently rest on the book in Riven's hands—and her eyes sank down to his chest. "You've been going over that book like it's an obsession. How many times have you read it now?"

Riven's mood darkened. "I'm just being careful, Athela."

"How many times?" Athela pressed softly, staying where she was and letting her fingers touch his.

He looked down at the physical contact, somewhat surprised, and let her words sink in. "Probably fifteen times."

She nodded but said nothing.

They stood there like that for some time, and Fay gave them a curious look while nudging Azmoth in the side and whispering something to the larger demon.

"You know . . ." Athela began, then pulled the book from his grasp and tossed it to the floor behind her. Turning back around, she slowly pulled him into a hug, locking her arms around his back and resting her head on his shoulder. "You may not trust others like you used to, Riven. But there will always be people you can trust. Don't let the world get to you just because of who and what you are. When you're important, you draw the ire of other people who want to take you down a peg or completely get rid of you for no other reasons than jealousy, spite, or fear."

Riven stood rigidly in place, almost in a state of shock upon hearing Athela's genuine and heartfelt words while her warm body pressed against his in a firm but kind embrace. "I . . . Athela, what are you trying to say . . . ?"

She closed her eyes, heaved a deep inhale, and then slowly exhaled with a contented smile while resting her cheek on his shoulder. "That I'll always be there for you. Even if the world abandons you, even when the gods and demon lords of the hells try to push you toward a quick death, I'll stand by you. So don't ever think that you're alone, and don't change the person you are just out of fear that you'll one day be betrayed by all the people you love. Because, Riven, you'd be wrong to think so. I will never abandon you."

How Athela had known what internal emotions and struggles Riven was dealing with was beyond him. Why she'd decided to bring it up now was also beyond him. But her words resonated with his soul, and the awkward, rigid contracture of his muscles slowly softened as he felt a lump begin to form in his throat. Slowly enveloping Athela in an embrace of his own, he fought back tears and nodded wordlessly, focusing on the feeling of her body against his.

"Thank you, Athela."

She nodded, arms still wrapped around him. "No problem, twerp."

They held each other for over a minute, just standing there while Fay gawked in surprise and mild amounts of jealousy, before Athela pulled back, stood up on her tiptoes, and planted a long, drawn-out kiss on Riven's cheek.

The Arshakai demoness wiped blood off Riven's face along with a lone tear that'd begun to fall down his cheek, then brushed his hair back with her fingers and adjusted his hood. She gave him a pat on the shoulder and smiled. "Don't get the wrong idea about this, but come on. We have to get back to the surface now that you've done your exploring . . . We cannot help these rat-kin at all until we deal with our own problems topside. And, for the record, Riven, I think I'll be staying with you for a little while longer. Going into the underdark by myself, abandoning you right now to search for those other vampires in the state you're in is a bad idea. Maybe later, but right now, I think you could use a friend."

CHAPTER 22

[The Apocalypse Beasts, Chalgathi, Quest Update: Brenna Landish has fallen in battle to Tao Zhang. Tao Zhang has acquired two of five set pieces for Chalgathi's Inheritance. A new Chalgathi's chosen will be picked within one hour as a replacement for Brenna Landish.]

[The Apocalypse Beasts, Chalgathi, Quest Update: Venice Garcia has fallen in battle to Fred Talons. Fred Talons has acquired two of five set pieces for Chalgathi's Inheritance. A new Chalgathi's chosen will be picked within one hour as a replacement for Venice Garcia.]

Snagger snapped the small booklet shut, then looked up. His rodent ears were pinned against his head in shame and sadness, and he shook his large rat head in regret. "I-me sorry, friend, did not know-aware of plot-schemes you were caught in. I shall show-enlighten broodmother of this. Thank you, Riven-kin."

The rat-kin extended a hand, and Riven shook it with a nod. "Not a problem at all—it wasn't your fault. Perhaps after our own problems are sorted, we can help each other out. Until then, I wish you and your people the best of luck."

"Well-wishes to you, bat-kin friend. Come visit-seek me at your leisure-chance, or if find self able-willing to help us-kin. Dwarf-devils ever eager to kill-maim rat-kin of Deepnest." The muscular rat-kin bowed, clasping his gauntleted hands together in front of him while Mesha did the same at his side. Then they started to walk back through the sewers and toward the tunnels leading deeper into the underdark.

"Nice to meet-find you, Riven Thane!" Mesha's squeaky voice echoed through the tunnels, her small, pawed hands waving at them before the two rat-kin of Deepnest vanished from sight. "Keep safe-sound!"

Riven smiled, pushing his hands into his pockets while his staff floated in the air beside him. "It's nice to see that not everyone is an absolute prick out to get me. Maybe you're right, Athela."

"Of course I'm right!" Athela playfully smacked him across the back of the head with one of her spider limbs. "Now, let's go! We have a royal vampire to meet so we can ask about your malignant prophecy. What was her name again?"

"Kathrine Vonsilla Crushada, something or other of the eldest house, 107th in line for the throne."

"I think you got that wrong, but let's go with it for now."

Riven smirked and began climbing the ladder into the basement of the hospital. Pulling himself up and huffing, he glanced around the basement where he'd battled the horde of dream creatures. The bodies that hadn't been ripped apart in torrents of blood mana were still rotting here and there, and he'd already told Allie she needed to come collect them, at least for the bones. Materials for undead in the Thane Necropolis were growing in demand, with more and more undead traveling from other worlds through the bone garden or being created there atop the tower from souls drawn in out of the void.

"Come on Athela, let's—"

A nearby heartbeat quickened.

Riven's body lit up with red lightning, drastically enhancing his speed as he sidestepped a blurring projectile that would have taken his head clean off.

CRACK-BOOM

The room shattered around him, and something akin to a missile exploded on impact on the far wall. His body was scorched and he barely had time to summon Hell's Armor to avoid the majority of the blast before a shadowy figure launched from the adjacent hallway, glistening blades extended.

Riven's red eyes went wide, and he simultaneously tore a rift through space while creating a myriad of spinning blades around his original position.

The assassin missed their strike, blades slicing through nothing but air when the portal winked out and the Bloody Razors erupted after an influx of mana.

An unfamiliar feminine scream echoed out, and Athela tore up through the hole in the floor to launch herself at the new assailant just before the figure vanished—leaving Riven to evaluate his surroundings in more thorough detail.

"Fuck," Riven muttered, seeing nothing but not letting his guard down while Black Lightning crackled along Vampire's Escort. "Who the hell was that?"

Astrid's body went rigid when she saw the notification appear, and she continued to limp-run quickly down a long street in the dead of night while unnatural mists permeated the surroundings.

[Due to proximity, you have been notified of the following: Your Chalgathi Cultist Mask has been pinged by the unique ability

Ping Chalgathi Artifacts. This ability pings the locations of other Chalgathi Inheritance Set artifacts, only identifying pieces you do not already have, and may be used at any time without any mana requirement. This ability only locates artifacts that you are missing from the set. Due to proximity, this ability only gives an area destination of fifty square meters and not an exact location.]

"Shit!"

She picked up the pace, using her own ability to keep track of her pursuer as he closed in. Just who the fuck was that guy?! She'd had the drop on him; she knew she'd been completely stealthed up until the very last second because her bloodline had told her so, and yet he'd somehow had the reflexes to dodge one of her best high-speed martial art abilities. Then he dodged her dual viper strikes while teleporting out and figuratively backhanding her with magical mines of some kind—all as a MAGE?!

Weren't mages supposed to lack that kind of awareness and speed?!

Her mind raced and blood from her wounds dripped onto the pavement behind her. Despite her injuries, she was traveling fast and passing broken-down houses where eerie, bat-like creatures stared down at her from their perches and cats that'd been mutated into ghostlike figures glared at her.

She was still ahead of him by a good margin, too, but despite this he wasn't injured—and he was slowly closing in. Every time she pinged his amulet, the one she'd seen right in front of her face but had been unable to obtain, his position relative to her became closer and closer.

Astrid paused after turning a corner and coming face-to-face with some kind of skeletal zombie wolf that was eating a pig-size rat. It growled at her warningly, and she backed away, only to use the next alley over and dart down the thin passage between buildings into the next suburban road.

[Due to proximity, you have been notified of the following: Your Chalgathi Cultist Mask has been pinged by the unique ability Ping Chalgathi Artifacts. This ability pings the locations of other Chalgathi Inheritance Set artifacts, only identifying pieces you do not already have, and may be used at any time without any mana requirement. This ability only locates artifacts that you are missing from the set. Due to proximity, this ability only gives an area destination of fifty square meters and not an exact location.]

She cursed again, her body warping with the shadows around her and only producing a thin veil of black as she passed. This was not how it was supposed to be. She couldn't lose her only artifact now; she'd paid so much of her time and blood over the years to get here—especially when it was just some nobody who wasn't even part of the cult!

Another shadow, not one of her own, grazed the edge of her peripheral vision, and Astrid froze while blending into the darkness between a tree and an old dumpster that smelled like rot. Her body twisted and shifted, molding into a crevice underneath the dumpster as her heart started pounding wildly.

She knew something was there, just across the street from her and sitting on a windowsill—but the figure was just as black as she was, and Astrid could barely make out the many blades protruding from its back through the unnatural, Unholy-tainted mists of this cursed place.

A winged woman, a demon of some sort, landed on the rooftop of an abandoned old gas station at an intersection to Astrid's right, obviously looking for her, and a flash of black produced a rift in space just ahead of Astrid's position. The man she'd tried to kill stepped out, crimson eyes scanning, his staff of black wood and muscular flesh writhing with flowing blood and crackling black lightning.

Upon exiting the portal in the middle of the road, he abruptly stopped, cocking his head to one side as if hearing something, and Astrid tried to remain as quiet and still as she could while her heart pounded frantically in her warped chest, waiting for an opportune moment to assassinate him when his back was turned.

[Due to proximity, you have been notified of the following: Your Chalgathi Cultist Mask has been pinged by the unique ability Ping Chalgathi Artifacts. This ability pings the locations of other Chalgathi Inheritance Set artifacts, only identifying pieces you do not already have, and may be used at any time without any mana requirement. This ability only locates artifacts that you are missing from the set. Due to proximity, this ability only gives an area destination of fifty square meters and not an exact location.]

"She's here . . . somewhere . . ." the caster muttered, glowing eyes combing the dark and settling on the exact spot where Astrid hid in the crevice of the dumpster. "Right . . . there . . ."

Her shadow-formed eyes widened, and she froze in shock for only a moment while her mind went into overdrive. He shouldn't be able to see her—he should only be able to ping a general area—so how did he know she was there?!

Like a lightning strike, his staff lifted, and a torrent of crackling black energy intermixed with a lance of blood exploded toward her position.

Using one of her escape martial arts, Astrid barely managed to get away and nearly vomited in fear when the position she'd been in only a half second ago was devastated—turned into a smoldering pile of rubble and a cloud of debris.

The other dark figure on the opposite rooftop screeched and launched itself over the street, giving chase as Astrid glided like water over the tiles, hopping frantically from house to house.

She dodged left, avoiding a claw swipe and turning to launch four throwing knives at the figure pursuing her. Eyes went wide, and she narrowly avoided a long, black tongue that crashed through the rooftop she stood on—coming face-to-face with nothing other than some kind of demon.

The throwing knives made contact and punched into the demon's gut, but the monster kept coming through the pain and Astrid whipped out her dual combat daggers to engage the monster.

That was a bad idea.

In a blur of exchanging blades, Astrid's left hand flew off her body in a spray of blood, eliciting a scream of horror and making her backpedal—shadowstepping off the roof and landing on the ground before sprinting ahead through the mists again in an attempt to lose her pursuers.

Then she got the ping notification yet again, and she let out a frustrated scream when necrotic poison began visibly climbing up her severed forearm. "GOD FUCKING DAMN IT!"

Realizing she was going to die here unless she was able to lose her trackers, and knowing the artifact wasn't worth her life, she tore it off. Flinging the mask to the side through an unhinged open door, she vanished into the haunted city like a ghost, intending only to figure out her next move and treat her injuries.

Riven bent down, picking up the sinister mask with a small smile creeping across his lips. There weren't any heartbeats nearby, the assassin obviously having left it to throw him off her trail, and he flipped it over to wipe off the blood.

[Chalgathi Cultist Mask: ???]

So they'd finally come.

The mask itself was very intricate, with numerous carvings that shifted and roiled under his touch—but to his surprise, the mask actually began to change while he grasped it. From seething, shadowlike textures, it evolved into some-thing else entirely. Smooth, white porcelain replaced the shadowy texture until it became a very plain but sleek-looking full-face mask without any identifying features at all. There weren't any holes for the eyes or mouth, either. The only other thing notable about it was that the back side, the one that was supposed to fit onto his face, shimmered with red wisps now that trailed along his skin and pulled—almost as if it was trying to latch on to him. It was completely different from the item it'd been only a minute ago.

"How odd."

He set off another ping, finding out that there weren't any other participants in Chalgathi's trials nearby for hundreds of miles . . . then quickly corrected himself. Not only was this unknown woman still here, somewhere, and she could track him while he couldn't track her—but it was certainly possible there were others of Chalgathi's chosen and he just couldn't ping them. The ability only worked to identify those with artifacts he didn't have, and now he had two of the set.

[The Apocalypse Beasts, Chalgathi, Quest Update: Astrid Fested has been defeated in battle by Riven Thane but has escaped pursuit with her life intact. Riven Thane has acquired two of five set pieces for Chalgathi's Inheritance.]

Within only seconds of having acquired the notification, the communication bauble started pulsing, and he picked it up to answer Allie's call. "Hey-o."

"Riven!" Allie's voice echoed through the mists and deserted streets of the Brightsville suburbs. "Were you attacked?! Are you okay?! What happened! I had no idea they were that close to us! Where are you now?!"

"Calm down, I'm fine. Almost got assassinated by some bitch because I was off my guard. I'd been pinging their locations, but she somehow cleared nearly eighty miles in less than a day, and it threw me off. She must have some kind of traveling or movement ability aside from the ones I saw."

"Which were?"

"She's a stealth type, uses something akin to my Riftwalk via the Shadow subpillar and can blend into dark areas or mold her body to fit into tight spots. She has a couple escape abilities—I'm not entirely sure how they work—but she's very mobile. Be careful, she's still around here somewhere, but I managed to cut off a hand. So unless she has some kind of means to heal herself, she'll be maimed."

"Well, at least that's a plus. But where are you? Are you back from the underdark already?"

"Yeah. Visited Snagger's city of rat-kin, was neat to see. I'll tell you more later—I'm in Brightsville now and headed to the altar to get some answers on malignancy points. I also need to identify these Chalgathi artifacts."

"Oh . . . I probably need to do that, too. I have the pauldrons, but I haven't been using them, because I wasn't sure what they did and they gave me odd tingly sensations whenever I put them on."

Riven snickered in amusement. "Odd tingly sensations? They're artifacts for a world quest—surely they can't be bad."

"You never know! Don't laugh at me! And I already have these legendary-tier soul-woven pauldrons built into my outfit—okay?! I went with what I knew!"

"Well, at least it doesn't make you a target. Where are you keeping the Chalgathi pauldrons?"

"In a guarded vault in the tower. Tell you what, I'll have Mara grab them for you and meet you at the altar. Have the Blood Moon Requiem identify them for me, too, and since I already have a pair of pauldrons with the soul-woven outfit, you can have the Chalgathi set. It's probably better if we combine ours anyway—gives us a better chance of finishing this stupid quest and getting the next Chalgathi quest update before other people do. It'll also allow me to monitor more people involved with the quest line, because I won't have any of the items. One more thing—do you mind helping Mara clear the prison sometime in the next day or two? I told her I'd be back to lead the attack, but I've been busy killing elves the past two days."

Riven's eyebrows raised. "Killing elves? I hope you're not talking about my slaves. They're supposed to be treated well, Allie."

"No! Idiot. Dawn's northernmost town, Bradshire, is under siege. Or it had just begun when I arrived; I'm routing these pointy-eared pricks now, adding to my legions with their bodies, and I'm going to discuss terms with some of Dawn's ambassadors, so I'm kind of busy."

"Just be careful, Allie."

"I have an army of undead with me, along with Vin and Nin. I'll be fine. Talk to you later!"

Allie's voice cut out, and Riven hummed in discontentment.

"She's in the S tier of natives on this planet, too, you know," Fay stated from behind him, adjusting her crop top and clearing her throat as she folded her large black wings behind her. "She'll be okay!"

"It's not her that I'm worried about," Riven said, putting the newly acquired Chalgathi artifact into his Satin Bag of Holding. "We have rules about engaging any truly strong opponents—if we think there's a chance at losing, we're to retreat and group up. It's just that Allie can be . . . a little bit kill-happy."

CHAPTER 23

Kathrine Vonsilla Crushada the Ninth, eldest daughter of the duke and duchess of House of Crushada, 107th in line for the vampiric throne, was not in a good mood.

"Yes, Instructor Pladius . . ." Kathrine said for the twelfth time that night while brushing a comb through her long locks of brunette hair—staring at a slim figure wearing a black dress in the mirror. She barely recognized herself. "I realize it's important, but there's simply nothing I can do."

"You're obviously not making this a priority!" Kathrine's teacher scolded, irritation flaring in his words as the older vampire glared at his pupil over a stack of books on a polished wood desk. "It is your responsibility as mouthpiece to initiate contact!"

"I know that, Instructor Pladius . . ."

"Then do something about it!" Pladius snarled with fangs bared, slamming a thick book onto the table, glaring over the rim of his glasses, and steepling his fingers. "It is not just you and your family that will feel restitution if this succeeds, and you are CERTAINLY not the only ones who will feel the queen's scorn if we fail! My entire family's fortunes are riding on my success, Your Highness! Please keep that in mind!"

Kathrine's eyelids drooped, and she smoothed out the formfitting black silk before turning on her backless stool to glare coldly at the older man. "Need I remind you just who it is you speak to? Instructor?"

Pladius opened his mouth to speak but thought better of it after meeting the unflinching gaze of the young royal in front of him. Sighing, shaking his head to stare at the desk underneath him, and running his fingers through his graying hair, he only ended up mumbling something under his breath.

"As I thought," Kathrine stated coolly. "Now, please have patience. I am confident one if not both of them will come speak to us in time."

"What makes you so sure of that?" the old man asked angrily, glaring up at her again with a sniff and sipping on a goblet of blood.

"Because they haven't kicked us off the planet yet." Kathrine turned confidently back to the mirror, trying out different types of Dao flowers in her hair that she'd been gifted by her mother for acquiring this position in the first place. Despite her outward appearance, she too was worried that Riven and Allie would simply never come. But just as the old man's—her family's—entire fortunes as well as her own future were riding on this mission, and she couldn't fail no matter what it took, she was at a loss for what to do, and the instructor's ramblings didn't help her feel at ease when she was battling with her own internal demons.

A rapid knock at the door caused her to turn, and the door to the dimly lit study opened to reveal a half-panicked vampire maid wearing a red and black dress of her own, with a red veil to cover half her face from the nose down like most of the maids here did. Her red eyes were wide, her blond hair disheveled, and she was breathing heavily, as if she'd sprinted up the stairs to get here.

"My lady!" the maid said, bowing low with a curtsy.

Kathrine frowned at the woman, not remembering her name, and tapped a finger against her folded arm with irritation evident on her features. "Since when is it okay that you just walk in without asking for permission first? What is your name?"

The maid froze, then looked up hesitantly from her bowing position. "My name is Cherna, Your Majesty . . . It's just that—"

"Just that you should be reschooled in the appropriate manners of your class and rank, Cherna. Peasants do not just waltz into the abode of a royal, and it is an offense that some would punish by death," Kathrine stated flatly. "Be happy that I am no such tyrant, but keep in mind that I will not tolerate such behavior, either."

The maid stuttered a whispered acknowledgment, standing up to a normal posture with hands clasped in front of her when Kathrine bade her rise.

"Now tell me, Cherna," Kathrine continued, still irritated at the complete lack of manners on the maid's part, "why did you enter this room in such a vulgar way?"

The maid stilled, then caught her breath. "I tried to come earlier, but the others—they stalled me! My lady, Riven Thane is downstairs. The other nobles and children of the great houses who came across the portal are already beginning—"

"*Curse those incompetent DIRTBLOODS!*" Kathrine whipped herself into a frenzy and out of the chair, Instructor Pladius quickly scrambling after her. "Of COURSE they wouldn't tell me! Their insufferable political games just HAD to follow me here!"

Kathrine stomped past the maid, who was trying to make herself look small and even paler than normal for a vampire—being well aware that getting a peasant such as herself involved in the power plays of the nobility would likely see her dead one day.

"Pladius!" Kathrine glared over her shoulder at the older man, pulling up her dress to begin half running down the steps so that she'd hopefully get there before her political enemies caused too much damage. "Pladius, I need you to put on your best behavior, no matter what you actually think about them! Understand? None of your pompousness today, AND DEFINITELY NONE OF YOUR PHILOSOPHIES, or I swear by the blood god, I will have your head!"

"What's wrong with philosophy?!" the old man protested with a scowl while he raced after her down the spiral staircase.

"NO! I don't want you to bore him to death! Not yet! UNDERSTAND?!"

Riven stood in the dining room of what had to be the most extravagant place he'd ever set eyes on.

Gold and platinum trimmings decorated the walls and ceiling, where carved monuments to creatures of all kinds were set in marble. Overhead the chandeliers sparkled with types of gemstones he had no name for, and though it was well lit, the light here had an unnatural feel to it. It was a room far too large for the keep it was contained in, making him think there was some kind of spatial magic going on, and some of the vampiric or thrall servants were already beginning to set up a feast on the single long table, which was adorned with finely made glass cutlery.

"Your Majesty, it is an honor that you grace us with your presence!" the sing-song voice of the female vampiric noble said with a charming smile. She wore a brilliant red Victorian-style dress with a corset that contrasted starkly against her pale-white skin, and her orange hair was cut in a punk-rock style: very short and almost shaved on the right side of her head, very long everywhere else.

A very tall, muscular man with a raven ponytail and dressed in silver-trimmed, monk-like black combat robes gave a poor attempt at hiding a sneer while he eyed the woman. "Yes . . . I finally find myself agreeing with Lady Muren at long last."

The man with the ponytail shifted his red gaze back to Riven, then bowed at the waist with a hand on his front and the other on his back. "It is a true pleasure to finally meet you, Prince Riven of House Wraithtide. My shorter name is Duke Blemrich, but you may call me Blemrich. Will your beautiful sister be joining us this night? I was hoping to meet her as well!"

Wraithtide. There was that family branch name again that Riven and Allie apparently belonged to.

Riven's face betrayed a scowl, and he shook his head while keeping them at a short distance. "Unfortunately, Allie will not be attending tonight's meeting. The last interaction we had here was less than receptive, so I thought it'd be better if I came alone."

The third person, an incredibly handsome but rather thin man with long blond hair trailing to his shoulders, glared at the obvious social blunder of the two people standing behind him. He wore something akin to what Duke Blemrich had on, the formfitting robes of a cultivator, but his were colored royal purple with gold inlaid into the fabric in various draconic designs.

He'd briefly introduced himself as Lord Carsion but otherwise hadn't talked at all—he'd merely observed the interactions.

"We humbly apologize for that attempt on your lives . . ." Lord Carsion said warily, staring daggers at Duke Blemrich with a clear signal to shut up about Riven's sister. "The man who attempted the assassination was dealt with, not only by the system, but he was thoroughly tortured and executed on a public stage for the entire empire to watch. The queen wishes for us to send her deepest apologies, as we only wished to establish positive contact with the two of you."

"The lack of oversight on the part of our esteemed expedition leader is under scrutiny by the crown even now," Lady Muren mused, waving away a veiled servant girl who'd brought over refreshments. "It is truly a shame—we had such high hopes for her."

The bustle of activity in the dining hall was growing, with guards in full plate armor bearing halberds and tower shields positioned all around the room. They gave Riven respectful nods whenever he looked their way. Servants, both thralls and vampires of lower status alike, were setting up jugs of blood wine and extremely high-quality food—slabs of steak, cakes, tarts, cheeses, and other foods Riven didn't have names for.

Riven glanced Lady Muren's way. "You're saying the attack was Kathrine's fault? The woman I met earlier?"

Lady Muren winced slightly, then gave a hesitant frown in exchange with Lord Carsion. "I spoke out of turn . . . It is just that she is very . . . Oh, how should I put it? Well, if it had been me, there would have been little in the way of such oversight. To think that she'd not assume an attempt on your lives would be made . . ."

Lady Muren gave an exaggerated huff and fanned her face with a handkerchief.

"She should have checked the thralls, as she was the one in charge of assigning duties," Duke Blemrich stated flatly. "If anyone is to blame for what happened—other than the man who attempted to take your lives—it is her."

Brutal.

Riven exchanged looks with Athela and Fay on his right, and Azmoth continued to stand silently behind him with his maul on the floor.

"And who exactly are you three? Aside from some random nobles who just happen to be here off-world in the trade commune," Riven said eventually, curiously tearing his eyes away from Athela.

Lord Carsion cleared his throat in feigned embarrassment. "Oh dear, we did get caught up in the excitement, didn't we? The three of us are representatives of great noble houses very close and loyal to the queen. She thought it wise that, due to our influence across the empire, our houses should send the young elite for representation."

"They paid an extreme amount of money and exchanged many favors to be here," a familiar feminine voice called out across the extravagant dining room, and all heads turned to see Kathrine Vonsilla Crushada gracefully entering. Her long, formfitting black dress flowed out behind her, and a red flower adorned her perfectly combed, silky brown hair. "They are not as important as they might try to make themselves out to be."

The two men scowled, Duke Blemrich clenching his fists, and Lady Muren snorted in derision while tossing her hair to the side and clasping her hands in front of her. An older man scurried behind Kathrine, clutching a book and pen to his chest before bowing low in Riven's direction when he came to a stop.

"My prince!" the old man stated with a huff. He stood up straight again, adjusted his glasses, and glared at the other three nobles. "The princess and I were not made aware of your arrival until just now. We apologize for not having a formal entrance or tour prepared; this was most unexpected."

Princess? Ah, yes. Kathrine was technically in the line of succession, though she was near dead last, from what little Riven understood.

"Those are rather petty insults, coming from someone who can barely call herself a princess—one from the equivalent of lower nobility at best. Wouldn't you agree, Lord Carsion?" Lady Muren mused, glaring heatedly at Kathrine, who only stared coldly back.

Lord Carsion coughed into one hand, seeming unsure of what to say—but was saved by Duke Blemrich as the bigger man crossed his arms.

"I agree wholeheartedly."

Kathrine's smile twitched, and she gave Riven an apologetic smile. "I am truly sorry. We shouldn't be getting into the politics of our nation or the feuds between families in your presence, Riven Wraithtide. It also appears that some people cannot remember just whom the queen appointed expedition leader, or what the chain of command here is. Would you mind following me? I wish to speak to you in private, cousin to cousin."

"We have already begun dinner preparations—" Duke Blemrich stated with a scowl, but he was cut off by a wave of Kathrine's hand.

"Later," Kathrine said dismissively, turning heel and beckoning Riven to follow. "Please, this way. We will have dinner after I speak to you in private."

The fog and dark clouds hanging over these haunted lands wasn't always present, but it had certainly been a weather favorite ever since the altar's terraforming. Even now, at midday, the sky was overcast and thin mists dotted the landscape in patches.

Riven sipped a tea that included blood and some kind of berry with a sweet aroma. He sat on a balcony in a fluffy brown chair overlooking the rest of the altar, which was buzzing with activity. Orcs, undead, and demons all conversed with one another in or around Dungeon Negrada's enormous red tent with the black eye symbol etched into it, which encompassed the dungeon's trading commune. There were even a few goblins and humans down there, too, though in smaller numbers than the others. No doubt the humans were residents of the city that Allie had brought on board, or at least he'd thought that until he saw some of them pulling wagons with various goods and dressed in peasant attire from a medieval civilization.

Traders from Dawn had already gotten this far? That was his only guess.

As for the goblins . . . Well, most of them were downright stupid, but a few were more intelligent than their counterparts—according to Gurth'Rok, there were other, smarter goblin species that were just as intelligent as other enlightened races.

Maids brought refreshments and burning incense sticks to the table at the center of their balcony, and Kathrine set down her own glass to lean back and breathe in deeply. "Again, I wish to extend my most sincere apologies for what happened. To think that one of our own would attempt to kill you is beyond me. I would have never thought it even a possibility, and I take full responsibility for my failings."

Riven stared out across the fields adjacent to the altar, where he could see his guild hall in the distance on the southern edge of the city. People kept coming and going to and from Brightsville, crossing a dirt road between greenskin cabins and tents and the fields his high elf slaves were tending to. Trade was bustling, and a true, thriving community was starting to appear in the ashes of the old world.

"It's not okay, but I do forgive you," Riven stated solemnly, turning his attention back to his distant cousin—who visibly sighed in relief, judging by the slumping of her tightened shoulders. "It appears that you don't get along very well with those other royals."

"They're not royals," Kathrine quickly corrected with a shake of her head, picking up a smoking pipe from a dish, letting it emit a dull purple vapor with each exhale. "They're high nobility. Our society is divided into royals at the top, high nobility directly under them, and low nobility at the bottom for the ruling classes. They all come with titles and responsibilities of various sorts, but in the end it doesn't really matter—what does matter is that you must realize these people are not your friends."

"They seemed friendly enough."

Kathrine set the pipe down and gave him a raised eyebrow. "They are opportunists."

Riven smirked at her expression, then smiled warmly at a nervous servant girl who almost tripped on her way over to give him a pipe of his own. She flushed behind the thin veil she wore and scurried away after delivering the item, covering her face and whispering to the other maids, who giggled or laughed softly at their friend's poor coordination.

Kathrine watched the interaction with growing amusement of her own. "You make them nervous."

"You're royalty, too. Wouldn't you make them just as nervous?" Riven asked with a side-eye.

Kathrine shook her head. "No, they've been my servant girls since I was little. We all grew up together, so they never act this way around me."

"Why use vampires for servants when you can use thralls? I see you have a mixture of them here. Wouldn't it just be easier to have more submissive *mind slaves* to do your bidding rather than other vampires?"

Riven said the words *mind slaves* with a tinge of distaste that was obvious to anyone with ears, and Kathrine frowned.

"Do you have something against owning thralls?" Kathrine asked, her tone rather curious.

"Absolutely. I think it's disgusting to warp someone's mind like that. Plus, it really rubs me the wrong way that my sister already has two hunky sex slaves she'd changed into thralls. Really pisses me off, actually."

Kathrine's jaw dropped slightly, then she sputtered a laugh and held up a hand over her mouth with a flush of amusement. "Your sister created thralls just for that? Are they human?"

"Yes."

"How erotic! I've always wanted to do that, but my parents said it was beneath my station." Kathrine refused to hide her grin much longer and placed her hands in her lap, ignoring the old man at her side clearing his throat with a disapproving frown. "To sleep with cattle, I mean."

"Perhaps you'd get along with Allie after all," Riven muttered, sighing and taking a long inhale on the pipe. It gave him a buzzing sensation, and his spirits immediately lifted. "You never answered my question."

"Oh! About why I keep vampires as servants? Vampire servants are more expensive to maintain, it is true, but they're also one of us. It adds prestige to enlist other vampires in such a position as well—gives your house recognition that you are able to afford such things—and it allows me to speak with them frankly, rather than just having thralls, who agree with anything and everything you say. Have you ever had a conversation with a thrall?"

Riven shook his head. "I have not."

"It's not very enlightening," Kathrine mused thoughtfully, tapping her chin with a slender finger. "They're good for manual labor, a useful food source, or for being obedient slaves. They are still somewhat their own people, but only to an extent. They can think abstractly, but when it comes to their masters, they will immediately switch opinions to match your own. They are all pleasing, which I suppose is why your sister enjoys the two men she's taken."

Kathrine winked Riven's way despite his loud snort of discontentment. "Ha-ha! I am sorry. Enough with the teasing! I would say that I'd deliver the queen's gifts, but they were very short-lasting Dao fruits that have already expired . . . and we cannot bring any others across at this time due to system limitations. Above all else—what can I do for you? Why did you come here now? What changed your mind about speaking with us?"

Riven shrugged, scooting over in his seat to make room for Athela when she yawned and transformed into a spider to curl up next to him. He stroked her head fondly as she buried her arachnid face in the crevice of his arm, then looked up at the mildly surprised royal across from him. "Three reasons. First, I wanted to see what you could offer me in terms of aid. Secondly, I want to know more about malignant prophecy and malignancy points. Third, I need help identifying some world-quest items. A ghoul woman by the name of Mara should be arriving with an undead escort soon; she'll be carrying another piece concerning the world quest, and I need your identifiers to look them over. I figured it's the least my long-lost family can do after almost getting my sister and me killed."

The old vampire next to Kathrine winced at the outright accusation, but Kathrine nodded sagely. "Of course. I'd be more than happy to help with all three of those things. Should I address them in order?"

"Address them however you'd like," Riven said flatly.

Kathrine cleared her throat, steepled her fingers, and leaned back into the soft cushion of her chair. "In terms of aid . . . the most valuable we have to offer isn't anything tangible, and system limitations are set to prevent us from giving much out for free until the integration is over. Instead, we've prepared quite a lot in the form of knowledge and training. We have a legion officer and general's son here to teach you the strategic arts of warfare and physical combat, three magical instructors who were some of the best for their given levels across our empire, as well as a historian and Dao theorist, who happens to be standing next to me."

She gestured to the old man with glasses next to her. "This is Instructor Pladius, historian and Dao theorist, who is hoping to teach you and your sister about the happenings of our universe as well as give you insights on how to expand your Dao pillars to new heights. He's been a family friend and my own teacher for quite some time."

Riven's eyes focused on the old man, and Pladius bowed low.

"My prince, it is an honor to be assigned to tutor you." Pladius straightened again and smiled widely, exposing his fangs. "It is a great opportunity for both you and me to pursue. I hope that you will take me up on my offer—you shan't be disappointed if you agree. I have many things to teach you."

Riven nodded to the man. "I may take you up on that."

Pladius beamed in turn.

Kathrine's own grin widened, too. "I hope you do. To be trained by some of the best the empire has to offer is no small feat. True, it is within a level-90 restriction set upon us for people we could bring to this world, but our empire spans hundreds of worlds. The talent here is very real, and it would be a tragic waste of resources if you and your sister didn't utilize them. The queen personally handpicked these people because she is very invested in getting her favorite granddaughter's children up to par with the rest of the royal family."

Riven remained silent for a time upon mention of the queen and his own long-lost mother, and Kathrine looked like she was preparing a reply if he was to ask about it—but he moved on to the more important subject matter instead. "What about malignancy points?"

"What about them?"

"I've used Malignant Prophecy twice." Riven held up his pointer and middle fingers in a peace sign. "And yet I've acquired four points. The first prophecy cost me one point, but the second prophecy that saved all our lives when the assassination attempt happened cost me three. I have a gut feeling that acquiring them isn't a good thing. Would I be correct?"

Kathrine opened her mouth to reply, but then frowned and then shut it again. She turned to look at the scholar beside her. "Pladius?"

The old man stepped forward. "It would be my honor to explain these things to you, young prince. I have had the honor of tutoring many of the royal family's young, including Kathrine here, but unfortunately not all the royals have the gift you and your sister have acquired. Most of them don't, actually, and the secrets pertaining to your Malignant Prophecy are a well-kept thing indeed. The gift is an invaluable resource to the empire, so the two of you having this gift makes you both a very strategic resource for the queen."

He held a hand up to his chest while looking at the gray sky, as if he was about to recite poetry. "To outsiders and the general public, Malignant Prophecy is just a way our empire has climbed to the top. It is a thing of legend and myth that sways the tides of fate in our favor, it has won many wars for us in the past, and it is a thing to be feared. It is a way to change the future before it happens by giving routes and avenues to success where they'd otherwise be lost. However, it does come at a steep cost. Each time you use Malignant Prophecy, you alter fate—and in doing so you acquire bad karma. These malignancy points you have are symbolic of that bad karma, with more points being given for more drastic changes to the future. Spontaneous combustion of your points will happen at random, with more probability for combustion with the more points you accumulate."

"Spontaneous combustion?" Riven repeated, a little unnerved. "What exactly does that do if it's supposed to be bad karma?"

Pladius frowned, and his shoulders slumped slightly. "My boy, it means that something very bad will happen to you, your interests, or the people you love. It is not an unavoidable thing, but it is often a trial set up by the system to punish you for intervening in fate—which is on the borderline of heresy where Elysium's laws are concerned."

That did not sound good at all.

"Any examples?" Riven asked, shifting in his chair to put Athela's spider body in his lap.

"That . . . is unfortunately beyond my knowledge. I only know that we have lost royal family members twice before because of this, and many of the royal family have experienced significant loss in other undisclosed ways. Secrets like that are kept close to the chest, even from people like me, due to many under-the-carpet rivalries between different royals who have the ability. The general idea is that you only want to use Malignant Prophecy if you absolutely have to, but many times it only activates when you're in dire need—so there isn't often a choice in the matter.

"More important than avoiding its use is overcoming the trials that Elysium will administer to you as punishment. What or when that may be is never known to us."

CHAPTER 24

It didn't take long for Mara to arrive.

"Was it odd? Finding out that you were a prince, of all things?" Kathrine asked while sipping at her tea again and giving Riven an appraising glance. "Did it faze you?"

"It doesn't mean much to me, honestly. I was more interested in finding out about my mother and father than anything else, but it appears none of you know what happened, either." Riven yawned, covering his mouth, and then waved Mara over from where she was being escorted onto the balcony by a set of vampiric guards. He could see her undead had been forced to wait outside and were standing at the fortress gates, but she'd come, nevertheless. "Hey. Did you bring them?"

The ghoul woman knelt with her head bowed, a large linen bag at her side. She gave the other vampire a side-eye of distrust but quickly averted her gaze when set upon by Kathrine's own. "Yes, my lord. As Allie commanded."

Riven gestured for Mara to rise, and she did so while pulling out a pair of pauldrons connected by a thin strand of shimmering black mana.

They were each very . . . engaging to the eye, and the pauldrons changed in size to fit his body when he picked them up. Why these items shifted or morphed to fit their owner was beyond his knowledge, but he hoped to get answers from his off-world compatriots very soon.

[The Apocalypse Beasts, Chalgathi, Quest Update: Riven Thane has acquired three of five set pieces for Chalgathi's Inheritance.]

Each pauldron was an ivory-white porcelain like the mask he'd taken off the rogue earlier that day and crafted in the shape of a horned devil's skull. The eye sockets actually flickered with infernal flames, which was a rather neat trick, in Riven's opinion, and with just a thought they whipped around and latched across his head and onto his shoulders with a thunk.

Immediately he felt a difference in how his body felt, though he couldn't place just what that was. Was it a stat boost? Some other bonus? He had no idea.

Which brought him to his next question for the Blood Moon Requiem.

"I was hoping you'd be able to identify these things," Riven stated, pulling out his dragon amulet and then the smooth porcelain mask with red tendrils of power wafting off the inside—only for the three items to abruptly interact with one another.

[The Apocalypse Beasts, Chalgathi, Personal Quest Update: three of five set pieces for Chalgathi's Inheritance have been acquired. Checkpoint reached. Participant under evaluation, identifying weaknesses, strengths, and orienting artifacts to the most powerful affiliated build.]

Pladius's eyes went wide at seeing the artifacts, and his jaw slowly started to drop while taking a step back. "Those . . . Those are dangerous to have on your person. My prince . . . Why do you have these items?"

Riven gave the old man a frown. "What do you mean by dangerous?"

WHAM

The mask in Riven's hand slammed onto his face, the tendrils of red power off the backside beginning to claw into his eyeballs and mouth—forcing their way into his body as he let out a scream of pain and surprise. He clawed at his face, only to be attacked by the other two items next. The amulet lurched downward onto Riven's chest and began tearing through his shirt to dig into his skin, and the pauldrons clamped down around his shoulders with jagged teeth that sank into his muscles.

"RIVEN!" Athela immediately whipped into her humanoid form and tried frantically to pry the mask off, but she was blown back by a pulse of power that shot her straight off the castle walls and to the ground below a hundred yards away.

"PLADIUS! DO SOMETHING!" Kathrine screamed, getting to her feet while maids cried out for help and guards rushed over to try and help the prince—only for the older vampire to hold up a hand to stop them from approaching.

"STOP!" Pladius yelled out over the sudden turmoil. "These are soul-binding items! DO NOT TOUCH THEM unless you want to do harm to the prince! We do NOT know what will happen if you rip them off during the fusion!"

"Fusion?!" Kathrine choked out, hands shaking and no doubt wondering just how her family would be murdered if the queen found out her great-grand-child had died horribly in her custody after only barely escaping with his life on the first visit.

"Fusion!" the old man repeated, physically pushing her back with a warning waggle of his finger. "I said, do not approach! Let it finish first. He'll be fine . . . I hope."

Kathrine froze in horror and shock, reliving the day her charges had almost been assassinated—only to watch now as Riven writhed on the floor, screaming and thrashing. Guards looked on nervously, awaiting orders, and Riven's two remaining minions clearly didn't know what to do, either.

Azmoth bent down over his thrashing master, watching the mask shift and mold, its red tendrils spreading down Riven's neck. Watched as the amulet warped and twisted, the ivory etchings of the dragon changing into something else entirely, and watched as the pauldrons twisted with new features.

The blazing infernal eyes of the pauldrons became glowing red orbs similar to Riven's own, balls of blood magics that radiated sinister intent. The horns along the pauldrons elongated, becoming much sharper and sleeker than their originals, and the demonic visage of a devil warped down into the more skull-like appearance of the original, vampiric teeth protruding from an open mouth.

Riven continued to scream.

The porcelain mask still did not have any holes on the front surface. It remained smooth and covered the entire front of Riven's head, but it now sprouted seven peacock-like feathers made of glowing crimson blood mana along the edges that protruded from his hood, making it look somewhat like a headdress.

The amulet's dragon visage had completely disappeared, and spikes of bone ripped out along the circular jewelry piece and gouged into Riven's chest like anchors just below the sternum, where his demonic pentagrams were located. In the center where the circular amulet had originally been, a large gaping hole opened up, razor-sharp teeth expanding up and down to create a vertical maw that split his chest in half down the center. It grew to about two feet in length and led into an abyss of black. The mouth in the center of his chest opened and closed, expanded and contracted, letting wisps of black protrude from Riven's center until the sharp teeth of the maw closed over the hole to seal it shut in an interlocking pattern.

Afterward, all along Riven's skin, a thin, woven layer of bloody threads began lacing themselves up and down his body. They covered him completely, creating a lattice of skintight fabric under his clothes that in turn connected all three of his Chalgathi artifacts over the course of a few minutes.

[The Apocalypse Beasts, Chalgathi, Personal Quest Update: three of five set pieces for Chalgathi's Inheritance have been acquired. Checkpoint reached. Participant has acquired the most powerful affiliated build available based on soul aspects for current acquired pieces. Item set is now sentient and is linked to your Core of Original

Sin—Gluttony. Item aspect attained: Gluttony. Participant must acquire remaining set pieces within six months' time or participant will be consumed by the worn items due to pathway's requirements.]

Allie's gauntlet crunched into the face of the elvish warrior, splitting his skull open along with the winged helmet he wore in a snapping of metal and bone.

"HAAAHAAAAAAAAA!!!!" she shrieked with a gleeful laugh when the body hit the earth, radiating death mana that pulsed and surged along her figure while the screams of innocent and guilty alike echoed through the air.

Huts burned, shadows moved on the outskirts of the firelight, and weapons clashed in the roar of battle as she stood over the enemy commander's corpse, glaring down with red-tinged eyes.

Two shimmering spots shifted in the air in her peripheral vision, and she whirled, six neon-teal flaming skulls erupting about her position and launching toward the incoming assassins.

The attacks broke the sound barrier, causing sonic booms to radiate from her position. The skulls shrieked and catapulted into the two stealthed enemies, blowing one hooded elf's chest clean out of his back and causing him to drop his daggers. The other hooded figure, dressed in leathers, managed to dodge with a dash ability that blurred his body to her right, but a flickering black ribbon of power whipped out of her wand and eradicated him with extreme prejudice.

The nearby screams and crackling of flames were interrupted by a loud crash, and looking left, she saw one of her bone giants use an enormous club to crush a nearby hut with all the people inside it. The small house was utterly decimated, and the giant slowly turned to the next target while lumbering off into the dark, seeking out hiding prey.

Her excited breathing ticked up a beat. All around her in the firelight under the night sky were dozens upon dozens of bodies, combatants and civilians alike. "Just look at all this material we get to use!"

Vin, who'd been watching from the shadow of a still-standing cabin and scribbling down notes about an experiment he was performing on a twitching elf, looked up to her. He motioned for his skeletal minions to keep the flailing, frothing elf in place and headed over to stand beside his queen. "You get nearly as excited as Nin does about seeing new bodies!"

She gave him a chuckle and raised her hands out to either side while black and teal mana shimmered and ripped from her fingertips to enter nearby bodies. Flesh began to melt off in swaths of necrotic tissue. First it was five corpses, then ten, then more than twenty corpses as blue lights started flickering to life in their eye sockets. Groaning and gradually pushing themselves to their feet, they stood to look at their new mistress in silent decorum.

"War is profitable; it makes harvesting that much easier," Allie muttered, waving her hand toward the remaining lines of defenders at the back of the elf village they were tearing apart, and the undead scattered—off to find their old brethren to eat, claw, and rip apart the living. "How goes your experiment?"

Vin clicked his teeth together in irritation, and the skull's lower jaw twisted to the side. "Poorly. I cannot seem to keep their souls intact. Progress is slow, and I don't know if we're even on the right path. Perhaps your newfound allies, the vampires from afar, could enlighten us? Do you think they have knowledge of such necromancy?"

Unholy sigils flashed up above in the sky where her ritualists were calling down meteoric showers of offensive magics—raining down hell on the hill where the last group of elvish defenders was quarantined. She watched her skeletal minions rush forward in a wave and listened to the singsong screams of her enemies as they begged, pleaded, and died under the green flag of a white doe.

How funny that they ask for mercy when they'd almost wiped a human town clean off the map before she'd gotten there. If it wasn't for her, the town of Bradshire would be nothing but a smoking husk in the wake of the elvish forces calling themselves the kingdom of Tereen. Saving the town and purging the elvish forces attacking it had been a strategic move that gave her an excuse to essentially annex Bradshire entirely, its citizens not only thanking her for the help but outright praising her as she walked through the streets—even though she was a vampire. Now, after removing the closest elf threat in this small village where the routed Tereen forces had congregated, she'd found abundant supplies for the war effort. She'd taken more corpses to create undead, body parts for modifications that were in high demand back in Brightsville, and more slaves to work the farmlands her brother was cultivating. If anything was to be said about these elves, it was a certainty that they had a knack for growing crops—and she'd be damned if she let that go to waste.

"What do you think the kingdom of Dawn will say when they realize I'm not going to give Bradshire back?" Allie asked with an amused hum, turning back to Vin with a sadistic smile. "Do you think they'll want to fight us, too?!"

"I think making such rash decisions without Riven's input is going to cause you to butt heads with him again," Vin stated while scratching his head. "If you truly do want to rule in conjunction with him, it would be wise to ask his opinion before claiming the town as your own."

Allie paused, thinking it over with a scowl, and then motioned for Vin to walk with her. Killing the convulsing man on the ground as they walked by with a flick of her wrist and a pulse of mana, Allie headed back toward where Bradshire was located a few dozen miles to the east. "I will speak to him first. Though I don't think he'll be around much longer."

Vin abruptly stopped in his tracks, eyeing his queen with a sour expression even for a skeleton. "You don't mean you're going to kill him, do you? He's your brother!"

Allie's jaw dropped, and she let out an abrupt laugh. "No, you fucking idiot! Of course I don't mean that. God."

She shook her head and rolled her eyes, turning back around with Vin close behind her. "Moron. I'd rather off myself before killing Riven—he's everything to me. No, what I meant is that he's likely to pursue events that take him far away from this place. We both see the writing on the wall—the world is changing. We cannot just simply stand by and let rogue forces go berserk, tearing our new world apart, so one of us must leave to address the problem. And one of us is going to have to stay behind to make sure things here are run right. That person who stays is likely going to be me."

"You speak of the world quest?" Vin asked dubiously, stepping over an armored, bloody elf corpse that was missing its arms. "Would it not be wise for both of you to pursue it if the results of failing are so grim?"

Allie paused in her stride, then shrugged and shot a wide, fangs-bared smile over her shoulder. "Riven is strong enough to do it by himself, and I have an empire to build."

CHAPTER 25

[The Apocalypse Beasts, Chalgathi, Personal Quest Update: three of five set pieces for Chalgathi's Inheritance have been acquired. Checkpoint reached. Current Chalgathi artifacts have had their stats partially revealed and unlocked based on the aspect they bonded to within your soul. Full stat pages for each item that has acquired your aspect will be further revealed and unlocked after all five set pieces have been acquired.]

[<u>Chalgathi Cultist Amulet</u> (Legendary Heavy Armor, Gluttony Aspect) (Parasitic) (Unique Soul-Bound Sentient): The Gluttony aspect absorbed into this amulet has transformed this artifact into the Great Maw. This artifact is currently in an unstable transformation state and will consume you unless the item set is completed soon. This artifact set can attack and defend on its own. Set Piece: one of five. This item is part of the <u>Chalgathi Cultist Set</u>. Acquire three items of the Chalgathi Cultist Set for additional bonuses. Acquire five items of the Chalgathi Cultist Set for all bonuses.

- The Great Maw: ???
- Devour: This amulet can use shadowy tendrils to attack and pull in prey for devouring. If bitten, a potent paralytic poison is applied to your enemy. Devouring enemies allows this item set to grow slowly.
- ???]

[Chalgathi Cultist Pauldrons (Legendary Heavy Armor, Gluttony Aspect) (Parasitic) (Unique Soul-bound Sentient): The Gluttony aspect absorbed into this Pauldron Set has transformed this artifact into Twin Cannibals. This artifact is currently in an unstable transformation state and will consume you unless the item set is completed soon. This artifact set can attack and defend on its own. Set Piece: one of five. This item is part of the Chalgathi Cultist Set. Acquire three items of the Chalgathi Cultist Set for additional bonuses. Acquire five items of the Chalgathi Cultist Set for all bonuses.

- Twin Cannibals: 1,290 defense to shoulders. +10% to all stats. +60 flat points of Sturdiness. ???
- Blood in the Eyes: These pauldrons passively absorb blood mana from your surroundings up to a maximum of double your normal mana pool. They act as a reservoir for both your passive vampiric regeneration and a mana font to pull from as you would environmental resources. Once the pauldron's eyes dim, your extra resource pool has run out.
- ???]

[Chalgathi Cultist Mask (Legendary Heavy Armor, Gluttony Aspect) (Parasitic) (Unique Soul-Bound Sentient): The Gluttony aspect absorbed into this mask has transformed this artifact into Fallen Apostle. This artifact is currently in an unstable transformation state and will consume you unless the item set is completed soon. This artifact set can attack and defend on its own. Set Piece: one of five. This item is part of the Chalgathi Cultist Set. Acquire three items of the Chalgathi Cultist Set for additional bonuses. Acquire five items of the Chalgathi Cultist Set for all bonuses.

- Fallen Apostle: +900 defense to face, +325 defense to whole body via additional bloodskin layer that can be used underneath any other armor. Natural sunlight does not bother you while wearing this item, and all your senses are enhanced by 40%.
- Identifier's Clause: Wearing this item increases your ability to identify information concerning items or living creatures, being the equivalent of a low-tier identifier class. Your own basic information will be much harder to identify.
- ???]

[Checkpoint update: In the past, you have made A Choice of Selflessness. A branching quest has been unlocked based on your previous choice, Savior of the Weak.
Chalgathi Side Quest, Savior of the Weak: You, Riven Thane, have proven yourself to be one of a bleeding heart. A rare case amid your kind, you seek to bridge the gap between the damned and the saved.

It is a path few walk, and even fewer succeed in their attempts. Some would even call it a fool's errand. Nevertheless, your previous choice of selflessness has landed you here—and now you will reap the rewards to play hero to those less powerful than yourself.

- **On the opposite side of the world of Panu, one of Chalgathi's previous chosen is wreaking havoc among your kin of Earth and other humans in the area. This chosen is a blasphemer, having taken Chalgathi's artifact to warp and distort it into a cursed item. This in turn caused it to become useless in the world quest entirely, and it will not count toward your five set pieces, but it is also an item of great and corrupting power. Your assignment is to kill this blasphemer who has strayed off the path and disregarded the world quest to rampantly kill without cause. Completing this quest will please Chalgathi, save many thousands of innocent lives, allow you to take this item for yourself or destroy it at your leisure, and establish portal points you can access both here in Brightsville as well as across the world through the staff you carry. These portal points will only become accessible after you kill the blasphemer. Abandoning this quest by using your guild hall's teleport will result in angering Chalgathi immensely.]**

[Your minions have been temporarily banished to the nether realms and you have been transported to the next probable site of conflict. Good luck.]

Riven woke to the sounds of birds chirping overhead and men arguing fiercely about . . . something.

God, his head hurt.

He blinked, only barely absorbing the information contained in the notifications before letting out a breath. To his surprise, his surroundings were crystal clear to all his senses—far clearer than they'd ever been before at any point in his entire life. It was like he'd been awakened yet again, beyond the vampiric and into something truly divine.

He was in a prison cell, an old cement one with metal bars like the ones back on Earth. He could see the specks of sand and dirt on his surroundings in vivid detail, could smell the sweat of people nearby, could hear their heartbeats and the shuffling of feet, and a skylight overhead leaked in streams of dimming daylight that he did not shy away from.

Slowly, he reached out a hand—illuminating what should have been the bare skin of his fingers. Instead, he saw a thin veil of bloodred silk coating his body; it fit over his skin like a tight glove. He looked down from where he lay on a rickety dirt-stained bed full of holes and saw that he was essentially wearing a tight bodysuit. But everything else was gone.

His staff was gone, his bag of holding was gone, his clothes were gone—everything was just gone, with the exceptions of his mask, the bodysuit created by his mask, the monstrous maw of teeth etched vertically down his chest, and the two pauldrons, which were gored into his shoulders with spikes of ivory. Along his wrists were locked a pair of basic iron manacles, which must be enchanted somehow, based on the faint white runes glowing on the iron, but they weren't attached to one another and were probably only there to suppress his mana.

How laughable, considering he could feel just how weak the enchantments were. He did notice a slight dip in his power output when he flexed his mana channels, but he was easily able to conjure two Blood Lances along either arm. Blood mana flickered along his already-red body like ribbons of power up to his shoulders, and he heard each of the manacles pop with a crackle of electricity when the white runes were extinguished.

[Broken Iron Suppression Manacle: 13 defense. Enchantments extinguished. Forged by low-level crafters of the native populations on Panu.]

His mask lit up with the information he'd missed since the Chalgathi starter trials had ended, and a large smile spread across his face. Sitting up and turning his body, he turned his attention away from the cell bars and toward a mirror.

Seven bright-red peacock feathers, or their equivalent, protruded from the outer perimeter of the blank, white, completely smooth mask covering the entire front of his head. There was one vertical feather at the peak of his head, one on either side at a diagonal, and two more on each side of his face for a total of seven. However, upon closer inspection and when standing up to get closer to the mirror, he realized that the peacock feathers actually had . . . Were those eyes looking back at him?

He saw one of the eyes divert its attention from where it was positioned at the end of the feather, glancing out toward the cell door, then shifting its attention back to him.

That gave him the creeps, and he involuntarily stepped back while pawing at his face. His hand touched the front of the mask, but when it made contact, the effort was like he was looking (and even breathing) through a layer of thick glass. It was like he had a HUD of some kind, where he was trapped inside some advanced mecha suit—and when he tried to peel the mask off, it wouldn't budge at all.

HOW WAS HE SUPPOSED TO FEED LIKE THIS?!

Shit. Hopefully the mouth on his chest would take in blood?

Otherwise he was in for a really bad time.

The rest of his head, neck, and body were covered in the newly acquired bloodred skin, and the teeth along his chest occasionally shifted from their interlocked positions to open—revealing a black abyss beneath them from which shadowy wisps flowed out, only to retract when the demonic mouth closed. The porcelain pauldrons, an ivory color similar to his mask, had glowing red eyes infused with blood mana, the depictions of horned vampiric skulls with open mouths and fangs protruding along their surfaces.

If he'd had his black wooden staff of flesh and flowing blood, he'd really look the part of the evil sorcerer. Hell, even now he looked like a storytime villain of extreme proportions.

A knock on the cell door caused him to turn his head right, and the feathers all swayed and adjusted to look with him—peering their red eyes at the figure that'd made the noise with as little interest as when Riven viewed an ant underfoot.

Holy shit. Riven could feel the INTENT of the thing he was wearing . . . of the incomplete item set he had on. It was all one entity, a will of its own—yet one that was subservient to him . . . at least for now.

Standing at the cell door was a man in an army uniform bearing the American flag on his shoulder, outfitted with grenades and a fully automated machine gun. He had a crew cut and a strong jawline and was Caucasian. He was also likely in his late thirties or early forties by the looks of it.

"You're awake," the man said gruffly before two more soldiers stepped up behind him on either side with hands on their own machine guns. "You are something of a freak. You know that?"

Riven stared back, expressionless due to the porcelain mask, and turned his body to face ahead fully. He walked up to the bars and looked side to side, finding out that he was on the lowest floor of a two-story complex. There were at least a couple dozen prison cells here, with inmates banging on the bars up above and a scuffle breaking out in one of the others, which was largely ignored by the soldiers on guard duty.

Riven turned his attention back to the man in front of him. "Where are my belongings?"

The echoing yells of the scuffling inmates caused the lead soldier with the crew cut to scowl, and he verbally cracked the whip at his nearby compatriots who were slacking in their duties. The guards snapped to attention and rushed ahead, unlocking a cell door to stop the bigger man inside from murdering the smaller one with a shiv.

"Your belongings are being held for study and evaluation. The government of Chicago needs every bit we can get in these trying times. I'm sure you understand," the lead soldier stated, eyeing the shifting vertical maw along Riven's chest. "You had quite the set of equipment, and we couldn't even get most of it off you when you mysteriously dropped into the downtown district from fifty feet in the air. Senator James didn't want it damaged when we realized you were actually a person underneath it all and not one of the monster spawns in this area, but you're going to have to give it up if you want out of here."

"Is that so?"

"It is. If you give it up, we can start talking about getting you out of here."

Riven snorted in amusement at the man's steely gaze, then he crossed his arms and shook his head. If there was another of Chalgathi's chosen here, he had to be very careful. He couldn't waste time like this; who knew when the man or woman would attack? And without his staff, he'd be at a disadvantage. "I'll give you thirty seconds to let me out of here to speak to your boss or whoever has my things. Then things will start to get dirty."

The two soldiers behind the leader stiffened, and the man who'd been talking to Riven narrowed his eyes while undoing the safety on his automatic rifle. "I don't think you understand the situation you're in. You're locked up, have suppression manacles on, and have no weapon. What're you going to do? Spit at me? You'd have to take that mask off first."

"It's only a safety precaution," one of the other soldiers said with a scowl, lifting his weapon and aiming Riven's way. "Don't make us shoot you, man. No matter what kind of shit you have going on with that outfit, you're not going to survive 7.62 rounds to the head."

That was actually very inaccurate, and Riven knew it, as long as they were just plain, normal bullets. Based on the defensive perks he had on this equipment when compared to Breath of Valgeshia—his other mask with a defensive rating of forty-eight—he was more than certain even the weaker, thinner blood suit he had on could withstand at least a couple of bullets like that. Not to mention he'd be able to heal whatever did make it through via passive regeneration.

Riven paused, then sighed. "Go get your boss and get me my things or I tear this prison apart. There will be no negotiations."

Riven's arms flared with blood magic again, ripping off the manacles and shredding the iron like paper while dozens of spinning razors bloomed around their position. His aura exploded out of his cell, causing the soldiers to go rigid with shock as blood frost began accumulating along the walls, guns, ceiling, and floor—and when Riven concentrated briefly on the cell bars, they literally cracked and shattered. A palpable intent to destroy and kill was etched into their psyches, and the sounds of the other inmates in the other cells immediately silenced when the air inside the prison started to ripple with random cascades of red mana.

The soldier who'd been jittery from the get-go, the one who'd aimed his rifle Riven's way, pulled the trigger, but the weapon jammed due to the frost. His boots stuck to the floor where they'd been frozen in place, which caused him to stumble and fall when the ice shattered under his weight.

"Pathetic and embarrassing," Riven said coldly, arms pulsing with mana while he stared down at the terrified man still fumbling with his rifle. "As I said, you have thirty seconds. The count begins now: Thirty. Twenty-nine. Twenty-eight. Twenty-seven . . ."

"OPEN FIRE!"

The city lights of Chicago still shone brightly even after all it'd been through, a bastion of the old world under the dying light of sunset; the tall buildings and sprawling suburbs now stood adjacent to a patch of land along a new ocean's coastline. Ah, how Richard hated this city while growing up. A den of corruption, crime, and hate was what he'd come to know as a child, and things had only gotten worse after his incarceration and shunning from normal society many years later.

He wanted to purge it. All of it. And with his newfound power, he was finally able to make that dream come true.

Looking back at one of his hatchlings, a newborn insectoid that'd crawled out of one of the corpses of a local patrol, he smiled with sinister intent. With a yellow gleam to his eyes, Richard stood up—clutching to his chest the black orb he'd created from the remnants of Chalgathi's artifact. His chitinous, insectoid legs shifted and groaned, splitting the earth underfoot with pincers that could crush cars, men, and even tanks.

He knew because he'd already done it. His awakened bloodline was just that powerful.

At level fifty-one, Richard was at the apex of strength here on Panu. He would harvest these disgusting creatures he'd once called kin; he'd slay them all and use them as fertilizer to plant his eggs. Then he would create a society where he and his children could thrive.

The time to strike would be soon, and after he was done with Chicago, he would head to the other cities farther down the coast, just like he'd done with the smaller towns here in previous weeks. The ones that hadn't already been ransacked by creatures or internal strife would meet a quick demise under his grim claws, and they would know the pain they'd inflicted on him during his past life.

All humans were naught but lambs to the slaughter.

CHAPTER 26

Senator James was usually a composed man. He was in his late forties, young for a man of his position in the Senate—though not much of the Senate was left if he had to guess at the whereabouts of the old government. Still, he'd done a good job of maintaining order after calling the present military into action and setting up systems for food distribution.

But that food reserve was running out, and without a supply chain that worked properly, he was in for some real problems unless he figured out how to go about getting almost a million people access to foodstuffs. That didn't even include the other cities, Rockford and Milwaukee, which had been put under Chicago's military protection but whose mayors were otherwise fending for themselves.

Senator James grimaced at the idea that the last estimated count was placed that low. Chicago was nearing three million before the integration, but after the tutorials, monster attacks, anarchy, and hostile neighbors they'd had to put down, they'd lost almost two-thirds of the population.

He shook his head in silence under the bland light of the prison interior. Today he wore a typical black suit, well pressed, with a red tie and dress shoes. His hair was combed back in the usual gelled style he liked most, emphasizing the single gray streak in his otherwise dark-brown hair that was borderline black. He sat in a chair across from the prison warden's desk, waiting impatiently as the balding old man sifted through papers. It was unfortunate, but the warden had very recently become a person of importance in the city, whom Senator James had to deal with all too often.

"Surely it can't be that hard to find a paper on a man who was just admitted into the prison today?" Senator James stated sourly, tapping his finger against the padding of his armchair while glaring across the room.

The old warden glared right back, adjusting his navy-blue baseball cap, but didn't reply and went back to sifting through papers.

Senator James sighed, but thankfully the search only lasted another couple of minutes before the files were pulled and handed over.

"That's what we have," the warden stated sourly, leaning back in his rolling chair and looking out the window to the sunset along the skyline. "Our best identifiers couldn't get any read on his person other than the class of warlock, but they did get partial reads on each of the things he's wearing, along with that wicked-looking staff he had and the contents of his spatial bag. All the details are right there in those documents—pretty nasty stuff. These items make our own weapons look like children's toys, and the general isn't too happy about it."

"General Florence?"

"Is there another general I should be aware of?"

Senator James pursed his lips, closed his eyes, and tried not to be too snippy. "No, Warden. You are correct, there is only one general. Now, tell me . . ."

The senator laid a picture of Riven's passed-out body on the desk. "The notes here say that this warlock . . . someone mistook him for a monster and tried to shoot him?"

"A civilian, yes," the warden said with a head nod. "Nine-millimeter bullet right to the head, which promptly bounced off to hit someone else in the shoulder. Didn't even leave a dent."

"Jesus."

"Gets worse. That weapon he has? It's higher grade than anything anyone in the city has—that's for sure. And look—" The warden pointed to a line highlighted in yellow marker on the description written out by their intelligence officers. "'Requires vampiric heritage to wield.'"

Senator James blinked, scowling, and flipped the page over to get another look at the snapshot of the staff. "So you're saying this man's a vampire?"

"We don't know, but his staff implies that he is one."

"I didn't realize vampires were real."

"Is it really something you want to question at this point, after all that has happened?"

Senator James shook his head, continuing to scan what little information they'd acquired on this stranger. "No. I won't question it. I just find it very weird that he was teleported into the middle of downtown by a magical disturbance that caused power to go out for entire city blocks. Bringing the power lines back up is going to be a real pain in our asses, considering how long it took the first time. Are you sure we him properly restrained?"

"Yes. He's got the suppression manacles on, and we've posted soldiers outside his cell. The general gave them strict orders to fire . . ." The warden's voice trailed off, and both men looked to the door leading out of the small office when they heard gunshots erupt farther into the prison.

A terrifying cold sensation swept over them both, a palpable presence settled onto their minds like a titanic weight of pressure, and a thunderous boom rocked the prison—shaking the very walls of the large structure. Red frost began form-ing along the furniture, ceiling, chairs, and even their hair as the men's breath started giving off visible vapor. Senator James held on to his chair as the quaking of the prison got more and more violent, gritting his teeth and staring wide-eyed at the window that was being covered in this new onslaught of abnormal red ice—until, all of a sudden, everything stopped.

The sound of gunfire was gone. The frost stopped accumulating. The heavy feeling of pressure subsided, and only calm remained.

The warden wheezed out a gasp, eyes wide and hands shaking. "What the fuck was that?!"

Senator James got up, not bothering to wait for the older man, and headed for the door. Putting his hand on the cold metal, he winced at the subzero tem-perature—and pulled.

But it didn't budge.

"The door is jammed!" He tried to yank harder, but it still didn't budge. Ice had covered the door's hinges, and all he got was a grating sound whenever he yanked.

The warden shambled over, almost slipping on the ground and cursing aloud before leaning in and taking a hold of the door handle himself. He pulled once, twice, and then three times before the handle completely snapped off—and the warden fell backward to the ground with the metal piece clutched in his hand.

"Shit!" Senator James looked around for another way out. He went over to the landline—the only types of phones that worked here anymore, ever since the satellites went down. Cell phones were nothing but little pieces of garbage now. But when he picked up the receiver, he heard a dead signal—likely due to damage from whatever kind of freakish event or attack was going on. "Goddamn it! We're trapped in here!"

On the other side of the door and far down the hallway, beyond a solid door held in place with keypad access, where he'd stationed his personal escort, more shots rang out. He stiffened when the shots abruptly died, then turned around when he heard a monstrous crash of metal on cement.

Senator James exchanged looks with the warden, who'd just gotten to his feet, supporting his weight on the desk. "Something just took the barricade off its hinges."

"You think I don't realize that?!" the older man hissed in terror, fumbling with the drawer in his desk and pulling out a handgun to cock and load it. "By god, this world has gone to hell!"

Steps echoed, crunching through the long hallway one after another. The ground shook underfoot, and the senator's heart shook with it while he quivered and backed up to the frozen window. He briefly thought about trying to throw a chair through the glass behind him, but it was bulletproof. He could only hope that he'd be able to negotiate with whoever or whatever was on the other side.

CRASH

Thick, metallic-black claws tore through the cement on either side of the door, gripping the entire thing in four different places. Dust and debris shot into the room, and Senator James watched in awestruck horror as some gigantic brute ripped the door right out of the wall, part of the cement still clinging to it.

The warden didn't bother waiting, rapidly firing his pistol into the dust cloud that washed over them and sending sparks off his target with every bullet that hit. A deep, demonic chuckle echoed into the room, and Senator James paled to a deathly white when the visage of a huge, armored THING appeared out of the debris.

It was absolutely massive, having to hunch over in the relatively small confines of the hallway behind it, with four muscular arms that effortlessly tossed the door aside. It lacked any eyes and had two slits for a nose; it only had a spiked, helmetlike metallic head that matched the rest of its obsidian body. Thin lines of sinewy red muscle could barely be made out between the large plates of armor fused to its body. Its smile was what creeped Senator James out the most, though, as it had rows of very long, very sharp obsidian teeth that smiled wickedly back at him while it continued to laugh.

"My god . . ." the warden said, stumbling back and shakily fumbling to load another magazine. "Oh my god, oh my god, oh . . . my . . . god . . ."

From behind the large monster, a humanoid figure stepped out, and James immediately recognized him as the previously unconscious warlock they'd subdued and imprisoned earlier that day. He looked around, the feathered headdress-like mask turning left and right before settling on the warden, who lifted his hand to fire.

The warlock lifted his own hand in turn, and red ice quickly encompassed the pistol as well as the warden's hand. The man screamed in pain.

"Oh, shut up. I guarantee a little bit of cold is far less painful than being struck with a bullet." Riven snickered, walking toward the screaming old man and backhanding him to send the warden toppling to the ground. "I hate dealing with idiots, and there are oh so many of them. Fay, ask which one of them has the goods."

The Succubus entered next, alongside Athela, and the two demons pulled a bound man who'd been halfway cocooned in red threads. It was the same military man with the crew cut who'd tried to tell Riven he had to take off his stuff and hand it over.

Quickly she whispered something into his ear, the Succubus using her Silvertongue ability to get a drugged half smile and a head nod from the warden. She straightened, proudly pointing to the man Riven had just backhanded.

"Oh, so it's dopey, then." Riven walked by Senator James without even a sideways look, pulling the warden to his feet and knocking the gun out of his hand—shattering ice and a finger with it. The old man screamed even louder, but Riven shook him back and forth rapidly like a rag doll to get his attention. "Hey, idiot, shut up for a second! I SAID, SHUT UP!!!"

Riven stopped manhandling the poor guy a few seconds later when his cries died down into a whisper, and then he looked around the room. "I've been told you're the dumbass who took my shit. Where is it?"

"Your shit!?" the warden repeated, quivering in Riven's grasp and being held by the neck of his shirt, which was slowly ripping at the seams.

"My shit! Like, my staff and my bag and all that other stuff that you cockwombles stole from me." Riven unceremoniously dropped the old man with a thud, then walked over and ripped open a closet door, only to frown underneath the porcelain mask he still couldn't take off. "Goddamn it. Not here. FAY! Your version is better than mine—get over here and ask."

"Yes, Master!" The Succubus skipped over to the old man, the two large objects she always had on her getting his attention instantly, and bent down while infusing mana into her words. "Where is my master's stuff? You can tell me!"

Instantly the old man's eyes hazed over, and he stiffened as his minimal Willpower tried to combat the demon's ability. It was not nearly enough, and he gave a sidelong look at a large, lidded metal box on the far side of the room. "There."

"Good boy!" Fay patted the old man on the head, then let her ability go as the man sputtered and fell back, horrified.

"Mind magic!?" the warden gasped while Riven walked past him to the metal chest.

Pulling off the lid and flinging it halfway across the room, he cackled delightedly and yanked his staff out. The magic item pulsed in his grasp, fleshy tendrils embracing him tightly before the weapon was placed to the side and hovered midair while he sifted through the other goods.

Riven quickly became irritated again, though, and one by one started putting stuff back into the bag of holding that these idiots had taken out. "They pulled out a lot of stuff to examine. This is going to take forever to put back inside. I swear to god, if anything is missing . . ."

"Ahem . . ."

Riven straightened, and for the first time since entering the room, he looked over to the man in the nice suit who was trying to put on his best impression of confidence. "What is it, Pops? Got something to say?"

"Pops . . . ?" Senator James repeated with furrowed brows. Becoming slightly more confident in his assumption, he straightened his tie. "You're from Earth, aren't you?"

"And you're quite the Sherlock Holmes," Riven stated sarcastically, turning back to the box and rummaging around again while pushing stuff into the satin spatial bag and setting aside his clothes. "What gave it away? The good old American accent or the fashionable outfit that so many millennials nowadays try on for sport? I'd like to say I'm a trendsetter, but I don't think I'm the first guy to try out kinky, formfitting cosplay."

Senator James almost forgot his current predicament when he started to grin, but he quickly shut that down when he remembered that this man had torn through a heavily guarded facility to get here—and likely killed many people. This man was incredibly dangerous, and he commanded equally dangerous creatures. A wary frown quickly set onto his features, and he hesitantly took a step forward while side-eyeing the obvious Succubus not far off. "Just by the way you speak . . . I realize that we're not speaking English anymore, but the mannerisms and the way you structure sentences is the same as me."

"Goodie. Perhaps you people should have tried talking to me first before putting me in a prison cell and stealing all my shit, then."

Senator James winced, casting a sidelong look at the warden, who was babying his broken finger. "Yes, that was obviously a mistake . . . I assume the men I stationed outside that hallway are dead?"

"Dead?" the warlock repeated, standing up and pulling out a pair of dark linen trousers as well as some leather boots. The magic vanished from the fabric of the frost-covered couch when he sat down—and he began to put the pants on over his skintight jumpsuit. "No, I didn't kill them. They were weak enough that my demons and I were able to subdue them without much fuss."

Again the senator winced. "Demons? Too weak? This is one of the most secure places in Chicago . . . we keep most of our hardened, higher-level criminals here."

Riven paused, having put on one boot halfway, and he looked up through the blank face mask with body language that imitated surprise. "Seriously? Chicago?"

Senator James nodded slowly. "That's right . . . Oh, and my name is Senator Rufus James. You may have heard of me if you're an American—"

"Nope. No idea who you are. Don't care, either." Riven went back to shoving on his leather boots. "You motherfuckers ruined the country because you were all so greedy. I'd half hoped you all were lost to the system tutorials. Did you know that many people with type 1 diabetes—who were born with the condition—couldn't even afford insulin and died due to your bad policies? And that's just one of a billion bad things you people did."

The senator's face reddened, and his fists clenched. "I am well aware of the failings of our Senate. I, for one, never voted—"

"Oh, I'm sure you're not the problem. None of you senators ever were; it was always the other side, right? Always the OTHER political party. God help

Chicago if they have one of you cockroaches already leading them. I assume you're the man in charge here?" Riven grunted, standing up and pulling on a dark, baggy shirt. In order to put it on, he needed to literally tear off the sleeves and cut down the side so his pauldrons would fit. Immediately after that, the maw along his chest ravenously tore through it in a miniature temper tantrum until the teeth were exposed to the air again—and Riven looked down, dumbfounded, at the shirt his amulet had just ruined. "Oh, goddamn it, this better not happen to all the shirts I buy."

Trying to change the subject and realizing that this warlock obviously had a very poor view of the government back on Earth, Senator James spoke again. "So . . . these are your demons, then?"

He stared at the two beautiful women, who were sitting on the desk chatting in low whispers, and then looked warily over to the living armored tank that was glaring at him with a wide, toothy grin.

"Indeed. Now . . ." Riven tried to put on his cloak next, struggling to find a way to get it on without ruining it like the shirt. He made sure it stayed open in the front so his great maw wouldn't eat through the fabric there as well. Thankfully, and to Riven's own surprise, the pauldrons actually lifted up off his shoulders to hover in place temporarily—allowing him to place the cloak back down and underneath the pauldrons with just a thought—which was certainly going to make dressing easier, considering his Twin Cannibals had been spiked down to his flesh only earlier that day. Then, when he tried to remove the pauldrons manually again, they simply didn't budge.

Must be the sentient item set sensing what he wanted. It didn't want to let him go. Would it want to let go when all five of the set pieces were put together?

That would definitely be a problem he'd have to address sooner rather than later.

Riven grabbed his staff from out of the air, pulled his hood up to the edge of his porcelain mask where the peacock-like red feathers stood out in seven directions, and waved a hand over the window to clear it entirely of frost so he could check out his reflection. "I have a busy schedule ahead of me and some jackass to find. Then I have even more jackasses to find . . . fucking Chalgathi out to ruin my day. You wouldn't happen to know of any roaming person killing civilians by the thousands in this area, would you? Any mass murders you can't explain? Any evil-looking baddies that need taking out because they've gone mad with power? Anything like that? I'm looking for someone fitting that description, and I have no idea where to start."

Confusion. That was the emotion Senator James was feeling right now, and he shook his head rapidly when Riven turned his way. "Uh . . . Um, no. We've had monster attacks and a lot of infighting during the anarchy after our tutorials, if that's what you mean . . . but a single person killing civilians by the thousands? I can't say I've heard of anything like that."

A thought crossed the senator's mind, and sweat began to slowly accumulate on his forehead. Dabbing at it with his sleeve, he tried to regain his composure while the other man stared him down. If this man had just ransacked the prison so effortlessly, and he had a friend in the area with that kind of description . . . there wouldn't be anything Senator James could do to stop him. It was very likely that it would take an entire battalion to kill this man, just from the show of force he'd already displayed, and he didn't even know the warlock's true extent of power yet. "If I may ask . . . why are you looking for this particular type of person? Is he or she an acquaintance of yours?"

Riven cocked his head to one side. "No, nothing like that. It's a long story, but I'm here to kill them."

CHAPTER 27

A steady, familiar thrum started to descend on Riven's position. It came from outside, up above, and the sound only got louder as the seconds ticked by.

Slowly turning his head, Riven watched the air beat against the bulletproof glass of the second-story window. The remaining patches of frost there shuddered, and the machine of war he'd been very familiar with as a kid for the very first time in his life made an appearance, which caused him to go giddy. He'd always wanted to see one up close . . . but perhaps being the target it was locking on to wasn't all that great.

A heavily outfitted Apache helicopter settled into a hovering position just below the third floor, where the chain guns on either side of the absolute beast of a war machine lined up to face him on the second level. The helicopter blades whirred steadily, missiles were locked and loaded, and it had obviously been modified to fit into this new magical world with sleek yellow enchantments engraved onto its thick armor. Instead of the runic symbols of the Unholy pillar he was used to, these ones were . . . blockier. Less archaic and more futuristic, and he had some ideas—especially considering they were plastered on the side of a war machine—as to which pillar these enchantments came from.

"Now that's fucking sick."

Riven had assumed that because he was standing next to Senator James that the Apache wouldn't fire. He was only a few feet away from the man, after all, and he was supposed to be the guy in charge of Chicago—was he not?

But Riven assumed wrong.

The bulletproof glass shattered when bullets shining a brilliant yellow sprayed out of the machine guns on either side. Riven's eyes widened only for a brief half second before a wall of thick red ice ripped out of the floor in front of him to block incoming projectiles. But Riven hadn't been the initial target—and that was more than enough time for Senator James to be plastered against the wall in a spray of blood and viscera. Meanwhile, the wall of ice was chewed away in seconds as the helicopter unloaded hundreds of those glowing yellow bullets into the room.

He heard Fay scream out in pain when her left leg blew off, and he heard Azmoth roar, but Riven had to move. With a thought, he tore a rift through space and vanished—reappearing outside in midair behind the helicopter and swinging his staff in an arc. The fleshy tendril whipped out from fifty feet away, flashing crimson under the light of the sunset, and Vampire's Escort ripped through the helicopter with its blade like a cleaver's knife through soft meat.

The modified Apache helicopter exploded and shrapnel went everywhere, and Riven let himself fall thirty feet to the ground, landing near the crashing wreckage in a superhero pose, one arm slamming into the dirt. Whatever runes they'd inscribed into the Apache, they either hadn't been defensive ones or they'd simply been far too weak to withstand his attack.

He looked up to the devastated second floor and could still hear Fay screaming in agony from up above. He didn't even need to see just how bad it was to dismiss her to the nether realms for healing; the pentagram of Succubus wings on his sternum flashed as she portaled out.

The sound of grating metal caused him to look left at where three tanks, of all goddamn things, bulldozed over a fence at high speed and started to turn their cannons toward him. The shouts and approaching heartbeats of men beyond the corner of the building alerted him to even more enemies, and his eyes narrowed behind the porcelain mask.

"So we're playing hardball."

Azmoth crashed into the first tank from up above, crushing it in a spray of magma. The maul made contact with the machine of war, flattening most of the central cockpit and no doubt leaving all the occupants dead. Riven's body crackled with red lightning, and he sidestepped a projectile with a blur of speed, retaliating with a blast of Black Lightning from his staff that shredded the second tank.

The third tank was already backpedaling over the crushed fence, a machine gun on its side riddling Azmoth's armor with sparking bullets as they glanced off—only to blow the flaming demon backward into a spiraling fall with an antiarmor shell that left a large dent in one shoulder.

Riven was about to intervene, but bullets started plastering him from the side when an entire firing squad in American military uniforms unloaded on him from the prison's first floor. He'd only barely heard the heartbeats over the din of battle, and though his pauldrons, great maw, and face mask easily deflected the bullets, the rest of his clothes and red bloodskin layer were another story. The clothes were shredded in the first two seconds, and though the bloodskin did take many of the hits, it was unable to sustain more than a few shots to the same area. Holes began forming where bullets had punctured through, causing him a lot of pain and spiking his anger as he began to see his assailants as more of a real threat.

He cursed, encasing his body in Hell's Armor as flames blazed to life around him to eat up more of the incoming bullets, and he launched a volley of spinning crimson blades that ripped the soldiers apart. Heads, limbs, and innards splattered across the wall and ground, simmering blades embedding in the building and dirt, only to erupt again when another wave of soldiers tried rushing through the door spraying machine-gun fire.

The blades blew in a wave of shrapnel, annihilating the reinforcements and causing a small part of the building to groan and sag when the support structures beneath the top floors turned to dust.

"This is not how it's supposed to be." Riven angrily turned his head and dismissed his flames, glaring with frustration at the last remaining tank; Athela had ripped its hatch off and was clambering inside to the shouts and screams of the service members in it. "We're not supposed to be fighting one another."

In the distance and over the suburbs of Chicago, Riven saw five more Apache helicopters flying their way. They were small dots now, easy to pinpoint with the backdrop of the ocean at sunset but would no doubt be at the prison within minutes.

The sound of a bullet leaving his body to hit the dirt beneath his feet met his ears, and he looked down at the damaged armor and numerous oozing wounds. But his body had started pushing the bullets out as his wounds started to seal, and the red bloodskin layer of his armor was already starting to repair itself. Lifting a hand and curling his fingers, he summoned a flowing, ribbonlike wave of mana along his left arm and—without looking their way—fired at the two men preparing an RPG behind a shed.

The Blood Lance blew through their bodies in a flash of crimson, and he called out to his demons to get their attention while picking up a walkie-talkie from a corpse. He only paused briefly when the maw across his chest opened up, unleashing tendrils of black that pulled in the arm of the corpse and snapped down to eat it. "Azmoth! Athela! We need to leave!"

[You have gained one level. Congratulations! Be sure to visit your status page to apply points.]

Athela jumped off the tank she'd infiltrated, covered in blood, and Azmoth's two eel-like maws blew flames into a third-story window from which gunfire had been raining down on him. The horrified wails of the shooters died out, and the large demon snapped his dislocated upper left shoulder back into place before hefting the huge stone maul.

"Let's leave before we get more innocent people involved," Riven said sourly, staring into the sunset where the Apaches were fast approaching. "These people don't know what they're doing; they're just following orders, and I really don't like the idea of killing my own countrymen because some ass clown is telling them to attack."

"So what's the plan, then?" Athela asked curiously, stepping over a simmering piece of metal that had once been an attack helicopter. "Hide for now and try to ping the Chalgathi artifact to find the blasphemer?"

Riven hesitated at the question.

"I'll call you back later, Azmoth—you're too big. Sorry, bud." Riven dismissed the armored monstrosity and motioned for Athela to follow. Still crackling with red sparks due to his Blessing of the Crow, he and his minion shot over two more barbed-wire fences and a thick cement barricade before advancing onto a large road leading west. Civilians were staring wide-eyed at the commotion from beyond the barriers, and Riven turned right to avoid the crowds—setting his gaze on an abandoned-looking business district that seemed like a promising start.

They rushed through street after street, alley after alley, passing through multiple districts and neighborhoods and eventually coming to a run-down motel that had been ransacked and halfway burned to the ground. Breaking open one of the doors to a room that looked more promising than the others, Riven waited for Athela to go inside before shutting it behind them and drawing the curtains. Barricading the door with a desk that would at least give him a heads-up in case some stupid kids or local refugees tried to break in, he let out a groan and walked over to the bed.

Letting his body fall, he landed on the soft cushions with a bounce.

"You didn't answer my question," Athela stated with an amused smile, hopping onto the bed and poking him in the side while the red peacock-feather eyes shifted her way. "Are we just going to hide for a while? And have you tried pinging the Chalgathi artifact to find the blasphemer yet? The faster we do this job, the faster we can get back home."

Riven grunted, facedown, then nodded into a pillow. He pulled out his communication stone, the black orb that Allie had given him, only to put it back in his spatial bag again. "It's too far for this to work. The ping-Chalgathi-artifacts ability lights people up, but they're all quite a ways away from here. My guess is the cursed object that was once a Chalgathi artifact isn't being picked up by the ability because the system no longer registers it as a world quest item."

Athela frowned, sighed, then lay back beside him with her hands behind her head. Scooting over and pushing her side up against his, she closed her eyes and let out a content huff. "Well, it could be worse. Hey, do you mind taking that armor off? It's creeping me out."

"You're a demon—you shouldn't get creeped out by things like this."

"Well, I want to see you naked. We're in a dirty old motel room, after all."

Riven cackled while turning his head to look at her, then pushed Athela aside when she started laughing, too. "Shut up, Athela, don't tease me like that. You know damn well that I can't take this off—I've already tried. You're doing that on purpose to mess with me."

Athela leaned onto her side with one arm holding her head up, smiling deviously and chuckling while wiggling her eyebrows in the dark. "Yeah, you're right. I'm bad, I know. Think the armor will come off when you get all five set pieces?"

"Probably, but that's just a guess."

"Well, we need to start that hunt as soon as possible after this blasphemer is killed. It's a priority, above all else. If we don't find him fast enough, we need to just abandon this quest altogether. Your life is more important than a silly side quest, and angering Chalgathi by not finishing it is an easy price to pay if these items are going to devour you if you don't get the other set pieces."

She laid a hand on one of his vampiric, horned-skull pauldrons, looking closely at the swirling vortices of blood mana in the eye sockets. "But you do look pretty damn cool. How are you going to feed like that?"

"I ate an arm earlier with the demonic mouth on my chest. It had blood in it, and I'm already satiated. It appears that this suit actually can and does settle my vampiric needs by consuming things . . . as creepy as that is."

General Florence took the stage in full, stacked black body armor, high-powered snipers and Machine foundational pillar engineers placed at various intervals around the media gathering there. There was even one small mech behind the stage just in case, outfitted with technology he'd only dreamed possible pre-integration, but the Mecha subpillar of the Machine foundational pillar offered a new route to glory and military dominance even above the other related subpillars. His aircraft were also being outfitted with upgrades day by day, and it'd only be a few months before his military was up to the task of conquering other nearby cities not already under his control.

Nevertheless, he was very aware that the monster was still out there in the city and could strike at any time; he was taking no chances after it had torn through three tanks, an already modified Apache, a locked-down prison, and two squads of his men.

His dark-gray hair was neatly gelled back in the crew-cut style many of his men had, and his strong jawline was clenched rigidly as he took the stage, flanked by armed soldiers wearing sunglasses. Only his face and head weren't covered, the rest of his body garbed in thin plates with white, orange, and yellow markings emblazoned on their surfaces, the best quality his engineers could create. Engineers were the equivalent of mages for those under the influence of the Machine foundational pillar, with classes given to those who utilized this pillar.

They had different but still somewhat similar abilities to the magical casters he'd heard reports about in other civilizations across the coast.

He tapped the microphone to make sure it worked, squinting slightly and motioning for the overhead lights to be dimmed so he wasn't blinded while addressing the reporters who sat or stood in the aisles of the college auditorium he'd commandeered.

"General Florence! Is it true that the vampire in question killed Senator James in cold blood?! After breaking out of a prison that has been holding some of our most dangerous criminals?! How did this happen?!"

Other questions echoed the first reporter's own, and the general briefly muted the microphone while touching a coms unit placed in his ear. "Are the cortex channels active?"

His intelligence officer on the other line buzzed back. "Affirmative. All news channels are active and live-streaming across the Panu cortex forums related to Chicago, Rockford, and Milwaukee. You're on air."

General Florence didn't bother nodding, just flipped the microphone switch back on while clearing his throat to silence the blubbering idiots in front of him. The reporters representing the new-world news networks quickly went silent, and he gave a long, stern look out to the crowd. "It is my solemn duty to report to all the fine people still residing in the cities of Chicago, Rockford, and Milwaukee that our beloved Senator James has been killed. Assassinated by a monster, a warlock, a vampire. We've uploaded surveillance footage of the unjustified attack to Panu's cortex as proof, showing him blatantly killing the brave men and women of our armed forces who so selflessly sacrificed themselves in an attempt to save the man leading us into the new world."

Gasps and solemn mutterings echoed throughout the auditorium, but General Florence held up a hand with a grim expression to make sure no one interrupted him. "We did not provoke him or start this conflict, but our forces will certainly end it. Our military might is greater than it ever was pre-integration, with new technologies being unlocked by the day. The sacrifices of our people will not be in vain, and we will bury this vampire by the end of the week—mark my words. Even now we have classers such as mana hackers, system engineers, and even our elite cyborg hunting him down to bring him to justice."

"Will Lieutenant Cliff be enough if the vampire was able to break out of a maximum security prison so easily?" one of the reporters, a pretty middle-aged Asian woman in a business suit called out, holding up a microphone.

General Florence nodded confidently, the stern look never leaving his gaze. "I have absolute confidence in Lieutenant Cliff's capabilities. He is on the cutting edge of the merging between machine and man, and he is already a level-39 S-tier ranker. He will be more than enough to bring this vampire down, especially with the support our other classers are providing him."

Smiles and impressed raises of the eyebrows met the general's proclamation, and there was even a small amount of clapping from the crowd before General Florence raised his hands to settle them down one final time. "However, due to current circumstances and a gap in the chain of command, it is my solemn duty and responsibility to all of you that I take up the mantle of leading our newfound country. I have already spoken to the mayors of Milwaukee and Rockford, and they agree that it is in our best interest that I—for at least the time being—enter into a full leadership role with complete authority being invested in me. Until this threat is dealt with, and until we can set up a working system that better provides for all the needs of safety, food, shelter, and the other basic functions of society, I will do my best to protect you all. Pray for us. Pray for our children so that they may grow strong, pray for our prosperity so that we may find a path to greater heights, and pray for our military men and women so that they return safely to their loved ones every night. May God watch over our souls, and may the sun shine brightly on our fledgling civilization."

CHAPTER 28

Riven, on the bed, yawned, still unable to take off his mask or Gluttony-modified Chalgathi items, much to his irritation, while replaying the recorded scenes over and over again. "What a two-timing, cocksucking motherfucker."

Azmoth grunted his acknowledgment from across the small hotel room; he barely fit even while hunched, and the sound of giggling in the shower nearby caused Riven's eye to twitch. Somehow the water was still running here, and Riven was really fucking pissed that he wasn't able to enjoy a hot shower right about now because he was stuck in this evil contraption encasing his body.

He glanced over to where Fay peeked out, long white hair dripping wet, to wink his way while wringing water onto the floor. "Stop getting so worked up about some human spreading lies. They're rather good at that kind of thing, and you're an easy target. How about you relieve some of that pent-up stress and come join me, hmm?"

The sky-blue woman stepped out of the bathroom, spreading out her wings, raising her chin, and crossing one leg in front of the other—putting her bare body on full display for the first time since Riven had contracted her. Riven had done a pretty good job at ignoring her teasing up until now, but he nearly died of a nosebleed and coughed back a quick retort. Despite all the previous banter, she really was incredibly pretty.

Azmoth's head turned, a growl echoing through the room as the Hellscape Brutalisk pointed two clawed left hands at the dripping-wet Succubus with intent. "I will catapult evil Succubus out window if tempt Riven. Riven not simp. I smash Succubus if try!"

"Oh, come on!" Fay said with a brilliantly white smile, bouncing on her tiptoes while smirking Riven's way while she—for the first time ever—had Riven's undivided attention due to the shock-and-awe tactic she'd just pulled. "Don't be such a buzzkill, Azmoth. It's not like he can even take the suit off anyways—I'm just teasing!"

Azmoth thought about it for a moment, cocked his head, and settled back down with a nod. "That true."

"What a walking, talking chastity belt . . ." Fay rolled her eyes, checking for Athela and seeing she still wasn't back—only to put on a seductive grin and waltz over to Riven on the bed. Casually swinging her bare legs over the motionless vampiric warlock who continued to stare with his hands behind his head and notification screens buzzing in front of him, she swiped a hand through the cortex prompts to dismiss them.

"Hmm . . ." Fay muttered with a chuckle, aggressively pinning Riven's left hand when he reached up to push her off. Her smile grew, and she pushed her face closer to his and flexed her toned abdomen while clenching his hand in excitement. "I'd been under the impression that you may not like girls . . . but I see now that isn't the case . . ."

Hand trailing down to where she was straddling him, she came to a stop just below his stomach to a growing bulge. Her smile faded, her eyes softened, and she took on a serious look, retracting her hand. "Thank you, from the bottom of my heart, for getting my brother out of there. It means a lot to me, what you did—most warlocks wouldn't even consider it unless it benefited them. When we get back to Brightsville, I'd really like you to meet him . . . So again, thank you."

Riven, who still wore the porcelain mask that hid the complex series of emotions crossing his features, was suddenly very thankful for the item. "You're welcome, Fay. Though I have to admit, you're a bit mean, doing this to me."

Fay's smile returned, and the Succubus let out a singsong laugh, caressing his chin with one hand before sliding off and lying down in the crook of his arm with folded wings. "It's rather fun, knowing you can't do anything about it. However, I don't believe you even would if you could. Would you, Mr. Chastity? You're too righteous to use your demons like that, aren't you, Mr. High School Hero? God forbid you take a willing servant because of that power dynamic you keep talking about!"

Her narrowed black eyes looked up teasingly as she pushed her soft chest into his side, and one hand settled on his rib cage to play with the carnivorous teeth that randomly shifted with occasional low hissing sounds.

He paused, thinking it over, and didn't reply for almost twenty seconds. "I don't really know anymore. Maybe I would do it."

Fay's eyebrows lifted in surprise, and genuine shock was evident underneath her small black horns when her mouth started to drop.

The door swung open, and Athela, in her spider form, barged in from the night with a cackling laugh. She wiggled her two front arachnid feet in front of her, bags of groceries in either foot, and screeched out her victory. "I AM THE ONE! THE BRINGER OF ALCOHOL, THE TYRANT OF THE CHICAGO GROCERY STORES, THE STOMPER OF BABIES! I—"

She quickly shut up when she saw Fay lying there on the bed next to Riven, and she dropped the grocery bags with a thud. "You're in MY SPOT, BITCH!"

With a screeching lunge, she transformed into her humanoid Arshakai form in midair and landed on top of Fay before roughly—albeit playfully—flinging her off the bed. "BEGONE!"

Fay crashed against the wall and scowled, rubbing the back of her head with visible irritation and extended fangs that she rarely put on display. Her shoulders heaved in scarcely seen rage, and her right eyebrow twitched. "You can have the OTHER side, Athela. I was there FIRST!"

The Succubus launched herself back, putting all her meager strength into a slap that cracked across Athela's cheek, pulling a surprised yelp from the arachnid woman. "Don't be such a JERK!"

The slap was so loud it caused a brief moment of silence, Fay breathing heavily and glaring at Athela with almost murderous intent—to the surprise of the other three.

Athela was stunned, realizing how obviously pissed Fay was—and not in a funny or teasing way, either. Athela's own face dropped seconds later, and she met her friend's gaze with a stern coldness while rising up off the bed to square off with the other woman. "Oh? Does the pretty little Succubus want to play dirty? Are you mad because of my interference with your little schoolgirl crush? Maybe you should rethink your place in all this—I'd be happy to give you a tiny reminder about the hierarchy here."

Athela's claws extended in a threatening flash, and her six bladed arachnid limbs ripped out of her back, only for Fay to hiss with Unholy curses rippling across her hands. The Succubus extended her wings in challenge, and Azmoth looked on with startled curiosity—starting to step over and pull them apart before any serious damage was done.

But Riven intervened first with a contractual command.

"Stop it immediately. Both of you."

Both women turned their heads to stare at Riven, who was swinging his feet around and getting off the bed.

He cracked his neck, stretched, and pointed to a corner of the room devoid of anything but a small wastebasket. "Athela, you're in spider-princess time-out."

"WHAT?!" Athela gasped, utterly appalled—and obviously irritated that he seemed to be taking Fay's side. "You can't be serious, AND SPIDER-PRINCESS TIME-OUT IS NOT A THING!"

"It is tonight, and you'll sit in that corner until I say so while you figure out how to be nicer to Fay," Riven stated flatly, then turned to the beaming Succubus, who looked like she'd just won a lottery jackpot. He pointed to the bathroom, where the shower was still running. "And you, you're in time-out as well. Sit in that room and think about how much you overreacted to Athela's shenanigans until I come get you."

Fay's beaming smile dropped like a cinder block, and the Succubus's bare shoulders immediately slumped. "But she—!"

"Not a word." Riven cut her off with a wave of his hand, looking back and forth between the two demonic women with an eventual shake of his head, not wanting to show any favoritism. "Azmoth is the only one here not behaving like a child, so he and I are going to go enjoy all this alcohol Athela stole by ourselves for the next little while until I feel like you've both had sufficient time to grow up. Got it?"

Fay sputtered something unintelligible, then glared angrily over at Athela, who was making a face at the Succubus while sticking out her black tongue.

"You just earned yourself another hour after Fay gets out," Riven stated, pointing a finger at Athela, only for the Arshakai demoness to scowl fiercely and harrumph with folded arms. "Meanwhile, I'll continue to monitor the cortex forums for any sign of the impending attacks. I'm sure they'll happen sooner or later, but that may be hours, days, or even weeks out. Who knows. If you both want to be useful while in time-out, you can do the same. Come on, Azmoth. Let's go to the roof. The stars tonight look rather nice."

Riven sat beside his large, armored minion while running over all the numerous topics in the cortex forums. There were hundreds of forums for Chicago, most of them talking about recent events concerning him—and many others talking about forming groups to go monster hunting to cull the local threats. There were topics on bartering, trading, crafting using the new system-related pillars, and theories of how different pillars worked, and it very quickly became apparent that there was a strong orientation toward the Machine pillar all across the city here. There were certainly mixes between the other pillars, too, though, with discussion groups on literally every single pillar available—including his own Unholy foundational pillar, but that was by far the smallest group of people here when compared to the others.

- **The Unholy Foundation Pillar, with the major subpillars of Blood, Shadow, Death, Infernal, Depravity, and Chaos.**
- **The Holy Foundation Pillar, with the major subpillars of Light, Heaven, Grace, Moon, Sun, and Judgment.**
- **The Fae Foundation Pillar, with the major subpillars of Volcano, Storm, Ocean, Glacial, Swamp, and Forest.**
- **The Archaic Foundation Pillar, with the major subpillars of Arcane, Void, Metal, Illusion, Alteration, and Time.**

- **The Harmony Foundation Pillar, with the major subpillars of Body, Mind, Primal, Chi, Karma, and Zodiac.**
- **The Machine Foundation Pillar, with the major subpillars of Hacking, Armaments, Integration, Mecha, Interweb, and Sci-Tech.**

Literally every single pillar and all their subpillars were represented in the forums, though. There were groups of civilians who hadn't picked classes yet trying to figure out how to best approach their choices and routes to acquiring different classes, as well as groups talking about ways to expand pillar orientations to better fit the molds they wanted to buy in to. There were groups of varying classes here, too, with experimental builds already being copied or expanded upon by up-and-coming people who were showing incredible enthusiasm for the magic and mystery these system classes held potential for. There were discussion groups on whether or not physical-, magical-, or miracle-based classes were best, including specialist subforums for groups of individuals with the same classes, and he even found a group for warlocks, which piqued his interest immensely. However, all the warlocks here were far below his own level, and not one had been granted more than their very first demon due to a lack of demons wanting to bind with them—which was kind of hilarious to Riven and made him feel good about himself. Some of the warlocks here were even having trouble binding a *single* minion.

Regardless, most of the classers here were oriented to the Machine foundational pillar, which was what the Earth-made military had apparently adopted for its main branch. There'd been an army reserve base here, as well as an air force base, and there were talks about engineers—which were essentially the equivalent of mages, but for the Machine foundational pillar and all its subpillars—modifying fighter jets. It was quite fascinating to read about, and Riven had often found himself over the past two days getting lost in magical theories that made his own will to explore magic come to light.

He'd always thought magic was pretty neat—who wouldn't? But it'd also been a tool for him to survive. Here, these discussion groups had reignited a spark of wonder about what the future held for him. Magic was . . . fascinating, intriguing, awe-inspiring, and he found himself getting almost giddy while talking under an alias to other online theorists about how the pillars worked. He often was the one giving them insights because he was a lot more advanced than any of the others, but with dozens of other people picking his brain, it was rather stimulating for the mind.

"Man . . . This would have been a much nicer place to start out," Riven muttered, pulling a wine bottle from one of the bags Athela had brought. The teeth of the great maw on his chest casually popped the cork off, and little slithering wisps of darkness encircled the handle before bringing it up to his lips and starting to drink.

Riven watched under the starry sky, sitting there on the rooftop overlooking the city, rather amused that the gluttonous amulet was so careful to not spill any of the alcohol at all. It also reacted to his own thoughts, allowing him to almost communicate silently with the Chalgathi artifacts in a way he hadn't experienced before other than with his staff.

Feeling a very slight buzz come on, he set the bottle to the side and glanced over at Azmoth, who was playing with a Rubik's Cube barely big enough to survive the demon's large claws. "Not feeling it?"

"Alcohol not work on Azmoth—just taste gross," Azmoth stated with a shrug, noting how Riven was motioning toward one of the vodka bottles that'd been drained. "Disgusting."

Riven spluttered a laugh, resting on his elbows and kicking his feet out. "Well, I suppose it isn't for everyone."

"Did you try again?"

"Try what?"

"Upload images to forum."

The vampire sighed, then pulled up his notifications again. "Yeah, but maybe I'm missing something. Let me try again."

[Welcome to the Panu Cortex!

Here you will find forum categories and branching categories; you can scroll through subjects, post your own topics, acquire or share video feeds, create enemies or alliances, and even bargain for goods like a marketplace. Be warned that each has strict sets of rules, and you will receive a notification if your content is prohibited. Most prohibited material involves key events in the world of Panu or even in your local area, secrets of Panu that the Elysium administrator wishes to be found rather than publicly exploited, information released too early regarding worlds outside Panu, and spam content. Video feeds can only be uploaded by request. You must ask the administrator directly to upload content, and your request may or may not be recognized. Sometimes the administrator may also post video content even without an express request. In order to request video uploading, just mentally think of the time and place you want to upload and wait for a response.

Please note that restrained or imprisoned personnel may not access the forums of Panu's cortex. Forums extend only to places you have visited and guilds you have joined, with the exceptions

of the main page discussion board and the World Quest message boards—both of which are world-spanning and more heavily moderated. No forums outside key areas visited and guilds can exist other than Global Forums.

Feel free to select from one of the already categorized subjects, or you may use the search function for more in-depth selections of guild forums. Your options are as follows:
- **Main Page and Announcements (Global)**
- **Power Ladders, Guild and Individual (Global)**
- **World Quests and World Quest Ladders (Global)**
- **Brightsville**
- **Deepnest**
- **Chicago**

NOTE: Continental differences on Panu have been detected in optional selections. To acquire access to continent-wide forums or map-sharing specs, please visit more locations on the continents where you have traveled.]

Riven frowned, already knowing this probably wouldn't work due to earlier failures, but hey—maybe persistence was key.

[You have failed to post in Brightsville's forums. You may view these forums but are too far away to add any content yourself.]

[You have failed to post in Deepnest's forums. You may view these forums but are too far away to add any content yourself.]

Riven grimaced harder when he saw topics on Allie's war, the integration of more elvish slaves, the acquisition of a new elvish town, talks on the purging of the prison back in Brightsville with public beheadings of the inmates there, and large rewards for any information on Riven's location. A public notice had been set up with details of how he'd disappeared, with massive sums of Elysium coins offered as a reward for clues that led to his finding.

Allie must be pretty worried because he hadn't used the guild hall's teleport-home option after being swept away. He wanted to reach out and let her know he was okay, but that wasn't really possible. He had to wonder just what she thought and if she'd banished the Blood Moon Requiem from their planet after this second mishap on their turf. No doubt she had serious suspicions about them, but at the same time, that could also mean she would keep them around to try and peel whatever information she could from the people who'd been there when his Chalgathi artifacts had mutated.

He went back to Chicago's forums next and again tried to upload footage from his own memories. He concentrated hard on recent events, trying to display the thoughts and images flashing through his mind, only to scowl in irritation at the next pop-up concerning his attempt.

[Your request for uploading video content has been denied. Reasons for denial: Lack of control over this area. Conflict of interest with parties holding control of this area. Lack of defined footage.

For higher success rates concerning uploading video content, please review the following: Gain control over this area. Destroy conflicting interests holding sway over this area. Ask the administrator directly for preapproval of an event or approval to record an event prior to event happening, providing defined footage and less strain on the administrator's systems.]

Riven's glare circled back to one of the forum topics, where news networks were blasting him as the villain who'd killed Senator James. Knocking his knuckles against the side of his porcelain mask and adjusting his hood, he continued to stare toward the downtown area, where city lights illuminated the tall, steel buildings across the backdrop of the ocean and night sky.

"This is bullshit."

CHAPTER 29

Athela chugged a beer in one quick go, gasping for breath and wiping her mouth with a wide smile and a loud belch. "Why so grumpy, my guy?! We're having fun! Be happy!"

"It won't allow me to upload footage of the senator's death to prove myself innocent," Riven stated grimly, popping another bottle of wine to feed to the vertical maw across his chest. "It's beyond irritating that I was framed for this."

Athela shrugged, kicked out her long, slender legs, and popped another beer can with a fizzling sound. "You should be thinking of the cortex as more of a propaganda machine than anything else. The forums are controlled by those who govern the given area, with contested territories requiring a large fee to upload footage—or they may even deny it outright. If you want to upload footage, it usually can't be antagonistic to the dominant party in a sector. That's how it's always been."

Farther out to sea, the shimmering lights of the starry sky above reflected—giving an image of calm before the storm that was no doubt to come. Fay flew far overhead and farther to the south, her figure only barely visible from here even with Riven's keen dark-sight.

"Are you and Fay all right?" Riven eventually asked, lying back to stare up at the cloudless heavens and crossing his legs. "I haven't ever seen you two go at it like that before."

There was a pause, and Riven's gaze shifted over to where Athela had stopped with a beer can halfway to her lips.

She met his gaze, frowned, and let out a sigh. "Yeah. It's fine."

Athela's right hand extended above her, and her flesh began to shift. Slowly but surely, the tiara Riven had given her not long ago started to come out of her hand like she was giving birth to it.

[Tiara of Silent Killing (Blood/Shadow Trinket): After successfully killing a target without being noticed by anyone else, gain

**a charge of critical strike. Your next unseen attack has a 100%
chance to be a 2x-8x critical hit, with multiplied damage coming
in the form of kinetic burst energy from the strike site. Requires
a 26% or higher Blood or Shadow pillar affinity to wield, and the
wearer must be female.]**

"That's a neat trick," Riven mused, watching Athela put the black tiara with inlaid rubies on her head, a bright smile adorning her features. "Is that a new ability?"

"No!" she replied softly, tapping the tip of her tiara with her fingers daintily. "I'm just progressing my shape-shifting abilities and found out I can store small items like this. Not in dimensional storage like that bag you have, but rather, I can physically keep it on my body if it's small enough."

"Gotcha. I've seen Fay wear her feathered boots and Azmoth keeps that large maul on him all the time, but I rarely see you wear the tiara. I'd thought you just didn't like it."

Athela gave him a surprised look, then let out a laugh. "Riven! I love it . . . I keep it hidden away because I don't want to accidentally lose or damage it."

"But isn't it supposed to be used?" Riven frowned in confusion. "It has great stats."

Athela pondered this, then nodded. "Yes . . . but I'd rather not wear it during fights in case it falls off when I'm hit hard or something causes it to fall off! Just let me do my thing, okay?!"

"Doesn't that defeat the purpose of having it, though?"

Athela smiled, then took the tiara off again and softly patted it. "No. It's a keepsake. It's the first gift you've ever given me, and I want to keep it safe."

A warm feeling started growing in Riven's gut, and he merely stared back and didn't reply. There was nothing that needed to be said, and the three figures on the rooftop continued to drink until morning, when Fay returned from her scouting trip.

But despite the feel-good energy Riven was experiencing now, this was merely the calm before the storm. And a very big storm it would be.

Lieutenant Bradley Cliff was a young man, aged twenty-four, who'd grown up in a military family that expected nothing less than excellence. He'd attended one of the best military academies in the United States, had become an F-35 fighter jet pilot, and was well on his way to making his father proud when the integration hit. Before he knew what'd hit him, Bradley found himself dogfighting wyverns in the sky over Chicago's airspace as they breathed fireballs his way.

Killing a few of the monsters using the tech he had was the key to unlocking the cyborg class when he eventually hit the tutorial. That, and the fact that he'd had a microchip implanted in his right arm as part of an experimental trial for some of the military's more advanced communications systems back on Earth. It'd ticked off the boxes he'd needed, and the Machine foundational pillar—along with the Integration subpillar—had unlocked.

The Integration subpillar, funnily enough, had nothing to do with the actual integration of the planet. Rather, it had everything to do with integrating machinery or mechanical parts into one's body. His first skill had changed his right arm into a part flesh, part mechanical energy weapon, and he'd found it in a tutorial seemingly made just for him. Then he'd upgraded his body with bionic limbs and a titanium skeleton, and he'd acquired a new skill that gave his physical attacks kinetic energy blasts. He'd acquired a built-in engine-fueled plasma shield that could encompass an entire side of his body with a half orb of light-orange energy at will, and his body's nanobots repaired damage far faster than normal humans could heal.

All in all, he'd gone down a route far different than normal people. Most of the classers had focused on acquiring new skills, with many of the classes either just supplying new skills at random or giving them a choice between skills and traits. When given the option, most people chose the martial arts, miracles, or spells that the system supplied rather than the traits—but he was different.

He had nine traits, all focused on making him an unkillable half-machine beast.

Which was why he wasn't at all afraid while hunting down the monster that'd killed Senator James. Carving a path through the dark tunnels in the hillside, mowing down the creatures that lived there to find the vampire and exact vengeance was so far proving rather easy. The vampire's minions were relatively weak compared to him, and he just made sure to keep ahead of the strike team at his back by a good distance so they were put in the least amount of danger at any given time. He could only hope the other strike teams were also faring this well, but he couldn't be everywhere at once.

CRUNCH

Bradley's half-titanium fist smashed through another of the wolf-size insectoids, splattering its green guts across the hive tunnel floor before he pulled his arm out of the large creature and threw the corpse aside. Then it shifted back from a hand into the energy-cannon version of his limb, glowing as it charged up another round of ammunition. The tunnel behind him occasionally sounded out or lit up with automatic rifle fire and targeting lasers sweeping from side to side, and Bradley continued on through the maze of passages while firing off pulses of energy from his right hand whenever he saw movement.

Bradley touched his ear, opening up communications with the home base, where General Florence, his most trusted officers, three of their best hackers, and their most skilled mapper were organizing the assault on the hive of mantis-like creatures at a safe distance. "Still no sign of the vampire, just more bugs. Are you sure this is the place?"

The patchy coms unit rang with static for a moment before the voice of General Florence cut in. "We're certain. Our hackers tracked him here through the unique items he was wearing; we got a brief signature read on them for analysis before the vampire broke loose and took them back. A very similar signature is coming from this hillside. We've also received reports that people have been disappearing from this area for a while, and after interrogating that other vampire we found a few weeks ago, it makes sense that he'd set up here. It's a perfect location to attack from—on the border of the city, where he can pick off prey to feed on easily. Just focus on your job, get it done, and I'll be sure to make it known just how much of a hero you are, Lieutenant Cliff. Your country needs you. Do not fail us here."

Lieutenant Bradley Cliff nodded to himself, stepping around a corner into the darkness of a large, cavernous room that he couldn't see the end of. His right arm's energy cannon pulsed with neon-orange light to illuminate farther ahead, and upon feeling a sudden drop in the temperature, his plasma shield bloomed, encasing him with a half orb of energy.

He scanned the area, still not seeing anything, but hearing the shifting sounds of something farther back in the cave. He opened up coms again. "I just don't see how or why a vampire would be able to control so many of these creatures. They aren't registered as demons, and from what we know of the warlocks in our own city, he shouldn't be able to control more than a handful of creatures right now. It doesn't make any sense."

Static again.

"You have your orders, Lieutenant. Let us know when you've found him."

General Florence ended the coms, leaving Bradley frowning and alone at the head of his strike team while the lasers and flashlights of dozens of guns spread out across the room. Despite being a good soldier who followed orders to a T, Bradley couldn't help but be a little irritated that the general was so dismissive of the oddities here.

Something just didn't feel right about all this.

"Lieutenant?" one of the strike squad members asked to Bradley's left, a flashlight attached to the front of his weapon pointing into the dark of the cave. "Are you okay?"

Bradley glanced over, nodded, and was about to reply when he stopped midsentence and peered harder into the gloom. Holding up a hand, he motioned for the rest of the strike squad to remain where they were—and he slowly walked forward with his energy cannon charged to max.

The translucent orange plasma shield in front of him caused the air to shimmer as he moved. His footsteps echoed throughout the cave, only interrupted by the distant sounds of gunfire or explosions in other areas of this strange hive. Ever more cautiously, he approached the side of the cavern wall, dismissed his shield, and reached out a hand to where a slimy gray substance was plastered to the stone.

The fingers of his left hand touched the substance, and he pulled his hand back to examine the semisticky goo that dripped off and splattered against the floor. Looking back up, he reached out again and pressed more forcefully—noting how soft the substance was. It felt like a biological thing, a membrane, and this was further confirmed when the metal tips of his fingers punctured the membrane to reveal white skin underneath.

He gripped the camouflage membrane, tearing at it, letting gallons of fluid spill out and wash over the stone floor. With the fluid came the body of a deathly white woman—only barely alive. She hit the floor hard and remained there, motionless, somehow still breathing despite the strange fluid leaking out of her mouth. Her bloodshot eyes stared ahead without registering his presence; she was completely naked and had swollen green egg sacks growing out along her body—each ranging in size between a quarter and a bowling ball.

There were dozens of them, and inside the larger eggs Bradley could see the insectoid embryos of the armored, mantis-like creatures he'd been fighting through the tunnels. Then, looking around, he realized that there were dozens upon dozens of these camouflaged sacks lining the wall. "Holy shit . . ."

One of the men who'd been closer to the scene pulled off his mask and vomited, while another shied away—not wanting to look upon the grotesque figure in front of them that'd once been a pretty woman.

A clicking sound echoed off the stone walls, and shadows in Bradley's periphery moved in a blur. He whirled around, not finding the source of the motion—but then heard the sound of guns and bodies hitting the floor behind him.

"Level 39. An S-rank classer . . . A cyborg. How cute."

Bradley turned around, eyes narrowed, as the light of the flashlights on the ground illuminated the decapitated bodies of his entire squad. Blood was oozing from their wounds, and a sensation of cold dread overcame him when he stared back into the peripheral shadows, where four eyes were gleaming a sickly yellow.

A huge frame, larger than a truck, stepped forward on large, sharp, chitinous legs—snapping spines and crunching stone in stark contrast to the silence the creature had moved with only moments before when it had assassinated his people. Rows of sharp teeth smiled devilishly back at him, and Bradley started to sweat when he took a step back.

"You have entered my home uninvited. I do not know how you found my lair, but I thoroughly welcome this." The figure in the dark snickered, and from all along the ceiling and walls, dozens, then hundreds of armored, gray insectoid bodies with yellow eyes started peeling off the stone to glare at Bradley. "Without aerial support, and trapped deep underground, you will be far easier to pin down—Lieutenant Cliff. Hero of Chicago's sheep. I had been planning various ways of luring you into an enclosed space so that I might more easily kill you before ransacking the city. Being a ranged artillery specialist with your primary weapon an energy cannon, it surprises me that you'd walk into a battlefield that so obviously suits you so poorly. Despite your rumored traits that amplify your defensive capabilities. But I digress . . . you've made my job all that much easier by waltzing down here of your own accord."

More and more of the creatures began to move, encircling Bradley's position with blades flashing. Things Bradley had thought to be stone boulders were actually in fact creatures, far larger and many sporting abnormal evolutions beyond what he'd witnessed in the weaker of their brethren up until now. His eyes were wide, his heart beat furiously, and the energy cannon on his arm that'd brought him victory through so many battles up until now suddenly seemed very inadequate.

There were too many.

How had he not picked up on these creatures before?

Static reached Bradley's ears. "Lieutenant, we've just lost contact with five of the seven other strike teams. They are unresponsive, and . . . Hold. It was just reported that one of the other strike teams encountered an ambush and is in full retreat. Give us a status report—are you able to pull back and assist? We have reinforcements gearing up to head in, and we'd like you to rendezvous with Captain Marshal at the nest entrance."

The cavern shook, when the largest of the creatures, the one that had been talking to him, flashed forward and slammed into Bradley's side, shattering the plasma shield and sending the usually sturdy cyborg crashing into the stone wall with a sonic boom. Bradley's cannon discharged everything he had in an orange beam of plasma, ripping through dozens of enemies simultaneously as a swarm of hungry predators tore in from all sides—plunging him into darkness. Ripping, tearing sounds could be heard amid muffled screams as pieces of flesh and metal flew through the air.

An electrical discharge began to spark beneath the piling bodies. It surged, writhed, and built over long seconds of agonizing torture, while the man struggled with desperate swings to kill as many of the enemy as he could—but they kept on coming.

Until he let it loose.

Power erupted in a storm of lightning around Bradley, frying dozens and then hundreds of the large, scythe-bearing creatures in a torrent of energy that left the cyborg gasping for breath. His hands shook, his mana levels were at rock bottom, and desperation was beginning to etch itself into his soul. "I need to get out of here!"

"Lieutenant!" The coms unit in his ear rang again, the communication officers back at base much more urgent this time. "Command is under attack! I repeat, command is under attack! We have thousands of incoming hostiles—we are in need of your assistance!"

He pushed off corpse after corpse with rasping breaths, digging himself out of a mountain of fried bodies. He only hoped he'd killed all of them after expending all his resources to deal with the ambush, and ignored the further desperate requests for help over the coms until he found himself face-to-face with four gleaming yellow eyes while still half-buried in an army of enemies.

His face paled, and rows of gleaming teeth smiled back with sinister intent.

Then the deep, sinister voice echoed through the cave one more time. "Overconfidence is a flimsy shield, Lieutenant Cliff. A very flimsy shield indeed."

CHAPTER 30

"Here's the list," Fay said, handing over a booklet of names and dispelling the illusion she'd placed on herself. Her body shifted from that of an overweight, bearded guard in a police uniform to her usual self—and she smiled at Riven's nod of approval.

"Great job as usual," Riven stated, getting an eye roll from Athela when Fay clicked her feathered boots together, adjusted her crop top, and bashfully tossed her hair to the side. "Have you ever thought about becoming an assassin? Those illusions you cast are quite handy for infiltrating places. Perhaps you and Athela could team up and support one another, and when Athela gets her shape-shifting abilities under control, she'll be able to change forms as well. Right now she can only shift between her basic spider and humanoid forms, but eventually she should be able to change her features on a more refined level—even allowing her to change her face. You'd be quite the duo."

Athela raised an eyebrow, silently evaluating the Succubus, who hesitantly glanced her way.

"I don't think I have the qualifications to become an assassin . . . I'm more of a mage, and my curses don't kill very fast," Fay stated, frowning slightly and avoiding Athela's stare. "And they're technically hallucinations, not illusions, but if you want to call them illusions, that's fine. Hallucinations have a direct effect on a mind; illusions are not directed toward the mind but toward external sources. It really only matters when you get into how the curse works rather than the outcome. Usually, anyways."

Athela nodded. "If she picked up some high-powered strike magics, she'd be a mana assassin instead of the traditional kind like me. And she'd need to improve her hallucinations considerably if she would want to utilize them against higher-level enemies who have more Willpower and Perception."

Riven nodded, flipping through the charts listing the inmates down below. The prison whose roof they now stood on was a much smaller version of the highly guarded one he'd been put in, but it still had what he was looking for. "Thief, drug dealer, drug dealer, battery and assault, ah—here we go. Rape, home invasion, and double homicide. Checkmate."

Riven pointed to the name. "Where would this one be located?"

Fay, who'd memorized the layout, looked at the room number, then glanced around the prison grounds and pointed to a jail cell on the second story. "That one!"

Riven gave a thumbs-up, then tucked the booklet into his bag. "Thanks. I'll be back in a few minutes."

A rift opened up in space, and in a blip of shadow, he was gone. Instantly he found himself inside a prison cell, where a bald, shirtless, middle-aged white man was brushing his teeth and a bulkier Latino guy wearing a wifebeater tank top lay out on a bottom bunk.

They both startled when Riven flashed into their room, the bald guy yelping in surprise and the Latino man quickly taking out a shank and standing up— eyes wide and cursing under his breath. "What the fuck?!"

Riven took the book back out, planted his Unholy staff into the floor, and flipped open to the page he was looking for. His crimson feathers flared out to the sides of his hood, seven eyes peering out at the inmates, and the maw along his chest hissed with excitement. "I'm looking for a Timothy Ransen. I assume that's you, Baldy?" Riven snapped the book shut and pocketed it again, waiting expectantly.

"Who the fuck are you!?" the man replied, only for his bunkmate to step back against the bars.

"You don't know?" Riven asked curiously. "Footage of me has been all over the Chicago cortex."

The Latino man shook his head rapidly, shiv still clutched in his right hand. "Prisoners can't access the cortex—it's part of the system rules."

Ah.

Yes.

Riven had forgotten about that. Anyone considered captured or bound lost all access to forum functions.

"What's it to you if I am Timothy?" the bald, shirtless man asked hesitantly after glancing over at his cellmate. "Why the fuck is a mage coming to meet me, of all people, in this prison cell? Did Gramps pay you to bust me out or somethin'?"

Riven raised an eyebrow underneath his porcelain mask, and an amused chuckle echoed out from behind it. He shook his head. "No, nothing like that. I was just looking through the prison roster because I'm a vampire and I need someone to die for me. Someone who can be my next meal."

Riven spread his arms out to either side, and the maw along his chest opened wide—revealing rows of teeth leading into an abyssal, black hole. Both men screamed in absolute terror when cords of black tore out from the abyss, latching onto Timothy's neck, arms, ankles, and waist.

"WHAT THE ACTUAL FUCK!?!!???" Timothy screamed, starting to thrash and struggle as he was dragged across the floor, and the other man started frantically yelling for help while banging on the cell door. "WHAT THE FUCK! WAIT—WAIT—WAIT! PLEASE!!!"

The maw grew, becoming wider and wider while Riven's ribs cracked painlessly to adjust the size. Riven saw the fear, the sweat, the piss the man had just released onto his pants, and he could hear the thunderous heartbeat of the horrified human while Riven dragged him forward.

"PLEASE, NO!!!"

Riven's maw yanked an arm in first, snapping down and tearing off the forearm in a bloody spray of bone and muscle. Timothy howled, renewing his attempts to thrash free while hyperventilating and being eaten alive, only to lose more of the arm when the black cords yanked it in farther.

CHOMP

"AAAAAAHHHHH!!!!"

CRUNCH-SNAP-RIP

The man's screams immediately died to nothing when Timothy's head was torn off his body. Half of his upper body was now being devoured. The other inmate, who was still up against the bars as far as he could physically push himself, sobbed and shook while holding the shank as threateningly as he could. Shouts from outside began to reach Riven's ears, and he heard their heartbeats coming down the hallway at a quickening pace.

At the same time, he felt his body rejuvenate as the man's blood soaked into his vessels . . . and he sighed with a long, contented exhale. "That hits the spot."

[You are now well-fed.]

A thunderous echo rolled out across the night sky, and a shock wave brought Riven's attention upward. Looking out the window, eyes widening, he riftwalked back onto the roof where his two female demons stood—leaving the remains of his meal behind.

Fay and Athela both stared upward as well, watching in confusion as myriads of colors bloomed over them, rapidly encasing the entire city and landscape for miles out in an enormous dome of energy.

"The fuck is that?" Athela asked with furrowed brows.

Fay shrugged. "That's what I was about to ask you two . . . Any idea, Riven?"

"Not a clue."

[A CLASH OF FATE HAS BEEN FORCIBLY INITIATED.]

CRASH

The entire city shook, and a pillar of dusky gray light tore skyward from just beyond the city's perimeter. Immediately alarms went off all around the city, and searchlights positioned along the skyscrapers and military base farther in illuminated the air.

WARNING
WARNING
WARNING
A CLASH OF FATE HAS BEEN FORCIBLY INITIATED BY RICHARD LONGHOLLOW THROUGH THE ACTIVATION OF A CURSED SANCTUARY STONE. THE CITY OF CHICAGO HAS BEEN TARGETED AS THE PLACE FOR THIS SANCTUARY'S CREATION.
RICHARD LONGHOLLOW HAS SET TARGET ACQUISITION TO CHICAGO'S ENTIRE HUMAN POPULATION. ALL DECEASED SOULS WILL BE ABSORBED BY THE SANCTUARY STONE TO FEED ITS CREATION.
CHICAGO HAS BEEN SEALED OFF. THE BATTLE FOR CHICAGO IS ABOUT TO COMMENCE.
ATTACKERS: AZAG HIVE CLUSTER
DEFENDERS: THE POPULATION OF CHICAGO

Riven sneered in distaste, then glanced up at the dome above. Seconds later, a series of booms erupted from the place where the gray pillar of light was shooting up into the multicolored sky, and even from here, Riven could see a swarm of . . . something tearing down hillsides all across the western border. They came rushing toward the city like a tidal wave of gray, though their figures were hard to make out at this distance in true detail. Whatever these things were, they were met with hostility immediately. The humans opened up their heavy artillery and gunfire, meeting their charge from numerous points where military units had been stationed to fend off monster attacks.

"So he's finally made his move. Didn't think there'd be so many enemies, though."

Blinking in surprise, Riven's brows furrowed, and his attention shifted when another notification appeared. He read rapidly while his demons watched the battle unfold. Attack helicopters began to scramble from the military base farther east, no doubt to be followed by the fighter jets Riven had seen earlier that day, and lights all along the city started flickering to life where the suburbs had been kept in good enough condition to house the civilian population.

[A clash of fate has transpired in your vicinity. You do not meet the requirements of the sanctuary's targeting system; you have been given the option to leave the sealed city if you wish to do so. If you do not leave, you will be considered a hostile presence to the attackers AZAG HIVE CLUSTER and their leader, RICHARD LONGHOLLOW. Do you wish to stay? Yes or no?]

Riven selected "yes."
"Didn't come all this way just to run away now."

[A clash of fate has transpired in your vicinity. Elysium's administrator has designated this clash as a battle of supremacy. You have been added to the defenders' side: THE POPULATION OF CHICAGO.]

[AN OUTSIDE FORCE REPRESENTING THE THANE NECROPOLIS HAS VOLUNTEERED TO JOIN THE DEFENDING SIDE. THE BATTLE FOR CHICAGO HAS NOW COMMENCED. THE ELYSIUM ADMINISTRATOR HAS RULED THIS CLASH OF FATE TO BE A STRATEGIC BATTLE. RULES FOR SYSTEM-REGULATED STRATEGIC BATTLES ARE AS FOLLOWS: EACH TEAM'S PARTICIPANTS ARE MEASURED BY FATE IN TERMS OF INFLUENCE. THE TOP FIVE INFLUENTIAL PEOPLE HAVE BEEN DESIGNATED AS BATTLE TARGETS. IF ALL FIVE OF ONE SIDE'S BATTLE TARGETS ARE KILLED, THAT SIDE WILL BE PURGED BY THE SYSTEM INSTANTLY.

PROTECT YOUR BATTLE TARGETS AT ALL COSTS. ALL TARGETS WILL BE HIGHLIGHTED BY DOTS IN THE SKY— RED SYMBOLIZING THE ATTACKERS, BLUE SYMBOLIZING THE DEFENDERS.

Battle targets for ATTACKERS: AZAG HIVE CLUSTER
- Richard Longhollow—(Azag Overmind)
- Clidra Mutishbane—(Azag Broodmother)
- Scythewalker Trik Trak—(Azag Broodfather)
- Tiklik Longjaw—(Azag Broodfather)
- Everkill Gorgemonger—(Azag Bull Champion)

Battle Targets for DEFENDERS: THE POPULATION OF CHICAGO
- General Florence—(Leader of Chicago's Military Forces)
- Lieutenant Cliff—(Cyborg Champion)
- Lieutenant General Bruner—(Human Military Officer)

- **Governor Banks—(Human Civilian Authority)**
- **Riven Thane—(Pure-Blooded Vampire Prince, Allied Unit: The Thane Necropolis)]**

[You, Riven Thane, have been designated one of five battle targets on the defending side for the clash of fate ongoing in this region. Should you and the other four battle targets die, the side you represent will be purged by the system immediately. Good luck.]

[Richard Longhollow has been engaged in battle. Click to view.]
[Lieutenant Cliff has been engaged in battle. Click to view.]

"Oh, look! The system called me a prince. That's neat."

Both demonesses nearby got the follow-up notification about the battle commencing and how Riven was now a battle target. They turned slowly, staring wordlessly his way, when a pillar of blue light skyrocketed from all around his position, and he held up both hands to either side with an innocent shrug, bouncing his large horned pauldrons up and down as he did. "WHAT?! Don't look at me like that! We were potentially going to die here anyways if we decided to stay, and finding that asshole is what I came here to do!"

Four other pillars of blue light around the city illuminated the darkness. Two of them were already on the front lines, where the battle was raging, one of them was in the military base, and another was in the eastern suburbs on the opposite side of the city. Five red pillars, four of them in the oncoming swarm of gray bodies, shot skyward next. And a moment later, all ten pillars dissipated, leaving only blue and red dots that glowed brightly along the multicolored dome overhead to symbolize the positions of the battle targets.

Athela's eyelids drooped. "You *volunteered* for this? Don't you think it would have been smarter to just wait this battle out, and when Chicago fell you could have come and cleaned up afterward?"

"I was more . . . voluntold, rather than volunteered."

"How so?"

"Gotta kill this guy if I don't want to anger Chalgathi, and I can't just let all these people die. There's almost a million people living here—I don't have a choice."

"You have a choice if you stop giving a shit about these nobodies! And if someone is powerful enough to wipe out an entire city of that size, even more reason to hold off and strike after the battle."

Riven rolled his eyes, but the only indication was the way he rolled his head along with them for emphasis. "No more discussion. We have a battle to fight."

[General Florence has been engaged in battle. Click to view.]
[General Florence has been killed in battle by Azag Hive Cluster forces. Four of five battle targets for the defenders remain.]

A pop-up window showing the same man who'd framed Riven not long ago appeared in front of them next. It was a video feed, showing the man in a hybrid suit of mesh and metal with intricate engineering enchantments. He was being torn apart, eaten alive in a bloody display of carnage by large mantis-like bugs as he screamed and cursed. The men nearby, in some kind of base camp tent, were firing off whatever bullets, energy weapons, or explosives they could, shredding the oncoming swarm of armored, chitinous insectoids, but the monsters were far too many. Their thick hides, bladelike limbs, ripping pincers, and yellow eyes soon dominated the scene—burying the general underneath a wave that swept over him in seconds. The footage ended with two tanks and a large sci-fi–looking mech engaging the swarm—leading a counteroffensive push with guns blaring and insectoids blasting apart.

[Lieutenant Cliff has been killed in battle, slain by Richard Longhollow. Three of five battle targets for the defenders remain.]

Another pop-up window displayed next, showing a huge, dark figure in an underground cave impaling a wide-eyed cyborg outfitted in American military gear on a clawlike leg of sharp, spiked chitin. Blood and another plasma-like fluid leaked out of the man, but despite the kinetic blasts from every desperate punch he made, he was doing little damage to the leg that had impaled him through the chest.

The dark, shrouded figure grinned with piercing yellow eyes and with a blur slammed a large stinger through the cyborg's skull. Abruptly the man stilled, his brain matter plastered against the ground next to him.

Riven blinked as the window winked out. "Wasn't that guy supposed to be S-class, too?"

Fay pointed skyward, drawing Riven's attention to a red dot along the dome that was very quickly closing in on his own blue dot's position. "I think we have incoming."

CHAPTER 31

The red dot overhead was traveling in a straight line, and Riven didn't have a hard time finding it due to the size of the creature.

Six legs in the back, four bladed arms along the sides, two sets of yellow eyes, a long, wingless carapace of gray chitin armor, and long pincers were all set onto the body of a gigantic mantis that was rushing over the rooftops and roadways toward him at breakneck speed. Easily the size of a tank and likely just as bulletproof, it was closing in fast, the air shimmering around its body.

Riven's eyes narrowed, and the enemy activated a martial art that sent it tearing through the air with a thunderclap toward his location on the prison's roof.

"If he's going to send one of his lieutenants, I'll match it with some of my own. Don't want to give away all my tricks just yet now, do I?"

Calmly watching the bullet-like creature ripping through the air, Riven raised his hand. "Azmoth."

A portal of fire flared around him, and the titanic demon launched out of it to meet the Azag mantis. Riven saw the creature's yellow eyes go wide in alarm just before they met, and a pulse of fire and magma erupted when Azmoth's infernal maul crashed into the monster's skull.

[Riven Thane has been engaged in battle. Click to view.]
[Tiklik Longjaw has been engaged in battle. Click to view.]

The recoil was the equivalent of a baseball bat hitting a home run. One moment the large mantis was rocketing toward him, the next it was rocketing in the complete opposite direction, aflame, with a third of its face caved in.

Riven cackled loudly in amusement, watching the streaking, flaming, screeching creature bounce like a stone on water through roadways and ruined buildings. "Athela, Azmoth, kill it. Fay, you stay here."

Athela's black tongue whipped out of her mouth when she screeched with glee and blurred forward—jumping off the roof and tearing toward the injured monster, which was still writhing on the ground blocks away. Azmoth pursued them, landing with a boom after a two-story jump, then effortlessly bulldozed his way through the layers of barbed-wire fences while bursting into flames.

"You don't wish to kill it yourself?" Fay asked curiously, side-eying her master with a cocked eyebrow and folded wings.

"Nope. We have other targets to draw out."

Tessa clutched her two small daughters in the corner of her family home's basement. Her red hair was frazzled, her kids were crying, and the house was literally shaking from the battle being waged right outside their doors. Being woken up in the very early hours of the morning by her husband to the sound of blaring sirens, system notifications, gunfire, and unearthly screams from a monster swarm was not something she thought she'd ever experience—but here she was.

"We've barricaded the door down here with everything we have!" Derrick, her husband, said with a grimace, breathing heavily. He looked over his shoulder to where Tessa's stepfather was still inspecting the makeshift barricade—adjusting things here or there on the pile to feel useful in a situation where they were all rather useless.

Derrick grunted, then leaned against the stone wall of the basement and slid down to a sitting position next to his eldest daughter—wincing when the house shook again under the crash of a large body outside. His daughters were crying silently, and he patted both their heads with a loving smile—one that'd won over Tessa's heart when they were younger. "It'll be all right, girls. The military will save us."

Off in the other room, the rest of the family, including Tessa's mother-in-law and two sisters-in-law, were all huddled together around the cortex forums, which were rapidly uploading video feeds and information with live streams of the battle. System notifications had been coming and going as different battle targets were engaged or killed off, and two on their side had died only a few minutes after the battle started. Being caught in the crossfire was certainly a worry, but they may all be goners regardless of whether monsters found them if the military couldn't hold these attackers off. If that were to happen, Tessa could only hope the system's purge would be quick—because by the looks of things, it wasn't going well outside and she couldn't bear the thought of her children dying horrible, agonizing deaths.

They were such good little girls, and they deserved to live. They deserved to grow up and find husbands, bear children of their own, laugh and cry and enjoy all the little things that were important in life. But Tessa wasn't sure if they'd make it. Even after all they'd been through with the tutorial and frequent monster attacks up until now—they still might not make it.

Not with this army of carnivorous creatures tearing through the outer suburbs, killing and devouring anyone they came across.

"You should go watch with the others . . ." her husband said, smiling Tessa's way and gripping her hand. "I'll stay with the kids. You keep looking over at my mom and sisters—I know you're nervous and want to watch it. It'll make you feel better."

Tessa's pale face shifted his way, lips quivering into a smile of her own, putting on a brave face for little Elsie and Milly. "Yeah, I think that'd help a lot. Thanks, honey."

Kissing each of her daughters for a brief goodbye, she then bent over and gave Derrick a long, drawn-out, passionate kiss—one that they hadn't shared the likes of for a long, long time. "If we make it out of this alive . . ." she whispered, putting her forehead against his, "let's spend more time together. We let work get in the way of the important things—let's not make that mistake again. Okay?"

Derrick choked up, but nodded and pushed her away. "Go, watch. You can bring me updates from time to time. Hurry! Go!"

Cries of horror and outright denial abruptly erupted from around the corner, and Tessa startled, only to realize why her husband's family was so upset a split second later.

[Governor Banks has been killed in battle by Azag Hive Cluster forces. Two of five battle targets for the defenders remain.]

Derrick and Tessa shared a pale look, only for Tessa to dash around the corner and bring up the notification showing Governor Banks's demise.

It'd been an assassination. Although the governor had been on the opposite side of the city, he'd been run down in the street, an entire escort of military personnel being ravaged while trying to protect him and escort him to one of the towers downtown. The scene was bloody, gore-filled, and just outright horrible—and Tessa had to cover her mouth while watching the people there get eaten and slaughtered as they fought back to kill as many of the Azag hive cluster as they could. Even some of the braver civilians had come out of their homes with shotguns, pistols, submachine guns, or whatever else they could find—and the groups of adventurers, mercenaries, and makeshift guilds that'd formed in preparation for the coming guild system had also taken to the streets to help defend their homes.

Tessa collected herself and was offered a seat at the table by her teary-eyed sister-in-law Amanda. Her twin sister, Samantha, was on her left, and Tessa's mother-in-law, Debbie, was across the table—all of them looking at a series of screens and scrolling walls of text.

"Can you catch me up?" Tessa whispered, looking over her shoulder at the corner she'd just come around, where her daughters were still crying and clutching their father. "What's going on? Is it as bad as it looks?"

Samantha sniffed, using a quivering hand to wipe away her tears, and cleared her throat. "Um . . . It's pretty bad. Only Lieutenant General Bruner and that Riven Thane guy are left on our side. Bruner is holed up in the air force base, and they're carpet-bombing the major roadways that are leading into the city—that's where the swarm originally went. Most of the front-line defenses we had set up for monster attacks are overrun, except for a couple, and the army is preparing a last stand with the police and whoever else can come help."

"A lot of civilian groups have bravely gone out to fight," Debbie said with a nod, her eyes glossy while staring at the screens and her hands white-knuckled to grip the table's edge. "The forums are talking about how they've stationed all their new mechs there, and they hope the fighter jets and helicopters will be able to provide enough support that the swarm can't just roll over the ground forces. So far, it's only working because of that other guy . . ."

Debbie shifted the screen so the others could see. Tessa's father-in-law came into the room just as her bloodshot eyes went wide, and she took in a quick inhale of breath.

"Whoever he is, he's definitely bringing the heat," her father-in-law, John, said while sitting down next to his wife with a firm jaw. He pulled his wife in by the shoulder and kept a brave face on for them just like Tessa had done for her own daughters. "And those demons he controls are something else. We may just make it out of this battle yet. I just wish he'd been at the front line when all this went down. Maybe the general would still be standing . . . but then again, the general had been hunting him down not long ago for the assassination of our senator. That doesn't really make a lot of sense to me, looking at what he's doing now . . . And it makes me wonder why this Riven person stayed."

"The front lines were overrun in less than five minutes; he wouldn't have made it to the outskirts in time," Amanda muttered, gazing at the screen with a mixture of amazement and anxiety, her hands clasped. "He's doing what he can, and the system notifications said he didn't even have to stay. He volunteered to fight for us. The forums are going wild right now, speculating about who he is and why he chose to fight, or if the allegations against him were false and a power grab on the general's part. You know how the conspiracy theorists were getting even before all this, when the military only released pieces of the footage and not the entire thing. Anyways, Elysium said he's a vampire prince, from somewhere called the Thane Necropolis— but no one has heard of anything like that around here. It's all very confusing."

Tessa only nodded silently, more awestruck as time went on.

The cortex screen in front of her was split into three parts. One was of the roiling forums that were going crazy with viewers, mostly noncombat civilians, who were hiding and waiting anxiously for the battle's outcome. The second part of the screen was a live feed of two demons—one the forums were calling Athela, after they'd heard her talk to her companion, and the other one they were calling Azmoth.

Tiklik Longjaw, which was supposed to be an Azag broodfather, was currently engaged in a battle of epic proportions inside a burning landscape as it desperately fought off the smaller of the two demons in what was mostly one-on-one combat. The broodfather was much larger than a lot of the other Azag mantis creatures and had an extra pair of scythe-like arms in the front, but it wasn't quite a match for the speed of the pitch-black woman with blades coming out of her back—and the furious exchanges of blindingly fast strikes between their limbs was like watching a cyclone of swords crash into one another over and over again. Usually the demoness Athela would come out on top—scoring deep gashes along Tiklik's body to add to its oozing wounds, which bled profusely and started spreading black poisons across the Azag's flesh. Occasionally the demoness would activate a martial art of some kind that caused her to glow green and land a combination of strikes that were so fast no one was able to keep up with the hits—but the mantis creature would retaliate by activating a martial art of its own that would harden its body over the course of two seconds to counter her flurry, resulting in a blinding spray of sparks when her blades met the temporarily hardened carapace. Then, whenever she switched over to spraying red needles or threads to try to pin the creature down, the mantis would counter by spraying acid at her webbing to dissolve it in midair. Still, the demoness had the upper footing—though it was a war of attrition; the Azag mantis was slowly being worn down.

Meanwhile, hundreds of the smaller mantis monsters had come rushing in from all sides, and occasionally they'd get to Athela to take away some of the pressure she was putting on their larger commander—but most of them were being ripped apart and smashed to bits by the titanic, flaming tank of a demon that had set entire blocks of abandoned neighborhoods aflame. His maul crushed, his claws ripped, shock waves erupted underfoot, and most of the scythe's attacks just bounced off his obsidian plates as he cackled and bowled over the monsters by the dozens.

It was incredibly impressive, seeing two allied demons fight off hundreds of other monstrous creatures in a battle of competing nightmares—no doubt to see which type of nightmare would win out. But what was even more impressive was the next screen over, and Tessa couldn't help but gawk at the absolute display of might and power.

The vampire prince, Riven Thane, stood on the edge of an abandoned five-story office building. Beside him an absolutely stunning Succubus with blue skin and black wings stood by, weaving her hands through the air to produce a fine black mist, and all around the two of them an absolute storm of chaotic energy crashed into a horde of enemies, ripping them apart the moment they got too close.

The Succubus's black mists were swept up in a tornado of crimson energy that billowed about them in the form of ice and blood, causing the bodies of the insectoids to soften and wither away with rot before being eviscerated by the madding howl of blood. Some of the armored insectoids made it through the outer storm of black and red, only to enter a minefield of invisible sigils that'd flash green and explode on impact. Those that made it past the minefield and tried climbing the building found themselves torn off in sprays of viscera when spinning red discs with serrated edges came billowing down at them—ripping the hardened armors of the Azag monsters into scraps before rising again to circle the warlock overhead.

"Jesus Christ almighty . . ." Tessa gasped, holding a hand over her mouth in absolute astonishment. "Just how strong are these things?"

"The demons and their warlock master? Pretty damn strong!" John gave a nervous laugh, trying to lift the mood, but Tessa could easily tell he was just as worried about the outcome as any of the rest of them. "Just look at him! He could take on the entire swarm by himself!"

Amanda grunted—eyes glued to the screens. "Why do you think he just stays up there on that tower? Do you think he's waiting for them to come to him?"

"Definitely," John said with a stern nod. "Why go to them when he has the high ground? None of these creatures seem able to fly, which is why our aerial units are doing so well—aside from the few that've been shot down with acid projectiles or spines that some of the stinger variants have. If I was him, I'd stay up there, too. Eventually the Azag big shots are going to have to go meet him, otherwise he'll just continue mowing down their forces like he's been doing for the last thirty minutes."

"Won't he run out of mana, though?" Tessa asked hesitantly. "He is a mage, right? Warlocks are a type of mage?"

John opened his mouth to reply, then gave an uneasy smile. "Not sure."

"The forums are talking about how he's utilizing the blood of the fallen creatures to draw more mana out," Debbie said, scrolling through text boxes. "One of our own native warlocks has been talking about it while he waits with the military at the base for the Azag assault. He says that this warlock has to be an S-tier classer as well, probably on the higher end of S-tier, otherwise there'd be no way he could hold off that many monsters at once for this long. And none of the warlocks here have been able to get more than one demon companion, while this vampire has three."

"Why would a vampire want to help us, though? Aren't they evil?" Tessa asked

"*Evil* is a relative term—who knows? All that matters is he's here and has chosen to help. Realistically speaking, the base would probably already be overrun by now without him —and we'd all be dead. Let's just hope he and his minions can keep it up, because the enemy side hasn't lost a single target yet," John replied.

Athela was growing frustrated.

Blurring left and avoiding another pincer strike from more of the smaller mantis creatures, she fired off hardened needles of her threads to impale them like a Gatling gun—only barely dodging another lightning-fast strike from Tiklik Longjaw.

"WHY DO YOU RUN FROM ME, TINY DEMON!" the Azag broodfather hissed through mandibles that reminded her of one of her uglier sisters back in the nether realms. "STAY STILL AND FIGHT ME!"

Tiklik was obviously a poor sport and venting because of the necrotic venom debuffs she'd repeatedly stacked. Each strike with her blades, tongue, or claws added more and more stacking damage over time. And although this monster had some sort of poison resistance as well as a regeneration property, it wasn't nearly enough.

One of her limbs shot out a thin red thread, sticking to the wreckage of a burning building to her right when she launched herself into the air. Tiklik began spraying acid again when she feinted with another offensive cloud of needles, but she tugged on the string and caused her body to abruptly jolt right. Clear of the acid burst and activating her martial art Flurry when she had a clear line of sight, Athela ripped forward into a combination attack she'd preset.

It was one of three combination attacks she could program into the ability. Flurry drastically increased the speed and strength of any preprogrammed ninemove combination, moving faster than a normal brain could process or her normal body could move without the martial art. This particular version of Flurry included a lunge forward that was meant for aerial attacks, not needing any kind of solid footing to do it, as the stamina literally propelled her like a rocket would.

CRASH

The Azag mantis activated its own hardening ability just in time to avoid most of the flurry, but not all of it. Athela smiled when she felt one of her claws rip through the front of the armored thorax and into softer tissues right under one scythe-like arm, only to feel the rest of her slender arachnid blades bounce off the quickly hardening body in a spray of sparks.

She cackled and kicked off, backflipping dozens of yards away onto a tiled rooftop and abruptly rolling to rip the throat out of another mantis with a wicked grin Tiklik's way. "GOTCHA THAT TIME, BITCH!"

Azmoth's maul exploded with flame, and a shock wave of kinetic energy blasted through another wave of the incoming enemies farther down the street—leveling an entire burning block of the neighborhood in an instant with a shower of debris.

"AAAAAAAAHHHHHHHHHHHHHH!!!!" Tiklik screeched in agony, stomping the ground with its six legs and cursing in a language she didn't understand while its limp upper-left arm snapped off by the thin thread of meat she'd left behind. "MAY YOU BE BLASTED BACK TO THE HELLS FROM WHENCE YOU CAME, YOU DIRTY BITCH!"

"Hey, only my master gets to talk to me like that!" Athela winked, then cackled again when she imagined what Riven would say after reviewing the footage later. "I am quite hilarious, I know. Don't mind me!"

Her hand blurred again, knocking aside a spine projectile that'd been launched her way from one of the stinger variants these monsters had for ranged units. The spines were covered in acidic goo, were anywhere between two and five feet long, acted as the actual stinger tips until fired, and were just as fast as bullets—but Athela's claws were faster, and it only took a slight nudge to push the spine off course and redirect the trajectory.

She retaliated with her own spray of threadlike needles from her six spider legs, jolting the mantis with the stinger that was starting to harden yet another spine in real time to replace the projectile it'd fired. The mantis screeched angrily and started yelling back at the demon as it died, but it quickly slumped over—riddled with holes and dozens of needle wounds that leaked blood.

BOOM

The tiled roof she stood on shook, and Athela's eyes widened in surprise when she saw Tiklik had used yet another martial art to close the distance in an instant while she'd been distracted. Her mind almost blanked upon seeing a blade closing in for her neck only a couple inches away, and with reflexes akin to a cat on crack, she bent her back at a ninety-degree angle to avoid the swipe and counterattacked with blades of her own.

The roof collapsed under the weight of the monster's landing, but a spray of blood and a loud gurgling sound met Athela's ears over the snapping of wood and rising dust.

She unloaded everything she had through the cloud of debris, swiping and slicing blindly at the flailing body in front of her while dodging retaliatory strikes that were just as blind as her own.

The two combatants crashed onto the stairway of the second floor, only for part of the stairs to give when the railing snapped off. The huge body of Tiklik Longjaw unceremoniously flopped and smashed face-first onto the cracked, burned side where Azmoth had hit it earlier—and it let out a pained wheeze just before Athela's claws shot forward into the back of its skull.

CRUNCH

Athela's evil smile widened from ear to ear, far wider than any normal human could smile, and she let out a delighted screech of victory as she pulled out the brain of the creature for the entire Chicago audience to witness. Doing a little happy dance, she flung the gray matter over the spasming body of the monster to splatter against the wall, then trotted out of the ruined building that collapsed behind her while she dusted herself off.

[Tiklik Longjaw has been killed in battle by Thane Necropolis forces. Four of five battle targets for the attackers remain.]

Athela could hear the faint, excited cheering that rose up in the distance as the notification appeared. It came from miles away and from multiple directions, and she posed for the system's camera she knew was there somewhere. "Yes, yes, I'm great—I know!"

She tossed her long black hair to the side and harrumphed, hands on her blood-covered hips to pose yet again. "Princess Athela to the rescue! HEY, ASSHOLE!"

She pointed to Azmoth, who was munching nonchalantly on a bug carapace while silently staring her down from a couple yards away. Raising his maul with his left hands, he smashed it down onto another bug that was trying to bite one of his flaming, armored legs.

"WERE YOU THERE JUST WATCHING ME THIS ENTIRE TIME?!" Athela screeched angrily, stomping over to the larger demon with a scowl. She then threateningly whipped one of her sharpened spider legs out to point directly at his face from an inch away. "THIS ISN'T SNACK TIME! THIS IS A BATTLE, GODDAMN IT. YOU GOTTA HELP ME OUT!"

Azmoth stopped chewing, then gestured over to a field of flaming, dead mantis monsters scattered among the remains of the burning neighborhood. "Azmoth did help. I fight many monsters. Athela just slow to kill big one. Not Azmoth's fault Athela is weak."

"YOU TAKE THAT BACK!"

"Azmoth not take it back. Azmoth stomp Athela like little baby. Now come, we go find Riven and help kill more."

Athela opened her mouth to retaliate, a quivering bladelike leg still pointed in Azmoth's direction, but eventually she harrumphed and started walking toward the storm of blood magic and the cursed cloud that'd intermixed about half a mile away. "This is not over, you goddamned Sasquatch wannabe! When we're done here, we're having a one-versus-one battle to the death! Then once one of us is sent the nether realms, we'll see just who is the weak one and who is the pussy-ass bitch!"

Azmoth heaved his stone maul, etched with lines of magma, over one shoulder and grunted his agreement. "Fine. We make bet, though. If Azmoth win, Azmoth uses Athela as chair for whole month."

"And if I win, you have to be my little wee baby that I get to stomp on every night for a month! You'll have to pretend to cry like a little wee baby, too, whenever I do it—and you'll have to beg for my lullabies. IT'LL BE HUMILIATING! Now shut up and let's go!"

"I just said we go. You the one holding us back by taking long time to kill single bad mantis monster while Azmoth fight army."

"SHUT IT, TWERP!"

CHAPTER 32

The shrill cries and screams of the oncoming swarm echoed around him, like a faint memory on a wayward breeze. Flocks of beautiful red blades continued to wash away the enemies that dared to try their hand at ending his life, effortlessly wiping them off the face of the building and ending their existences. He only needed to think about it, and the blood magic reacted to his will.

Blood, Shadow, Death, Infernal, Depravity, and Chaos.

Out of all the elements in the universe, why was Blood one of Unholy's subpillars? Was blood an inherently evil thing, or was Athela wrong about what the Unholy foundational pillar actually was?

Unholy didn't necessarily have to be evil. That had been proven over and over again, time after time. Though Riven was an Unholy-oriented vampire, he'd say he was generally a better person than many of the humans in this city. He was certainly no godsent hero come to act as savior to the world—he was no bastion of moral excellence—but he was proud of who he was as a person. So what was the Unholy pillar, really? What was the Blood subpillar's relationship to it?

Despite the immense internal calm he felt as he contemplated these things, eyes glazed over and heart slowly pumping at the epicenter of untold carnage while his magics wreaked havoc amid the enemy, he felt confused. Ribbons of crimson whipped around him and his aura sang to the heavens in a storm of red that washed away the cursed clouds of black his Succubus produced— incorporating them into his own torrent of energy . . .

To make them his own.

He studied them, barely registering a spine projectile that somehow made its way toward him. The spine was utterly crushed, obliterated when it made contact with his living, thriving aura, which encompassed him and the area where he stood, looking down from the building's fifth-floor rooftop.

The clouds Fay was producing . . . they had an inherent code to their production. He could see it, see the way the mana roiled and folded in on itself—adding layers of restrictions and conditions to the spell before being gently incorporated into the massive typhoon of his own energy that cradled and used Fay's own.

His head tilted slightly. Why was it that curses created pain when cast? Why did they exact a price of emotional turmoil in order to create a cloud that would rot enemies to their cores?

Was it magnifying internal turmoil and pain, eliciting a strong emotion and pumping that emotional state to create something new?

Why was it that her clouds of Unholy pain and rot mingled so well with his blood magic? Blood was a biological thing, a life bringer, something that brought warmth to one's body and made muscles move and flow. It was the exact opposite of Fay's magic, which should by theory be eating away at his blood mana—yet that was not the case. The two entities twisted and swerved, the blood mana incorporating Fay's clouds like stirring sugar into coffee. The sweetness, the cold rot, the flavor of the Unholy curse was within his flowing ocean of red— swallowed to be made one.

Merged to be made one.

His eyes shifted from the moving whirlwinds and ribbons of mana back down to the oncoming swarm that continued to mindlessly and desperately push past his cyclone of death. He watched them wither and rot, watched their bodies shred apart, watched when even the best of them made it to the tower. Even when the flood of swirling blades sometimes failed to knock them off their ascent, he watched when they finally came into contact with his aura. He watched them rot, watched them disintegrate as piece by piece their bodies fed his growing storm.

Riven could feel how the area around them was infused with a slight under-current of Unholy power even aside from himself or his minions. It leaked out from the corpses, permeating the area with a taste of the profane as the blood of his enemies was drawn skyward to obey his will.

No doubt it was due to these creatures being related to the man he hunted here. Richard Longhollow, by definition, had to have an Unholy bloodline, just because he'd made it into Chalgathi's trials. So it would make sense that his spawn would be inherently Unholy.

Yet here they were, creatures with blood flowing through their veins and inherent Unholy properties permeating their very fabric . . .

Just like him, actually.

There on the rooftop overlooking the carnage, watching these creatures die by the hundreds, Riven had an epiphany.

He understood.

He held up his right hand: a crackling, snapping surge of red lightning traveled along his fingertips, then surged along his arms as he pulled blood mana into his Unholy ability Blessing of the Crow. The Unholy foundational pillar shifted and churned inside his soul apparatus, resisting the command at first—but within seconds, it started linking and forming new pathways with the Blood subpillar beside it.

The pillars . . . They were one and the same.

Fay's cloud of cursed mana, his blood typhoon, his aura, which wasn't even a true skill by the system's definition—they were all connected. Even his minions, who by contract were an extension of himself now, were connected to him—each of them a new appendage to utilize like a piece of his own body.

Rapidly his soul aperture began to shift, expanding, connecting threads, quickly tearing across the pillars to weave an intricate web from the Unholy foundational pillar, the Shadow subpillar, and his Blood specialty pillar—and a vision flashed before his eyes.

Six comets rocketed through the heavens, all coming together and crashing in an explosion of red, black, and green—creating an abyssal monument that radiated profane might.

Three hooded skeletons rotated around a floating vampire of immeasurable beauty with golden hair, pale skin, and brilliant golden tattoos that wrapped around her bare body. Each skeleton held a scythe that dripped with flowing blood—leaving patterns on the floor that began to congregate underneath the vampire's hovering feet.

The nude vampire in the middle of the room slowly lifted her red eyes toward the ceiling, and the roof of stone exploded—revealing another six comets that crashed into one another overhead amid a star-laden sky.

Riven felt his soul explode as a storm of black and red crashed down from the point where the comets had collided. He screamed, an influx of pain shattering his psyche and crumbling his bones.

As Riven continued that scream in an ethereal state of being, the vampiress slowly descended to the floor. The ball of crimson collected from the three scythes turned black and created a pool with the nude vampire kneeling inside—clasping her hands and a bowing her head. Then she started to pray before she too began to wither and rot, disappearing into the pool of black that grew into an abyssal maw while her body crumbled to nothing.

She and the pool were swallowed by the maw, and the world became silent.

Then, attempting to do what the vision of the six comets had done in their own merging, Riven attempted to replicate it with his own pillars—but the struggle was too great. He tried and tried again, only to fail repeatedly, until finally he reduced the number of pillars to three. His half fusion between pillars was a success, and he was able to control them, albeit at a lesser extent than the vision of the comets that were each imbued with one of the major subpillars that created the Unholy foundation—but he was happy.

He had seen the path, and it was glorious.

[Blood specialty pillar has gained an ascended ability modifier through Dao insights: The Path of Red and Black: Profane Cyclone (Ascended Ability Modifier), which is automatically applied to any and all Unholy/Blood/Shadow abilities for additional mana cost unless mentally choosing not to. All Unholy/Blood/Shadow abilities have been upgraded to Profane Cyclone's modified version of each spell.
Notice: Only one ability modifier may be active at one time. Mana channels have been enhanced. Meditate and contemplate upon the concepts you have understood to further evolve this path.]

The building underneath him shattered as the sky exploded into a red and black storm, and his body radiated with killing intent as his Succubus screeched in surprise.

BOOM

Fay was the only thing in the immediate vicinity not affected when a mighty shock wave leveled the building Riven stood on. The cyclone of blood surrounding the building pulsed and exploded—shooting off in all directions and ripping apart entire city blocks in a wave of black and red.

Thousands of Azag hive cluster forces succumbed in an instant, and waves of red and black mists with crackling Black Lightning were left in the aftermath that quickly caused any creature inside to wither into a necrotic husk or be ripped apart. Numerous mantises immediately attempted this, dashing across the decimated landscape toward their enemy, only for almost all of them to succumb in less than a minute.

Riven's ears rang, and he hovered dozens of feet in the air with rippling tides of crimson intermixed with smaller black clouds of sparking energy. The power of his blood magic pulsed and rose with new additions, rotting the very ground away as buildings cracked and roads decayed.

Lifting a hand as he floated in midair, he commanded the blood magic to come to him. Wisps of crimson mana instantly shot up his arm, with flickers of black inside the red like little worms or flames that refused to be entirely beaten down by the more dominant color. The intent behind his mana was more palpable, more malicious, and hungered with a craving that simulated the cravings of Gluttony in past experiences. The three Chalgathi artifact pieces oriented toward Gluttony all screamed with envy and approval, and Riven felt his still-forming Gluttony core shiver upon the mental touch of the Path of Red and Black. Blood was somehow connected to Gluttony, Unholy was connected to Blood, and the shadow was pulling at an aspect not yet gained.

The ringing slowly started to fade, and he abruptly became aware that Fay was shaking him roughly—wings flapping and outspread while she tried to get his attention. Below, Azmoth and Athela looked around in utter astonishment at the devastation Riven had unintentionally caused—gazing about a wasteland that continued to crumble and decay all around them. A crater was forming in the ground beneath where Riven was continually pulsing mana with power rising skyward in rippling, semitranslucent waves.

He ignored his minions—he couldn't hear them anyway—and he was still on the cusp of ascending even more . . . he could just feel it. The power was just one step away from achieving a bonding momentum with his Gluttony core, yet he couldn't quite figure it out.

His brows furrowed and he gently shrugged Fay off, concentrating on the inner workings of his soul. His aura was so palpable now, so alive, consuming everything around it to feed the growing power that he commanded at his fingertips. Bloody blades condensed and widened—forming shadowlike vortices with sharp edges that rather looked like spinning balls of the black and red storm—sharpened miniature balls of Profane Cyclone that shredded everything they touched. Multiple simultaneous rifts in space tore open around him, bathed in black and red that sucked and pulled things through with currents of the profane storm based on his will. Blood Lances were summoned, forming much faster and with thick black trails of lightning indicative of the very fundamental foundation of his ideology behind Blood magic—having integrated it with Unholy and Shadow upon achieving a step toward the greater truths.

The greater truths of oneness between the profane comets he'd seen in his vision.

Fay's clouds intermixing with his own had been the catalyst, and he felt like the potential to achieve more was there—but despite all the mental pressure and his racing thoughts, there were no further results. He was just so close . . . and minutes ticked by as he tried to corner the aspect of Gluttony that was still escaping him.

[Riven Thane has been engaged in battle. Click to view.]
[Clidra Mutishbane has been engaged in battle. Click to view.]

He saw it coming before it got there, like a buzzing fly coming to irritate him and draw him out of his budding insights. Blessing of the Crow, usually conjured with streaks of sparking red lightning, now rippled along his skin with red and black streams of blood that moved like silk ribbons and felt like death. Not only did his reaction speed up far more than usual, but his concept of time slowed down—and he casually tilted his head to the right with what appeared to be blinding speed to anyone watching in order to avoid an incoming strike of boiling, dark-green liquid.

He stared at the monster below him while power crackled along his body—all seven of his feathers focusing their eyes on the monster in turn.

[Clidra Mutishbane, Azag Broodmother, Level 35]

Clidra Mutishbane was even larger than the first offensive target had been. She had a large, elongated abdomen that dragged out behind her and three stingers that bubbled and oozed green liquid radiating Unholy power. Yellow eyes glared back up at him, and the basic casting staff in her claws was a stark contrast from the normal scythe-like attachments of the rest of her species.

"Who are you? All of you. We have no qualms with demons and vampires; we are of the same flock," Clidra's mandibles clicked, sneering toward the demons on the ground. She was like a beacon amid a gore-filled storm, dark-green mana rippling around her to combat Riven's own tide of blood and decay. A small horde of Azag warriors surrounded her position, bladed arms out to the sides and awaiting their commander's call. "We can still settle this peacefully. There are too many of us and only four of you. We do not wish further bloodshed between us and your own kind, and we are all of Unholy affiliation. Let us speak terms, and then we may negotiate a fee with the system to withdraw your volunteer ballot. Withdraw your minions and I will withdraw my own forces so that we may finish this discussion without—"

Riven's voice echoed across the landscape as his power began to rise, and the visage of a great semisolid maw appeared behind him—as if to swallow them all whole. "I do not negotiate with genocidal maniacs. Chalgathi has sent me. I come for the artifact your master has—as well as your master's head."

Clidra's mandibles abruptly stopped clicking when her eyes went wide upon witnessing a surge in power above her, and she took an involuntary step back when the vampire's aura spiked. "Chalgathi?! You are one of the cult?! You should not have been able to find us here! Our allies—"

Riven's sinister laugh tore through the building storm and cut Clidra's speech off. "Cultist?! No, I will kill all of them, too. I am merely caught up in a greater play on Chalgathi's grand stage, but as an involuntary side character. But I must say, what my choice of selflessness has led to is both amusing and satisfactory. Your master and the cultists will all have the same fate—you are all destined to become fertilizer for my path."

A clap of thunderous power exploded overhead, causing many of the Azag mantis monsters to flinch and duck instinctively. Meanwhile, Riven continued to stare down at them like a vengeful god of judgment as more and more power began to accumulate in rippling waves around him for hundreds of yards in all directions. "Do you think yourself strong? Do you think yourself among the powerful in this world? Let me show you what true power is. And when your souls are ground to dust and your spirits enter hell, tell my friends there that it was Riven Thane who sent you."

Hundreds and then thousands of spinning storm orbs and crackling red and black lances congregated in the sky above them in a rapid flurry. The storm of crimson heightened, creating snowflakes and ice shrapnel that crashed across Clidra's green barrier with rot applications, causing her own power to quickly decay.

In an instant, two dozen portals ripped open through space, and the offensive projectiles were launched. Hundreds tore through the portals—exiting out at different angles all around Clidra's position to fire on the Azag from all directions with shock waves of ice, lightning, and berating waves of decaying mists and blood.

The city shook underfoot, and Riven looked to the west.

[Clidra Mutishbane has been killed in battle by Riven Thane. Three of five battle targets for the attackers remain.]

CHAPTER 33

**Battle targets for ATTACKERS: AZAG HIVE CLUSTER (three of
five remaining)**
- **Richard Longhollow—(Azag Overmind)**
- **Clidra Mutishbane—DECEASED**
- **Scythewalker Trik Trak—(Azag Broodfather)**
- **Tiklik Longjaw—DECEASED**
- **Everkill Gorgemonger—(Azag Bull Champion)**

**Battle Targets for DEFENDERS: THE POPULATION OF
CHICAGO (two of five remaining)**
- **General Florence—DECEASED**
- **Lieutenant Cliff—DECEASED**
- **Lieutenant General Bruner—(Human Military Officer)**
- **Governor Banks—DECEASED**
- **Riven Thane—(Pure-Blooded Vampire Prince, Allied Unit: The
  Thane Necropolis)**

Officers shouted orders while machine guns rattled. Heavy artillery explosions
and plasma-weapon fire consumed the other noises outside. Large mechs of various designs stood tall over the defenses and projected one-way barriers to help
negate the oncoming horde's barrage of acidic spines, while both helicopters and
fighter jets zoomed overhead, trying to beat back the ocean of enemies using
missiles.

Lieutenant General Bruner, the second-in-command concerning Chicago's
military and the graying man at the head of the rectangular table, continued
to get feedback reports from his scouts on the outside. Even with the live feed,
many eyes and ears gave him an advantage over what the system showed from his
operatives—and for the first time since the battle started, he was hopeful. Morale
had been shattered across their entire force when General Florence and their

most powerful combatant, Lieutenant Cliff, had been killed almost immediately, but now that morale was skyrocketing again.

"His magics are actively ignoring our operatives, sir," one of the intelligence officers farther down the table confirmed with a nod of his head. "At most it's just an uncomfortable pressure. They're able to move freely inside the blood storm without much issue, and we also have recently confirmed reports that groups of independents are using his blood storm to kill off the invaders more easily."

"Independents?"

"Guild mercenaries and civilians, sir."

"I see. Then I want all sniper teams to support him at a distance, too," Bruner said gruffly, his hand shakily rubbing the stubble of his beard while he glanced between various screens—both system-made and not. "They should be safer inside his field of influence anyways."

"Should I call in the F-35s and drones to lend aid as well?"

"No. Keep them here; we're barely holding the swarm back from overrunning our base defenses even now, and the last two jets we used to target their leaders were blasted out of the sky instantly." Bruner held up his robotic right hand, grimacing down at his cyborg appearance and hoping it would be enough if things came down to close combat. But if the defenses didn't hold here, there was little hope for the residents of the interior, as most of their scattered forces on the outside were disjointed and recollecting themselves after the sudden ambush on their city.

His eyes lifted, gleaming with orange light as the cyborg half of him analyzed the forums at a rapid speed. It was one of the perks of using the Machine pillar, and in this unique situation, it suited him wonderfully from a command perspective.

But just who was this Riven Thane?

He knew little of the man other than his superior officer, General Florence, had named Riven as the assassin who'd attacked their senator. But Bruner had had an uneasy feeling about General Florence from the get-go, especially after integration, and his suspicions of the general planning a treasonous takeover had run high ever since they'd arrived on Panu.

Now, seeing the man who was supposed to be the enemy of their city fighting entire armies of these creatures, bringing earth-shattering waves of death and destruction on a level he'd not even thought possible, Lieutenant General Bruner found himself at a loss. He watched as swaths of Azag hive cluster forces were cut down in the blink of an eye, rippling waves of black and red magics carving a path toward the point where the remaining three battle targets on the enemy side had congregated.

They were out there, somewhere just outside the city's perimeter, waiting for Riven and his demonic servants to meet them in battle. They had no doubt realized, just as Bruner had, that this man who faced them was uniquely suited for killing armies. It'd taken him ten or so minutes, but after watching this war-lock continue to grow in power as he collected more and more blood from the bodies of the fallen, Bruner had finally confirmed it.

What they'd all thought was a limited mana pool was something entirely different. This warlock was somehow using environmental resources to feed his magics, with far greater efficiency than any other magic user the Chicago intelli-gence unit had ever heard about before. So it took until far longer into the battle than the hive cluster would have liked for Richard Longhollow—overmind of the Azag hive—to order his forces to completely avoid Riven. They'd only been fodder for Riven's building storm, and the spike of energy had significantly declined in rate ever since the retreat. All weaker units had been sent toward the military base, where Bruner was now, and Richard Longhollow had condensed only his most powerful people to meet Riven in battle over the upcoming hour. That way Riven would have fewer bodies, less blood to feed on to build his ever-increasing storm.

Bruner regretfully applauded Richard Longhollow for the insight. He'd hoped the hive overmind would not notice it, but unfortunately that'd not been the case. The graying cyborg sighed, looked out over the walls of the military base, over the explosions and din of battle, where mountains of bodies flooded toward them with reckless abandon—to where a writhing cyclone of ominous energy ripped across the city limits on their western border under the multicol-ored dome.

Bruner could only hope Riven would win. He hoped the warlock had col-lected enough of the energy to end these monsters just as fast as he'd ended the last one, or that Riven would at least kill one or two of them. Because if not, Bruner wasn't sure Chicago's forces would last the night.

Dearest descendant . . . You have chosen poorly, and I am not sure it is not a choice you can take back. The Path of Red and Black is a boundless road leading into the eternal maw of oblivion. You have been tricked, you have been swindled, and you have been led astray. Gluttony awaits you, sin bearer . . . And though I hope your soul is up to the task, I doubt that you will make it out of this alive . . .

Riven snapped back to reality as the whispers faded, and he blurred left, dodging the strike of another mantis elite and countering with a whiplash of his staff. The fleshy cord flexed and extended, tearing the monster and a chunk of concrete apart instantly, only for the blade to slam back into the black wooden shaft of Vampire's Escort.

Then all went quiet, with only his minions and the swirling mana around him causing ripples of air in the surroundings as he beheld the carnage.

Thousands of mantises lay dead, permeating the area with an Unholy taint that was so thick the people who'd been following Riven at a distance to lend whatever support they could had to stay back. Crowds of Chicago's citizens with various weapons, classes, and build compositions had come out of the woodwork to help him crush the invading forces despite losing hundreds of their own—but the enemy had lost far more thanks to Riven.

"The overmind has figured out your trick . . ." Athela mused while licking one of her bloody claws—frowning as the remaining blood was sucked off it to add into Riven's swirling vortex overhead. "They figured out how you tick. They are waiting for you . . . Will you go to them? Or will you wait out here?"

Azmoth slammed his maul headfirst into the ground, waiting expectantly like an Unholy paladin of legend, and Fay hesitantly swayed back and forth in the air while repeatedly adjusting her invisible land mines to keep ahead of Riven's position at all times.

Whispers from beyond echoed through Riven's thoughts, and the visage of a great maw screeched inside his head—causing him to clutch at his mask while his soul apparatus shivered.

Athela gave him a concerned look, but he shrugged it off and looked back over to where the three red dots were positioned in the sky not far off from his own blue dot. To match the congregation of three was a large hill with numerous newly created cave entrances where the swarm had burrowed out to attack the city. Thick green mists wafted in abundance, clashing with Riven's own tidal wave of red as a deep aura of malice oozed out to rub up against Riven's soul.

Riven only sneered, his seven feathers flaring out to all sides and the great maw across the front of his chest shrieking in challenge. "I will wait here. And if they do not want to come out, I will force them to do so."

He closed his eyes, steadied his soul, and began to concentrate with his staff planted into the ground before him and clutched in both hands—using it as a conduit to better conduct mana through his pillars. Slowly, ever so slowly, his cyclone of rapidly swirling blood, Crimson Ice, necrotic clouds, and Black Lightning all came to a standstill. It was like he was trapped in time, everything around him almost completely frozen in space. He felt the runic inscriptions on his pillars flare, he felt the mana channels burning with power, he felt the newly formed connection between his pillars circumventing his soul's core to more rapidly process and integrate power with one another, and the magic let out a breath of contentment as the world around him sighed.

With the eyes of the city on him, Riven raised the tip of his staff overhead. "Come to me."

The world howled, and a roar of violent energy pulsed before rapidly beginning to condense. The miles-wide storm of mutated, twisted blood mana was sucked into Riven's position like a black hole—coalescing and packing into a globe of energy a few meters across at the tip of Riven's staff above him.

Ribbons of red liquid, flurries of crimson shrapnel, and torrents of dark lightning were all sucked in and crammed into a far, far smaller area than what should be able to hold a power of that magnitude.

The ground cracked underneath the weight of Riven's power, and the cement he stood on began to decay faster and faster—turning into dust that floated up into the air while the winds of incoming magic howled and crashed around him. His horned pauldrons glowed brightly, infused with as much blood mana as they could possibly hold, and his cloak whipped about him while he struggled to maintain the condensed storm.

And just as the last of the energies tore from his surroundings to feed his building spell, Riven settled his gaze on the riddled hillside from which the aura of malice continued to pour forth. He let go of his staff, maintaining the collecting power through a mental connection with his weapon. Fingers began to quickly turn and twist, incorporating two-handed patterns that unlocked profane seals necessary to complete the call.

Riven could feel the energies within the hillside retract just when he finished his necessary hand gestures, and he uttered the words to set it all loose: "Nefajia crecus Blood Nova."

It was unlike anything Riven had ever created before. The multicolored dome overhead went bright red for a split second, and the ball of power he'd collected blossomed into a cataclysmic strike that flashed forward to strike the hillside.

There was a brief, deep blast of sound before his eardrums shattered and caused everything to go silent but for a high-pitched ringing. The entire city shook under the impact, and the landscape along the western edge blew like a supervolcano.

Debris and roaring, searing power hit the outer wall of the multicolored dome encompassing the event before the backlash of power sent aftershocks into Riven's position. Riven's mending eardrums abruptly popped yet again, despite his vampiric regeneration, and the howl of his own energies rebounding off the event's domed cage nearly caused him to stumble back. He smashed the pointed end of his staff down into the ruined cement, the blade cutting deep, and he held on to keep his position while the onrush of power blew by.

**[Scythewalker Trik Trak has been killed in battle by Riven Thane.
Two of five battle targets for the attackers remain.]
[Everkill Gorgemonger has been killed in battle by Riven Thane.
One of five battle targets for the attackers remain.]**

As the dust and swaths of rampaging energy eventually cleared, the remnants of Riven's attack were finally revealed. A deep crater, crackling with red and black energy, had been left in the wake of his strike—encompassing well over two square miles of space with black and red glass forming along the crater's underbelly due to how compressed the magic had been upon release.

Two glass-encased figures, each far larger than the normal mantis monsters, had obviously perished underground where they'd attempted to draw Riven in. The figures were Scythewalker Trik Trak and Everkill Gorgemonger, Riven assumed, but Richard Longhollow was nowhere to be seen . . . and the system notifications indicated he was still alive somewhere.

Riven glanced up just in time to see the last red dot rapidly closing in on his position, and his eyes widened in alarm at the speed before a portal flared to life.

Riven vanished just in time to avoid a huge, chitinous claw whistling through the air so fast that it sent shock waves out from his old position—and he exited only to barely dodge by creating a pillar of ice underneath him that launched him skyward.

[Richard Longhollow has been engaged in battle. Click to view.]
[Your minion Fay has died. She will be returned to you twenty-four hours after you pay the blood price for your minion. To resurrect your level-27 Succubus, you will be required to pay Elysium directly with a sum of twenty-seven thousand Elysium coins. Simply will this transaction to happen and make sure you have the required payment to further this agenda.]

The pillar of red ice shattered from where it'd propelled him skyward along with the torn body of his Succubus, and Riven saw a blurring, hulking figure flash through the air only to have it disappear—and then he felt himself crash back down into the road below.

What was left of the road shattered in a spray of debris as Athela screeched in rage and rushed to meet the attacker, and Azmoth abruptly catapulted toward Riven's position before slamming a fist down into the ground beside them.

The shattered floor Riven was flattened into turned to magma, and a dome of flames encompassed their position just in time to intercept another incredibly fast claw swing from a shadowy figure.

Cursing and pushing himself up with a glare of irritation and aching bones, Riven picked up the staff he'd nearly dropped and glared out to where Athela had just been launched three streets over. Standing there, in the middle of the ruined suburb bordering the hills on the city's outskirts, was a grotesque half man, half monster hybrid.

Despite his speed, Richard Longhollow was abnormally large. Four chitinous legs with barbed ends, a thick, armored brown carapace, bulging muscles, and a humanoid upper body made this creature look like an insectoid centaur of some sort. Antenna that came out the ends of his forehead flicked back and forth, evaluating Riven and his minions with four yellow eyes, and three rows of mouths with sharp teeth stacked on one another while he hissed in irritation. He held a large black orb that swirled with Unholy green light in one of his two humanoid hands, while four scythe-like mantis arms also protruded farther out to the side. Lastly, a large stinger was positioned at his back—and it hovered like a scorpion's would right before the strike.

All this being said, and even after all that Riven had unleashed on the hillside, Richard was somehow completely unscathed.

"He he he . . . To think . . ." Richard Longhollow's voice echoed out in a deep, raspy laugh. "That another of Chalgathi's chosen has already been sent to hunt me down. That apocalypse beast is rather melodramatic over a simple artifact being stolen, wouldn't you agree?"

Riven turned, feeling his bones cracking back into place and the teeth of his maw grating against one another. His staff crackled with Black Lightning, but he remained where he was as Azmoth's barrier died out. This enemy was far faster and far stronger than Riven would have liked to believe, matching or even overpowering himself in both categories despite the wisps of black and red blood flaring off his body via Blessing of the Crow. Unlike Riven, this man turned monster had no doubt sunk all his points into physical attributes . . . that or his bloodline was heavily oriented toward Strength, speed, and defense. It was the exact opposite of Riven, who'd applied all his free points to Intelligence, Willpower, and, to a smaller extent, Sturdiness.

"You're rather stealthy for being so big," Riven commented, his right arm flaring with tendrils of mana and producing a Blood Lance that crackled with encompassing Black Lightning. "Just how did you survive that attack? Did you dodge it?"

"I'll answer your questions if you answer mine," Richard retorted loudly with another crazed cackle, and the sound of artillery fire picked up from deeper in the city, where the military base was under siege. "Tell me, how did you find me to begin with—and what did Chalgathi offer you to kill me? How did a vampire end up enrolled in Chalgathi's quest, when all the vampires on Earth had been long extinct according to the cult records? I'm curious, and before I cut off your head I'd very much like to know."

CHAPTER 34

"It appears the information your cult had was wrong." Riven cracked his neck and let out an audible sigh when his left arm snapped back into place with a click. He let out an amused chuckle when his staff hummed in anticipation, hissing and flaring with power as it mentally urged him to kill the creature in front of them. Flashes of images rippled across Riven's consciousness, and he grinned at what the weapon was telling him. "It appears my weapon wants to feed on you. Your body is going to allow it to evolve."

Richard Longhollow snorted in turn, and he readied his four scythe-like blades while channeling power into the orb he held at his chest. "Let us finish this and see just who feeds on who."

Minutes later, the entire western edge of Chicago had become a devastated wasteland that continued to tremble under the momentous clash between two high-end S-tier combatants.

Azmoth, for the first time in a long time, was just a little bit nervous. He'd never seen an opponent this fast, this strong, or this durable. Richard was as strong and sturdy as Azmoth, as fast and nimble as Athela, and every time he took a hit, the mantis-man creature would rapidly repair himself just as fast as Riven's own regeneration. The only advantage they had was Riven's ability to manipulate mana and cast hard-hitting spells, but his master was constantly on the back foot—constantly needing to portal out or defend with walls of ice and snares to avoid being cut in half. This made Riven unable to focus entirely on offense, and despite both Azmoth's and Athela's best efforts, Richard was set on taking Riven down over the demons.

CRUNCH

Azmoth flung Riven out of the way and snarled when a five-foot-long stinger penetrated his left chest plate. The roaring demon's maws snaked around to snap onto the stinger and hold Richard in place. "STAY STILL!"

Azmoth violently bodychecked his enemy and simultaneously swung his maul up to crush the stinger that was stuck in his body, and he felt the weight of his huge stone weapon cleanly smash the appendage off with an audible snap.

A blurring side kick with one insectoid leg sent Azmoth's head backward into the ground, too fast for the large demon to react, only for Athela to undercut Richard's posterior legs with her blades. A long, pointed lance of crimson sparking with black electricity broke the sound barrier and tore a hole in Richard's chest, but the monster shrugged off all the attacks and aggressively moved in Riven's direction while healing his injuries in mere seconds.

"GET UP!" Athela screeched at him while passing by to tear after the creature chasing their master.

Azmoth's head was dented, and one of his long, sharpened obsidian teeth was lying on the ground. He shook himself to clear his mind, grunted, and roared while pushing himself off the ground and turning to find the threat. He needed to give Riven time and an opening to let out another full-force strike, because despite Athela's speed and Azmoth's strength, Riven was the real heavy hitter when it came to damage output.

BOOM

A shock wave radiated out from where Riven's magic-infused staff knocked aside a blade-strike martial art that left fifty-meter gashes in the earth behind him. Portaling away again and charging up dozens of swirling red and black balls of mana, Riven sent off a swarm of chaotic, sharpened projectiles. They were upgraded versions of his bloody blades and thus locked on to Richard and tore left when the mantis overmind tried to evade.

Athela was there to intercept, too, and she tried to slow the creature down—a flurry of attacks flinging sparks and blood off Richard's body with her limbs before she yanked herself out of the way of a counterattack with bloody strings, avoiding a life-ending strike.

The half-man insectoid screamed in anger when the swarm of red and black balls crashed into him, sending pieces of his chitinous armor in all directions as his three serrated mouths bared teeth. He flashed forward, ripping through space itself with a dual-strike cleaving attack from abruptly shimmering scythes.

Azmoth saw Richard refocus on Riven's position and charged with a vicious lunge. The demon slammed his maul into the earth, causing it to quake, while a wave of magma blasted forward to rip up the ground.

Richard dodged easily, retracting his attack and countering with a pulse of Unholy energy that blasted out of his chest. Azmoth was flung backward, head over heels, and came to a screeching halt with claws digging into the cement, only for a shadow to close in on him with a flash of black.

Azmoth grinned, and he poured everything he had into his Infernal pillar while roaring at the top of his lungs akin to a Tyrannosaurus rex. Just before the advancing shadow was in striking range, Azmoth's body exploded into a pillar of flames.

The landscape around him exploded, and a searing heat caused all plant life even outside the immediate radius to wither and die. The shadow was blasted backward, sending Richard's body speeding out of the shadowy dimension he'd entered while still aflame and crashing through a small office building beyond Azmoth's line of sight.

"AZMOTH WILL CRUSH YOUR SKULL AND FEED ON ENTRAILS!"

Activating his kinetic shock wave and infusing his clawed feet with explosive flames, Azmoth inadvertently created a new skill.

[You have created a new Infernal-based martial art, Propulsion (Infernal): Activate this ability to infuse Infernal energy into the stamina channels in your legs, launching yourself at high speed in one direction. This ability empowers any physical attack with additional flame damage. Medium cooldown, high Stamina cost.]

BOOM

A shock wave erupted from Azmoth's position, a cloud of flaming debris shot out the back, and a trail of embers followed his wake as the armored demon launched himself through three brick walls to slam a huge stone maul right into Richard's face.

"PAYBACK."

CRASH

An explosion of flames rippled out of his maul with the remnant energy of the martial art, and he returned the gift Richard had given him earlier with a scream of satisfaction. Riven followed up with a well-placed snipe—using a supercharged, long-range Blood Lance from over ninety yards away and tearing off one of Richard's legs in a spray of body fluids.

But Richard only laughed and glared up at the flaming demon as Azmoth began to bring around the maul with all four clawed hands for another swing. "Not good enough."

Richard's body exploded with rampant Unholy power, black and green light effortlessly lifting Azmoth off the ground before hundreds of acidic spines appeared out of black portals all around Richard's position. A sea of projectiles ripped forward in all directions, and Azmoth was thrown up into the sky, numerous spines impaling him while he heard Athela's pained scream.

[Your cocontractor Athela has fallen. Your master, Riven Thane, must pay the Blood price to have her resummoned back into the mortal planes.]

Riven watched helplessly as Azmoth's smoldering figure continued to sail farther and farther away. Then, watching Richard pull himself up out of the burning wreckage of the nearby city, Riven couldn't help but frown. Richard's regeneration grew his leg back in real time—frankly, it was even better than Riven's regeneration, and he simply didn't understand how it was possible.

Regardless of how, this posed a serious problem for Riven. Two of his demonic familiars were temporarily dead, and the other was no doubt seriously injured and probably would have to stumble back here across half the city. He'd been holding on this entire time because of the help of his minions, but Riven had to admit, he'd be hard-pressed to fight Richard one-on-one even with his recent Dao insights and spell upgrades. He'd roasted, lacerated, frozen, blown up, and electrocuted this guy dozens of times already. He'd torn off limbs, twice blown a hole in Richard's head, and had even annihilated the man's insectoid body from the chest down. Each of these interactions had resulted in the same outcome: Richard had regenerated almost instantly.

But that didn't make sense. Riven knew that even his own regeneration had limits, and the same rule must apply to Richard. It had to; Richard couldn't just regenerate fifty times over like that under normal circumstances, and so unless he had a source he was drawing from to fuel his regeneration . . .

Riven's eyes locked onto the black orb with swirling green lights that Richard always kept on his person. He hadn't seen the Chalgathi blasphemer use it or activate it even once; he'd only seen brief power fluctuations being infused into it, so just what was the purpose of the orb?

Was that the key to this battle? Was it somehow enabling Richard to continually heal, or was it fueling his own natural perks to a greater extent and allowing the insectoid monster to keep his energy stores high? At first Riven had only assumed this item was the profane artifact Chalgathi had sent him after, and that it somehow created the sanctuary the system had talked about. But that sanctuary hadn't been created yet, so Riven had also assumed it had value later instead of now. Perhaps he was wrong.

Riven didn't have much more time to contemplate this; the familiar shadowy blur of Richard's movement skill activated, and Riven muttered a curse while flinging up a wall of spiked ice in Richard's direction.

Richard easily jumped over it when exiting the skill, but this gave Riven ample time to create a reinforced Wretched Snare and fling it like Spider-Man. Up until this point, Riven hadn't been actively targeting the orb, and whenever attacks had been launched Richard's way, the insectoid would defend with his hand while attacking using his scythes. When the orb had been knocked out of Richard's hands once or twice, the man had simply picked it back up quickly. But now, as Riven flung the snare over, latching it onto the black orb in Richard's arms, Riven was attempting to steal it. The snare was reinforced with the Profane

Cyclone modifier from his new path, and the net began to electrify his target on top of the burning, acidic effects it usually had.

The reaction was far more immediate than Riven had expected.

Seeing Riven's ability latch on to the orb to try and pull it away, Richard let out a screech of rage and used all four of his scythes to cut the snare off. He also rebounded backward off his original rush and released blades of energy in a medium-range attack that tore through the air and left Unholy wisps in its wake.

Riven's staff spun in the air and smashed the waves of energy apart, hissing with hunger and urging Riven to kill this man faster. Vampire's Escort desperately wanted to feed on this man, and it kept sending images of Riven impaling Richard's heart with the bladed tip with increasing momentum.

"I'm trying my best!" Riven grunted at the weapon, sidestepping another energy blade and jumping onto a nearby rooftop while releasing another swarm of spinning storm balls. "I'm going as fast as I can!"

The building he stood on shattered when the auras of the two S-tier combatants collided, Riven building his own to counter the building pressure from Richard. Whereas Riven's aura was a pressure that felt of predatory hunger, blood, and cold violence, Richard's stank of mutation, change, and cannibalism.

Cannibalism?

It was an odd sensation to feel, as Riven was usually the one putting his aura out to others and hadn't experienced many if any others using their auras on him before. The concepts were tangible, though, and they spoke to Riven of alternate paths that he could have chosen if he were to abandon the recent Dao insights he'd acquired not only today but over the past few months.

"THIS IS MINE AND IT BELONGS TO ME!!!!" Richard screamed, his whirling aura of green pulsing and rocketing skyward as a thick layer of energy slammed into Riven's own aura zone of rippling red tides. "DIE!"

Riven landed just as Richard opened his mouth, and out of it came a swarm of . . . hornets? The swarm immediately grew to enormous proportions, not only coming out of his mouth but soon peeling off his very body. The chitinous armor he'd been wearing warped and shed from his outer layers, moving into an offensive ability and tearing away his defenses in the process. The swarm grew until it clouded out the light from the multicolored dome overhead, creating a shadow that spanned for hundreds of yards and then well over a mile. Thousands of winged insects with claws and little stingers rushed about Richard's position, creating a literal whirlwind of tiny bodies that each hummed with Richard's aura. It was then that Riven realized these insects were actually smaller pieces of Richard's real body—otherwise that aura wouldn't be present on them. It was also here that Riven realized Richard was going all out in an attempt to end the fight.

Richard then stuck out a hand to point Riven's way, and the buzzing swarm rocketed toward him in a dark cloud of wings.

"Oh, shit."

Riven's eyes widened and he tried to portal away, but his portals abruptly sputtered and died when he tried to summon them. They simply wouldn't work, even after four attempts to open them up, and he wasn't sure why that was. He began to run at breakneck speed.

He was traveling far faster than any normal human could, but it wasn't fast enough. Looking over his shoulder and speeding by broken buildings and decimated streets, he pumped his legs and cursed while trying to think of what to do next. The swarm was gaining on him, fast, and just as the first of the insects got to him, he burst into flames.

Hell's Armor bloomed along his body with an explosion of heat, covering him with obsidian plates and hellfire that killed most of the insects that got close without much problem—but a few of them latched on anyway and started to chew away his clothes or the skintight, blood-laced layer his mask provided. Whipping around to face the oncoming cloud of insects, his body crackled with Black Lightning and he unleashed a torrent of energy from his staff that shredded thousands of them—only to be outdone by the maw on his chest.

The vertical, sharpened rows of teeth spread wide—causing his rib cage to crack open to extreme lengths as tendrils whipped out to devour the incoming insects. Simultaneously a black vacuum from inside the mouth began sucking the cloud in.

Riven watched, dumbfounded, as the vast majority of the millions-strong cloud was simply sucked away and eaten by the Gluttony-attuned Chalgathi artifact on his chest. Those that weren't sucked in were either burned to ash by the flames coating his body or dragged in by the thousands of tiny black wisps reaching out from the abyss within the maw.

Seconds later they were all gone, and the maw snapped shut with a crunch.

The area was very silent after that, with Richard just looking, equally dumbfounded. It only took Riven a second to realize that he was out of hot water, though, so he pointed over to Richard and began to laugh loudly.

Meanwhile Richard, who was now devoid of his outer chitinous armor layers, glared at him with all four yellow eyes. He looked far less bulky this way and no doubt would take a lot more damage than he had now that the outer layers were gone—unless he could somehow regrow them. That's also probably why he turned to run with a hiss of rage—only to meet Azmoth's claws.

CRASH

The flaming demon had leaped from atop a building across the city, activated his new martial art Propulsion, and exploded forward to land sharp, daggerlike fingers right into Richard's unprotected neck.

Richard's soft body was slammed backward into the stone, and he quickly began screaming in agony as Azmoth's flames burned him alive. He flailed against the larger demon, only for Azmoth to double his grip with other sets of claws as he began to yank on Richard's spine.

Riven didn't waste the opportunity and charged ahead, portaling forward now that he could suddenly use the ability again. That cloud of insects must have had some kind of spatial locking trait, but he doubted he'd ever find out the real truth.

There would be no interrogation here.

In a flash he was on top of the struggling duo, and without pausing, he speared Richard in the rib cage. His staff shuddered and let out an audible screech of delight, and the dagger-tip end began to dig and worm itself into Richard's body, wrapping around vital organs while sucking out the man's life force.

Yet even now, Richard was still beginning to regenerate.

"GET THAT ORB!" Riven yelled, attempting to blast it out of the man's hands, only for Richard to yank it out of the way in his flailing. "NOW!"

Azmoth, who was struggling to keep Richard down, nodded and swatted at the black and green ball with one of his four hands.

The item was knocked free, and Richard's burning eyes went wide with alarm as he began to scream far louder than only a half second ago. But if the insects that'd been part of Richard didn't come back even when he'd had the orb, perhaps the orb had nothing to do with it. Richard was able to heal his softer, fleshy wounds even now to some extent, but he couldn't regrow the armored outer layer? Even if the item was influencing Richard's ability to heal, giving him the ability to continue that regeneration, something about Riven consuming those insects with the maw of Gluttony had left Richard unable to grow his chitin again.

Azmoth continued to roar, using all his strength to keep the flailing monster pinned down underneath him while the stinger and scythes continued to stab at him frantically. Meanwhile, Riven's staff kept draining and sucking energy out of Richard with a hungry hum, and Riven himself created a three-foot-long blade of red ice along his right arm. Not wanting to accidentally hit Azmoth, he chose to close in for the kill and quickly made his way over to the head that Azmoth was trying to pry off by the neck.

With a couple quick lacerating jabs of the sword attached to his right arm, Riven helped behead Richard with a malicious grin. "Gimme that, and hold the body down in case he regenerates again!"

The screaming head of the insectoid literally spat blood at them, and Riven took the large face from Azmoth by the sides of the skull with a shrewd, cruel laugh. "I'M NOT TAKING ANY CHANCES! IN YOU GO. ADIOS, MOTHERFUCKER!"

Riven opened the abyssal jaws on his chest one more time, the maw of Gluttony peeling his ribs apart with a hungry growl.

"NOOO!!!! FUCK YOU! FUCK YOU AND EVERYTHING YOU STAND FOR!" Richard's head screamed while his body still thrashed on the ground. "BURN IN HELL! BURN IN HELL!"

"Been there, done that!" Riven guffawed merrily as he let the black tendrils from his chest encircle the screaming head. He watched with a giddy smile as they dragged Richard in by the neck, and then jaws snapped shut, abruptly ending Richard's screaming.

The body immediately went limp underneath Azmoth, and the scythes digging into Azmoth's body slowly fell out with a clattering sound. Then, from the depths of the city and the surrounding landscape, where thousands of people had come out to watch, a roar of excitement was sent to the heavens. In the distance, where the remaining mantis monsters still tried to swarm the military base, rays from the heavens began burning them away with lightning-quick efficiency.

The purge of the losing side had begun.

[Richard Longhollow has been killed in battle by Riven Thane. Zero of five battle targets for the attackers remain.]

CONGRATULATIONS
CONGRATULATIONS
CONGRATULATIONS

THIS CLASH OF FATE HAS ENDED. DEFENDERS THE POPULATION OF CHICAGO HAVE COME OUT VICTORIOUS. ALL ENEMY TARGETS HAVE BEEN DISPATCHED. ALL ENEMY FORCES NOT ALREADY DECEASED WILL NOW BE PURGED. THE CURSED SANCTUARY STONE HAS BEEN SET BACK TO DORMANT. CHICAGO HAS BEEN UNSEALED; ALL DEFENDING SURVIVORS WILL NOW BE GRANTED BOONS BY THE SYSTEM BASED ON PERFORMANCE.

[You, Riven Thane, have been deemed the one who contributed most to this battle. You have been awarded the following: the Snipe upgrade to your Blood Lance spell has been added. All Elysium coins dropped by Azag hive cluster forces have been placed in your bag of holding with an additional one million. The rest of the Valgeshia Armor Set is now available to buy from your Elysium Altar (one of five pieces already obtained). Once bought, all vampires in your empire will have the opportunity to buy the Valgeshia Armor Set for themselves directly from the system.]

[You have gained 23 levels. Congratulations! Be sure to visit your status page to apply points.]

[System Notice: You have ascended tiers and have climbed out of the S-rank. Elysium has reassessed your level of power when compared to the many billions of souls living on your planet, and you are now ranked as a Paragon on this world's power ladder. You are currently listed at spot No. 72 on the power ladder. This shift of power on the world stage is noted by Elysium, and video footage of your climb to the peak has been uploaded to the world forums along the main page for anyone to view. With this increase in rank will come better opportunities for you as Panu's integration continues. Congratulations! The ranking categories are as follows: Apex rank (top 10), Paragon rank (top 1,000), S rank (top 0.0001%), A rank (top 1%), B rank (top 15%), C rank (top 30%), D rank (top 50%), E rank (bottom 50%)]

[Chalgathi Side Quest Savior of the Weak has been completed. You have killed the Chalgathi blasphemer and may take the cursed sanctuary stone and do with it as you see fit—but beware its corrupting power.

You have once again successfully played a hero's role to those who do not deserve it. That is the path of the selfless, I am afraid. However, your success will still reap you rewards even aside from the cursed sanctuary stone.

- Completing this quest has pleased Chalgathi, has saved many thousands of innocent lives, and will establish portal points you can access across the world through the staff you carry. These portal points can also be made into permanent, stationary portals that allow travel between the different sides of Panu if you choose to do so, but this is up to your discretion. Please notify the system of what your decision will be.
- You have been given a Tier-3 Infernal spell scroll, Blaze of Profane Glory.]

[Your staff, Vampire's Escort, has consumed the essence of Richard Longhollow. Vampire's Escort is now evolving through its trait Sacrificial Kill. Your staff is entering a stasis mode and will be unable to wield in battle until it exits the stasis.

- Sacrificial Kill: Killing strong opponents has a chance to imbue this weapon with additional attributes, stats, or bonuses.]

[Your previous request for uploading video content has been reevaluated and accepted. Reasons for acceptance and reevaluation: the population of Chicago sees you as a hero and is willing to follow at a percentage of 96%. Control over this area has been established based on reputation and influence. Conflict of interest with parties holding control of this area is no longer an issue. Footage of Senator James's assassination will now be posted to the cortex forums.]

CHAPTER 35

[The Apocalypse Beasts, Chalgathi, Quest Update: Revo Mani has fallen in battle to Fred Talons. Fred Talons has acquired three of five set pieces for Chalgathi's Inheritance. A new Chalgathi's chosen will be picked within one hour as a replacement for Revo Mani.]

[The Apocalypse Beasts, Chalgathi, Quest Update: Pam Orni has fallen in battle to Nora Lang. Nora Lang has acquired two of five set pieces for Chalgathi's Inheritance. A new Chalgathi's chosen will be picked within one hour as a replacement for Pam Orni.]

[The Apocalypse Beasts, Chalgathi, Quest Update: Jin Lee has fallen in battle to Justin Mather. Justin Mather has acquired four of five set pieces for Chalgathi's Inheritance. A new Chalgathi's chosen will be picked within one hour as a replacement for Jin Lee.]

Three days had passed since the battle for Chicago.

Riven stood on the balcony of the Margrave Hotel with his back to the railing. It was a very high-society building that'd been built just before the integration, and it'd been well-kept even afterward, with many of the fancier things in life still available. His weapon, Vampire's Escort, was encased in what Riven could almost describe as a brick of red ice while it underwent evolution and was lying on a table in the room behind him, where various staff members for the leadership of Chicago bustled about. Beside the chunk of ice was the black and green orb that'd once been a Chalgathi artifact, held up on a pillow—the same one he'd taken off Richard.

[Cursed Azag Sanctuary Stone: this sanctuary stone enables the bearer to create an Azag Hive Cluster Sanctuary and will list the

creator of this sanctuary as this hive's Overmind. This sanctuary will seclude an area of the planet in a protective layer that has permanence for one year and can only be passed through by the Overmind, Azag, and whomever the Overmind deems allies. Becoming the Hive Overmind will enable the creator of this sanctuary to create a hatchery immediately upon creation and will open up the queen and drone pathways to breed units with. More units will be available upon creation of the necessary biological modification facilities. Warning: this item is cursed; it afflicts the owner with compulsions that are in the best interest of the Azag Hive Clusters and links the owner to the galactic hive minds for communication purposes.]

Riven dismissed the screen with a thought. It appeared that there was more to the backstory of Richard Longhollow than he'd originally thought, and they weren't just simple monsters. Whatever these Azag were, it appeared that they had a far greater influence than just the local area or even this planet. Had they sent this sanctuary stone here or helped Richard to get one somehow through changing Chalgathi's artifact in an attempt to gain a foothold on the planet? It certainly appeared that way through context clues.

"Riven." The newly appointed General Bruner, who'd replaced General Florence as chief commander of the military, saluted him. He immediately went at ease after Riven's nod of approval and approached to stand beside Riven at the railing. The older man's graying hair was swept back, and his orange cyborg eyes combed the surroundings far below in the bustling central district before he cleared his throat. "Sir. Are you ready for the press conference?"

"Are they already good to go?" Riven asked, a little bit surprised by the speed at which things got done around here. "I'd been thinking it'd be another few hours."

"Well, the civilians are all riled up and wanting to know how things are going to proceed from here—so things got a bit hasty. They're calling you a hero, you know, and most of them want to join without question. Everyone was scared after the city was almost overrun, and having someone like you at the head of things, protecting them, doesn't sound like a bad option to most." General Bruner adjusted his uniform, frowned, and waved away an assistant who offered him refreshments. "They've lost faith in us after the video footage of Senator James's assassination went public, and finding out that you're from the USA only helps your standing. There'd be riots in the streets if we didn't go ahead with this, and the mayors of Rockford, farther inland, and Milwaukee, down the coast, are both ready to pledge as long as you guarantee our citizens certain rights. But may I be frank, sir?"

Riven raised an eyebrow from underneath his mask, then nodded lazily. "Go ahead. You know I'm anything but formal."

"Your sister is worrying," General Bruner stated flatly, straight and to the point. "In the very little time I've known you—and after witnessing your conversation with Senator James before he was killed in cold blood by our own people—you seem like a decent man. It was also a breath of fresh air to get so much honesty out the gate, concerning how you've treated those elvish war criminals, even if there are many in the city that don't necessarily agree with it. The forums are abuzz with what-ifs and worries about losing our democracy in favor of a kingship, but without your intervention, we'd all be gone. People are willing to bet on you. I just hope that you're as straightforward as I think you are, and I would hope that if your sister does anything rash, you'd stop her. We are pledging because of you, Riven. And because we need to be stronger than we are. We are not pledging because of her—I just wanted to reiterate that."

Riven gave him a sad smile. "Try to get to know her before making any assumptions, General. When we open the gate later today at the press conference, I hope to introduce you soon."

Riven winced as his body shuddered again, and he coughed before glancing up at the blue sky overhead. It was nice, being outside in the daytime without needing to look away. His mask allowed him to do just that, and it was rather refreshing.

"Are you okay?" General Bruner asked. "Is it the stat points again?"

Riven nodded wordlessly.

He'd leveled twenty-three times to settle at a combat level of sixty-eight, which was frankly absurd. But given the number of mantises he'd killed, he could understand it. The power spike he'd had due to the Dao insights had made all his abilities far faster to cast—and far more powerful than they had been just days before the fight. The mere shock of having all those base stat points flood his body at once had been rather violent, and he was still in recovery days later—not daring to use his free stat points yet due to fear of what would happen if he allocated them all at once on top of the baseline stats he'd already gotten. He still had 161 free stat points just sitting there, but he was going to add them slowly so he'd avoid the violent downsides to abrupt stat acquisitions again.

Casually pulling up a screen and looking over the forums of Chicago, Milwaukee, and Rockford again, he touched base with what of his countrymen were saying.

The city was still in mourning due to their losses, but many of them were excited by the new developments. Videos of the battle and General Florence's assassination of Senator James were rampant, and even the front page of the world's cortex had it on display while highlighting Riven's rise to the number-seventy-two spot on the power ladder out of tens of billions.

The populace had received Riven very well, even going so far as to burn pictures of General Florence while sending death threats to his family for killing the senator—which Riven put a stop to immediately. Riven had been almost unanimously hailed a hero, and when it was learned he had been an American prior to his vampiric change, he'd essentially been put up on the pedestal of leadership without much of a say. The forums practically demanded it, which was a big surprise considering his negative Charisma, but it went to show that Charisma only went so far. Actions could speak for themselves, and memories of Mara's explanation on Charisma or speaking with Ethel and Senna on the subject before their betrayal only reinforced that it was something that mattered far more with first impressions than anything else.

And it made him feel very good that his old country, or at least part of it, had accepted him back as one of their own.

Lieutenant General Bruner had given a public speech yesterday regarding the transfer of power to Riven—and today Riven was going to publicly accept the position of king of the three cities. It was . . . interesting how easily people's worldviews and priorities shifted when their safety was at risk. He hadn't even asked for it, but rather he'd had it shoved onto him through desperation and public outcry when they thought he might leave them.

Two men in business suits, one in blue with a bald head and the other a very burly man in a black suit, came up to the door together with smiles typical of used car salesmen. The other people in the room behind them got out of the way rather quickly, and it was apparent that both of these people were of a higher social standing.

"Mayor Bret Rawling, Mayor Eric Parker," General Bruner said with a curt nod to each of the arrivals. "Good to see you both. I hope the trip was both uneventful and safe?"

The bald man in blue chuckled, causing his shoulders to bounce, and he shook his head at both Riven and the general. "We were attacked by some kind of dinosaur birds on the way . . . but the armored convoy easily dealt with those beasts. Still, it does me little good to complain after what happened here in Chicago. It must have been downright terrifying. Plus, the roads between our three cities are largely intact and the newly modified cars that run on new-world energies work just fine . . . so I shouldn't be complaining when so many others have it far worse than I. By the way, name's Bret. Bret Rawling, mayor of Milwaukee."

Bret held out his hand to Riven, which Riven took. The mayor's eye twitched slightly when touching the slick red suit covering Riven's body, and he glanced hesitantly to the maw across Riven's chest, visible between the black rags of his shirt. "Ahem. It's nice to meet you. Should I start calling you *liege* now?"

Riven saw the slight grin on Bret's face, and it was obvious the man was trying very hard to look friendly here. "No. Just Riven is fine."

"Eric Parker, mayor of Rockford," the burly man in the black suit stated next, holding out a hand of his own with a more stoic expression. "I hope you'll do right by us. Never thought I'd see the day when we went back to the rule of a king, but that's what the people want. So that's what the people will get."

"I take it you're against the idea of joining the necropolis?" Riven asked casually, letting the man's hand go.

Parker shrugged. "Not necessarily. If life becomes better, I'm all for it. I just have my doubts. Prove me wrong and I'll be more than happy about it. Regardless, it's not really my say. I'm just a small-town elected official, nothing like the big shots in Chicago or Milwaukee."

"Over ninety thousand people still live in Rockford after the integration," Rawling stated with a drawl. "I'd hardly call that a small town. Small city, maybe, but not a small town."

"The specifics are meaningless to me," Parker shrugged again. "Anyway, we were hoping to get a rundown on the new laws. Stuff we can bring back to our own cities to discuss with our police force and citizens. Anything out of the ordinary that we need to know about? I'm also curious about this elf situation that you've got going on back in Brightsville—seems a bit Dark Ages to me. Care to explain that in more detail?"

Riven let out an exasperated sigh, then motioned for the three men to follow him inside. The staff, rearranging papers and talking to their contacts in the media outside the hotel room, and the soldiers standing guard all paused briefly and made room at the table. Quickly a hotel maid provided by the owner set down some cookies and cheese and a bottle of wine with glasses.

Riven sat down and reached for the cheese, only to hesitate as he looked down at his maw. "Goddamn it."

Bret Rawling, mayor of Milwaukee, began to laugh. "So it's true then? You really can't take off your mask?"

"Nope. I can't, and the maw on my chest doesn't taste anything, so eating stuff like this is just bland. As I said in my video on the cortex addressing the three cities, I kinda fucked up and now have an evil set of armor strapped to my body that I can't get off . . . for now, at least. It'll probably come off eventually— if I don't die completing the apocalypse beasts quest first."

Rawling snorted with amusement. "That's hilarious!"

Riven slowly turned his head, and General Bruner nearly face-palmed. "What's so funny about that, may I ask?"

"Oh, come on!" Rawling said with a cheeky grin. "You're rank number seventy-two in the world! You just wiped out an entire army! You'll be fine. There's no way you're going to fail that Chalgathi quest."

Riven gave an unamused grunt. Little could be hidden from the populace after his talk with Richard concerning the cult and Chalgathi had gone viral, and afterward Riven had come clean on just what was going on. It was both fascinating and scary to most of the people here, and another hot topic that was rampaging across not only Chicago's forums but apparently the world forums, too. Not many people across the planet had openly discussed or had knowledge of the apocalypse beasts quest to Riven's knowledge—which General Bruner had confirmed.

Though Riven hadn't had the time to look over the world forums himself just yet. He had his own stuff to contend with, but when he wasn't swamped he'd make time to delve into the massive expanse of Panu's main page later this week. No doubt he had both haters and fans out there somewhere, but he also cared little for public opinion now as long as he had a core set of people he could rely on. Especially after he'd tried so hard to win over the opinions of the elves of Greenstalk, only to be betrayed. There was only so much you could do to make people like you, so he'd do what he could for the people that he got along with, and the people who didn't like him for what he was could go fuck themselves.

Riven folded his arms and leaned back. "Anyways, there'll be little in terms of changes to the laws just yet, with a few exceptions. I know you want to talk about guild activities or taxation, and we'll get to that, too, but for now it's this: the undead part of our faction is going to need bodies. That means all bodies lost to death, from old age or in battle, will be given to the necropolis government for processing, either for parts or for raising. Bodies are valuable resources now—no more burying them. Other than that, the prison systems need to be redone. We aren't going to have leeches that feed off the rest of society, especially in a postapocalyptic world like this one. The worst prisoners we have now will be made into slaves or outright executed, and the ones whose crimes aren't that bad will be put into indentured servitude. Both slaves and indentured servants will only be owned by the government, and there will be no personal slaves whatsoever."

"Not too terrible," General Bruner muttered.

Riven nodded. "To address your question from earlier, Mayor, the elves of Greenstalk tried to kill me. Their people apparently have a deep-seated hatred for vampires, so they struck out at me even after I saved their lives. I struck back. What remains of their village is enslaved to the government, but they will be allowed to pursue happiness in many aspects of their lives—it won't be as bad as you'd think. Their children won't be born into slavery, either, but rather are being reeducated and allowed full citizenship rights unless they cause problems. That's pretty much the gist."

Both mayors nodded. "Fair enough. Do you mind going over a few things that are at the forefront of problems we have now, though? Before you go off to your news conference and open the portal gate to Brightsville?" Bret Rawling of Milwaukee asked with a curious side glance at General Bruner. "May I?"

Riven and General Bruner nodded, and Bret took a small manila folder from his suit jacket and pulled out a list. "These are the things that I think need immediate attention in the wake of what happened in here in Chicago. Some of this was already a problem and just outright ignored by our late General Florence, God rest his traitorous soul, so I'm hoping to get some more input from you—Riven. Ahem . . ."

Bret shuffled through the papers, brows furrowed. "All right, here goes. We have bandits and gang problems along the trade routes between our cities. We have guilds of civilians who are proclaiming independence in small pockets of territories after we lost over half of the army in the battle for Chicago. The black market for sex slaves is skyrocketing, mostly involving captured peasants from the villages farther south and inland—which in itself is causing a lot of unrest with our neighbors. Monster attacks are on the rise, and I think we may have a dungeon problem on our hands . . . and food supplies are dire. We won't make it through winter without increasing our food stores, and it's already the beginning of autumn."

Riven was dumbstruck when he stepped out of the armored transport to the sounds of thunderous applause and screaming crowds. They'd chosen the professional football stadium as the site where Riven would set the portal up, as it'd be a major trading hub between the two sides of Panu and would be a permanent addition to the landscape.

It was also where he was to make his public address to the citizens of the three cities, and he'd expected there to be a couple dozen reporters working for the new-world press—but he hadn't expected this. It was one thing to see how the forums were ramping up positive vibes about him, but it was something else entirely to see tens of thousands of people chanting his name.

"They really seem to like you," Athela mused at his side, waving and putting a hand on his shoulder to the absolute roars of approval when she did. "OOOH, A FAN BASE! They seem to like me as well! Let's stay!"

Fay stepped out next, getting quite a few gawking looks from nearby onlookers, and Azmoth hopped off the tank he'd been riding on with a grunt.

"Avengers assemble!" some nerdy teenager wearing a superhero shirt called out from behind the barricade, getting laughs from both Riven and the others nearby.

Riven waved to the kid, then to the crowd, and followed General Bruner through the gates of the stadium.

The walk to the central field was a bit surreal. Despite dozens of soldiers with automatic rifles making sure the crowds didn't push in and outright swarm him with pleas for autographs, congratulations, or heartfelt thanks for saving the city, someone broke through to touch Riven a few times and once an old lady shoved past and swung her arms around his waist with tightly closed eyes. She sobbed her thanks loudly into his chest, talking about how her son had died protecting Chicago and that she knew he was up in heaven looking down favorably on Riven for what he'd done, and Riven had to stay the hands of nearby military personnel to stop them from dragging her away until she was done.

"I'm sure he was a fine young man. I wish there was something I could say or do to help your struggles . . . but I'll make sure that you and people like you don't go without if you're in need." Riven hugged the old woman back, and she let go, wiping tears away and smiling up at him as he waved back at her and continued to make his way to the field.

Inside the stadium, a wooden platform had been erected and a series of microphones set up, and the two mayors were already seated, waiting for Riven to make his entrance. They stood up to clap, followed by dozens of reporters and tens of thousands more people in the stands.

Again the uproar from the crowd was deafening, and Riven even began to get a little bit emotional as he gawked underneath his porcelain mask. Ever since coming back to Panu from the hellscapes, he'd been worried he'd be an outcast. He'd been betrayed by Jalel, betrayed by the elves, been shunned and hunted by Prophet's forces and the humans of Brightsville. But here and now, thousands upon thousands of people had given him their stamp of approval.

They called him a hero.

They called him their savior.

And they wanted him above anyone else to lead them into the new world. Yet again, it was a stark reminder that the forum posts praising his name weren't just text on a screen—those were real people with real feelings and ideas behind them.

The lump in Riven's throat grew, but he continued walking after the brief moment of clarity. Uniformed soldiers on either side of the path to the platform saluted him as he passed, and eventually he came to the wooden stage. He walked up the steps and waved to the crowd, coming to stand beside the mayors, who each shook his hand before General Bruner cleared his throat and spoke loudly into the microphone.

"Silence, please! Quiet down!"

It took a couple of requests, but eventually the people of Chicago settled into a more bearable state of excitement as the top military officer began to address them yet again.

General Bruner nodded in satisfaction, taking his time to eye the people sitting in the seats all around them. "Hello, people of Chicago. It is a pleasure to be with all of you here today, and even more of a pleasure that I have the honor of publicly introducing the man who saved our fine city only a few days ago. By now you all know his story; it is public knowledge now that he posted a video on the cortex explaining just who he is and what happened to him. How he was changed into what you see now, and where he began. And it brings me great pleasure to announce that he was and is one of us—born and raised in the United States of America!"

Again the crowds roared with approval, only to settle down again with a raise of Bruner's hands.

"But that brings us to today. Things are changing—even the physical world around us is completely different from the one you and I grew up in." Bruner's gaze turned, cameras flashing and voices murmuring. "We are now in a world where the United States of America sadly doesn't exist anymore. We are on our own. The cities of Chicago, Milwaukee, and Rockford have all been thrust into the world of Panu, one of many puzzle pieces of land mass shuffled into the greater whole, and we have enemies on all sides. Monsters of myth and legend roam our lands, killing our people at random. Kingdoms to our south and north from other planets with magics not known to us are encroaching on our lands regularly with questionable intentions. The weapons of our old world are not necessarily obsolete, but as you have all recently seen, there is much room for improvement to be made when things like magic exist. Not only that, but we have six world quests that need to be completed in five years' time, and if not, great calamities will befall not only us, but the entire planet we now reside on. They will be calamities far greater than the one you witnessed here in our tiny piece of the planet recently."

General Bruner let that message sink in, and the mood became more somber. "With that in mind, and with the will of the people having been expressed, I and my colleagues in the military brass believe that strong leadership is a must. Especially after the traitorous actions of my predecessor, General Florence."

Boos and angry shouts echoed throughout the stadium but quieted again after another pause from Bruner. "We have listened to all of you. We have heard what you have to say, and we agree. As I said, strong leadership is a key in these trying times. We need someone who can not just lead us, but someone who can protect us from the greater evils of this world that we cannot fight by ourselves. Who better to do that than the man who so selflessly fought for our city without being asked to do so? A man who was framed for a crime he didn't commit, only to turn around and help us when he could have run? A man who is one of the most powerful entities on this planet, a superhero not in the comic books, but in reality. And above all—a man who shares our origins and histories from Earth. He is one of us, and he did not ask this of our people, but he is willing to take on the responsibility we ask of him. Without further ado, I present to all of you the man we are now pledging our allegiances to. To our new king, the hero who saved our city, I present to all of you Riven Thane!"

The crowd went ballistic, jumping to their feet and starting to chant Riven's name as General Bruner stepped back from the microphone and started to clap along with all the government officials.

"Thank you, General Bruner," Riven said into the microphone while waving, and he chuckled as the people of Chicago continued to chant.

"RIVEN! RIVEN! RIVEN!"

"All right! All right. Calm down, everyone," Riven said with an amused grin while the uproar died down to a thrum. "Thank you all for being here today. As General Bruner said, I did not ask to be your king. I am even a little bit surprised that it was suggested, and I've gotta admit, I'm humbled by the idea. It is true that I'm technically a prince and one of two leaders of the faction you'll all be joining, though, so I'd like to welcome you all into the Thane Necropolis. Today marks the day that I'll be utilizing a system prize to join the two opposite sides of Panu with a permanent portal gate, making travel between Brightsville and Chicago an everlasting fixture, and I hope that you'll all have the time to explore the opposite side of the world with me over time when the city there is more secure. Now, with all that's happened, there are a couple things the mayors and I have talked about recently that I'd like to address—then afterward you'll all be witness to the portal's creation. I hope that I can fill the shoes you've all given me, and I look forward to making all your lives better through both policy and protection."

CHAPTER 36

The portal took up half of the football field Riven had chosen as its permanent spot. It was a lot different from the ovoid ones Riven could create himself; rather this one was very similar to a wormhole—suggesting it utilized some other kind of magic Riven wasn't familiar with. It faced directly down into the planet, drawing people into it when they stood nearby and popping them out on the other side of the portal, where they were expelled into an area empty of others with systematic precision. From Chicago's viewpoint, the portal also showed a starry night sky. But when Riven was flung through said portal and exited to stand on the familiar fields of death-attuned grasses, the mirroring wormhole portal on the outskirts of Brightsville not far off from the Elysium altar showed daylight and a blue sky speckled with clouds.

They were windows looking into opposite ends of Panu.

Riven blinked a couple times and oriented himself, ignoring the cries of alarm from nearby orcs and elf slaves working the fields. Examining the portal with his mask's basic ability to identify things, he even got a small grin and a pleasant surprise.

[Riven's Eye Wormhole: a permanent portal fixture on the world of Panu that allows one to travel instantly between opposite sides of the world. This portal is a system-made phenomenon, granted to the vampire Riven Thane in the early days of Panu's integration.]

Well, at least he could say he'd made his mark on the world.

"Lower your weapons or get smashed," Athela casually yelled out to a group of ghoul and skresh warriors who'd taken up a defensive semicircle perimeter nearby. "This is Riven Thane, you idiots, or do you want to piss off your doting queen by attacking her brother?"

"Athela?" Gurth'Rok called out, stepping out of the line of warriors, followed by a few orc soldiers. The old chieftain looked a lot more wholesome than he once had, with his cursed upper lip wound now showing signs of complete healing. His green skin had turned paler, though it still retained a tinge of green, and his tusks were noticeably sharper as he moved with a grace obviously due to a vampiric shift. "It is you! Athela, I am glad to see you here. And the rest of you . . . is that Riven?"

"It's me," Riven called out with a wave of his staff from underneath his mask. "I can't take this stuff off. Long story. Where's my sister? I've been wanting to talk to her. Also, I'm digging the vampire look you've got going on. Welcome to the club."

Gurth'Rok smiled, shot General Bruner a curious glance, then gestured for them to follow. "You have only been gone for a week or so, but a lot has happened in that time. Your sister is at the bone garden. I'm sure she'll want to fill you in on all that has transpired."

"RIVEN!" Allie cackled with a piercing smile, letting wine spill onto the floor in her alcohol-induced fit of laughter. "I WAS A THREE-YEAR-OLD KID! How was I supposed to know that toilets worked that way?!"

The stone manor, Riven's guild hall, was for the very first time hosting a party in the eastern wing, near the large indoor pool, the dining room, and the kitchen. Allie had installed a large crystal chandelier for tonight's celebration of Riven's return, candles were placed all around the perimeter of the room on shelves and other fixtures, a live group of musicians who'd been stationed in one corner were playing classical music, and food was being brought out regularly to resupply the long redwood table, where fancier glass cutlery had replaced the stuff this guild hall had come with.

The people most important to the Thane Necropolis were all present, along with a couple of others, such as two nervous-looking diplomats from the human kingdom of Dawn, a small brown-robed rat-kin diplomat from the underdark city of Deepnest, and yet a third diplomat from a mix-and-match faction that was located farther to the west bordering the conflict between Dawn and the elvish kingdom of Tereen.

Tereen had become the mutual enemy of the Thane Necropolis and Dawn, after Dawn had accepted Allie's demands and handed over two of the larger elvish settlements conquered during the war in exchange for her help. The other option had been to give up Bradshire, the large town under Dawn's rule to the southeast of Brightsville, which Dawn's leadership had staunchly refused.

All in all, there were quite a few people here. Vin and Nin were animatedly talking to the Deepnest diplomat about necromancy. Mara was engrossed in a conversation about herbs with Dr. Brass, Gurth'Rok, and three of the orc warrior elites that always followed Gurth'Rok around. Fay and Athela were swimming in the pool below, wearing rainbow-colored swimsuits that left little to the imagination—which only proved Dr. Brass's previous claims correct; Athela actually did wear around a thin, formfitting layer of chitin around on the regular, because today her skin was a lot more human-looking than it usually was. Then there was Azmoth, who was playing chess with Mayor Bret Rawling, to the amusement of General Bruner and the other human military officers who'd come over from Chicago—because Azmoth had beaten the mayor three times in a row so far. Outside of these were a good number of undead soldiers stationed around the room, various human and undead officials Allie had appointed to help run Brightsville, Allie's two playboy thralls, wearing Speedos and bow ties and attending to her every need, to Riven's disgusted expressions, and more than two dozen staff members, who were being ordered around by Tupper.

Tupper, Fay's incubus brother, had taken it upon himself to get things around the manor running properly in his downtime. Upon his initial arrival, he'd stayed in his room, with only Fay visiting him occasionally, as he'd needed time to heal from whatever traumatic undertaking he'd gone through prior to being assigned to this guild hall. Tonight was the first time he'd really come out when Riven had been around. Tupper was a very handsome demon, with white hair and short black horns similar to his sister, only he had a more masculine build—though he was still somewhat thin even by human standards. He was currently in the kitchen, making sure the chefs were doing things in a timely manner and that all the guests were taken care of. According to Fay, it'd given the incubus a small but necessary sense of belonging here—and she'd actively encouraged Tupper to take up the mantle of pseudo-manager of Riven's estate after getting Riven's permission to do so. In fact, Tupper had been the one to acquire the chandelier for Allie upon her request for tonight's event, and he was also the one who'd found uniforms for all the maids and butlers present.

French maid outfits for the women, and English butler outfits for the men. The maids and butlers, mostly consisting of elvish slaves, had been handpicked from the more trustworthy group of conquered people to serve here. It'd apparently been a very sought-after position among the younger generation of elvish adults, with both young men and young women desperately trying to get out of the farming duties the rest of their kind had been assigned to.

Riven leaned back in his cushioned chair, jealously casting gazes at the food on the table that he was unable to taste. He was especially eyeing the cheese wedges with crackers in front of General Bruner. His mouth watered, but with his current predicament regarding the Chalgathi artifacts, it was a big no-go.

"My lord." Tupper as he tapped Riven's left pauldron timidly and bent low so he could whisper. "I hope you don't mind that I selected Genua as one of the maids . . . She was a good candidate and passed my questions while using Silvertongue. However, given your history with her and her family, I can always send her back to her cell. I just want to confirm that my choice was all right by you, my lord."

Riven looked left to the incubus, who was wearing a butler outfit like many of the young elf men were, and then shifted his gaze to where Ethel's mother, Genua, was cleaning dishes at a sink behind a kitchen counter. The blonde elf momentarily looked up, caught him watching, and blanched before going back to furiously scrubbing and trying to look small.

Riven blinked, and the maw along his chest hissed slightly as he pondered Tupper's question. "You said she passed your Silvertongue questions? What exactly did you find out about her while you were interrogating her for this position?"

The incubus cleared his throat. "She is very willing to be loyal, even to a fault, as long as she is given freedom to explore the manor. And as long as she is able to see her daughter soon."

Riven's memory shifted to the little girl, Len. A pit of guilt started to form, and he reached a hand back to rub at his neck where tension was beginning to build. "You're sure Genua won't cause problems?"

"It is very unlikely a mortal of her caliber would be able to successfully lie to my Silvertongue ability. It is possible, but very unlikely."

"Then that is fine. Do you know anything about how the children's reeducation is coming along?"

Tupper paused, then straightened and shook his head. "I do not, my lord. Do you want me to ask Mara? She's the one overseeing such things."

The incubus gestured farther down the table in the ghoul necromancer's direction, and Riven nodded. "Yes. If you could, make sure the visitations are started sooner rather than later. In fact, have Mara give the entire day tomorrow to the children to see their parents again. If the elves behave over time, we may even lift the restrictions entirely."

Tupper shifted his stance. "I will pass the message along."

Allie's drunken cackling as she talked to General Bruner caused Riven to grin, and he watched their interaction unfold with mild amounts of curiosity. On one hand, General Bruner was a pretty straight-to-the-point man, and he'd been wary of Allie based on the things Riven had told him. It wasn't that Riven had embellished or lied about anything, he'd just told General Bruner the truth, but the older man had been on guard since getting here. However, in the moment it seemed like they were really getting along. Despite Allie's drunken state, the general was occasionally smiling and laughing himself.

So far this meet and greet was a real success, and Riven really hoped there wouldn't be any problems with the integration of Chicago and the two adjacent cities of Rockford and Milwaukee with Brightsville. Tonight was more relaxed, but tomorrow was going to bring talks concerning military integrations, problems concerning both sides of the portal and political maps, supply shortages, and more. Most of those issues, other than the war with the elvish kingdom of Tereen, were located on Chicago's side of the portal, since Allie's forces had crushed all other factions inside Brightsville's borders, putting Brightsville entirely under the control of the Thane Necropolis.

"Uh . . . um . . . Riven, right?"

The meek, feminine voice of one of Dawn's diplomats asked hesitantly from behind him. Riven sat up, turned, and shot a look over at the two Dawn diplomats, who had largely been ignored since arriving here. Personally, he hadn't really been in contact with anyone from Dawn aside from the roc-riding knight who'd visited the manor a while ago, and he'd subtly given the responsibility of dealing with them over to Allie since she was the one heading the war efforts and claiming new lands in elvish territory for the necropolis.

"Yes, that's my name," Riven stated, the crimson feathers along his porcelain mask twisting and blinking at the short, plump brunette woman who'd bundled her hair up into a bun and wore a clipboard across her robed chest. "I don't think we've been introduced ourselves yet."

Looking relieved that someone was finally giving her the time of day, the woman held out a hand to shake—though Riven could tell it took her a lot of courage to do so by the way she flinched at his touch. "Marin. I'm one of the diplomats from Dawn, and this is Theodore Munchamp, court wizard to the king and practicing scholar of the sun arts."

The skinny, orange-haired old man next to Marin, also robed in yellow and white, gave a half smile and a timid bow while scrambling to his feet. "Lord Thane! I have heard so much about you, and your accomplishments on the cortex have already been noted. To know that one of our neighbors, who holds us in such high esteem, has such a powerful warlock is truly inspiring!"

Theodore Munchamp. This was the man who'd initially sent the roc-riding knight to negotiate a peace pact and request help in the war against the elves. He certainly looked a lot less impressive than Riven had imagined.

Riven leaned back in his chair to evaluate the skinny, robed man with hands folded over his lap. "Oh, so you've seen videos of my exploits, have you?"

Theodore nodded quickly. "I have! We all have. The world forums are a vast place, but our kingdom's scholars keep a keen eye on the happenings of the world in case any of it relates to us. It just so happens that when your battle with the Azag hive cluster was posted by Elysium, and your rise to the Paragon ranks was recorded after your Dao insights, it became a very attractive topic to talk about in the kingdom. We were all very impressed . . ."

Riven silently waited for the man to continue, but Theodore looked like he was at a loss for words. "Well, thank you for the compliment. Let me ask, are you new to the diplomacy thing?"

The court wizard stuttered a reply. "U-um, why would you ask?"

"Just curious."

Hesitantly, Theodore Munchamp glanced over at Marin, who just stared back at him like a deer caught in the headlights, then he slowly nodded. "Um . . . why, yes. Diplomacy is not necessarily my first calling . . . I am more attuned to practicing or experimenting with sun magic than anything else, as my title implies."

"What made you the one to come, then? I'm not trying to insult you—I'm just curious. Also, please sit. There's no reason to stand; this is an informal dinner and you're more than welcome to eat whatever you want in the meantime. Please be at ease."

Theodore wiped away sweat that'd begun to accumulate on his brow, nodded, and sat down, taking a long swig of ice-cold water. "I'm sorry if I seem inadequate for the job—"

"I never said that," Riven cut in with a smile that the man couldn't see. "I'm sorry if I came off rude. You're just very nervous, and it shows."

Marin let out a long sigh, putting her face into her hands.

Theodore glared at the woman next to him but didn't comment on her obvious display of irritation. "Most of our professional diplomats were already attending other kingdoms and empires on Zazir before the integration and merging of the three worlds. We have to make do with what we've got, and I just happened to be one to fill that role at the request of the king. As for my nerves—it is hard not to be."

Theodore gestured over to Allie. "When you're sitting at a table with someone as bloodthirsty—and simultaneously gorgeous—as that, those are just two big reasons to be nervous."

"Theodore!" Marin gasped, going pale and wide-eyed with a stiffening posture in her cushioned chair.

"It's the truth, Marin!" Theodore exclaimed with exasperation, again dabbing at his forehead. "And you, my lord! How am I supposed to be anything but terrified after seeing that tremendous display of power! You two siblings running this necropolis are downright scary!"

Riven's grin wasn't visible, but his sputtering laugh came fast and turned into a hearty bellow. "I see! Well, Theodore, at least you're honest. I like that quite a bit, actually—honesty goes a long way with me, and it's a hard trait to find in many people."

He gave a pointed look Genua's way as she passed by, and her eyes shied away from him while she adjusted her French maid outfit to deliver more slabs of meat to where Azmoth was rapidly devouring food.

"Tell me," Riven eventually said after there was a lull in the conversation, and his attention shifted back from the enslaved elf to the two humans nearby.

"What do you think about the war with the elves?"

"They're pompous, arrogant, evil bastards," Marin immediately replied with a hot rage simmering behind her brown eyes. "They attacked us for no reason, butchered an entire town without cause, and raid our supply caravans every chance they get. They are racist, bigoted, and they deserve to die. All of them."

Riven's eyebrows rose, and his left hand settled onto the table to begin tapping at it with his fingers while the laughter of his two female minions echoed from the splashing pool below. "Really . . . that's a rather aggressive stance to take."

"What other stance would you take if your family was killed by them for no reason?" Marin shot back, venom in her words as her knuckles went white on the clipboard she carried.

Theodore's features softened into a look of sad contemplation, and he let out a sigh, nodding. "I must agree with Marin's assessment. The elves of Zazir were always arrogant, but we'd never had any real dealings with them before now. But due to the proximity of Tereen to Dawn after the merging, it appears that we have no choice but to fight. Otherwise they'll enslave or kill us to take our lands for their own. They think of us humans as a lesser race, a flawed race, and their inherent racism is drilled into their young from an early age. They will either need to be put down or completely subdued . . ."

Theodore motioned to where numerous butlers and maids bustled around the room. "You're treating your conquered enemies rather well. We've seen your farms, we've seen how you operate, and we've seen the school you set up for their children. But the people enslaved by the kingdom of Tereen are quite the opposite of this—they live and wallow in mud while dying like flies for the amusement of elvish masters. To be quite blunt, we were worried you'd decline our request for aid. The king is very grateful, and if he weren't on the front lines regularly, he'd have come to thank you in person. With your forces protecting our northernmost town, Bradshire, and after Allie defeated the elvish commander at the battle of Longhill, we've been able to focus our efforts on the core of our remaining kingdom."

Riven nodded mutely, then snapped his fingers in Allie's direction. "You said we acquired new elvish settlements to rule over, is that right?"

Allie stopped laughing at one of General Bruner's dad jokes, turned her head, and squinted. "Yes . . . why? We've occupied two medium-size towns and had a village under our control that we ended up burning down for a tactical retreat. They're to the southwest, near where the mountain range ends, past where Greenstalk was, and we're ridding the area of guerrilla fighters before figuring out what we're going to keep. It's likely that we'll destroy one of the towns and consolidate the populations of both into one, after most of the defenders are killed. It'll be easier to keep an eye on the subjugated that way."

General Bruner, who'd not been in on any of these talks concerning the military agenda on this side of the world yet, perked up with interest. "If I may, I would like to get a rundown on what's going on with the war efforts here. Riven informed me that you have enemies in the area, and although we have our own problems near Chicago's borders, we may be able to send some flying units for scouting and striking purposes."

"You're not bogged down by the moral decision of whether or not you should participate?" Riven asked curiously.

General Bruner looked confused. "Sir, we pledged to you. If you decide to go to war, you're our king now—we will do whatever you want us to do after you saved our city from annihilation. Aside from that, I think it's a moral obligation to unite the planet."

"Oh-ho!" Allie crowed, turning back to reevaluate the general with a new gleam to her eyes. "And just why is that?! I think I like this guy!"

General Bruner grinned slightly, then placed both hands confidently on the table and clasped them together. "If I'm speaking bluntly, a united front across the world means two things. One, it means fewer wars for future generations. In the past, back on Earth, war was a rampant plague that destroyed the lives of people over countless generations. So it is, in my opinion, the moral high ground to conquer everything to prevent wars like that from occurring over future decades, centuries, or even millennia. And with vampiric heritage like yours, you'll be able to live long enough to see it through and keep it stabilized."

Riven hadn't ever really thought about it like that, but he couldn't necessarily argue with that logic. There were certainly flaws behind it, but the overall premise wasn't a bad one. "All right. What is the second thing?"

General Bruner didn't take long to think it over. "This is the multiverse now. Our planet is just one of many, and we already have invaders from other worlds coming to take over, according to the world quests. If we don't unite as a world, someone from off-world will do it for us. And it is likely that things will end very badly for our people if that comes to pass."

CHAPTER 37

Lahn Lucio sputtered and coughed, clutching his bruised forehead where his wavy chestnut locks were plastered across his face. He had slipped trying to get out of the bathtub again and tipped the porcelain tub over while simultaneously landing face-first with water rushing over him onto the tiled floor.

Being born with a deformity had caused him many problems growing up, and among the least of them were his regular slips in the bathroom. His left leg was slightly short, looking rather withered, with scrunched-up green and gray tissues, while his left arm wasn't as afflicted but was still abnormally weak and shriveled. His back curved with extreme scoliosis, and he had the misfortune of being very, very weak on his left side with overall poor balance. Thankfully his mother was a kind woman and often helped him dress in the morning or eat when he couldn't hold his utensils properly.

"LAHN?!" his mother called from the next room over. She was always watching out for him, even when she knew he hated to be babied at the age of twenty. "LAHN, ARE YOU OKAY?! DID YOU FALL AGAIN?!"

"I'M FINE, MOTHER!" Lahn cried out in frustration, though he couldn't help but smile that his mother still cared for him so much. She was such a good and kind person.

The same couldn't be said for his siblings and father.

His father was a war hero and esteemed inquisitor for the crown, while his two siblings were rising stars at the Imperial Academy. The house name of Lucio was well-known throughout Dawn and the surrounding remnants of their kingdom as one of the most esteemed households in court. His siblings were worshipped as future leaders in the army, already having achieved great feats in the war against Tereen, while he was akin to a ghost. A ghost to them all, a ghost to be ignored, all looking down on him—save for his mother. But as long as he had her . . . that was all he could ask for.

"HURRY! LORD AND LADY BORTROST HAVE BROUGHT THEIR DAUGHTER TO MEET YOU!" His mother sounded excited, which spurred him on as he struggled to merely get up off the floor. A minute passed before she came into the bathroom, where she saw her struggling son. She wore a pretty dark-green dress, had her brunette hair pulled up into a ponytail, and wore a large pendant across her chest. Putting a hand over her mouth and trying not to damage his pride, she helped him to his feet and let him regain his balance without too much help.

"This is a bad idea, Mother . . ." Lahn stated solemnly, avoiding eye contact and allowing her to dry him off. "Perhaps I should just stay in my room while they're here."

"Nonsense!" Lady Shovi Lucio insisted. Her radiant smile always lifted Lahn's spirits, and she helped him into a white shirt before putting on his under-garments and pants. "Their daughter is supposed to be very cute, and her parents wish her to marry into a good household! Be sure to tell them about how you're doing in classes at the academy! I'm sure they'll be impressed."

Lahn's nervous grin showed briefly, and he cleared his throat as he felt his hands get sweaty. "Don't make me out to be something I'm not, Mom. The only thing I can do at the academy is magic—"

"And there are PLENTY of men and women who make a good living doing just that!" exclaimed his mother as she kissed his bruised forehead. "Some people have very low affinities or no affinities at all, making them unable to cast any-thing! Be grateful for what you have—there are always those worse off, and you're a catch for any woman!"

Lahn rolled his eyes.

"Yeah. Maybe one day, if I study magic hard enough, I'll even figure out how to stop my body from . . ." Lahn's words trailed off as his eyes fell to his shriveled limbs. His mother frowned, and her lips quivered just briefly before she kissed him again and held his handsome face in her hands.

"You are my son," she said as she wiped away a tear and sniffled. "Never forget that I will always love you. I will always be there to support you when you need it, and even if I have to spend the entire family fortune doing it, I will find a way to fix this."

"We've already tried many times. The cure isn't there." Lahn smiled at his mother and put his good right hand around her shoulder to hug her warmly. "I love you, too, Mom. But there's no need to spend any more money on healers; the best have already been hired and failed. If there is a fix for my . . . disfig-urement, it will have to be through new magic not yet discovered. That's why I went to the academy in the first place, right?! It's not like they'd ever let me into the military like this. And I only got into the Imperial Academy because of our family name."

"You wouldn't like it in the military anyways. Your brother and sister are crazy for following in their father's footsteps—he's miserable all the time, and those Tereen monsters are so bloodthirsty! Not to mention the new monsters around here since the integration!" insisted his mother as she finished buttoning up his vest. Going over to a mirror trimmed in gold, she reached behind it and pulled out a bottle of men's perfume, which she sprayed all over her son, causing him to cough. She laughed and kissed him on the forehead again just as a uniformed maid rushed in and bowed.

"The lord and lady Bortrost have just arrived with their daughter! Their carriage is pulling up now!"

"Shit!" Lady Shovi Lucio exclaimed as she finished dressing her crippled son. She motioned for the maid and was quickly brought a wheelchair from his bedroom. The plain-looking, freckled maid and his ever-sweet mother helped him into the chair. They then wheeled him through the large, well-lit halls decorated with paintings of Lahn's father's triumphs to the front entrance of their estate, just as the servants finished escorting the guests to the marble arch of the front door.

"SHOVI!" Lady Lucio's childhood friend Lady Niltini Bortrost exclaimed she as rushed over to greet her. The two well-dressed brunette women looked quite similar as they embraced and kissed each other's cheeks while exchanging a myriad of compliments.

"It has been too long, Niltini! And how is your handsome husband doing this fine day?!"

Lord Armando Bortrost, a tall, well-built man with dark hair wearing a Victorian-style suit, smiled widely at the compliment and bowed to kiss her hand in the shadow of the Lucio manor. "Always a pleasure, Shovi. Who is this fine young man we've got here?"

Armando winked at his wife and motioned toward Lahn, who was directly in a blinding ray of sunlight, causing him to blink rapidly.

"Lahn! It's been almost a year, hasn't it?!" Niltini stated with hands clasped in front of her—bending down to be at eye level with her best friend's boy. "You're looking good! I heard you got accepted into the Imperial Academy? Is that true? We can use all the good men we can get in these trying times!"

Lahn's face blushed bright red, and he looked down sheepishly to hide his eyes under his wavy brunet locks. "My mother talks too much."

"Nonsense! I've heard you're doing very well in your magic classes!" Lord Armando Bortrost laughed as he patted Lahn's shoulder. "Lahn, we've brought someone we'd like you to meet! This is our daughter, Marsia!"

Lord Armando Bortrost motioned to the carriage parked on the cobblestone path nearby, and the door swung open to reveal a young woman that Lahn had seen before in passing.

Marsia, nineteen years of age, was in her prime years to marry another of the court. She wasn't spectacular to look at for most people, but she certainly wasn't ugly, with brown hair and large dimples, just like her parents. Wearing a bright-blue dress, she came forward from her hiding place behind Armando and curtsied reluctantly.

"Hello, Lahn. I've heard many things about you."

Lahn bit his lip and tried not to choke. This was actually the first time he had ever spoken to a girl his own age since his childhood years, and he squirmed under the pressure. "H-hi, Marsia. You look amazing."

His mother, Shovi, rolled her eyes as the Bortrost parents giggled to one another.

"Come inside! Come inside. We'll have the servants fetch some tea and pastries and eat out on the back porch!" Shovi exclaimed as she ushered everyone into the greeting hall. "I'm not sure if you remember, but we have a very nice view of the lake from here!"

The back porch was much larger than what most people would consider a porch—it was many times the width of a small house and was decorated with well-carved tables. Servants had already set up refreshments in anticipation of the House Bortrost's arrival, and they were quick to stand at attention as the noble families all sat down at one of the larger tables overlooking their backyard gardens.

"So tell me how your investments have gone since the merging of worlds! Are you bringing back a good haul with mining copper in the outlands? I've heard we're in dire need of new weapons material." Lady Shovi Lucio was quick to delve into her good friends' happenings.

Lord Armando Bortrost rolled his eyes and sighed with unspoken misfortune as he picked up a pastry and shoved it into his mouth, pouting. "Not good. The mining company we sponsored was butchered by Tereen raiders a few days ago. Those damned pointies are completely ruining us—and we're not the only ones."

Lady Niltini Bortrost frowned deeply, smoothed her dress, and sipped her tea.

But Shovi would not be dissuaded or dismayed. Their country had already survived quite a few challenges and hurdles, and if one didn't actively pursue happiness, it would quickly escape you after so many had senselessly been lost to the tutorials, local wildlife, or the elves.

"Oh, come now, give me the details! I must know what my friends have been up to. And at the very least provide me with some good gossip on this fine autumn day!" Shovi remarked casually as she too picked up her tea in a fine porcelain cup, very ladylike, and winked to her compatriots across the table.

"Gossip?" Niltini asked slyly, adjusting her dress and setting the cup back down. "That I can provide. I will spare you the boring details of our failed trading efforts and focus on the things that matter . . . Did you hear about how two ladies of the court were found to be involved in the illegal slave trades?"

"WHAT?! What are their names?! Surely they're in prison now. A shame. Do we know them?!"

"Well, yes . . . we do, actually! I'll tell you, and you won't believe who it was . . ."

The banter between the two women overtook the stage, and soon Lord Armando Bortrost was losing himself to sleep as his wife and her best friend gossiped. Meanwhile, Lahn was doing his best to think of things to say to their daughter, Marsia.

The young woman next to him at the finely made table hadn't glanced at him even once. Perhaps she was bored . . . his mother had always told him that he was fun to talk to, though. Maybe he could make her laugh? Maybe then she'd talk to him!

"M-Marsia. Do you like jokes?" Lahn asked in a hesitant whisper.

"What was that?" Marsia asked, barely turning her head to glance at him. "I wasn't sure what you just said."

Lahn felt his hands getting sweaty and tried to sit up straighter, but the extreme form of scoliosis was working against him. He tried to adjust his positioning in the wheelchair so that he could look at her straight on, but with his weak left side he was only able to kind of flop to one side before the maid had to adjust his frail body for him. Marsia didn't say a word as the plain, middle-aged maid pulled him up by his armpits.

"Sorry . . ." Lahn muttered, flushing thoroughly with a bright-red tint to his cheeks. "I said, do you like jokes?"

Marsia shrugged unenthusiastically, barely giving him a sideways half glance that was filled with impatience. "As much as any other person, I suppose."

"Well, would you like to hear one?" Lahn asked with a small, truly innocent smile. He was just happy to have someone his own age to talk to other than his pompous siblings.

"No. I'd rather not; I have a rather harsh headache at the moment."

Lahn's small smile quickly faded, and he was left twiddling his thumbs. "I see. Um . . . Are you enrolling in the academy, too?"

A bird flew overhead, and as it passed it dropped a small load of shit that landed on Lahn's left hand. Startled by the bird and filled with a mixture of disgust and embarrassment, he cursed his luck and used a napkin to wipe away the bird dung as Marsia eyed him with raised eyebrows.

"Yes . . . I'm actually a class ahead of you and have already been accepted . . ."

"Really?!" Lahn replied excitedly as he threw the napkin in a side pouch attached to his wheelchair. "Wow! Maybe you could help me with some of the classes I'm in now! Do you think—"

Marsia cleared her throat loudly and stood up as her eyes drifted to where their parents were talking enthusiastically. She then turned back to Lahn. "Do you mind showing me to the ladies' room?"

Lahn nodded eagerly and motioned for the maid to wheel him out, and without a word they began to backtrack into the mansion. Going through a set of large wooden doors and entering a large living room, they turned down one of the hallways toward the kitchen. He looked back excitedly and watched as Marsia walked by his side, looking straight ahead.

"That's the door!" Lahn exclaimed, smiling again as they came to the spot where one of the bathrooms was located. He looked her up and down just briefly enough so that she wouldn't notice, appreciating how pretty she was. "May I wait here for you to finish?"

The inside of the mansion was rather quiet. Marsia took a long look at one of the portraits of Lahn's handsome father before replying. As she spoke, an air of disgust overcame her.

"No. You may not."

The quick and blunt retort shocked him, and his face betrayed his emotions moments later while she continued to speak.

"Let me be clear . . . Lahn. I am not interested." Marsia's face was cold and stern. "I certainly think you are a nice boy. But I am the daughter of an esteemed noble family. My parents may approve this potential arrangement because of their friendship with your family, and your family does have a good name . . . but I will not allow myself to marry a cripple."

THUD

Lahn's heart almost stopped in his chest, and he looked like he'd just been struck across the face.

Marsia resumed her normal posture and placed a hand on the door handle. "Maybe your family's status will be enough to land you a peasant girl. Maybe one of your maids. But you need to leave me alone—and that is the end of it. Good day, sir."

The door to the bathroom shut quietly behind her as Marsia gracefully parted ways with him. Lahn just sat there, stunned and ashamed, as he looked over his crippled body in dismay. He wanted to cry.

"Entitled bitch," the maid who was wheeling him around said under her breath. She looked down in pity at the young man and frowned. "Should we go back outside, young sir?"

It took a while for him to get the words out, but he shook his head and said in a quivering voice, "No . . . just take me to my room. Tell my mother I felt ill. And please, do not speak of this. It would only cause my mother unnecessary grief."

The maid nodded reluctantly, and with a sigh she began to wheel him away. The excitement Lahn had felt when he had first laid eyes on Marsia was long gone, and all that was left was a pit in his stomach made of self-pity and depression. Off to sleep he went.

Things were gearing up. Riven was preparing to leave even though he'd just gotten back, he needed to get out and about to find the other Chalgathi artifacts before he was killed—and he was on a shorter timeline than the others. Meanwhile, Allie had a war to continue, so they'd set up a short goodbye breakfast. It was bittersweet, drawn-out, and the two siblings basked in each other's presence while knowing that it'd likely be a while before they were reunited. They'd stayed up late talking after everyone else had gone to bed, but they each had their own path to take—if only temporarily. Neither of them was very worried, though, not after spending an absolutely massive amount of money from their treasury on a certain pair of items from the Elysium altar last night in case of emergencies.

But at least they'd be able to talk if one needed the other.

Things had taken an abrupt right turn when the wizard Munchamp posed a question concerning a trip to Mandon, Dawn's capital. Apparently the king had given him a letter addressed to the Thane Necropolis leadership, and the old man had forgotten about it entirely last night due to his nervous breakdown at being in the presence of so many vampires and Unholy entities at one time.

Theodore Munchamp patted down his robes and pulled out the letter he'd mentioned. It had the king's red seal, the symbol of the sun, sealing the parchment shut. Cutting it with a small knife, the orange-haired older mage cleared his throat and handed it to Allie as Riven watched from the side.

Allie took it, scanned it up and down, then raised an eyebrow and handed the letter to Riven.

The room remained silent after that, with Dawn's other diplomat staring hopefully at the two vampires from across the table as Athela snarfed down scrambled eggs nearby.

"He wants one of us to attend the royal academy?" Riven said skeptically, turning the letter over to make sure he hadn't missed anything before pushing it into one of Allie's pockets. "I'm out. I have to find Chalgathi's other artifacts before I'm eaten by this goddamned suit. As for you . . ."

Riven eyed his sister suspiciously. A thinly veiled grin was creeping across her face. "I don't know about this. If you wanted to learn, you still haven't visited the Blood Moon Requiem's trading commune since I was accidentally banished to the other side of Panu."

"I have nothing to learn from them," Allie stated sourly. "Those incompetent relatives of ours have only brought us misfortune. First they almost got us killed, then they were less than capable when you were forcibly zapped away. I have lost faith in them."

"I see. But don't you have a city to run?"

Allie nodded and gestured out the window toward the portal in the distance. "More than just one now. Including the three cities you brought into the fold and the elvish town we conquered, that makes five. But I think you're failing to see the big picture here."

Allie adjusted her position in her chair to fully face her older brother as he gave her what she knew to be a judgmental frown despite the mask he wore. She could tell by his body language. "I'm already moving our armies farther into Dawn's territories for a back-line defense in case the dungeon Tereen is allied to attempts to strike out at Dawn's capital city, Mandon. I was going to set up a base camp there anyways with General Bruner, Gurth'Rok, Vin, and Nin, so why not? It'll give me some insight into how Dawn is run, what its people are like, and will allow me to make political connections with the nobility and give me some much needed off time. Mara will run things in my stead through the communication stones. Right, Mara?"

The ghoul necromancer nodded in agreement. "I will not fail you, Mistress. I have become very adept at running Brightsville while you wage war on the tree lovers. I've improved trade relations with Negrada and the Blood Moon Requiem, culled the remaining forces that opposed you in the prison and gang wars to the north, and I have integrated the remaining Brightsville humans without much hassle. I also have already drawn up plans for civilians to freely travel between Chicago and Brightsville through the portal with checkpoint setups and registration cards for safety measures—with many of the officers from General Bruner's police force coming over soon to get the layout of our twin cities. I do believe I've demonstrated at least some measure of competency."

Riven snorted at the comment about "tree lovers," especially when Genua shot the ghoul a glare while she was cleaning up after breakfast. "Hmm. I see. Well, I don't see any reason why Dawn would betray us . . . So it shouldn't put you in danger while I'm out hunting Chalgathi's chosen. Just be careful, okay? I don't want to have to come in and wipe out a neighboring city because you get into trouble—and I won't be able to communicate with you when I get out of range. Satellite phones or cell phones from Chicago still aren't up, so I'll be checking the Brightsville forums regularly if you have anything important to impart."

"I assure you!" Theodore exclaimed nervously, holding up both hands in wide-eyed alarm. "We would never DREAM of attacking your sister! The king merely thought that, since you two were of courting age, perhaps you'd find someone within our kingdom that may suit your fancy . . ."

Theodore's voice trailed off uncertainly as both vampires slowly turned to stare, and Marin, the other diplomat from Dawn, face-palmed hard.

"Well," Riven stated flatly. "I guess . . . Just try not to kill anyone while you're over there?"

"It'll only be a temporary thing while we finish the war," Allie stated with an amused nod. "I'm rather curious about what our neighboring allies are like, so this little trip should be rather fun."

CHAPTER 38

The Elysium altar's general system store was . . . overpriced, to say the least. Its options were also low quality, but at least it gave vast amounts of them. Even the basics were in high demand concerning their little necropolis kingdom, with dozens upon dozens of adventuring guilds or mercenary groups taking up government-posted contracts to cull beasts in the area or scout out resources of interest, like Unholy herbs and ores. There were even system-sponsored quests for such things that could be picked up at the altar. This meant Riven's altar—and Brightsville in turn—had become a major trading hub. There were even a couple of orcs, humans, and goblins exchanging their pillar affinities for the Unholy foundational pillar as well as randomized subpillars, which in large part reset what people could take in terms of classes, and it was a very popular choice due to the Unholy-attuned environments in this area giving people bonuses to leveling and Dao insights for the Unholy brands.

Riven touched one hand against the obsidian spire in the middle of the now-expansive trading hub, where people from Brightsville, Milwaukee, Chicago, Rockford, Deepnest, and Dawn's northernmost town of Bradshire all intermixed with one another. That didn't even include the vampiric host of the Blood Moon Requiem, who'd opened their metaphorical doors to the budding kingdom with items as dirt cheap as the system would allow while simultaneously avoiding consequences—a desperate attempt on Kathrine Vonsilla Crushada the Ninth's part to make amends with the Thane siblings. It also didn't include the various Jabob demons, gargoyles, and other hellscape creatures that were found in or around the large tent Dungeon Negrada had set up.

"This stuff is all so expensive . . ." Riven heard some poor sod from Bradshire mutter under his breath while touching the central altar's spire to access the general store. The young man glanced his way and abruptly paled when seeing Riven looking back at him, then quickly scurried away without buying anything.

Others, including various undead, orcs, a few of the smarter goblins, and the Earth-born humans, were all scrolling through their own screens that'd been displayed on the obsidian monument like individual computers that they and others could view. Watching the rows upon rows of people waiting in line to access the system store was rather interesting—with many of the people here conducting transactions by mentally selecting items and the system removing coins and then depositing whatever items the person bought. Usually this was low-tier adventuring gear for almost any or all classes, unique items like bonded pets, ability tomes or scrolls, information missives, tools, crafting materials, or foodstuffs—which was what Riven had primarily used it for in order to secure vast amounts of food for the growing empire.

In fact, after learning that Chicago was in dire need, Riven had nearly spent all his massive fortune from culling the Azag swarms and clearing the dungeon he'd saved Hakim from. Tons upon tons of rations of preserved food, seeds for planting, and even livestock had whittled away at Riven's funds until only a small pile of money remained from his once grand mountain of wealth.

[Elysium coins: 1,253,508]

Riven groaned internally when he saw just how low the cache his spatial bag had fallen. To a normal person, over a million coins would have been enough to be considered rich. But he'd topped out at over eighty million after his recent battles.

"The price of a bleeding heart!" Athela said with a wink, laughing when he glared her way. "What?! It's true! If you'd just let all these people starve, you'd have been able to buy all kinds of neat stuff!"

Despite what Athela was saying, Riven could see his efforts had been appreciated—and they'd been widely publicized due to his sister's efforts. Everyone here knew just how much he'd spent to feed the cities they controlled, how much he'd invested in planting crops for the next year, and if he'd been hailed a hero in Chicago before all this, now pretty much everyone who lived under the umbrella of their empire had a deep-seated respect for him that bordered on awe or fear. By now the world forums had been blasting Riven's fight across Panu, and it was a known thing in the necropolis that he was a Paragon—and that he was also involved in one of the major world quests. The power display had been impressive, to say the least, and would no doubt act as a nuclear deterrent to some while quickly garnering attention from leaders and diplomats in other start-up nations around here. Their intelligence gathering wasn't perfect, and the political landscape around Brightsville's area of influence was heavily contested, with several different wars going on, but nothing very solid had come up other than a few major outliers like Dawn, Tereen, or the nation bordering on their conflict that was still deciding whom to support, if anyone at all.

What was its name again?

Riven couldn't remember. He'd even talked to that country's diplomat over dinner, yet for the life of him he couldn't bring himself to really care when so many other more important subjects were on the table. He'd leave the politics to Allie.

Riven shook his head and focused, continuing to scroll through lists of equipment in preparation for the journey into unknown lands. He was going to go hunt down those other artifact pieces, and he had to be prepared for anything. It was obvious, especially after his fights against both the assassin in the hospital basement and the heretic, that these people in Chalgathi's trials were another level of dangerous. Even for someone like him, it was nothing to scoff at, and there was a good chance that many of them would give him a run for his money.

"There's nothing in the general store that interests me beyond the healing, stamina, and mana potions we got," Riven muttered, letting his hand drop and dismissing the screen from the obsidian face of the altar.

He ignored the stares and hushed whispers directed his way from the crowds around him, nodding to Azmoth and snapping his fingers to get Fay's attention. "Find anything good? Or should we make a stop nearby and then head over to the communes?"

Riven gestured over to where three buildings stood in between the two trade communes. They each belonged to prominent adventuring groups, one comprised mostly of orc warriors and some undead mages, while the second was mostly made up of humans from Brightsville. Both of these guilds had their own start-up crafting sects, and these parts of the guild had set up shop here on the Elysium altar's grounds after getting permission from Allie to do so. The third building was actually a ragtag collection of rat-kin from Deepnest, who had been able to create a hill full of caves and interior rooms like the ones Riven had seen in the underground city weeks ago.

From what Riven had heard, the prices were far better at the native stores when compared to anything you could find in the communes of Negrada and the Blood Moon Requiem—and they were WAY cheaper than anything from the general store. So it was always in one's best interest to check out the locals first, due to the taxation practices and price hikes the system enforced on outsiders and its own wares. The problem was that Riven highly doubted these locals had anything of value for someone like him, as most of them were below level 25 and he was now level 68, so until people started to catch up, he'd most likely focus on the trade communes from off-world.

Fay grunted her acknowledgment and flapped her wings in irritation. "There's only bad-quality stuff here, and it's all way more pricey than it should be! How can the system set these ridiculous prices?!"

"First time at an altar?" Athela mused with a grin, and the three of them started off in Azmoth's direction.

The large demon stood stoically with two hands resting on the shaft of his Infernal maul, and people didn't dare get near him lest he flare up. Beside him, bound to one of his large wrists was Genua—who'd been more or less *voluntold* she'd be coming along as Riven's private meals on wheels. The elf was outwardly terrified, her blue-green eyes darting around and sweat visible on her forehead.

Azmoth snorted. "Did find goods?"

"Just some basic mana, health, and stamina potions. Everything else was either subpar or priced so goddamned high it would have hurt my soul to buy them."

"Okay. Negrada has good stuffs. We go there next?"

Riven glanced toward Genua—who was nervously fidgeting and scratching at her neck, where the iron collar kept her shackled. Then he looked up at the large demon with furrowed brows. "You went to check it out earlier?"

Azmoth nodded. "They make special gear for us to buy. You want outfit us three demons, yes?"

Riven nodded. "Yeah, that's right. The goal here is to get each of you new equipment, traveling supplies, and some new abilities. Whatever I can buy with what I have left."

"Uh . . . Um . . . Master?" Genua asked, almost in a whisper while raising a hand to get his attention. "Are you really taking me along? I believe I'd be better suited here as a maid in your household . . ."

"Yes, you're coming," Riven stated flatly. "You're the one I'm going to be feeding on."

"But—"

"But nothing. You don't get to choose anymore—be happy that you're even alive right now. Be happy that I let you see your daughter before we leave. Other than that, be quiet unless spoken to."

Genua paled, then let out a shuddering breath to calm herself. "All right. Will I be able to see Len again when we get back?"

"What did Riven just say about being quiet?" Athela hissed, yanking on Genua's long blond hair and causing the woman to yelp. "Speak only when spoken to, Sandwich, because we're definitely not bringing you along for the company."

The tent Negrada had supplied for its tier-one trade commune was spatially enhanced inside—there was far more room within than should have been possible, with multiple floors of wooden stockades or platforms underneath the red roof. Locals bartered with many of the red-skinned, three-eyed Jabob demon merchants, who were rather shrewd in their dealings—and the peace was kept intact by armored gargoyles who'd throw any rowdy customers out. Hundreds of people were inside, with booths, stalls, and elevated walkways leading up to the more grand stuff overhead.

"Prince Thane! Or should I call you Prince Wraithtide of the Blood Moon Requiem, eh?!" an excited and shifty voice called from up above, making Riven and many of the others look or pay attention to the one shouting and the one being shouted at.

Above them and on a huge third-story platform was the red-skinned old Jabob demon Fred. He had a long white beard, was robed in purple, and hunched over a gnarled staff. He was the head of the trading commune here on Panu, and beside him, peering over the edge, was his assistant and the head identifier, Zelmont, the handsome orange incubus with his black ponytail slung over one shoulder.

"Come up! Come up!" Fred crowed, waving his staff in the air and causing a spiraling staircase created from red light to twirl down and settle at Riven's feet. "You are a special guest—do not mix with the rabble! Come see what stores we have for you! Azmoth has already given us a good idea of what you're looking for, and we've prepared some of the best we can offer on this poor, unruly, low-grade world!"

Riven smirked, then ignored the stairs made of energy and simply walked through a rift in space to step up onto the platform. His three demons followed, and they found themselves facing a rather lavish storefront that was secluded from the rest of the smaller shops, booths, and setups down below. Red banners inlaid with gold covered the entrance and walls of carved, polished wood—and some of Zelmont's Succubus wives stood at attention just outside.

"Traveling in style, I see," Zelmont stated with a head nod—letting his eyes fall over Fay just once to elicit a hiss before smirking and adjusting his plain white tunic. Pulling out a clipboard and a pen created from the same red energy as the staircase, he nodded over to the inner workings of Negrada's trading commune. "This is an exclusive trading area only for people on this planet who we deem . . . acceptable enough to enter. May I also add that I was quite pleased to see your rise to power on the cortex forums here? It did add some excitement to the boring tasks of overseeing this commune."

"Don't act like you do all the work. That would be me," Fred snarled with a flick of his wrist, ruffling Zelmont's hair with a blast of some kind of wind and getting a disgruntled glare from the incubus. "Anyways, I am very excited to see you finally make your appearance in our small and humble commune, my prince. It is an honor to not only have an esteemed progenitor of this planet buy from us, but also to do business with one of the royal house of the Requiem is beyond a simple demon like me. Please, come inside so that we may discuss the wares we have! Was Azmoth correct in saying you're looking for specialty items concerning your demonic familiars?"

"That'd be correct," Riven stated with a head bob over to the three familiars behind him. "Weapons, armor, outfits, supplies, trinkets, new ability tomes or scrolls—anything that'll help us on a long journey. You name it and I'll consider buying it."

"And what is your price range? Surely you gained quite a bit of wealth after your recent battle!" Fred's eyes gleamed with greed, and his little red hands rubbed together excitedly in anticipation.

"I spent most of it," Riven said honestly, getting a frown from the smaller, hunched demon in front of him. "Only a little over a million coins left. I spent over seventy-eight million at the system store on acquiring foodstuffs and getting our economy started. I'd heard that you didn't deal in food, so I just went to the source."

Fred's eyes bulged, and his voice rose to a squeak of disbelief. "SEVENTY-EIGHT MILLION?! Are you INSANE?! Why would you spend that kind of money on . . . Ugh . . . Never mind! Just follow me. At least tell me you still have the cursed sanctuary stone?"

"Yeah, I still have it. Why?"

"Negrada is interested in buying it. Getting our hands on an Azag hive sanctuary that can be harnessed isn't unheard-of, but it is very rare and potentially valuable to a dungeon core if we're able to crack its code."

"Huh." Riven had seen what the system store would pay for such an item. He'd also read up on some of the lore concerning the Azag, which were essentially planetary parasites that ate the cores out of worlds and left them as smoking husks after draining their mana. The Azag hive clusters were a very feared force in the multiverse, but just how they'd gotten a foothold on this planet through using Richard as an overmind was unfortunately beyond Riven's knowledge. Regardless, he could see why a dungeon would want it. Using it to build up a force of personalized Azag would without a doubt be of great benefit to Negrada, and perhaps a dungeon like Negrada would be able to resist the compelling sensations the curse of the stone would give.

That didn't mean Riven would part with it for anything less than a monumental price, because the price the Elysium altar's general store had proposed was immense. Hell, Riven wasn't even sure he wanted to part with it at all—in case he could somehow find out a way to control the start-up hive cluster himself one day.

Fred's irritation died down when he realized the Azag sanctuary stone was still in Riven's possession. Waving Riven forward, the Jabob went through the gold-inlaid flaps with Zelmont the incubus behind. Azmoth roughly yanked Genua forward by her chain, and the three familiars followed as Riven passed into the interior of the elevated third-story platform.

Inside was a long hallway with closed-off rooms on either side. And at the end of the hallway was a rectangular room with four sets of outfits already positioned on wooden mannequins. Each had a name carved into the wood below, with very fine detail noted to each carving.

Athela.

Azmoth.

Fay.

Genua.

"Genua?" Riven stated, eyeing the outfit and glancing between his slave and the mannequin. "Really? You prepared a set for her, too? The rest of this is rather impressive, and I'm sure it's expensive, but I won't be paying much if anything for her. She and her family betrayed me and tried to kill me. If she dies, she dies."

"It's on the house!" Fred stated with a wide grin, ignoring the wide-eyed look of shock on the elf's face. "And trust me on this, vampire: you should invest more heavily in creating a thrall. A proper thrall can be just as good a weapon as a contracted familiar, and with a bloodline like yours flowing through her veins, I'm sure you would not be disappointed."

CHAPTER 39

"I agree with Fred," Athela stated promptly, glowering over at Genua with distaste. "We'll need a solid supply of blood for you while traveling, and things will be dangerous. Creating a thrall will allow her to take more of a hit and maybe even be useful, as opposed to this sniveling creature we have on our hands now."

Genua's eyes had tears collecting underneath them, and with a fearful look shot Riven's way, she adamantly shook her head, fingers going white as they tightened against her palms. "Please . . ."

Hmm.

It probably was about time he created a thrall of his own. The problem was they took a long time to make, the process of continually feeding on them taking weeks, months, or even years if their Willpower was strong enough to resist the vampiric taint. Pulling up the old system quest from his screens, Riven reviewed the thrall-related quest.

[You have been offered a guiding system quest from the administrator: Acquire Cattle and Create a Thrall—As a newly born vampire, you will need to acquire cattle, or in other terms, people to feed on regularly. It does not matter if you do this through persuasion or force. Then after this, select one of these cattle to create a thrall. Thralls are mortals bent to a vampire's will and are essentially more subservient and powerful cattle, as many vampires like to say.

Though they do retain their Intelligence, personality, and to some extent their own free will, their desires are instinctively and heavily oriented to align with your own. This places them in the minion category of your status page when acquired successfully. Thralls also acquire some vampiric strengths, while they are able to retain their own pillars and abilities outside of the vampiric

influence. However: retained pillars and abilities will be corrupted—sometimes modifying them slightly for better or worse.

Lastly, thralls are able to provide greater amounts of nourishing blood than normal mortal cattle do, and their bloodlines may be modified over time to evolve to your liking. To create a thrall, you must feed on them regularly for an extended period of time, and they must in turn feed on your blood numerous times throughout their initial evolutionary cycle. Reward upon acquiring thrall: one combat level, a stable food source, and a new avenue to acquire minions.]

Riven let out an exasperated sigh in Genua's direction, then turned to Fay while Negrada's ambassadors waited patiently. "If we can't find anyone else to volunteer, I'll turn Genua. But we'll see if there's anyone else more willing first. Your brother vetted people to serve in the guild hall. Right? Would he know of anyone?"

Fay hummed in thought, rubbing her chin, then lifted a finger. "I can go check! Are you looking for anyone in particular?"

"What do you mean?"

"Do you want them older or younger, female or male?"

"Doesn't matter, as long as they're adult elves and they're willing or even wanting the change. Tell them it'll be a good opportunity for a power-up, a better life, and potentially a lot of excitement—but also danger. Just bring the first one you find, and if there happen to be multiple, bring them all. I don't want to waste time while this evil suit I'm wearing threatens to feed on my soul, so hurry. And thanks."

While they waited, Riven and Negrada's merchants made small talk, as he didn't want to go ahead with the transactions while Fay was out.

When she returned, the Succubus was followed by her incubus brother, Tupper, who glared in Zelmont's direction when their eyes met, but neither incubus said anything to the other. Behind Tupper was a single old man, an elf with silver hair in a ponytail, who was missing his right eye and supported himself with a cane. The man's wrinkled features were set in a determined yet also hesitant expression as he blinked.

"Master," Tupper stated, still dressed in a butler's suit as he bowed at the waist and extended his wings out to either side in a show of respect. "My sister has informed me that you were looking for a thrall, specifically one to create from a slave who is willing or wanting the change? Unfortunately that limited our options—we found only this single man after checking dozens of our captives."

Tupper rose when Riven gestured with a hand to do so, and the incubus stepped back to present the old elf, whose arthritic fingers tightened along his cane. "He isn't the greatest of specimens, but he is the only one who volunteered."

A snicker from Zelmont drew everyone's attention. The orange incubus was covering his mouth with one hand while looking the old slave over. "Rather pathetic, isn't he? Are you sure you'd rather not just take the woman you have chained here? Imagine all the fun you'd be able to have with her. Or if you'd rather not, at least sell her to me. I've always wanted an elf."

The old man's eye fell along with his expression, but he remained silent—and Genua's face paled more.

"Personal slaves are outlawed here," Riven said unemotionally as he walked up to the old man to evaluate the hunched figure. "They're only owned by the government for crimes committed. I won't be selling anyone, especially not to a sex demon."

Zelmont's look of disappointment was immediately mirrored by Genua's expression of relief.

"What is your name?" Riven eventually asked after moments of staring down at the old elf, who was avoiding Riven's gaze. "And what are your affinities? Or will I have to go get Zelmont here to tell me what they are? He should have the identification class to do so."

Zelmont nodded in confirmation of this, and the elf gradually lifted his good right eye up to blink at Riven's well-postured form.

"My name is Luke. Luke Blissfallen. My affinities are 43 percent of the Fae foundational pillar, 39 percent for the Forest subpillar, 48 percent for the Storm subpillar, and 28 percent for the Ocean subpillar. I did have the subpillars of Volcano, Glacial, and Swamp, but unfortunately lost these affinities in a battle many decades ago where my divinity channels were burned away and my soul was damaged. I also lost access to my bloodline . . . a true shame."

Riven's eyebrows raised. Most of the slaves from Greenstalk village were in the 15 to 30 percent range for their affinities and had only one or two. A lot of Allie's undead had Unholy and Death affinities ranging from 20 to 30 percent as well, while the greenskins had mostly Fae, Swamp, and Volcano affinities with similar numbers. "Those are some very good percentages. Zelmont, can you confirm?"

Even the incubus was quite surprised, and his look of disgust with the old man abruptly shifted to one of respect when he reached a hand forward to touch the old man's shoulder. Lights flashed across his eyes, and Zelmont gave a nod of confirmation. "He's telling the truth, though his energy channels aren't just burned away concerning his lost subpillars. They're burned out across his entire body; he won't be able to utilize any abilities at all, despite his percentages."

The incubus withdrew his hand, looking curiously down at the hunched figure. "Just what happened to you?"

The wrinkled old elf gave a hesitant smile and glanced Riven's way. "I used to be a well-known battle priest. I was caught in a life-and-death situation, back before the integration, and though I came out on top . . . I was forever unable to heal my body and soul entirely. I was hoping that . . . just perhaps becoming a thrall would fix me. Perhaps even give me a longer life. That is why I volunteered. I am a shadow of the man I used to be due to my disfigurement in both body and soul; even before being enslaved, my life was a living hell. I have no family that were killed in the battle of Greenstalk, as I was merely a traveler passing through when the integration came. My grandson, Ren, was the only remaining family that I kept in contact with, and he wasn't present at the battle. No doubt the young lad is off elsewhere in this world still trying to figure out what path he needs to take . . . but as for me, I am hoping that this one is mine."

There was a long pause as Riven considered the old man's words. "Does anyone here know if it is possible to heal energy channels and soul damage through becoming a thrall? I'm not even sure if it does."

"No idea," Athela replied.

Fay shrugged, as did her brother. Even Zelmont didn't give any input.

"I believe it is possible . . . but it would be hard to do alone," Fred, the bearded Jabob demon, stated while scratching his chin and looking over at the hunched elf thoughtfully. "Turning him into a thrall would certainly help his physical condition correct itself to an extent, and it would also prolong his life and modify his pillars and energy channels—be they stamina, divinity, or mana. However, whether it would fully fix these channels and pillars is unlikely without help. It is possible that the vampiric curse you afflict him with over time will eventually continue to shape his body so that he fully regains whatever it was that he lost—modified by your vampirism, of course. But I wouldn't bet money on it, and I'm a gambler at heart. Therefore I propose that, if you choose to make this man your thrall, you should buy some soul-healing Dao treasures or pills."

Fred gave Riven an evil grin. "We have them in stock, too!"

Riven snorted in amusement, then motioned toward Genua. "Take her back to the mansion. She is not needed here anymore, and thank you for the help, Tupper."

The incubus smiled widely at the acknowledgment of his success, bowed, and grabbed Genua's chains from Azmoth before leading the blonde woman out of Negrada's trade commune.

Riven watched Luke's expressions change, a conflicted pattern that settled down into a hopeful grin. "Do you know what you're signing up for, old man?"

"To become a thrall is to become a blood-bound slave to a vampiric master," Luke stated with an indifferent grunt. "But if it heals me, why would I say no? If it gives me another chance at life, one of excitement and adventure, why say no? You never did me wrong personally, nor the ones that I care about. The racism of the elves of Greenstalk got the better of them this time. Logically what you did by not purging them outright, and by treating them relatively well considering they are slaves, speaks to your character."

"You say *they* like you are not one of them."

"That's correct. I am not," Luke replied flatly. "As I said, I was merely passing through their village on a trip when integration struck. They are what I like to call country bumpkins. I always lived in the cities growing up."

This got a snort from Athela and a grin from Riven.

"I see. Well, then, Luke—I'll take your word for it. And what about your eye?"

"What about it?"

"Were you not able to heal at least your body?"

Luke shook his head. "Couldn't afford it. Didn't have the money, and it takes a high-level healer to replace body parts rather than just mend them."

Riven's gaze drifted back to Fred. "Get me some Dao treasures and soul-healing pills to look over. Also, if you have any slave-binding collars to use while his thrall transition is still being cultivated, I'll need some of those as well. Can't have him trying to betray me midway through becoming a thrall when his energy channels renew. Luke, you said you were a battle priest? What kinds of miracles do you have?"

Luke's look of excitement was palpable, but he settled himself down and let out a huff in reply. "I . . . I'm not entirely sure. I had many, but most of them were partially destroyed when I took soul damage. Even my remaining percentages were decreased. The fractals imbued onto my pillars are at the very least in need of repair, and at the very worst completely unusable. It'll take time to realize what I can and cannot access in terms of my old abilities."

"Got it. Well, welcome to the group. I hope you don't regret it."

Luke nodded. "I doubt there'll be anything to regret. Thank you for helping me."

The Unholy slave collar etched with green runes clicked into place, binding Luke to the owner of a bracelet now strapped along Riven's right wrist.

"This should keep him in check to obey anything you command of him as long as his Willpower is below eighty, which it is," Fred said while stepping back to evaluate the item. "That'll be forty thousand coins."

"Roadside robbery. I'll give you twenty thousand," Riven replied without missing a beat.

"Thirty thousand."

"Twenty-five thousand, and even that's a rip-off, you greedy fuck."

"Fine."

Riven mentally selected the number of coins he wanted to transfer out of his bag of holding, and a stack of coins flashed into existence moments later. Fred quickly deposited the coins into a sack of his own, grinned victoriously, and shot a command to one of the succubi standing nearby, telling her to exchange the female-oriented equipment set out for Genua for some stuff that'd better fit Luke.

"On to bigger and better things; the girls will get Luke his equipment, Dao treasures, and soul-healing pills while we go over the handcrafted pieces made for your own demonic minions." Fred's eyes gleamed enthusiastically, and he bade Riven's group follow him. Stopping at the end of the row, where a rather large mannequin matching Azmoth's size was positioned, Fred's red hand pointed up at the pieces adorning its figure. "This one is obviously for the brute you have with you!"

Azmoth snarled. "I smash you, little red ape."

Fred ignored the Hellscape Brutalisk and turned to face Riven head-on with all three eyes sparkling wide. "We've included many features! Hellscape Brutalisks are often very hard to find, and they're already heavily armored, so it makes their equipment hard to come by. Even more so for the one you have, who's acquired traits to make his bulk and armor even more noticeable than the average brutalisk his age. However, that does not mean we didn't get some things—so go ahead and take a look! The prices are matched up with the pieces; all identification information is also on display courtesy of Zelmont here."

The mannequin wore only three distinct pieces. The first and most noticeable was a very large, round shield, big enough for even Azmoth to hide behind it with over half of his body. It was made of a darker shade of gray steel, was many inches thick, and looked like it could have been the door to some kind of massive machine. Bolts and screws had been drilled into the external perimeter, and the sigil of a black hand had been painted onto the front.

Painted?

Maybe not. Riven saw the fingers of the hand twitch, causing the iron to creak and groan when the gray metal bent slightly, only to re-form to the way it'd been moments before.

[Immortal's Grasp (Tier-1 Awakened Shield) (Heavy Armor): 640 average defense, 83 average damage on strike. +209 Sturdiness, +42 Strength.

- **Grasping Fingers: A hand can launch out of the shield to grasp enemies, pulling them toward the shield or you toward an enemy.]**

That one was definitely interesting, but if he'd been complaining about the prices at the altar previously, he was certainly doing so now. The price for the shield was listed 140,000 Elysium coins, so mentally noting it as an item of interest, Riven moved on to the next.

Which was essentially a very large black loincloth.

The loincloth was created from numerous very small metal links. It only came down the front end, being strapped around the waist by another kind of metallic fabric that gave the lower abdomen some additional protection, and three very prominent red runes were laid into the front end; they looked like Japanese sigils or something similar.

> **[Cansun Loincloth (Medium Armor): 78 average defense, decreases the amount of energy spent from any fire-type abilities regardless of pillar by 8%.]**

The price was significantly lower than the shield—only nine thousand. Not that bad, but Riven couldn't help but think this piece wouldn't survive many battles with Azmoth wearing it. He was always on the front line, and Riven was doubtful it could take many hits before being torn up.

Then the very last item was a large amulet. It had a very large orange and black gemstone set into the front, held in place by rings of metal, but instead of being hung around the neck, it had four straps of metal that went under and over the arms to hook around the back.

> **[Flaming Beholder's Tear (Amulet): This medallion uses the core of an evolved fire-attuned Beholder demon to fire off high-powered beams of Infernal energy at enemies in between charges.]**

The price was six hundred thousand, and Riven whistled at the amount before shaking his head. "Hmm. Got any ability scrolls or tomes for him?"

"We selected two scrolls that Azmoth may be interested in and one tome. Go ahead and look." Zelmont held out two rolled-up scrolls, which each had literally flaming insignias written onto their seals, and an orange book that was a couple dozen pages long. "We only provide the best for our most treasured customers, but remember that the best comes with a cost!"

CHAPTER 40

Time went by quickly as Riven sorted it all out. Athela was presented with a list of five different martial arts, with various unique weapons and black, gray, or brown rogues' outfits oriented toward shape-shifting abilities. There was even a Dao treasure that allowed one to acquire the Shadow subpillar affinity, which she was very heavily considering.

Fay was presented with a wooden caster's staff that could amplify curse damage, a corset-and-skirt outfit in various shades of purple that gave bonuses for any mind-related magics, and a crooked black witch's hat that matched her horns, tail, eyes, and wings. She was given the choice of two spells, too, and a few enchanted rings with various properties related to curses as well.

Lastly, for Luke, who'd volunteered to become Riven's first thrall, it was mostly utility stuff aside from the five brightly shining soul-healing pills and a single Dao treasure in the form of a brilliant red flower. There was some cooking gear, another spatial bag to carry stuff in, a magical tent that pitched itself, a glass jug that Luke could store blood in as it leeched off his hand just by touch, and, above all else, an outfit that collected more XP points than normal while in a party, converting these extra XP points into healing energy that helped mend various types of damage.

Including soul damage.

"We can do this one of two ways," Fred stated, hopping up onto a nearby chair behind the four displays. "The first way is you trade that Azag hive cluster sanctuary stone for everything here. You won't have to pay anything else, just the stone. We'll even throw in another three million coins, too."

The red-skinned, apelike demon held up two fingers. "The second way is you can haggle for the items here and buy what you can, though as you already know it won't be nearly as much as all that is displayed here. And honestly, Negrada is very much wanting that stone. We could use it—we even somewhat need something like this."

"Need? Why?"

Fred frowned, then exchanged a look with Zelmont. "We're currently under siege. Negrada and one of our allied dungeons are fighting a war with five other hellscape dungeons, and one of our previous allies has already had their dungeon core destroyed. This stone will ramp up our production of military forces by a lot. It is useful to a dungeon core but very dangerous for a mortal who cannot deal with the hive minds trying to manipulate you when you link to the inner clusters of the multiverse."

There was an awkward pause, and Riven's was quite surprised. Then he folded his arms. He certainly would like the gear, and Negrada had helped him out by getting rid of that damnable ghost in his soul aperture, but the deal wasn't in his favor either way. "The system store will buy the Azag sanctuary stone for sixty-four million coins. There isn't any way I'd take your first deal."

Fred blanched a bit at the price but tried to keep himself calm when he straightened his posture and tried to regain control of the situation. "Ahem . . . I see. I didn't realize the Elysium general store would value it that much. All right, then . . . We can offer an additional eight million on top of these items."

"Still not enough," Riven stated with a shake of his head. "No chance. The stuff here is great, but it's only worth about three million total by itself."

"Then we'll throw in more items. Christia, please fetch the others."

One of the brunette succubi on the periphery of the room bowed, then turned to walk away. Doors opening, drawers being shut, and finally the sound of wheels turning drifted to Riven's ears before the Succubus came back only half a minute later, pushing a large cart.

It was loaded with scrolls, tomes, books on crafting, enchanted weapons and armor, jewelry, and odds and ends that Riven didn't immediately recognize. However, his mask enabled him to get the gist of what most of this stuff was— and he was left disappointed. This was all secondhand, low quality, and even the ability scrolls weren't anything to be particularly envious of.

Especially since he knew there were limits to what you could learn, due to soul fractals for each ability being engraved on your soul's core and pillars. When that space ran out, you either had to discard an old skill or just not learn the new one.

For half an hour Riven and his minions sifted through it, and Riven's best guess at estimating a price lay somewhere between twenty-five and thirty million for everything, including the eight million in coins Fred had promised.

Which was less than half of what the system would pay. And if what he'd learned about how the system sold high and bought low was true, he could accurately predict that the Azag hive sanctuary stone would be worth even more elsewhere.

"May I be blunt?" Riven asked after a time while the red Jabob demon anxiously looked on.

Fred nodded hesitantly, trying to keep his composure. "Yes, of course!"

"Is Negrada broke?"

Zelmont immediately frowned.

Meanwhile, Fred took in a quick inhale of air. "Well, . . . Perhaps the wars aren't going in our favor at the moment, so, yes . . . We aren't particularly in a good spot right now."

Riven nodded slowly. It appeared that Negrada was a lot less powerful—and a lot less rich—than he'd initially thought, despite intimidating forces like the lurker demons residing here.

But then again, Riven was different now. Those lurker demons on the first floor, like the one that had nearly eaten Athela back in the hells, would be nothing but fodder for his growth now. He could utterly crush most of them without much trouble after all the levels and Dao insight he'd gained, so perhaps on the grander stage of the multiverse Negrada might not be all that strong.

Then again, maybe these lurker demons were maxed out at level 90, instead of being in the forty to fifty range like the one he'd seen earlier. He hadn't checked.

"I suppose that's why you even came here in the first place, to help stimulate the economy. Most of the stuff I've seen are decent items for lower-level people or those who are just starting out, but none of this beyond what you initially presented is something I'd want for me or my minions."

Fred began to scratch his head, anxiety about losing the deal evident in the way he stiffened. "I suppose there is a third way. Otherwise we'll just have to forgo getting the stone and you can buy what you do like from the wares present."

"Oh? What is the third way?" Riven asked curiously.

Fred took his time to answer, likely because he wanted to create a dramatic effect, though Riven couldn't be absolutely sure. Perhaps there really was a reason why Fred was hesitating. Perhaps he lost out on the bonuses he'd otherwise get, as he knew that Fred, like many merchants using system communes, got a bonus cut for whatever they sold.

"I have been given permission by Negrada itself to forge a system-regulated contract." Fred steepled his fingers, eyes narrowing. "You may take one item scroll for each of your demons, some basic provisions that we supply with your thrall-to-be, and you will have 1 percent of all profits that Negrada makes, plunders, or steals. In exchange for the sanctuary stone."

Riven shifted his gaze to the pile of goods. "One percent of all profits?"

"Indefinitely," Fred confirmed with a nod. "Forever. Paid monthly starting a month from today, 1 percent of all profits for a given month by value of items or wealth. The money will be transferred to your bag of holding if I mark it, and I will even upgrade the bag for you so it can hold more to accommodate our tribute. I will be frank with you: when you first met Negrada months ago, we were far better off and far wealthier. Far more powerful, and with far greater allies. The tides are changing against us, and we need this stone. We are also willing to add to this contract a clause stating that if we survive this war, Negrada will owe you any single favor you can think of as long as it does not directly harm or endanger the dungeon. This includes asking for any item we possess, any sum of money we may have at that time, any minion you wish to acquire. Anything, just once, as long as we live through these trying times."

The offer was something of a shock, and Athela's eyes widened in surprise.

"And this stone would help you survive the war?" Riven clarified hesitantly, pulling out the black orb that crackled with green energy inside. "And I get to pick one item, and one ability tome or scroll per minion?"

"That is correct."

. . .

. . .

. . .

"You have yourself a deal, as long as you throw in the outfits for Fay and Athela. They have a hard time finding clothes that'll accommodate their more demonic features."

Fred guffawed with excitement, shaking a clenched hand in the air, and he smiled triumphantly like a man who'd just won the lottery. "VERY GOOD!!! You will not regret this, Riven Thane! Today, you have won yourself an ally in Dungeon Negrada—and we will pay this debt back a thousandfold! Mark my words, you have just done yourself a great favor indeed!"

Azmoth stood outside the Blood Moon Requiem's gates, an enormous new shield in one clawed hand while he commanded the black hand of the shield to extend and wiggle around in the air. The demon looked like a child on Christmas with a new toy. He'd actually selected the tome instead of a scroll, for an ability called the Burning Crusade, which boosted all members of a party with a martial art, giving them increased resistances and additional flame damage with physical strikes for a short period of time. He'd have to learn it on his own, which was different than scrolls, but the ability had been worth it, and he'd be able to reuse the tome instead of it just vaporizing like scrolls did.

Athela had been outfitted in a dark-gray assassin's outfit with studded leathers, vambraces, a hooded cloak, and an amulet. The outfit accommodated shape-shifters—absorbing into her body or meshing with her mutations as well as adding extra stealth boosts to her presence, meaning people would more easily overlook her even if she wasn't necessarily trying to hide. The amulet was a dark-black gemstone set into a backdrop of gray steel, and it increased the damage her physical-attack critical strikes dealt a 15 percent bonus. Her newest ability was a classic that Riven had seen in many games back on Earth, called Backstab. It was an ability scroll, so she'd learned it instantly, only to have the parchment evaporate soon after, and it allowed her to unleash a martial art that only worked on what the system considered the back of an enemy—and would only work when she was stealthed to her target. If she was noticed by her target prior to the strike, the martial art would fail, but if she successfully stabbed someone from behind before they were aware of it, the strike would cause an abrupt pulse of kinetic energy to rip through the victim's body, stimulating an automatic critical strike that would range from three to ten times the normal damage done. It was even enough to get her to wear the tiara she'd been safekeeping—now placing it underneath her hood and on top of her head, because it just meshed so well with her newfound upgrades.

[Tiara of Silent Killing (Blood/Shadow Trinket): After successfully killing a target without being noticed by anyone else, gain a charge of critical strike. Your next unseen attack has a 100% chance to be a 2x-8x critical hit, with multiplied damage coming in the form of kinetic burst energy from the strike site. Requires a 26% or higher Blood or Shadow pillar affinity to wield, and the wearer must be female.]

He could only imagine what Backstab would do when it stacked with the new amulet and the tiara. Aside from this, Riven had also bought *Heart of Darkness*, a Dao treasure that looked very much like a black coconut and that would allow Athela to also acquire the Shadow subpillar immediately upon consumption. This he'd paid for out of pocket with a whopping two hundred thousand coins flat, as it was outside the boundaries of the deal they'd struck—but it was actually cheaper than Athela's amulet. Without it, she'd have been unable to learn her new Shadow-affiliated martial art—so it'd been a given to buy and he'd brushed off her concerns about the cost with a wave of his hand.

Fay had acquired a wooden staff, the purple caster's corset and skirt, and the black witch's hat. They all gave bonuses that would benefit her, with the staff amplifying curse damage while decreasing the pain she felt while casting them. The hat amplified her mental defenses and mana regeneration, and the purple midwear gave bonuses to her mind magic. Namely, this was for her hallucinations, and they too could modify themselves to fit shape-shifting abilities. Fay wasn't all that great at retracting her tail, wings, or even horns, but as she got more powerful it'd come more naturally, and these clothes could benefit her then. Her one spell scroll was an Unholy-affiliated ability, though she was running out of space on her Unholy foundational pillar after applying it and would need to either start looking to the Depravity subpillar for new spells or start getting rid of old abilities to make room. This new ability was a curse called Dark Pact, which healed all allies nearby while simultaneously slowing enemies. It was a pretty potent tier-three curse that built up over time in both how much it healed and how much it slowed enemies. However, the adverse effect of the curse, which was mental anguish, would drastically increase over time as well—essentially torturing the mind of the caster until it started draining actual health from the user. If the caster used it too long, they'd even die.

Lastly, the collared, one-eyed old man who was to become Riven's thrall stood looking around curiously at the bustling activity. It was the first time Luke had been to the altar, only having seen it in the distance, as he'd been forced to work the farms before now, and Riven could tell by the smile that Luke was enjoying the relative freedom from his last predicament.

It made Riven sad, because he knew there were likely other elves on the farms just like this guy. Ones that hadn't agreed with what they'd done to Riven, but he just couldn't chance an uprising after what they'd put him through and how racist they'd shown themselves to be.

Kathrine's touch from behind him caused Riven to startle, and he turned to face his royal relation through the porcelain mask stuck to his face.

"I'm surprised you came, but I am relieved," Kathrine stated slowly, looking down at his minions talking to one another and the elf standing nearby. "They seem excited, but I for one am disappointed to see you go. I'd been hoping to talk to you in detail, set up a proper education and training program for you, and to deepen the bonds between you, your sister, and the empire. The queen is not very happy with my performance, and my family's name is being dragged through the mud due to my failures."

"That's not my problem," Riven stated simply. "But fear not—you can tell them that I have some things to take care of and I'll be back to hear you out. The last time I was whisked away was not your fault, nor should you let my sister's irritation rub you the wrong way. Even she knows that you couldn't have done anything—it was a system integration quest. Now, let us have one last talk before I leave to meet my sister and say my final goodbyes, as it is unlikely that I'll be back any time soon after this—potentially even years—and we have a lot to lay out for my time away."

CHAPTER 41

Three months later

"I love you, Riven. Don't stay gone too long, okay?"

Those were the last words Allie had said to her brother as she'd waved him off after a warm parting hug. He'd vanished through the portal to the other side of the world, and their forces in Chicago had reported they'd last seen him departing along the coastline into the northlands. She still remembered how he'd smelled, and it felt like it'd been so long now that she was beginning to become depressed. He only had another half year to find the next two pieces to the Chalgathi set, and although there hadn't been any notifications of his death, there'd also been no notifications concerning his success in acquiring another piece.

That worried her. She should have seen at least one message about it by now, as she'd already seen notifications about two of the contenders having acquired all five. What had happened beyond that . . . was anyone's guess.

Nevertheless, the game plan was set. Allie had her duties to run their fledgling country in preparation for what would no doubt become a worldwide war. Any one of the world quests could lead to billions of people dying, and she'd need armies to help get her agenda done—to literally save the world from catastrophe. If that meant crushing a few local enemies in the process, such as the elvish nation of Tereen, so be it. Meanwhile, Riven would complete and succeed in Chalgathi's subsection of the apocalypse beasts world quest. And if he needed her help, they always had that means . . .

"Allie?"

Snapping out of her trance, Allie realized the carriage had come to a stop. The zombified horses were becoming restless outside, and the black interior of the coach she rode in was still. Mara had originally been assigned to maintain Brightsville, but Allie had been so lonely that she'd replaced Mara with General Bruner—who was in between Brightsville and Chicago on a regular basis now.

"Sorry," Allie muttered, following Mara out of the carriage and wincing at the sunlight. Stepping onto the cobblestone street just outside the towering fantasy city, she gazed up at the many floors of elevated landscapes that supported different levels. Airships, rocs and their riders, and even a couple small drakes were swarming the upper city levels like bees to honey. "I just miss Riven."

Mara nodded, smiling and gesturing toward the opposite side of the road, where another carriage, escorted by high-profile warriors of Dawn's first legion, waited patiently at attention. "I know. He'll be back eventually—don't worry."

From afar, Dawn's capital, Mandon, looked to be an unbelievably tall stack of seven different cities—including the ground floor. Each of the floors was built on a very thick plot of elevated landscape. Mandon was a magnificent city; every layer spanned exactly 109 square miles, according to the government. According to the locals they had questioned, the city was a relic of the past, when necessity caused them to conserve space to limit their outside contact with enemy forces in the early days of its existence—back before the integration had culled the population in the surrounding area. Three levels of the city extended underground, and seven layers existed aboveground for a total of ten levels—ranked in order of number from the ground level when being described by the populace.

Generally the upper levels were for the better-off residents. Order and safety, along with beauty and splendor, could be found among the elevated gardens, farms, markets, trade schools, and communities of the top levels. Light from the sun passed down through the base of each top level via a magical screen that let you view the sky even while underneath—and the only way you'd know that you weren't looking up into the actual sky was the grid of the screen constructed with cables and stone, or the multitude of elevators, enormous pillars, and even larger spiral staircases that led up to further levels. In the very center of the city, a circle had also been carved into the landscape, many football fields across in diameter, and you could actually look up to see the palace on the top floor as its waterfall poured over the sides and fell down through all levels of the city to run into the sewers of underlevel three, where the water was recycled and cleaned for future use. Aqueducts imbued with magic were commonplace, and the pillars holding each level up often had tube systems for the transportation of water. The poorer citizens could be found underground, and slums were commonplace the farther down you went. Instead of magnificent grids with the sky overhead, here artificial lights were used to brighten the underlevels during the daytime and dimmed at night—the only exception was the large hole through which the waterfall entered.

Unfortunately Allie had done little sightseeing on her brief trips prior to today, but she was sure to do so now that she'd be spending more time here—if only temporarily. The city truly was a magnificent sight to behold and would no doubt have been considered the next wonder of the world if it'd been located back on Earth.

No, she'd not had time to sightsee. She'd been rather busy over the past season. One large city, three towns, and a large swath of land conquered—Allie had taken control of over a third of Tereen by herself. The war between Dawn and the elvish nation of Tereen was still raging fiercely, but the elves had been pushed back onto the defense and were becoming desperate thanks to the undead intervention. Not only that, but black ops teams, assault mechs, tank groups, and fighter jet squadrons were working in unison with the undead swarms to crush any opposition quite quickly. Trade between Dawn, Deepnest, and the Thane Necropolis had become the lifeblood of all three countries, with travel between them rampant despite Charisma clashes causing occasional conflict. The trust between the three small empires was ramping up, and measures had been taken to curb the effects of the system-based Charisma problems as best they could. It very much helped that Allie had essentially saved Dawn from either a long, drawn-out war or complete annihilation, and the citizens were reminded of this constantly, whenever their loved ones came back from the front line to tell their families of the undead who'd helped them survive the last battle. Meanwhile, the rat-kin of the underdark, who'd been lacking necessary weapons, food, and supplies after the dwarves had cut off their outlying farming posts, were now back in business. The Thane Necropolis had provided both local and system-based means of acquiring all those things, and the dwarves' initial strategic advantage was now gone. Caravans from the underdark regularly made it to the surface, and the tunnels facilitating trade between Deepnest and Brightsville were extremely well guarded at all times by both sides. Not only that, but Deepnest was so close to Brightsville it made travel very easy—with Brightsville already having sent some of its forces down below numerous times to help counter dwarven attacks. The rat-kin supplied the necropolis with bodies from both sides of the conflict, and Allie's forces continued to grow.

Meanwhile, on the other side of the world-spanning portal, the three cities of Chicago, Rockford, and Milwaukee were a center of attention for the surrounding factions rising there. It was well-known on the world forums that the Thane Necropolis was a rising powerhouse and that Chicago was associated with Riven—so the surrounding forces at play kept a wary watch. Two newly formed countries waged war to the south of Chicago, with a very sketchy faction up to the northwest sending spies southward regularly, and a couple of scattered independent city states had formed along the coast or farther inland. Allie truthfully just hadn't gotten around to exploring much over there yet, as she already had lots to do on this side of the planet. As long as Chicago and its neighboring cities weren't under attack, she'd let things remain as the status quo.

For now.

She closed her eyes and hummed to herself, trying to take her mind off the present and move it to a more peaceful place. It was time to relax, and she was finally going to try her best to do so after so much bloodshed and so much worrying.

Hopefully the king, whom she'd only met twice in very brief passing, was right on the money—perhaps attending college, or its equivalent at Dawn's academy, would be a good thing. It would give her a needed break, an interesting lesson on the politics and histories of Dawn, perhaps would allow her some insight on how to run her own kingdom, and would maybe even expose her to some new theories on magic. Her tutor at the Blood Moon Requiem was a very good teacher, but he was more focused on Dao theory than anything else, and he often discarded energy-based theory in favor of just understanding the Dao—which she didn't agree with. Magic had a rhyme and reason to it, just like science did, even if the Dao had a huge part to play. It wasn't just understanding the concept; it was understanding the intricate pieces that created a larger whole. Usually and in many other circumstances she'd call someone like her a fool to go against the mainstream teachings of an ancient empire, but she had a 100 percent affinity with the Death subpillar. It almost spoke to her, guided her in ways that were far beyond normal, and she'd take the Dao's teachings and promptings at the source over anyone or anything else. If it told her that there was more intricacies than what met the eye through compulsions and feelings, she'd trust it.

Given, those compulsions and feelings only ever came from the Death subpillar—so perhaps this only applied specifically to the Death subpillar. She couldn't speak for the others. Perhaps that really was how the other pillars worked.

"Allie, you're off in wonderland again."

Allie snapped out of it for the second time, getting her bearings and smiling at Mara—who wore a concerned look underneath the hood covering her patchwork ghoul features. "Sorry. Let's be off, then, shall we?"

Mara nodded, took the laptop she'd been using for administrative purposes out to check her private messages, and then waved to the undead escort who'd been riding in on zombified horses as well as the tanks and helicopters hovering overhead. Putting away her laptop again, she spoke into the coms unit attached to her ear she'd been given by the techies from Chicago and patched in to speak with the pilots nearby. "Thank you, we will be fine from here. Good hunting."

"Roger that," the voice of the escort leader replied. Shortly after that, the carriage turned around, along with the dozens of death knights, death-attuned mages, and heavy mechanical units, to make their way back north.

Heavily armored knights bearing the insignia of a yellow sun saluted Allie as she walked forward, and a decorated veteran with a feathered helm hopped off his own warhorse to address Allie with a low bow. "Queen Thane, my name is Sir Reford the Second—a captain in the king's service. It is my pleasure to escort you into the capital, the city of Mandon. Our destination is the tenth and top floor, where we have accommodations prepared for your attendance at the academy. It may take an entire day or more for the journey up if we go by land. Would you like me to call down an airship?"

Allie glanced over at the pristine white carriage waiting for her, embroidered with gold and decorated with flowers. Then she looked up to the different layers of city reaching high overhead, and the swarms of air traffic. She smiled, then shook her head. "No. I was hoping to see the city on the way up."

The feathered knight nodded, then stood up to his full height. "That's what I was told. I just wanted to make sure. We'll be certain to stop at many of the more interesting sites on the way; there's a lot to do and see here—and it will be my honor to act as your tour guide for the day."

He had traveled far across an entire continent, and he was finally closing in on not one but multiple other Chalgathi participants.

The desert sun beat down across the horizon, a barren wasteland of flat, cracked land suffused with extreme heat. The only sounds were that of the slowly flowing river nearby, the laughter of his two female minions as they splashed around, and the slow breathing of Azmoth and Luke beside him.

Riven hovered three feet above the ground, in a meditative, cross-legged pose. Light gleamed off the heavy steel armor that supplemented his Chalgathi outfit wherever it wasn't covered by his cloak—metal encasing his hands, arms, legs, feet, and even his chest surrounding the maw in the center, which was visible through a cutout in the breastplate. It was all custom-made, courtesy of a blacksmith he'd saved two months into the trip. He steepled his hands in front of him as wisps of blood mana spiraled gently off his body, and his eyes searched the dozens of bandit corpses that lay drying up under the blazing desert heat. They were merely husks of the bodies they'd once been after Riven had drained them to satiate his thirst. His hunger was becoming ever more ravenous.

And on Riven's lap was his spiritually bound weapon, finally coming out of its shell.

"Focus," Luke stated calmly, hovering beside Riven and opening his one good eye, which now showed an eerie red. It was one of the effects of having become a thrall belonging to a pureblood; a normal vampire wouldn't often get such results. Luke had changed only two months ago, and though his pillars and divinity channels were still damaged even after eating the soul-mending pills and divine Dao treasure. He would probably start to regain a grasp on his abilities soon. Things like manipulating his divinity, much like Riven manipulated his mana, were trifling things and easy enough to do for someone with as much experience as Luke. "Let your energy peel the layers back, but do not force them. With a transformation like this, you can think of it very much like you would your own Dao visions. Only that for the weapon, you are the guiding force—for you can mold these changes to be what you wish them to be. Feel it out, warp the essence stolen by this Richard person you slew, and let the weapon grow in ways that you feel would most benefit the build you want."

Flickering wisps of red and black coalesced, forming intertwining strings that slowly began to dig at the already cracking crystalline lattice encompassing his weapon. It'd been three months since he'd been able to use the staff, but now, behind the capsule closed around it, Riven could feel the staff calling to him. Pulling on Gluttony's shard and imbuing it into the weapon, Riven visualized the characteristics of what he wanted—and Gluttony replied.

It was finally time.

First the crystallized pieces began to flake off one by one, falling into dust as they touched the ground like red petals. Riven's strings of mana continued to gently nudge the capsule apart piece by piece, with small chunks falling off next—until entire sections began to flake and disintegrate. An audible sigh, like the wind on a night's breeze, escaped from the capsule as it finally vanished into nothingness—and in its place, a new weapon had emerged.

[Vampire's Escort has evolved into an ascended legendary weapon. As an ascended weapon, this item gains true intelligence and an awareness of self beyond what any other kind of totem, awakened item, or enchantment can produce. Most crafters only dream of creating such a masterpiece, and you have successfully done so. By utilizing high-grade materials, a piece of your own soul, Dao insights, and a piece of original sin, and by absorbing the essence of a high-tier enemy for your level, the system has granted this weapon access to ascendancy. As an ascended weapon, Vampire's Escort has given itself a true name, one imbued with power, that will forever remain a permanent fixture on the item. Ascended weapons cannot be soul-bound; soul binding has been nullified. Vampire's Escort has given itself the true name Jackal.]

[Jackal (Ascended Legendary Weapon. Type: Vampiric Artifact, Sin Artifact, Sorcerer's Spear-Staff): 894 average damage on strike with each physical strike dealing additional Shadow damage. Each physical strike steals health from the enemy, heals you, and repairs this item. Mana regeneration is increased by 305%. Stamina regeneration increased by 8%. All Shadow and Blood abilities cost 10% less mana while dealing 36% additional damage. This item has an abnormally high endurance and is hard to destroy. Requires vampiric heritage and a piece of Gluttony's Original Sin to wield.

- **Sacrificial Kill: Killing strong opponents has a chance to imbue this weapon with additional attributes, stats, or bonuses.**
- **Gluttony's Riptide: Passively builds up an elongated blade of sin energy that can extend by swinging this weapon in an arc. Recharge rate and damage output depend on control and insight concerning Gluttony.**
- **Black Lightning: This staff can passively build up charges of Black Lightning. Power of Black Lightning depends on the amount of charge emitted.**
- **Jackal's Lunge: Point this weapon in any direction and activate this innate and unique martial art, charging the blade with blood mana to create the visage of a jackal's maw and blasting forward. When your blade strikes an enemy, the red jackal will close down on them to deal additional blood and sin damage.**
- **Portal Master: This weapon can sync to any stabilized portal you allow it to use by the maker and master. Current locations available for access: Dungeon Negrada, Riven's Eye Wormhole. Takes one week of channeling in the same place to use this ability.**
- **Beastform: This weapon can turn into a shadow jackal. This form is not offensively compatible but is a way for the weapon to experience the world around it outside of combat—matching the will of the blade.]**

Many questions came with the awakening of Riven's weapon. Why was soul binding not allowed? What was sin energy? What exactly was an ascended weapon—other than one with self-awareness? Or was that all there was to it?

Regardless, Riven was not disappointed. The damage had increased almost nine times over, mana regeneration had more than doubled, each strike now leeched life from enemies and healed him, all Blood and Shadow abilities had even more umph than before, and Scorpion's Sting had been replaced with two new weapon-infused abilities: a riptide and a lunge. It now even gave him a very small stamina regeneration, which was kind of funny, because he really didn't use stamina much other than while sprinting. But it was well received.

Why it had named itself Jackal and why this was considered a true name were also a little odd. But the weapon certainly had that flavor, and it could apparently even turn into its namesake?

What Riven had once considered a true staff with a pointy end now was more like a Kwan Dao, or a Chinese halberd. It was a lot longer now, just slightly thicker, and was still made of black wood all along the shaft. The bottom end of the shaft was blunted, with a cap carved into a jackal's closed mouth, while the opposite end had another, larger jackal's head that produced a pitch-black blade.

In fact the entire weapon was a deep black, except for the swirling patterns of blood that trickled along its surface. It hovered above his lap horizontally just like he hovered over the ground, and when Riven reached up and clasped his hands around the polished black wood, the rushing streams of blood adapted and started flowing over his hands. The streams flowed along and into his skin, sending a jolt of awareness from the weapon as the mental entity touched Riven's mind, and Jackal's eyes along its carved faces began to glow crimson in a very similar way that Riven's own did.

The weapon shuddered, and a pulse of shadow over three miles in diameter swept across the land to blot out the sun for an entire five seconds. Then the darkness retracted, and Riven felt a feeling of acceptance wash through him.

I remember you . . . Father . . . a voice called out to him from the staff like a whisper. *I remember you . . . and I see you now.*

Riven smiled, sending a pulse of warmth back through his connection, and stood, gently touching down as he placed his feet on solid earth. "Show me."

Abruptly the staff shifted and warped, knowing what he was asking for, and formed the shadowy figure of a dog with red eyes that looked up at him from the ground. Slowly the shadows retracted and vanished, only to leave an abnormally deep-black—kind of creepy—dog staring at him. It was half the size of a fully grown golden retriever and would have perhaps been rather cute if not for the ominous aura and lack of a wagging tail.

Still, Riven felt only good intentions coming from the bond, which he still felt despite having lost a soul connection with the item. Somehow he could still feel its intent and knew that something kept their consciousnesses touching, even at an arm's distance.

Azmoth looked up from where he was contemplating the Infernal Daos and grunted in approval before turning back to meditation, and Luke smiled at the dog—reaching over to pet it before rapidly drawing his hand back. Riven felt a sense of dread sweep over Luke through his minion bond, when the two locked eyes.

"That feels rather dangerous." Luke chuckled, only for Jackal to look back to Riven and warp into the weapon form again—flying into Riven's hand without delay.

Riven nodded silently, running his hands approvingly over the black weapon and the flowing rivers of blood along its surface that constantly shifted positions into different sigils or no sigils at all. Without warning, Riven lowered the spear westward, activating Jackal's Lunge—and his body shot ahead, leaving a shock wave in his wake.

BOOM

Desert sands were blown apart underneath his feet, and the image of a jackal's maw, formed from blood magic, flashed forward ahead of Riven's blade before snapping down onto thin air with a resounding boom of power when the lunge stopped. Then, with a blurring vertical swing, Riven activated Gluttony's Riptide.

The visage of Gluttony's toothy maw roared from behind him with a flash of power. A black-and-red blade, sharp and fast, extended for dozens of yards off his spear staff and crashed into the ground ahead of him. The blow created a fissure and caused the ground to shake violently, getting the attention of both Athela and Fay, who'd been doing who knows what in the river farther off.

"HEY! RIVEN!" Athela called with hands cupped around her mouth, wet black hair plastered to her face as she laughed alongside Fay while half submerged in the water. "COME JOIN US AND SHOW US THE NEW TOY!"

"AGREED!" Fay intentionally turned around and stood up, topless, extending her wings and winking his way with a playful finger tug to motion him forward.

Turning, heavy armor glinting in the sunlight, vampiric horned pauldrons flaring along the eyes and his porcelain mask turning all seven feathers in their direction, Riven snorted their way. "Put on some clothes and stop flashing me, and maybe—just maybe I will!"

"THAT'S NO FUN!"

"Yeah, well, neither is being teased, and I can't even truly bathe with this stupid outfit on! SOOOO, fuck off." Riven ignored Fay's laughter and Athela's scowl and began to walk back to where his new elvish tutor sat.

Tutor? Thrall? Slave? Luke was all those things. The man was thankfully very knowledgeable about all sorts of things—weapons, hand-to-hand combat, magic, martial arts, and divine miracles. He said he'd been trained in all of them, too, but he'd had a major focus on miracles and combat with various types of weapons as some sort of battle priest.

"Mind giving me another sparring lesson?" Riven asked as he walked over and held out a hand to the one-eyed, silver-haired elf. "Staves and spears?"

Luke grinned, accepted Riven's hand, and pulled himself up from where he'd also been hovering above the ground. "Of course. But remember that I am still very weakened and have not had the opportunity to grow levels like you since getting here. Remember to pull your punches—the last time you almost killed me by accident. Even though I have the skills, I do not have the speed or power to repel any true attacks in our sparring sessions—so go easy onto his old fool. Especially now that you're going to be using a real weapon and not this old stick."

The old man bent down and picked up the walking staff he'd been using, then motioned for Riven to follow his example as he struck a pose. "Just like in previous lessons, go through the five combinations I taught you first as a warm-up. Then the three defensive stances. I'll come at you during the defensive stances, and after that we can really begin."

CHAPTER 42

Huffing and slamming back down onto the ground with a thump, Riven rested. His undersuit of red, silky bloodskin supplied by the mask Fallen Apostle kept his body cool even while wearing a cloak and heavy metal armor underneath a desert sun—but that didn't mean Luke couldn't still work him like a dog. The old man had become something of a drill instructor, and Riven could safely say he'd easily be able to kick his own ass from three months prior if his current self and past self had it out.

Learning close-combat tactics had been a long time coming, and it'd been needed, as Riven had often found himself at a serious disadvantage whenever enemies closed in. Sure, his magic was great and would still be his primary source of damage output, but that didn't mean it was unwise to commit to learning some close-quarters fighting styles. Already a couple of assassins had nearly offed him, two prominent ones being the orc from the Greenstalk village battle and the woman who'd tried to take his Chalgathi artifact in the basement of the ruined hospital.

"You're certainly getting better." Luke smiled down at the heavily breathing warlock. "I'm impressed with your performance. I only wish that I was in peak physical condition myself so it wasn't just you going at it with shadows or at my comparatively slower pace."

"Thanks!" Riven gasped, the weapon in his hands vanishing and whisking away to create a jackal beside him that started sniffing at his armor. "How does your new body feel?"

The dog glanced his way, nodded once in approval, then began to trot toward the river, where Athela was sunbathing.

"Not much of a talker, then," Riven mused, only to look up as he saw Fay's incoming form descending from the sky.

She landed a moment later, her feathered boots gracefully touching down as the wind blew her purple miniskirt about with a strong gust. Smiling and pulling the brim of the witch's hat down across her eyes to shield her from the blowing sands, she dusted herself off a moment after the wind died away and walked forward.

"How is it that you keep that hat on the entire time you're flying?" Riven asked curiously, pulling himself up when Azmoth walked over to give him a hand. "And did you find a caravan yet? We need cover to make it into the city."

Fay nodded and whipped her black tail out behind her to smack the ground with a *THWAP* before pointing. "Yes, sir! Another incoming caravan will be passing where the two rivers meet in about a day. We should be able to make it there beforehand by an easy margin."

"And you'll be able to disguise us as we go? How many minds can you effectively warp with your hallucinations? I know your spell is contrived inside the minds you want to move and not externally built like an illusion, so there's gotta be a limit."

"Somewhere over three thousand weaker minds—more than enough. Perhaps even four thousand, and the hallucinations work on status reads, too, but they get weaker and less convincing the more people I target. Stronger targets also take more effort."

"All right. My mask can also help; it stops other people from being able to identify me very well unless they have a true class—but I didn't want to bank on people recognizing me for what I am. Or at all, given how I look." Riven motioned to his unique outfit, images of which had been circulating on the world forums. Not many people in the top thousand had much public footage out there, only a handful, really, and Riven had only glanced at them once in a while to make sure. What he'd seen was that though he was only rank sixty and not even in the top ten most powerful people on the planet, albeit a few steps up from rank seventy-two, where he'd been a couple months ago, his battle for Chicago had gotten a very hyped amount of attention. Specifically from other vampires and from the people of Earth. He could safely say he was somewhat famous. "Anyways, let's get packed up. Athela, put on some clothes—it's time to move out. We've got a caravan to catch."

Riven stood disguised as a wrinkled old man, still cloaked but with human features and a slight hunch, using a staff for support. Behind him the hulking, tattooed, maul-wielding barbarian was the most intimidating of their group, as there was no way of realistically disguising Azmoth's movements without keeping him at least a similar size. Athela's outfit was the same, a dark-gray cloak with a black tiara underneath its hood and very recently added handheld crossbow strapped beside a quiver at her thigh—more than anything, she'd just been play-ing with it rather than using it seriously. Athela's skin was a dark brown instead of her regular pitch black with scattered white, though. Meanwhile Fay's wings, tail, horns, and black eyes had disappeared along with her white hair—revealing a still rather attractive blue-eyed, blonde witch. Lastly Riven's thrall, Luke, looked exactly the same as before but without the redness to his eye.

A caravan could be seen cresting a far hill on the path leading alongside the river. It'd no doubt take them a half hour or so to reach the spot where Riven and his crew stood, so Riven had time to burn. The members of his group chatted with one another or passed around flasks of water.

Pulling up his status page, he saw he had a level's worth of points to apply after his recent battle with some bandits.

[Riven Thane's Status Page:
- **Level 83**
- **Pillar Orientations: Unholy Foundation, Blood Specialty: Profane Cyclone (Tier 1 of the Path of Red and Black), Infernal, Shadow (subserviently linked to Blood Specialty pillar)**
- **Core of Original Sin—Gluttony: (Under Construction) (???)**
- **Traits: Race: Pure-Blooded Vampire (Extreme Darkness Regeneration) (Sunlight Decay) (Extreme weakness to silver weapons, Sun pillar, and Light pillar attacks), Class: Warlock Adept, Adrenaline Junkie (Blood) (+15% to Agility), Accomplishment Title: Bloodthirsty 1 (+5% increased blood mana from corpses, +1% dmg for blood magic)**
- **Abilities: Blessing of the Crow (Unholy), Wretched Snare (Unholy), Silvertongue (Unholy), Bloody Razors (Blood), Crimson Ice (Blood), Blood Lance (Blood) (Tier 2), Blood Nova (Blood) (Tier 3), Hell's Armor (Infernal), Blaze of Profane Glory (Infernal) (Tier 3), Riftwalk (Shadow), Ping Chalgathi Artifacts (Unique)**
- **Stats: 113 Strength, 308 Sturdiness, 772 Intelligence, 350 Agility, 10 Luck, -497 Charisma, 227 Vampiric Perception, 209 Willpower, 9 Faith**
- **Free Stat Points: 7**
- **Minions: Athela, Level 60 Arshakai [42 Willpower Requirement]. Azmoth, Level 71 Hellscape Brutalisk (Infernal Crusader Initiate) [58 Willpower Requirement]. Fay, Level 39 Succubus [29 Willpower Requirement]. Luke Blissfallen, Level 8 High Elf Thrall (Stormrazor Battle Priest) (Warning: 73% soul decay detected) [10 Willpower Requirement]**
- **Equipped Items: Basic Caster's Cloak (5 def, 3% mana regen), Jackal (894 dmg, 305% mana regen, 8% stamina regen, Shadow**

and Blood dmg +36% with 10% decreased ability cost, Black Lightning, Gluttony's Riptide, Jackal's Lunge), Chalgathi Cultist Amulet—The Great Maw (Devour, ???), Chalgathi Cultist Pauldrons—Twin Cannibals (1,290 def, +10% all stats, +60 Sturdiness, Blood in the Eyes, ???), Chalgathi Cultist Mask— Fallen Apostle (900 face def, 325 def with bloodskin, negates sunlight, all senses +40%, Identifier's Clause), Steel Boots (98 def), Modified Steel Breastplate (120 Def), Steel Greaves (104 def), Steel Gauntlets (91 def), Steel Arm Guards (90 def), Witch's Ring of Grand Casting (+26 Intelligence), Negrada's Modified Bag of Holding]

Riven glanced over his stats, realizing just how far he'd come since the beginning. Back when he'd fought that necromancer start-up in Chalgathi's trials and Athela had just been summoned for the first time, he'd been awed when casting his first spells. In some ways, he still was—but on an escalated scale. Now, if he'd been pitted against that man—or even against other opponents who'd given him problems in the past, like the fallen satyr warlord in Negrada's hellscape, the hive mind, or the clown dream creature—he'd crush them into paste with a flick of his wrist. The power gap between them and who he was then, versus who he was now, was astonishing—and even the drake he'd killed in the dungeon would have a much, much harder time landing any shots on him after his ascendancy to power.

Even so, he could tell that there were weak points in his build. Namely, his close-combat abilities were severely lacking. His vampirism gave him the great boon of being able to take a lot of hits, especially for a mage, and he wore heavy armor now that protected him beyond what his vampiric regeneration alone could do. However, there were other very powerful people out there in the world, and in his past experiences it'd been a very specific type of opponent that was most dangerous to him.

Those kinds of opponents were Agility based, be they the female orc rogue at the battle of Greenstalk, the assassin who'd nearly killed him after ambushing him in the basement of Brightsville's hospital, or, most recently, Richard, whose most serious threat to Riven had not been his hard-hitting attacks but rather the speed at which he chased Riven down.

That being said, Riven's Agility was pretty decent, as was his Sturdiness. He also had a defensive spell in the form of Hell's Armor and two movement spells with Blessing of the Crow and Riftwalk. So he usually didn't have much of a problem avoiding people or blocking attacks . . . but when he DID have that problem, it was a serious one.

Looking back on his fights time after time, he had a lot to improve upon outside the realm of magic; most specifically the realm of martial combat. He simply hadn't been trained in it, and he'd rightfully been focusing on magic as a dominant aspect to his build. But now that he had a true tutor in Luke, his thrall, a man who could guide him in how to fight using a stave, spear, or Jackal—it would probably be wise to start investing more points in Strength. His Strength stat was also one of his lowest, barely over one hundred points, and aside from the ten Luck and nine Faith, which he was completely ignoring—relatively pathetic compared to his other stats. Charisma was negative, sure, but that could be a good thing if dealing with the right kind of race.

Nevertheless he decided to put all seven points into Strength. The sensation was minuscule, but his muscles did tense and expand ever so slightly after the points were added. He never intended to be an absolute full-frontal fighter, but tacking some umph onto his physical attacks would probably be a good thing in the long run.

A pulse of hunger radiated from his soul apparatus, from the core of Gluttony that was still under construction. A visage of the great maw over a sea of corpses, rivers of blood flowing into the sky, and a blood moon in the background embedded itself in Riven's consciousness as his body went rigid—and a compulsion of extreme hunger rapidly came and went.

Athela's hand gently rested on Riven's shoulder. "Are you okay?"

Riven hesitated, realizing he'd visibly stiffened and had let out a long gasp with all four of his minions looking his way. "Yeah . . . Yeah, I'm fine."

"It happened again, didn't it? The compulsion?" Athela stated with a frown. "That's becoming more and more frequent."

"It's likely only going to increase," Fay added with a sigh. "Especially when your core is finished, but it also may be influenced by your new items. Your weapon and three of your Chalgathi artifacts are all touched by Gluttony. Did you ever talk to Kathrine about your sin core? I asked my clan in the nether realms about it, but they got very hush-hush."

Riven snorted. "Absolutely not. I don't think going around telling people I have a piece of original sin stuck inside me is a good idea, at least for now. What if the other vampires want to dissect me and rip it out?"

"Very possible."

"Yup."

"But unlikely. You are a prince of their empire."

"Not entirely off the charts, though. One of them already tried to assassinate me, remember?"

Fay scrunched up her nose with a rather cute expression, but nodded in acknowledgment. "I suppose you're right."

A lone man on horseback broke away from the front of the caravan and started toward them at a gallop. It was unusually fast for a horse, and flickers of some kind of energy radiated from the beast's hooves as it got closer.

Two minutes of silence later, the man finally came to a halt and pulled on the reins, stopping about twenty feet away from the five companions while eyeing them suspiciously. He was tall and wore a masked cowl over most of his face—likely to shield it from the sands. The scimitar at his side was decorated with gold but lacked any enchantments that Riven could see. He rode a white stallion with a golden mane, and oddly enough, its eyes shone a similar gold—as did the hooves, which actually let off a yellow-gold light.

The creature was truly beautiful.

[Sun-Blessed Sand Stallion, Level 19]

Interesting breed of horse.

"State your names and your business," the man called out, warily circling at a slow trot to get a better look at the five and gazing more intensely at Fay than the others. "You are obviously foreigners here, by the make of your garments."

Riven snorted, eyes shifting from the caravan back to the man as he played the role of an old and weary traveler. He even changed his voice slightly just to sound the part. "Aren't we all foreigners in these lands now? The worlds we once lived in have changed, and not for the better. Where do we call home, when our homes have all been taken from us and the system has thrust us into such odd places such as this?"

The horseman's eyes narrowed as they focused on Riven, and he briefly went over the rest of the party once before settling back on the group leader. "Yes . . . I will not disagree with you, traveler. However, I must be honest, you feel very wrong to me. Even looking at you causes my skin to go on edge, and I do not think myself a coward. The smell of evil permeates the ground you stand on. Part of me wishes to flee even now, and I cannot for the life of me understand why."

It was both a statement and a question, to which Riven didn't have an answer. It could be one of three things, the first being his shard of Gluttony. The second option was that this man could somehow sense pillar orientations. The third and most likely was that Riven's negative Charisma was at work yet again.

Thankfully, Riven had a pseudo-fix to this problem, which he'd already utilized a few times before his travels and even more while hunting the other Chalgathi participants. It wasn't a permanent thing, and it wasn't often noticeable as long as he didn't make big changes or force the target to completely obey a command. Small things like persuading someone who was already on the edge of a decision were usually easy enough to do as long as their Willpower was lower than his. The risk came with the knowledge that if someone's Willpower was equal to or higher than his own, or even close to his own but not quite there yet, it was possible that they'd be notified he was trying to use this spell, which could spell disaster. Thankfully, this man in front of Riven was not of a high

Willpower—and entering the caravan would be beneficial both in blending in and collecting information.

"We're of no threat to you and can even help make the trip safer. Let me be blunt and to the point: Would you mind it if we traveled alongside you? Assuming you are a trade caravan? We are on a long journey and wish some company along dangerous roads," Riven stated, infusing the words with his Silvertongue spell.

Immediately the frown on the horseman's face flattened out into a slightly dumb expression and his eyes faded out of focus—but then he quickly shook himself like he'd just woken up and nodded. "Yes, of course. We can bring you along with us—shouldn't be a problem after I've told the others I vetted you. However, which city are you intending to travel to? Our caravan is headed toward Daskus, city of canyons, watcher of the Cube Labyrinth. If you were hoping to go toward Jerildine, you'd be out of luck."

Riven grinned when he got a playful nudge of congratulations from Fay, despite the huff of annoyance from Athela. "Daskus is the way we want to go."

Riven pinged the Chalgathi artifacts, sensing two of them in close proximity far off where cliffs could barely be seen across the sand dunes—and where the river now led.

The horseman looked over, nodded once, and turned his horse around. "That would be the path to Daskus. The city is actually built into the cliff faces on either side."

"Mind telling me what the Cube Labyrinth is?"

The man gave Riven another confused look, but rephrasing the question with another influx of mana via Silvertongue caused him to not prod too much into exactly why Riven didn't know this already. "The Cube Labyrinth is a new feature the Elysium administrator placed in the canyon after integration as a prize for a quest the city's king completed. It is a permanent fixture and a reusable maze of sorts. It can be quite dangerous, but completing its puzzles and finding your way through it is very rewarding and has brought a lot of wealth to our lands. A person can only use it three times; each time the cube has harder problems, puzzles, monsters, and mazes to solve. After completing the cube three times, you can no longer enter it again—but you get a new trait dependent on what pillars you're oriented to and how well you completed the three trials."

Riven's eyebrows raised in surprise. "Really . . . Are people able to enter the cube together?"

The horseman nodded. "Yes, you can complete it as a group—but each group can only be up to ten people and has their own instanced area. That means that a different pocket of unique space is created for each group and it cannot be entered by others during that time. The exception is that if someone goes in with a group numbering fewer than ten, others can enter the cube's maze to fill in the spots and share in the reward. However, that can be rather dangerous to do without permission, because you might be killed for it—as you get a reduced reward if you have more group members, and crimes committed in the cube are not crimes at all by decree of the king. It's every man or woman for themselves in there."

Huh.

Riven pondered this for a time, but the horseman was getting impatient.

"I'm off to the caravan. I'll let them know you'll be joining us, but if there is any trouble on the road to Daskus, we won't hesitate to put you down. Do you understand?"

"Sure. I understand." Riven smiled and waved at the departing rider, only to turn fully around and face the distant cliffs. "This should be interesting. I did find it odd that we had two different Chalgathi participants in the same area for so long . . . At first I'd thought they'd teamed up. Do you think they're inside the maze?"

"Probably," Athela stated irritatedly with a sideways glare at Fay, who was pressing up against Riven's shoulder on the opposite side. "Maybe we can throw the Succubus into the cube to find out for us while we wait outside. I think that sounds like a great plan."

CHAPTER 43

Daskus.

City of canyons.

A sprawling fantasy metropolis located at the Y-junction of three intersecting canyons. Not only were buildings located on the ground level, but the rich of the city actually had palaces, manors, and castles built into the sides of the canyon walls or even on crest of the canyon itself. It was almost untouched by the devastation Elysium's integration had brought elsewhere, pristine and well maintained, though Riven couldn't be sure just how that was. Bridges crafted from sandstone and made sturdier with magic crisscrossed the thriving, breathing heart of the city. There was even a towering Elysium altar located in the eastern branch of the intersecting canyons that looked very similar to Riven's own, but instead of the Unholy attunement it was a generic one, lacking the halo of green fire and made of white marble instead of obsidian. And at the very center of it all, hovering in midair with constantly rotating slabs of stone panels displaying variously shaped carved insignias, was an enormous puzzle-box cube.

[Puzzle-Box Cube Labyrinth: This stone cube is a permanent fixture on the world of Panu, granted to this city by Elysium as a prize to the populace after the king of Daskus completed a difficult system quest with perfect marks. Rules: the trials are formed by outwitting monsters, mazes, and puzzles with a real possibility of death. Only ten may enter an instance event at once; instance events that are not full may be entered by outsiders at any time as long as they are within the same tier of trial. Any number of instance events between different groups may be ongoing at any time. You do not require sustenance while inside the cube, you may only complete the Puzzle-Box Cube Labyrinth event up to three times with scaling difficulty and scaling prizes via attempt tiers one, two, and three,

and you may leave the Puzzle-Box Cube Labyrinth instance events at any time—but only through the single entrance and exit points inside. Leaving the instance event will forfeit all remaining attempts at completing this system event or collecting its prizes. To create your own instance event or join another's, just stand underneath the cube and focus on it while thinking "Activate."]

Riven stood on a ground-level main street amid a bustling crowd of mostly humans and dwarves, all dressed in clothing suited for the hot, sandy weather. He'd call it Arabian attire; most wore cowls around their necks, ready to bring up over their faces if need be—yet otherwise most of them wore as little as possible to bear the heat of the desert. Sandstone and clay buildings holding apartment buildings, crafters' workshops, and general goods stores rose up on either side of the street, with the city's main trading district farther ahead. There were even occasional trees, though they were rather thin, very dark green, and very tall—definitely not species of plant that were native to Earth.

As he stood motionlessly staring up at the gigantic structure that cast a shadow over the center of the city, Riven intently watched the individual pieces of its body when they randomly separated from the main core to twist, turn, and then settle back down in a new orientation. It was almost like a Rubik's Cube, but there were more squares, and each individual cube piece had its own unique insignias that occasionally glowed a bright blue before settling down to a normal stone variant like the main core of the inner body. Occasionally entire faces of the structure would twist or turn, and just once Riven saw a party of ten heavily armed people distantly channel a beam of light from the monstrous thing—only to be sucked up into the cube like a UFO would do.

"Move it, old man!" the haggard voice of a fat, sweating dwarf merchant wearing a sleeveless, v-cut tunic stated as he pushed a small wooden cart full of vials. "You've been blockin' the road since I was all the way down near Billba's Smoke Shop! Stop gawkin' and move!"

Riven turned to look at the dwarf, ignoring the swarms of people around them to stare back without a care in the world. In a voice not native to a man appearing the age that Fay was displaying for him—Riven's cold words cut through the air. "Walk . . . around us . . . little piggy. And don't come back."

A pinpoint aura of cold dread crashed into the dwarf and only the dwarf, making him gasp and keel over in wide-eyed shock. He sat there in the middle of the road, getting sneers or jeers from the other passersby as he blinked repeatedly, trying to determine what had happened.

But when Athela turned to face the pudgy dwarf and fingered her crossbow, the man quickly got up and turned his cart around the other way—spilling numerous vials along the road—and rushed back the way he'd come, hyperventilating.

[The Apocalypse Beasts, Chalgathi, Quest Update: Rita Fellburge has fallen in battle to Fred Talons. Fred Talons has acquired four of five set pieces for Chalgathi's Inheritance. A new Chalgathi's chosen will be picked one hour from now as a replacement for Rita Fellburge.]

Frowning at the notification only he and the other chosen could see, Riven turned back around to stare up at the cube. Utilizing his Ping Chalgathi Artifacts ability, he saw both lights flare up to indicate the positions of the other participants of this Unholy quest nearby.

Both lights came from the inner core of the massive stone cube.

"They're inside."

Azmoth grunted, sounding very much like the hulking, bald, tattooed barbarian he appeared to be. "We go find if they with each other?"

"Hopefully they are," Luke commented with a frown, wiping sweat away from his forehead. "Otherwise it may be foolish to enter at all, as going inside may mean one of them could exit the event and disappear or lie in ambush for us."

Riven nodded slowly. "Agreed. Entering at all, even if they are inside the same event, could mean that. They've been inside the labyrinth for at least two weeks, because their locations haven't changed, and I'm willing to bet a lot of money that one is hunting the other. It'd make sense if they both pinged the other's location and the weaker participant decided to try to lose his opponent or buy time by entering the cube."

"Could it just be one man with two different pieces you need?" Fay asked curiously, pushing her witch's hat up an inch to get a better look at the bridges holding hundreds of traveling people crisscrossing above them between different sides of the canyon. "It's at least a possibility, right?"

Riven cocked his head to the side, pinged the Chalgathi artifacts again, then hesitantly shook his head. "It's possible, but if that's the case, he or she has split the artifacts into two separate places. I've heard from the locals in the caravan that this was a spatially warped event, but they're still moving in different areas despite this. No, it's more likely that there are two individuals."

Fay nodded in agreement after processing the logic behind his guess, then winked with a perfectly white smile and an intentional giggle. "Well, after we get the other pieces, I'm really hoping we can finally get that suit off you. For science, of course!"

Athela let out an exaggerated sigh. "Riven, why did you have to contract with a Succubus? Could you have not just chosen the shady Beholder demon instead?"

"I believe it was you who decided to pick Fay over the Beholder."

"Well, I take my decision back!"

Fay licked her lips and waggled her eyebrows at Athela next, then pointed her staff toward the other demoness with a seductive hip pop. "Don't be like that!

My darling Riven and I can always include you as well! In fact, I've been thinking about that for quite a while now, and I think it'd be best if I was positioned in between the two of you when we have our first. I think you'd like it—I'm rather good with my tongue!"

The mental image flashed into Riven's head unbidden as Athela simultaneously gawked, mouth open, and he combated a nosebleed while shaking his head in disbelief and started off into the crowds toward the floating cube without another word.

Meanwhile a feminine screech that turned into a gurgling choke from behind told him Athela had attacked Fay. Most likely by asphyxiation, by the sounds Fay was making. "I'm going to fucking stab her, Riven! I swear to all the hells, I'm about to fucking stab her!"

The king of Daskus, city of canyons, was a large, darker-skinned man with a well-kept beard who sat shirtless on his diamond-studded throne in an empty audience hall, barren of everyone except for the collared and otherwise naked brunette slave woman next to him who held his tray stone-still. Slaves were a bit rare in the city, but they were still legal as long as you had a license to own them or were of the nobility. And the king was no exception to this rule.

Darius Stoneshield remained in his palace positioned atop the cliffs while quietly watching the hundreds of images flickering about him. As the one who'd been gifted the cube in the first place, he was able to see the different instance events anywhere in their entirety—instead of the local populace, who only ever got to witness the end battles in the last room of the labyrinth.

Well, if people really wanted to, they could always watch it from beginning to end if they stayed underneath the cube and accessed the viewing features that way. Some people actually did this if they had loved ones inside, but most didn't have the time to spare—waiting weeks on end for people to finish if they did at all. There'd even been a few groups trapped inside the shifting, ever-changing maze for months now—but of all of them, there was one particular instance event that was more eye-catching than all the others.

He took a sip of wine out of the chalice at his right-hand side, placed it back on the tray the nearby slave was holding for him, and steepled his fingers while focusing back on the most interesting group of them all.

The creak of a wooden door on his left caused him to turn, and one of his advisers and a longtime personal friend dressed in gold silk began walking across the room. Chagin was of similar age, in his late forties, sported a longer black beard, had good posture and a thinner build than Darius, and he carried a slate, papers, and a pen. "Good day, Darius! Still watching, I see?"

Darius nodded casually with a grunt of affirmation, then turned back to the central image that kept shifting between scenes ahead of him. "You would be correct, old friend. The groups we sent in have died again."

The adviser frowned, glanced up at the main image, and sighed. "Unfortunate, but to be expected. They're rather powerful, almost on your level."

"Almost," Darius repeated flatly.

"Not to be taken lightly," the adviser stated with a sagely nod. "Quite a game of cat and mouse they're playing, utilizing the puzzle traps like that to try and corner one another and gain advantage. And the skills they both possess are quite fascinating, don't you think?"

The adviser's frown deepened when Darius didn't reply. "Do you intend to take the artifacts and enter the world quest yourself? Doing so would mean you'd need to leave the city."

"And who else, if not me?" Darius asked, shifting his brown eyes back to his childhood friend. "Even aside from the draw of power, which this quest no doubt would bring should I succeed, I cannot afford for them to fail. Billions of lives are at stake here. The future of our very world is at stake. Should I gain the power of one of the three apocalypse beasts, at the very least I will have a chance to defend my city from whatever other evils may lurk out there. The system spoke of a lich to the north, snow giants to the south, invaders from beyond, and word has it that the merpeople and naga have begun to attack coastal cities all over the world by the millions. Our allies of the Merivine have already lost two of their own cities, their residents butchered to the last child. It appears that the world quest regarding the sea dwellers is one of genocide, but specifics were hazy and reports differ between sources. Of course . . . you already know most of this, don't you?"

"Better than you, Majesty," the adviser replied with a soft laugh. "Regardless, the troops you've asked me to hide around the plaza have been positioned. Perhaps other groups of mercenaries or guilds will try their hand to take the heads of these Chalgathi's chosen, but despite the increase in pay, there aren't many people willing to take the bounty after so many have fallen. It is likely that we'll need to capture them with superior numbers after they actually leave the cube rather than attempting to kill them inside with only eight others being able to join their instance."

Darius frowned, nodded, then got up to stretch. "Perhaps, perhaps not. I'm still hopeful that some of the braver fools out there will strike it lucky and manage to kill one or both of them. I've put enough money on their heads to warrant at least the desperate to keep trying."

Glancing over at the stone-faced slave, Darius looked down her bare body and then back up to her glazed-over eyes. Putting one hand on the back of her head, he abruptly yanked her backward by her hair and threw her violently onto the throne as she yelped. The chalice and pitcher of wine spilled onto the floor with a clattering sound, and Darius began to unbuckle his belt. "Leave me, Chagin. I want privacy as I relieve some stress. Let me know if anything interesting happens with the cube."

The advisor nodded and bowed before turning heel. "Very well. Have a good time! I'll send another one of your harem up here to replace her, assuming you break this one like you broke the last. Try not to damage her too much, though—the quality of slave you ask for is always hard to find, and I'm tired of having to abduct locals with the excuse of treason against the crown when we run out of good foreigners."

The only response Chagin got was a high-pitched scream of horrified pain behind him, and he huffed to himself just once before exiting the audience hall and shutting the large wooden door behind him.

CHAPTER 44

Usually students didn't enroll halfway through the school year. In fact, it was unprecedented here at the Imperial Academy to do otherwise, but those rules did not apply to Allie. The kingdom of Dawn, namely the imperial majesty, was bending over backward to get her to attend the Imperial Academy at all costs—and the king had sent her a letter describing just how outright delighted he was at news of her attendance. He even said he'd personally come to speak with her before winter was over to discuss how things were going and added that he was very interested in meeting her brother whenever Riven eventually returned.

Allie was somewhat excited about the idea; she'd never attended college back on Earth and had always wanted to, but she was also weighed down by her responsibilities as queen of the necropolis and by thoughts that perhaps Riven wasn't going to meet his timeline and to survive. Flashbacks of Jose's death haunted her, and she shuddered at the thought that she'd lose someone else she loved to the plays of the system.

But she had to have faith. Riven was rank sixty in the world on the power ladder now, stronger than her by a good margin since acquiring Dao insights in Chicago, and if he couldn't do it, then no one could.

So here she was, day one of school as an exchange student equivalent—or so Mara called it—to start fresh and hopefully take her mind off the shit hand life had dealt her. Insistent on going alone today, she had refused Mara's company and had graciously accepted an enchanted brooch from the king per her own request to change the color of her eyes back to hazel. The reflection staring back at her was still pale, abnormally beautiful, and her locks of brunette hair over-shadowed one half of her face.

Her head leaned against the glass window of the decorated carriage as it drove by eloquent snow-covered gardens and fields of flowers that trailed out for miles. Snowflakes drifted slowly down from an overcast sky, remnants of a recent storm, and snow crunched underneath the wheels of the carriage as the landscape passed by. Large half-frozen ponds rippled in the light breeze on either side of the well-made road as they neared the esteemed estate of the academy on the highest level of the city. A couple of airships sailing amid flocks of birds far overhead calmed her burdened heart. She lost herself in the vast depth of the sky for many minutes, minutes that turned to hours, until the carriage suddenly stopped at its destination.

"We've arrived at the academy, Lady Allie Wraithtide," the driver said with a bow after opening the carriage door. "Do you want me to carry your bags, Miss?"

She shook her head. Allie wanted to remain anonymous while here—aside from her acquaintance with the king, of course—as having the pretentious title of *queen* on an outing like this would no doubt do the exact opposite of what she'd set out to accomplish: have some relaxation time while she learned about the inner workings of Dawn from the perspective of a low-tier noble. "No, I'm fine. I can carry my own bags."

The carriage driver looked slightly surprised but gave another small bow and got back on his seat. "Have a pleasant stay, Miss."

Soon the man was off to pick up other customers, leaving the earthborn woman standing alone outside the shining white gates to the academy. She looked very out of place amid such splendor in her intentionally basic cloth trousers, leather boots, and white linen shirt.

Allie took a long, deep breath and let it out slowly as she approached the two heavily armored knights standing quietly at the front watching her. She really wasn't sure if she should be here, now that she thought about it, and as she arrived directly in front of the guard on the right with her sack slung over her shoulder, she thought she might very well turn around right then.

Why was she nervous? She'd killed thousands of people and conquered cities, for god's sake. This was nothing in comparison.

It took a while for the armed soldiers to snap out of their trance and resume their duties. They'd been so caught up in Allie's good looks that they'd completely forgotten to speak, but their attitude toward her still reflected rather poorly. Minutes later, when their conversation had ended and she had time to ponder this topic, she had to question just how they'd have reacted if she didn't look the way she did.

"State your business, commoner." The knight was obviously making a reference to the way Allie was dressed and didn't seem to like the idea of the lesser class making an appearance here.

A flare of anger surged through Allie at the snide, demeaning comment, and for just a moment her body let out a compulsive and reactive wave of hostile energy. Allie hadn't commanded it to come to her, but the death mana radiated out in a wave of cold flames that scorched the earth about her feet. She quickly reined in her anger, though, as the guard backed away and reached for his weapon.

The knights stared warily at her for some time before Allie pulled out the sealed letter of acceptance the king had given her to present at this exact moment, handing it over without a word. The knight broke the seal and began to read, and seconds later the man completely changed his attitude.

"My apologies, Lady Wraithtide. I didn't expect someone with your reputation as a lady of the court to be wearing such clothes . . . or any student of the academy to wear such clothes, for that matter. Please allow me to escort you to the headmistress."

Allie simply nodded, clutched her sack more tightly, and smiled warmly at the knight. "Thank you, I would sincerely appreciate it."

Her response gave the knight pause, though Allie didn't know why, but he quickly opened the gate and motioned her to follow. Down the road they went, the glistening white gate closing behind them—and snow-capped buildings made of marble, polished wood, and gray stone began to rise up before them.

The sparring arena was the first of the buildings they passed, a monument to Dawn's achievements towering high above her with magnificent carved lions' heads bearing the symbol of the sun above every entrance. Flags emblazoned with the sun also waved along the top of the enormous theater and caused Allie to feel quite small.

"Classes are in session, so not many people are out right now," the knight commented while they made their way over the pristine cobblestone street. Glass windows both clear and colored decorated every Roman-styled building on campus, and most of the buildings stood many stories high.

Eventually they stopped in front of the largest of these structures. It had pillars supporting the flat roof many stories above them, where a living red drake was perched, a knight riding on its back.

"Admiring the drake? The letter did say you're a noble from outside Mandon. A lesser-known country noble, right?" Allie could hear the pride in the knight's voice as he looked up at the beast, too. "The breed is called a sun drake, after the sun god that blessed our nation long ago. They were native to this area before the integration and have been domesticated for centuries under the supervision of our military. Similar to the more common rocs we use."

"How big do they get?" Allie asked curiously. She was impressed—this sun drake was certainly big—twice the size of the rocs she'd seen knights of Dawn ride—but it still wasn't huge. Compared to the corpse of the drake Riven had given her, these sun drakes could have been chomped in half. They were likely just a smaller draconian breed, but then again, she didn't have a lot to go on other than the dead dungeon boss in her spatial sack.

"This is their adult size. The babies are much smaller. They come in handy as one of our primary airborne units when we go to war. They're often support units for the heavier firepower. You see the airships above us, do you not? Those are galleons of war patrolling overhead. Our aerial dominance using the drakes, rocs, and airships is the only reason we lasted against Tereen long enough to find allies in the Thane Necropolis to the north, otherwise we probably would have been wiped out by now. Our ground forces are simply inferior to the elvish cavalry in every way."

Mention of the Thane Necropolis got Allie's attention, and she side-eyed the knight as they started walking again. "What are your thoughts on the necropolis? As you said, I'm a noble from the outlands and have little experience with the undead."

The knight paused in his step, thought about it, and shrugged. "Kinda creepy bastards, if you ask me. I've personally seen a couple and up close—but as long as they're killing elves, then they're friends of mine."

The large double doors were already open and they walked inside to behold two carpeted spiral staircases on either side with a long hallway continuing straight ahead. Velvet chairs and couches decorated the entryway with tables full of refreshments Allie didn't recognize, and a detailed map of the continent was painted along the ceiling.

Walking farther down, Allie saw that most of the doors led to classrooms. Many had glass windows looking out into the hall and resembled small amphitheaters—seating anywhere from twenty to forty students—and every one of the students was far better dressed than she was, with many of them having servants waiting along the wall or taking notes for them.

Coming around a bend in the hallway, she was taken to a dead end with a locked door. The knight knocked on the door twice and waited patiently before it swung open to reveal a pretty, middle-aged woman with long black hair dressed in fine red robes.

"Archmage Zefima Navir." The knight bowed low while removing his helmet out of respect. "I have a delivery for you."

The woman eyed both of them curiously for a time and took the letter Allie had given her escort. The archmage's demeanor changed from curious to elated as she read, and she pocketed the letter to warmly hug a very surprised Allie.

"Allie! I'm so glad to finally meet you!"

The knight was flabbergasted, and his jaw dropped at the warm welcome, but he immediately straightened up and dismissed himself, turning around the bend shortly thereafter with a final curious look over his shoulder.

"Please come in so we can speak in private before you're set up with your dormitory and class schedule!" The archmage held the door wide and shut it behind them as Allie entered her private office. Books in varying languages and thicknesses lined the shelves on both sides, and an intricate wooden desk stood in the middle, twice the size of a dining table from back on Earth. A stained-glass window on the back wall lit the room, even aside from the orb glowing on the ceiling, and potted flowering plants were set regularly around cushioned chairs.

"So tell me! What's your first impression of our Imperial Academy?"

Allie watched the overly friendly and enthusiastic woman with suspicion but straightened her posture and brushed her long brunette hair to the side. "It's very well-kept . . . the limestone buildings especially add a nice touch, and the gardens surrounding the estate are very impressive. It must have cost a fortune."

"Many fortunes, I assure you!" Zefima winked at Allie playfully and took out five large books from underneath the desk. "I've had these all modified with more of the essential topics upon hearing you would be attending! Anything underlined will no doubt be tested on at least once, so keep that in mind—and don't tell the other students I did that for you."

". . . Thanks?" Allie muttered while she sat down in her own chair opposite the archmage.

Putting each book side by side, she scanned the titles: *Fundamentals of Battle Magic, Magic Theory Basics, Anatomy and Healing Techniques, A History of the Eternal War*, and *Illusions, Trickery and War Games*.

The archmage tapped on *A History of the Eternal War*, her brilliant smile radiating Allie's way. "The other books are relative to your classes, mostly on a broad spectrum to encompass many different pillar orientations—but this one I thought you'd take a personal interest in. Be sure to tell me what you think of it. Anyways! Our Imperial Academy is geared toward creating military personnel and officers for the army. This is not a normal school of magic, and we go at a fast pace . . . but your brother assured me that this would be okay."

"You spoke with my brother?" A frown of concern crossed Allie's features, and a pit formed in her stomach. How had this Zefima character spoken with Riven if he had left months ago?

The older woman suppressed a laugh and nodded enthusiastically. "He's quite a charmer! Even if he is a little bit scary. We had many in-depth discussions, and he paid for all three years of your education up front, along with significant donations to our studies and research department—even aside from the crown's own intervention. Riven apparently thought it prudent to show you two weren't taking handouts . . . and the research teams were very pleased, I assure you."

Allie raised an eyebrow but didn't press more. "All right. And what's your name again? Zefima, the knight called you?"

"Oh! I'm so sorry for my rudeness! I never properly introduced myself. My name is Zefima Navir, archmage of the academy! If you ever need ANYTHING, please feel free to ask! And your identity will be kept a safe secret with me, Lady Thane. Only the king and I know exactly who you are, as the crown felt it prudent I intervene on your behalf should anything out of the ordinary happen during your stay here. He very much values the relationship with your necropolis." Zefima leaned forward mischievously and winked, then leaned back and took out a parchment. Handing it over to Allie, she clasped her hands together with a cockiness Allie kind of liked. "Are you ready to start today?"

"Today?" Allie repeated, surprised. "I don't even know where my classes are or where I'm supposed to live. And I should mention that my companion, Mara, is still taking tours of the lower levels, so she'll need to be brought up later on."

The archmage smirked and clapped her hands loudly twice. A couple of seconds later, the door opened, and a young woman in a plain brown maid's outfit came in to bow low. She was very pretty, petite, a redhead, and had lots of freckles adorning her kind features. If she had been standing outside the door when Allie had arrived, she certainly hadn't seen her.

"I've prepared a handmaid for you ahead of time. Her name is Sherine, and she is one of the best servants we have here. Very capable."

Allie put on a brilliant smile and gave a small wave. "It's nice to meet you, Sherine."

"Lady Wraithtide, the pleasure is mine." Sherine curtsied and walked over to pick up Allie's books for her. She didn't smile, but she didn't frown, either, and she avoided eye contact. Perfectly straight-faced, she turned to Allie. "Your second class of the day has just started. Would you like me to escort you there now? Or would you rather be shown to your room?"

"Sherine, dear, Allie needs to change into some new clothes. They're all ready and waiting in her wardrobe back at the dorm. Please take her there first!" the headmistress said politely as the servant girl bowed again.

"Very well. Lady Wraithtide, please follow me."

CHAPTER 45

The plaza was filled with people trying to peddle goods. Weapons, armor, potions, enchanted jewelry, wards, totems, and more were all on display at expensive-looking shops surrounding the sandstone circle placed underneath the shifting stone cube overhead.

There were also pubs and smoke shops where people congregated to eat, drink, and watch participants in the Cube Labyrinth try to find their way out of an ever-changing maze full of puzzles and monsters. Being this close to the cube, Riven could see many family members of participants inside the cube watching their own individual instances. He saw mourners and celebrations—and many betting pools, as money exchanged hands.

Surprisingly enough, one of the hottest topics for the betting pools was none other than the one with both Chalgathi participants. Riven was even able to access the live feed himself this close to the puzzle box, but instead he decided to visit one of the smoke shops, where dozens of people were yelling and screaming at the video footage.

"This is where I'll be," Riven stated, turning his back to the room and looking his minions over. "You can all take some time for yourselves, but be back here within two hours or I'll have to collect you. Got it?"

"AYE, AYE!" Athela said cheekily, sticking her tongue out and giving a mock salute. "I know we talked about it a little bit earlier, but could we get an allowance? Not having any money to spend and walking around the city just for exploratory purposes isn't nearly as fun as actually going into the shops."

Fay scowled at the other demoness. "Athela, you can't be serious. We already have a great opportunity to level up without fear of a true death just by being here. Asking for money as well? That's absurd. Especially when he has already supplied us with items of our own—like the tiara you're wearing!"

But Riven only smiled. "You'll be able to keep your hallucinations going even at a distance across the plaza if we split up, right?"

Fay paused, then nodded.

Unhesitatingly, Riven drew out his bag—the one Negrada had modified for him to increase its space. But the only outward appearance change of the purple satin was an added sigil—a flaming black eye similar to Negrada's own. Out of it he drew four more sacks and handed one to each of his minions. "Already on it. Inside you'll each find a couple thousand Elysium coins. There are also health potions for each of you just in case of emergencies. Have fun, but stay in pairs."

Fay's eyes popped with surprise when Riven handed her a bag of her own, and Athela only cackled mischievously while fist-bumping the Succubus.

"Thank you, Riven. It is appreciated," Luke stated with a bow upon receiving his own sack of coins. He turned to look up at the barbarian at his side. "Azmoth? Do you wish to accompany me to the shops?"

Azmoth grunted his acknowledgment, literally flinging aside a smaller, drunk man who bumped into him. "Yes. I follow. You lead."

"Thanks, Riven!" Athela said, hugging him before she and Fay turned around and began chatting excitedly about what they wanted to find before blending in with the crowds.

Azmoth imitated Luke's bow and waved before the two departed, though Riven didn't have any trouble identifying them even at a distance due to Azmoth's sheer size.

Standing alone at the saloon-style entrance of the smoke shop behind him, Riven hummed in contentment. He glanced at the groaning drunkard Azmoth had thrown into a hay bale nearby, then shook his head and turned to walk into the establishment.

It was rather well-kept and very much like any hookah lounge he'd ever seen back on Earth, but patrons were indulging in liquor and drugs as well. Scantily clad maids served customers whatever kind of drug or drink they wanted, two male bartenders kept tabs on bets, and the central image conjured in the center of the room was magnified to show the two people Riven had an interest in.

They were why he'd chosen this place to begin with.

"I'LL INCREASE MY BID TO SIX HUNDRED ON THE LADY!" one of the customers called out, half high on the purple fumes he was inhaling from a hookah-like contraption. "SIX HUNDRED ON THE LADY!"

A shirtless young man in simple green linen shorts at the bar nodded, took up a piece of chalk, and changed the number on the board next to the older customer's name. "Noted! Cynthia, please collect the additional coins Rebbis wants to add!"

A petite young woman with blond hair trotted over to the table with the bettor, took a hundred coins' worth of money, and then walked back to the bar, where one of five bouncers scattered across the room was located. The large, muscular, dark-skinned man took the cash and placed it somewhere behind the counter before settling back into a watchful position to make sure no brawls or fights erupted between the intoxicated customers.

Riven hobbled inside while playing up the role of old man. Coming to an open seat at the bar and pulling out a stool, he huffed and yanked himself forward with exaggerated effort, to the amusement of another man on his left.

"You all right, old-timer? Looks like that took quite a bit out of you!" The friendly younger warrior in studded leathers with a long sword across his back grinned over. "What brings you out to the plaza? Looking for some good powder?"

[Swordsman, Level 13]

"You could say that!" Riven replied with a smile and a croak to his voice. "More than anything, I was just curious about the show going on! I heard from my grandson that some intense battles were being fought between these two strapping young'uns and felt like I might as well enjoy the rest of the day with a show. Name's Riven."

"Tahm!"

The other man extended his hand to shake, but Riven avoided the gesture by pretending not to notice and ordering a drink for both him and the swordsman. Riven had a heavy gauntlet on underneath Fay's hallucination, and he didn't want to give it away with a handshake.

Tahm's initial frown upon not having his gesture reciprocated quickly faded when the drink arrived, though, and the young man gave Riven a nod of appreciation while starting to sip on the ale—clinking glasses with Riven not long after. "That hits the spot! Thank you!"

"Not a problem!" Riven laughed, turning to look at the large display of the instance event he'd come here for. He'd already done a little bit of digging, though not much, but what he had found indicated that this particular trial had been going on for days now. "Tahm . . . I'll buy you another drink if you can give me some answers about these two."

Riven gestured up at the display, where a dual-axe-wielding barbarian was trying to catch a more nimble female rogue. The axe barbarian had a band of cloth over his eyes, was quite muscular, riddled with sigils he'd carved into his skin, and bulldozed over various spawning monsters inside an ever-shifting room of platforms. Occasionally he'd let out devastating attacks of Unholy might, shattering entire platforms and causing the vision to shudder—while the more nimble, hooded rogue, who was wearing goggles, fired off empowered high-speed shots from a Shadow-infused longbow. The rogue continually shifted between platforms, jumping up or down, dashing across chasms in the air as the swarm of tiles continued to change the landscape. It was very apparent, though, that the rogue was on the back foot, as even when she did land solid hits, the barbarian just healed and shrugged them off like they were nothing—and the body language of the barbarian made it very obvious that he was the hunter, not the hunted.

"Another drink, you say?!" Tahm grinned mischievously, sloshing the ale in his mug. "Sounds good to me! I've actually been here three days now waiting for my guild to take up a contract, so I've got to say, your grandson is right on the money. These are probably some of the highest-level people I've ever seen, and it's even rumored they're part of one of the world events and carry powerful artifacts. Has the betting rings in an uproar. That man with the two axes originally chased the woman into the cube after killing a bunch of bystanders in their fight, and he's been hunting her through the puzzle box ever since—going room to room. He's also killed every single person who tried to get in on the action when the king has placed a bounty on their heads—increasing the bounty twentyfold for whoever brings the bodies and all their items back for evaluation. I have no idea what they're going to do even when they get out, because whoever of these two wins is going to get swarmed when they leave. In fact, I think there's another group heading in later today to try and collect the bounty. It'll be the seventh group since the bounty came out."

Athela rummaged through the materials one by one as the watchful eye of the clerk made sure she didn't steal anything. Piles of various types of threads, wools, strings, and even plant-based ropes were tossed here or there with Athela huffing and puffing about how she couldn't find what she was looking for.

"He'll love it either way," Fay stated with a bright smile, ignoring the lustful looks they were getting from a group of six men at the shop's entrance. "It doesn't need to be perfect, you know."

"BUT IT DOES!" Athela exclaimed with an exasperated moan, flinging another ball of wool to the side in irritation as others in the shop shot curious glances her way. "I want it to be perfect, because it's the first thing I'll give him! He's so good to us—he even gave us our own gifts already—and I've been working on this for a long time now. It needs to be great."

Fay's smile softened, and she nodded once while looking in another crate. They'd already gone to the Elysium altar and had zero success, but then again, Elysium altars were more for the basics than they were anything else—at least until upgraded. And it was unlikely any Elysium altar on the planet was upgraded at such an early stage in the integration process. So, pushing one of her slender hands into the mix of wares, she started rummaging around as well. "Fine. But I think he's going to be absolutely head over heels for it regardless of if you find that particular ingredient to use. There are many substitutes, and he'll not even notice the difference if you use one of them instead."

Athela glowered at her friend but continued digging and huffing. "I just want it to last, you know? I don't want it to get old."

"Everything gets old, Athela, especially in the realm of items like these."

"But I don't want it to."

"Why?"

"Because I don't want him to ever throw it away."

Fay's smile widened, and she chuckled to herself. "I see. Well, then I guess we'll just have to keep searching, then."

Behind the two women, a gruff clearing of a throat was heard—and Fay turned to see a rather handsome older man in rich linens looking her up and down. He had many golden rings on his fingers, and he was flanked by two servants in similar but less gaudy attire. "Madam . . . Miss . . ."

The man bowed slightly to each of them and then straightened again when he had their attention. "Is there something you're looking for? I'm the owner of this shop, and I see you may be in need of assistance. If there's something that you need and it isn't here, I can send one of my employees to check other merchants for you."

Fay raised a suspicious eyebrow. "You'd check other merchants? That's very generous of you. My friend Athela is in need of something called Kenwit thread. Ever heard of it?"

The man hesitated, put on the fakest smile Fay had ever seen, then nodded quickly. "Of course! I have heard of it, though I am somewhat unfamiliar with the properties. We may have some in the back. Would you mind following me?"

Athela and Fay exchanged glances, shrugged, and then wordlessly followed the merchant and his two servants through the store and through a large door. Following the man deeper into the establishment into a storage unit through yet another door, Fay came face-to-face with a rather unexpected sight.

Hovering there above the ground and staring back at both women with many slowly blinking eyeballs was a car-size, purple-skinned Beholder demon—grinning wickedly back at them with a toothy smile.

"Do tell me . . ." the Beholder demon stated in a deep yet sophisticated-sounding voice as the central-most eyeball dilated. "What in the world are a level-60 Arshakai and a level-39 Succubus—both contracted to a master—doing in my fine establishment this wonderful afternoon? I must admit, I'm quite interested to see you both here . . . and if I'm right on the money about just who you are—I have a very interesting proposition for the two of you."

CHAPTER 46

The merchant and his servants bowed low, exiting the storage room and shutting the door behind them, leaving the Beholder demon alone in the dark with Athela and Fay.

Not that any of them had any qualms with being in the dark—they were demons.

[Beholder Demon, Level 28]

Athela glanced around casually, not seeing anyone or anything that could be a threat, then folded her arms. Fay's illusion dispelled a second later, revealing the horns, tail, and wings of a Succubus—as well as Athela's red eyes, pitch-black skin, and the arachnid limbs ripping out of her back.

"What do you want, eyeball? Don't just sit there—spit it out. I doubt it's about the ingredient I was looking for concerning my master's birthday present, so whatever it is, make it snappy," Athela eventually said after the two sides just stared one another down—evaluating each other in turn. She inspected her fingers, which one by one turned into a long obsidian claw. "There better be a good reason to call us in here like this. My friend and I are on a schedule—don't waste our time."

Fay nodded with a more polite smile and a brief bow of her head. "What she said. We don't have much time to waste. Please tell us what it is you desire from us."

Blinking a couple times with various different appendages, the Beholder demon pulled up the cortex forums. From there he navigated to the main page of Panu and scrolled through the forum posts until he found the one he was looking for. Selecting a video channel, he displayed Riven's battle in Chicago. Pausing the video feed when it gave a snapshot of Fay and Athela, the Beholder demon turned back to them.

"You are the same. Yes?"

Athela rolled her eyes. "Congratulations, you're not blind."

"That's correct," Fay confirmed.

The Beholder hovered in silence, took in a deep breath, and let it out slowly while casting his gaze downward. His demeanor changed to a strange and manic glee, and he even blinked away a cascade of happy tears—which was very much a surprise to the other two demons in the room.

"My name is Brezkevix. I need your help, and the help of your master. It's only right, considering you happened to show up at the wrong place and the wrong time . . . Could you not have just stayed away from the city for another day or so? That's all it would have taken . . . You should have been more careful!"

Athela's eyebrows raised in surprise; she felt very unsettled by the entire situation. Something about this wasn't right. "Um . . . and just what can we help you with?"

The Beholder's mouth widened to abnormal proportions, and a hiss of hot air escaped his lips as its iris began to glow. "You can help by dying for me!"

With a cackle, the Beholder self-destructed and unleashed a maelstrom of violent, Unholy energy that crashed into the other two demons like a freight train. Athela and Fay were both thrown backward, smashing into an invisible barrier coating the walls of the large room's interior. Fay screamed in pain as ethereal chains rapidly bound her to the wall and began to burn her alive, but Athela was too quick to be caught and blurred ahead—trying to find who or what was attacking her as a plethora of spells detonated around her.

CRASH

BOOM

THUD

Flurries of infernal spears, globes of blood, and a swarm of ravenous insects ripped out of spatial tears and tore into her like a hurricane of violence.

And despite how agile she was, Athela had been caught completely off guard.

RIP

TEAR

SPLAT

She was violently whipped around, half of her jaw hanging off and holes riddling her body as she gasped for air. Three of her arachnoid legs were ripped off completely, along with one of her arms. Burn markings scorched her body, and one femur was sticking out the side of her thigh when she slammed into the floor after the barrage was done.

A man's voice called out above the screams and cries of the flailing, burning Succubus. "STOP! WE MUST FINISH THEM WITH A BLADE!"

Athela's vision blurred, and blood began to pool around her as she tried to activate a portal back to the nether realms—but it was blocked.

Enchantments—having been inscribed into the stone walls, ceiling, and floor—were obstructing her passage back home. But she could still make out the robed, hooded figures of eight men and women circling her, with one of the older ones—a Japanese man with a neatly trimmed white beard—coming to the front. Two more demons accompanied them as well: a minotaur and a humanoid Cthulhu abomination from the outer realms.

The Japanese man turned to the Cthulhu monster, held out a hand, and was given a slender white blade with black runes that writhed with dark flames. The blade was only a few feet in length, but Athela's heart nearly stopped in absolute horror when she saw the weapon. She knew what it was before the man even told her.

"Hello, Athela. You put on quite a show with your master not long ago; we were all very impressed that one of Chalgathi's chosen—one of us—would have come so far in such a short time. To reach the top one hundred so early is beyond anyone's expectations . . . It is unfortunate that he is not part of the cult," the old man said slowly, coming to stand over the demoness while twirling the blade across his hands, only to rest it on Athela's neck. "Do you know what this is?"

Athela could barely move, but her loud whimper and wide-eyed horror was all it took to get the man to let out a malicious laugh.

"This . . . is a demon-slayer blade."

Fay, who was still strapped to the wall with flaming chains, let out a scream of absolute denial and blasted out every bit of mana she had left despite her flesh slowly being eaten away by Unholy power. Yet the chains soaked that up, too, and she stayed there—helplessly beginning to sob—as she screamed, "PLEASE DON'T! WAIT! WE DON'T KNOW WHO YOU ARE, BUT WE CAN BARGAIN WITH YOU!"

"Bargain?!" The head cultist laughed, as did the other hooded, robed figures around the room. "The sex toy wants to bargain. Isn't that funny. Let me ask you a question, Succubus—do you think your master would bargain with us, too?"

The old man grinned savagely at Fay, whose tears were actively streaming down her face as she trembled, knowing full well what the weapon in this man's hands did. "ANSWER ME, SUCCUBUS! WE OF CHALGATHI'S CULT DO NOT HAVE TIME TO PLAY GAMES WITH YOU!"

The man sank the blade an inch into Athela's neck, and she immediately began to spasm and scream in absolute agony. Her very soul began to burn away, bit by bit, faster and faster as the blade continued to grind down into her throat and then into her spine.

Athela shed tears of blood, seizing on the ground as Fay screamed and begged for this unknown man to stop.

"ANSWER ME, SUCCUBUS, AND PERHAPS I'LL MERELY VIOLATE YOUR BODY INSTEAD OF YOUR SOUL AS I DO TO THIS ONE!"

Athela coughed and sputtered on the ground, completely broken, but she managed to try and claw at the old man's foot—only to have the boot slam down and crunch onto her fingers, breaking bones. She glared up at the man whose blade was still stuck in her neck, managing to get only a few words out before the end. "Riven . . . *cough* will kill you . . . *cough* *cough* He will avenge me . . ."

The old man sneered. "It is certainly possible, but I doubt it. He wouldn't be the first of Chalgathi's chosen we killed that weren't true members of the cult—and he won't be the last. That being said, we don't even need to fight him . . . we only need him distracted long enough for us to accomplish our goal with the cube."

The blade punched through Athela's spine and then was ripped up into her brain—sending pieces of her face across the floor to be burned away with black flames as motes of light started crackling and fizzling away around her. Her soul complex was breaking down more rapidly now, and she gave one last look to Fay—then gasped and fell still.

Fay let out an ear-piercing scream of denial, arms and legs still burning against the chains that bound her to the wall, and then the scream faded into violent sobs and crying. Her head dropped, and the old man yanked the sword out of Athela's corpse to look at the others.

One of the other robed men stepped forward, gesturing to the Succubus. "What of her? We need to leave fast, before he gets here. We cannot beat him in a frontal assault or in a fair fight, and permanently killing these demons is only a temporary solution. The one you killed was a rarer and more dangerous breed—perhaps we really should keep this one for a bit of fun? That way he won't be able to contract other demons in the meantime."

The old man scoffed, sending a glowering look at the crying woman restrained on the wall. "There's almost no chance he could contract other demons so quickly, not in the time it will take us to kill him and the other two participants in the cube."

The ringleader glanced back over his shoulder to the others, only to receive looks of doubt and wariness. His eyebrows rose. "You truly think he'd be able to get more minions that fast?"

"I do," another hooded Chalgathi cultist stated solemnly. "We only have three advantages here. First is that the demoness you killed was a much more dangerous variant than what he'll likely be able to contract next. Second is that he doesn't know who or what we are—or where we are, as none of us are carrying our artifacts. That, however, could change at any moment if we don't get out of here right now. Third, we have the Succubus. Perhaps we can just mute the connection so he can't track her?"

"He's stronger than us and could just brute force the connection," argued another woman from the back holding a staff. "I for one don't want to end up as red paste on the ground—you all saw what he did in Chicago. He's an absolute monster. I say kill the Succubus, too, so loose ends are tied. We don't want him finding out who did this—even if he does realize it was likely a distraction."

"Nonsense," replied the second cultist with a scowl and a lustful glare toward the Succubus on the wall. "At the very least let me have her for a little while. Just cut the connection with that fucking blade and let's move. You owe me, Kenji, remember? This is what I want in return for the favor I did you. Give her to me instead."

Kenji, the group leader of this sect of the cult, scowled at his underling—but eventually scoffed and handed the blade over. "Cut the connection yourself. You have thirty seconds before we teleport out of here; no doubt he's already headed this way. Hopefully he hasn't realized the magnitude of what we've done just yet, because if he has, he's no doubt rushing. God help us if he actually catches us before we're gone."

The younger man grinned wickedly, then licked his lips and headed for Fay. "Fine! Prepare the portal ritual and let's go! I'll subdue the Succubus in the meantime."

He turned back to Fay, crashing a fist into her gut and causing her to sputter before pinching her cheeks with one hand. "Oh, am I going to have fun with you."

[Your minion Athela has been slain by a demon-slayer relic. Your minion Athela has permanently died. A demonic minion slot has opened up.]

Riven abruptly stopped laughing at the joke the swordsman at the bar had told him, going pale and dropping his drink to crash against the wooden countertop. Was he reading this right?

Shakily and with panic quickly beginning to set in, he rubbed his eyes and stared—his whole body beginning to tremble as he lurched back from the countertop. It'd only been an hour—just how the fuck had this happened?

WHAT THE ACTUAL FUCK?!

His aura began to billow out. Rage quickly was replaced with fear, fear was replaced by anxiety, anxiety was replaced with desperation, and desperation was replaced with extreme sorrow like nothing he'd ever known before. Even when Jose had died, it was nothing like this.

It was nothing . . . like this . . .

The mask temporarily opened up. Lurching forward and vomiting violently onto the countertop to the loud and angry or confused expressions of discontentment by nearby patrons of the bar, the hallucination around him began to flicker and then abruptly stopped working altogether when yet another message appeared.

[Your minion Fay has had her demonic contract forcibly severed. A demonic minion slot has opened up.]

The entire bar was now quiet as his aura slowly began to climb. Red frost began to accumulate along the chairs, cups, walls, and ceiling as he just stared, dumbfounded, at the system notification. Everybody there was staring wide-eyed at the fully armored man many of them recognized from the world forums. Red mana began to swirl around his body as the maw along his chest hissed with rage building to match his own. All seven feathered eyes began blinking rapidly, and the horned pauldrons on either shoulder glowed more and more brightly as the room began to shudder with power.

Why hadn't his Malignant Prophecy activated?

Was it still on cooldown from the last time he'd used it to save Kathrine's life?

But that'd been three months ago. Or was this event just not important enough to the prophecy for a trigger point?

No, that didn't seem right—the blonde woman he'd saved in Negrada had meant nothing to him! It should have activated! WHY hadn't it activated?! IT SHOULD HAVE FUCKING ACTIVATED!

His fingers clenched around the bar, smashing the wood to splinters as he began to whisper—with that whisper turning into a scream. "No . . . Nooo, no, no, NO, NO-NO-NO, NOOOOOOOOOO!!!!"

His body pulsed, and everything for over a mile around him erupted into a nova of red. Bodies and buildings were vaporized within seconds, and the resounding explosion sent a shock wave radiating for miles as his scream reached the heavens. All activity in the city stopped.

With it came an aura of malice and rage, and the hot sands of the desert froze over as Riven's body ripped through a tear in space and he raced toward the last location where he'd felt the two female demons with his soul aperture.

He looked down at Athela's broken, smoldering body, which still had black flames trickling along her skin. Her once beautiful features were now barely recognizable, and the tiara she'd prized so much—the very first gift he'd ever given her—was lying covered in blood a few feet away in a pool of her own viscera.

Riven dropped to his knees, ignoring the screams and commotion outside at the carnage he'd indiscriminately wrought in his moment of panic. He also couldn't care less . . . because right now, his very world was falling apart.

His best friend had died—again.

Riven let out a hiccuping sob as he buried his face in her unmoving chest. Bringing her body up to his own, he continued to cry while rocking back and forth—quaking violently while he continued to shake his head in denial over and over again. The words he wanted to speak were garbled both in his head and as they left his lips, and he was rendered little more than a mourning, bawling child—reduced to the same state he'd been left in when his mother had left him all those years ago.

On the other side of a pile of crates, the merchant who owned this shop was breathing fast. His heart pounded in his chest, and he held the communication stone up to his mouth to whisper a report. "Make your move to steal the cube now—he's preoccupied and probably will be for some time. His reaction was far more volatile than you anticipated and—"

The merchant's voice caught in his throat when all seven eyes along the glowing crimson feathers coming off Riven's porcelain mask focused on his location.

"You cut out. Continue the report." Kenji's voice came through at a hushed whisper—but even he, on the other side of it, stopped when a ravenous scream of hate roared across the sky—and the visage of a great maw darkened the land.

The roof above Riven and the merchant shattered, and the sandstone it was made out of was sucked skyward as Riven found a target for his rage.

There would be retribution for this.

There would be pain.

And in this realm of magic and miracles, he would find a way to bring Athela back if it was the last thing he ever did. Even if he had to tear apart the entire world to do it.

CHAPTER 47

The visage of the great maw in the sky echoed across the landscape with a roar that shook the heavens, and the landscape was painted red.

"I demand this sacrifice . . ."

Riven gingerly kissed the forehead of Athela's limp, bloodied corpse through his mask, picked up her tiara to put it away with her body, then slid them both into his spatial sack before slowly standing up. A boom of power tore apart everything around him—the ground, the civilians hiding nearby, the general goods store his minions had been ambushed in—everything except the merchant who'd been hiding behind the barrels.

Lifting one hand, Riven summoned Wretched Snares, which lurched forward and snagged the quivering man, who suddenly began to scream in abject horror. Those same snares ripped him forward, dragging him onto his knees to violently slam face-first into the ground at Riven's feet.

"Where are they?" Riven said, his voice only a whisper of cold fury—but it still thundered over the ruckus and chaos of the city around him. "I heard what you said. Where did they go?"

The merchant was panicking, screaming, and his flesh was being eaten away by the acidic black needles. "YOU ARE MISTAKEN! I DO NOT KNOW—"

CRUNCH

Riven's ice-covered fist smashed through the man's skull with a blur, splattering his brains across the floor, and he slowly picked up the communication stone the man had been holding.

When he inspected it and felt the connection wink out, Riven's fury caused him to abruptly crush the item into dust.

He looked left to a group of heavily armed guards rushing his way through the din of his maelstrom—spears and swords lighting up with energies as they began to charge martial arts in an attempt to stop him, to stop the whirlwind of agonizing red sleet that blasted everything for miles around Riven. Even now they took damage, but when Riven raised his hand and the warriors were vaporized in a whirlwind of storm blades—upgraded versions of his bloody blades that'd incorporated the Path of Red and Black.

The attacks were instantaneous, and the incoming guards were little more than scraps of metal and meat within a split second.

Something inside Riven had snapped. Something bestial had clawed its way to the forefront of Riven's conscious mind, something beyond right and wrong—something that just wanted to kill. Wanted revenge. Wanted to tear the world apart.

Seeing Athela's corpse . . . he simply didn't care anymore. It wasn't that he wanted to kill those guards, or to those civilians who'd been trying to hide from his storm. They'd simply been in his way.

They'd been in his way.

And he was done caring.

"Chosen bringer of sin . . . I can help you . . . if only you complete me . . ."

Looking up to the sky where the visage of the great maw of Gluttony continued to roar down upon Daskus, the city of canyons, Riven held out his hands wide. He could feel the tug, feel its pull; it wanted to speak to him, but he just couldn't understand . . . yet it felt important. It felt like a great hunger, a yearning for . . . something that he could not put his finger on.

Visions of murder. Thousands of bodies. A burning city. A swarm of souls ascending into the sky. The cube . . .

The cube.

The maw screeched, and Riven immediately turned his gaze to the cube in the distance, still hovering above the city and churning its puzzle-box pieces one after the other. He could see a number of hooded figures standing on it, performing some kind of ritual, as green sparks began to light up amid the red of his storm.

And there, gagged and bound with white glowing chains, was Fay.

The sky fell, and all hell broke loose as his wrath descended.

As one, his storm converged on the cube—thousands upon thousands of swirling shards of ice. Hundreds of spinning balls of black and red storm. Thundering arcs of Black Lightning. Dozens of lances crackling with electricity—they all sped toward it with an aggression far beyond what this world had ever seen.

The cultists atop the cube looked on in shock, and flashes of light from different spells and miracles lit up the cube right before his magic struck.

The impact was devastating.

A shock wave of enormous proportions radiated out from where his storm had converged, erasing the marketplace below and eradicating entire neighborhoods with cold wrath that billowed out like an atomic bomb.

"WHAT ARE YOU DOING TO MY HOME?!" screeched a voice Riven didn't recognize, and he turned slightly to see an incoming scimitar of blue flames rocketing toward him.

Riven's spear-staff, Jackal, met it with a snap of motion that broke the sound barrier and stopped the scimitar dead in its tracks. Staring back at a shirtless, bearded, dark-skinned man wearing a crown, Riven easily deflected the next blow, too, despite an empowered martial art attack.

Three more warriors of equal caliber, wearing exquisite golden robes, shot past the shirtless king after that to engage Riven next—but Riven stepped back and then activated Jackal's Lunge to double back with a cold, calculated blow. The black spear whipped forward, and the visage of a red jackal's maw opened up, three times the size of any man, before snapping down and instantaneously eviscerating all three men in a single strike.

Black Lightning pulsed from the spear-staff next and tore into the king, blasting him across the canyon to slam into the opposite wall—creating a crater that sent stone debris flying.

The exchange lasted only seconds, and Riven turned back to the cube—all seven eyes of his mask's feathers trained on the remaining occupants still alive on the stone surface. With a swift motion, he opened up a rift and shot forward—almost instantaneously stepping onto the large, floating, system-made construct to stare daggers at the targets before him.

Two of the hooded cultists lay dead, and a third was completely obliterated, body parts smoldering, along the large stone platforms that created the various pieces of the shifting puzzle box. One woman remained, injured and heaving in deep breaths as she bled out on the ground. It was a testament to just how strong they were that they'd even survived, but the others were gone.

Feeling the threads of blood mana around him, Riven closed his eyes and concentrated, searching. Pulsing rivers of blood swirled around him in an instant, bringing a vision that only he could see in a state similar to when he watched his soul complex change. Here, though, it was solely the Blood subpillar, the great maw above, and the whispers they spoke into his ear.

His eyes trailed the lines, listening to Gluttony resonate with his Blood subpillar—feeling them sync as he traced the remnants of Athela's blood that still lingered on the blade of her enemy.

They weren't here.

He looked down to the stone cube he stood on. He could feel them . . . inside.

They'd escaped his attack by going into the cube. Athela's killer was in there, and Fay was with them.

A bestial scream of rage echoed across the chasm, and in his peripheral vision Riven saw the king of Daskus rip through the sky on wings of blue fire.

He tore toward Riven's body like an angel of judgment incarnate, aura billowing out almost to match Riven's own. "YOU WILL PAY FOR THIS, CHALGATHI CULTIST!"

Riven didn't even look the man's way but merely opened a portal directly in front of the man and lifted Jackal to intercept.

The king didn't have time to react before he abruptly teleported right into Jackal's blade, and the maw of the blood jackal snapped the man in half. The king fell, lifeless, cut into multiple pieces that scattered across the torrential winds of Riven's aura.

"I can tell you . . . *GASP* How to find them . . . *GASP*!"

Riven glanced right, to where the last cultist left alive on the platform was struggling to breathe. He slowly began to walk toward her, and she nodded—gesturing for him to come forward so she could speak more clearly.

"Just help me! *GASP*" said the hooded woman, barely older than Allie, with a short pixie cut of red hair that matched the blood seeping from puncture wounds. She raised a shaky, lacerated hand, reaching out for him to take it. "Please help *GASP* me, and I will tell—"

Riven's blade snapped down, puncturing the woman's skull and abruptly ending her life. Yanking back the black blade with living, flowing streams of crimson encircling it, Riven turned his gaze back to the sky, where the great maw continued to whisper to him.

"Make my core whole . . . and I will show you the path you desire . . . You know what must be done . . ."

Azmoth landed on top of the cube next, having jumped an incredible distance to get here from god knows where while holding Luke in his arms. The elf scrambled down from Azmoth's hold, then looked around with wide-eyed horror at the carnage that was still ripping through the city around them. "Riven! What is this?! Why are you doing this?!"

Riven only spared the elf thrall a passing, uncaring glance. "Do I need a reason?"

His cold voice echoed across the canyons, over the din and howl of his building storm, growing again with every body that his aura consumed as screams of the innocent beneath him cried out for mercy.

"THIS IS SENSELESS!" Luke howled, trying to tug at Riven's armor to get his attention—but the maw along Riven's chest opened up, and a black tongue smashed him backward onto the stone floor. "WHAT IS THE PURPOSE HERE?! HAVE SOME SENSE! YOU ARE KILLING SO MANY FOR NO REASON! THEY WERE NOT THE ONES WHO KILLED ATHELA! I FELT HER CONTRACT LEAVE, I KNOW WHAT YOU FEEL, I HAVE FELT IT ONCE, TOO! BUT THIS IS NOT THE WAY!"

"I can save her . . . for a price . . ."

Riven's glare did not falter, and raising his staff high above him, he began to charge a ball of flames. Hellfire surged across his body and through his staff, blinding Luke and even Azmoth as the fires of the damned roared to life amid his storm of red and black. They crackled, licked at his body, and created a pillar many stories high that illuminated the darkness his storm cast on the world.

A sun began to take shape. One of wicked, writhing fires and Unholy might that caused the bodies nearby to melt or burn. The only reason Luke was left intact was because the mana actively avoided harming Riven's minions, and the vampire glared down at his subordinate only moments later after creating a raging, condensed inferno the size of the *Titanic* over the cube to dwarf them all.

Riven calmly watched the violent fires of hell swirling above his head, where his staff kept them focused. The weapon in his hand began to shudder, and soon the flames were too much even for Jackal to keep in one place. Fire began to flicker down its shaft and burned Riven's own hand, but still he kept charging.

"RIVEN! THIS ISN'T LIKE YOU!" Luke screamed above the din of the storm.

"Are you willing to pay that price . . . child of the blood god?"

The pure-blooded vampire smiled at the words Gluttony whispered to him, then he looked down to his elf thrall with indifference. "Luke . . . You barely even know me."

There was a silence between the two as Riven stared at the man he'd only recently begun to know.

"But you're a good man!" Luke croaked out with desperation, waving to the carnage and destruction Riven had wrought and was continuing to spill down onto the surrounding city. "What's the point of this, Riven? You're killing indiscriminately because you're upset? Because you're angry at the world?"

Riven slowly cocked his head to the side. Then he chuckled. "That isn't true at all. Let me pose a question, Luke. Just how far would you go, just how far would you push yourself, to save the ones you love? This . . . this is my answer to that question."

Not bothering to wait for a reply, Riven looked back up to the writhing ball of hellfire overhead—and his free hand began to move. It created a circle of flames, pushed through the center of that circle with a clenched fist, and then his forearm twisted while he chanted. "Rain fire upon mine enemies, cast doubt upon divine providence, and bathe the land in a blaze of profane glory."

[Blaze of Profane Glory (Infernal) (Tier 3)—Detonate a massive ball of infernal power overhead, devastating the surrounding landscape and burning your enemies alive. This spell seeks out all living creatures, avoiding nonliving material, causing soul damage as the fires of hell temper the innocent and guilty alike. One-week cooldown.]

The sun overhead exploded, and the supernova blew in all directions before turning into streams of flame that sought out all living beings below. Trails of liquid fire dived in between windows, blasted down doors, ripped into cellars, and chewed through stone to find and quench the life of every single screaming man, woman, child, and animal in Daskus. Immediately afterward, Riven's storm erupted to new heights—and a shock wave of black and red tore through the city with a silent finality that left everything around them as still as the grave.

Luke looked on in utter shock.

The city of Daskus was gone, and in its place was a silent, smoldering pile of rubble and ash.

"I am pleased. Bringer of sin . . . child of the blood god . . . I accept your sacrifice, and I will now provide a path as promised . . ."

[Core of Original Sin: Gluttony, has been successfully created. Bonuses: ??? Gluttonous Sacrifice (Sin Miracle) has been created and etched into your sin core.]

[Gluttonous Sacrifice (Sin Miracle): Perform a mass execution and destroy at least two hundred thousand innocent souls in order to bring a soul shard back from absolute destruction. Souls beyond this number will increase the effectiveness of this miracle. Cooldown: five thousand years.]

[Gluttonous Sacrifice (Sin Miracle) has been performed. Due to low Faith stat, you have only managed to bring a very small sliver of Athela's soul back from nothingness. Athela's soul shard is now bound to your core.]

Riven gasped in relief when a teeny, tiny light was created from nothing right in front of his eyes. Beginning to weep, he held out his hands—cupping the immeasurably small and fragile thing between his fingers to cradle it as if it were the most precious treasure he'd ever had. Watching it fade, he saw it bind internally to his own soul core, and from there it began to pulse.

He didn't know how to bring her back from this state of being, but he knew it was now possible. The damage done by the demon-slayer blade was now at least partially reversed, and that was all that mattered.

Athela could still be brought back . . . somehow.

Shivering, clutching his sides, and falling to his knees, Riven began to sob uncontrollably. His masked head hit the stone floor of the floating cube—the lone remnant of the city he'd so mercilessly butchered.

Only Luke, Azmoth, and Riven remained alive in the city. Only their hearts beat within the clouds of ash that encircled them, billowing out from the smoldering flames of wreckage that spanned miles of terrain.

Despite all he'd done, Riven wasn't finished yet. His eyes snapped open when he heard Fay's scream of horror and pain through the system's vision concerning the cube. He watched, eyes growing to a brighter crimson as she was dragged naked through another portal inside the cube's boundaries.

He watched as the remaining cultists, led by an old Japanese man, raced through the rift in space while carrying away the bodies of the two participants Riven had come to hunt—and their relics.

He watched as they all disappeared from sight.

His vision grew cold, and Riven slowly stood as the maw of Gluttony in the sky disappeared into nothingness—leaving only him and two of his minions standing above the burning wreckage of a once-great city.

His breathing picked up, and the silence was permeated with killing intent that flashed out of him like a tidal wave.

"We are going to hunt them down," Riven said with renewed hate, getting ahold of himself now that he'd secured Athela's chance at a future again. When he held out one hand, Jackal slammed into his grip. Feeling the mana leaking out of the tear in space from somewhere inside the cube, Riven knew he could trace the signal. "We're entering the cube, and we're taking Fay back."

Riven shuddered, ignoring the tears of disbelief streaming down Luke's shocked face. The vampire turned to Azmoth, who grinned wickedly back at his master, and with growing fury the warlock began to access the system commands to enter the puzzle-box event. Looking up right before he selected the option to enter, he addressed the system and the viewers he knew were likely watching all around the world. He could feel their gazes on him, could feel Elysium once again targeting him as a person of interest, and he began to speak clearly, addressing the cultists who'd come to take what was his.

"I'm going to find you. And when I do, I'm going to do unimaginably horrible things to your bodies. I'm going to tear your souls asunder, torture you until you scream and beg me for death. I am going to piss on each and every one of your corpses, and when it's all done I'm going to hang your bodies from the tower of my capital city for everyone to see as a reminder that you do not FUCK with Riven Thane. Run while you can, enjoy the short remnants of your pathetic lives while you can, because you are not long for this world. I'll be seeing you soon, Chalgathi's chosen. It will be me who stands at the top in the end."

CHAPTER 48

High Queen Nephridi watched curiously as the armies of the invading forces finally began to breach Panu's realm. These world quests always started later than the others due to the extreme difficulty the local forces often had in deterring professional armies of already-established factions, even if there were level caps.

Glancing lazily out over the capital city of her homeworld, where buildings of eloquent designs sprawled out toward the horizon, she chose an extremely high-quality piece of fruit—a blood-variant Dao treasure—out of a bowl and began to chew thoughtfully. Most people would want this kind of luxury for breakthroughs in the lower grades, but she merely enjoyed the taste and gained little to nothing from it.

Perhaps Riven or Allie could have used it?

Nephridi looked back down to the glistening crimson fruits in a basket nearby, her long white dress hugging her slender body as she lounged on the cushioned bench. Perhaps she'd prepare a gift basket for them when the integration finally ended—if they lived that long.

And although both Allie and Riven seemed to be doing wonderfully in their own progressions, that was not the case for Kathrine. Nephridi was half tempted to execute the little royal and her entire family for all the shame and failure she'd brought to such a simple task.

Bring them into the fold, Nephridi had said.

Support them in their growth, Nephridi had said.

But neither of those two very simple tasks had even come close to fruition. Instead, Riven and Allie had almost shunned the Blood Moon Requiem's trading outpost entirely—forgoing any training or tutoring in favor of their own pursuits after they'd almost been assassinated. Then things had only gotten worse when those damnable younglings Nephridi had sent failed to interrupt a simple low-tier system quest, resulting in Riven being whisked away against his will while Allie raged about how incompetent Kathrine and her ilk were.

It was outright humiliating for Nephridi to watch, because all this reflected on her. Truthfully, it was the first time she'd felt the sensation of embarrassment for millennia, as she usually didn't care what other people thought—she could just kill anyone she didn't like—but these were her favorite granddaughter's children. Nephridi wanted to impress them.

So much for that.

She let out a long sigh and covered her eyes with her right arm. "Oh, Sheline, if you're still out there somewhere, please forgive your grandmother for sending such idiots to help your progeny."

Raising her arm and lowering her gaze back to the visions over the table, her eyes rested back on Riven. "But perhaps they don't need my help. Who would have thought . . . a shard of Gluttony, in a newly integrated world?"

High Queen Nephridi snickered at the very idea of it. That snicker turned into an outright guffaw of laughter, and she had to clutch at her gut to stop herself from shaking from the forcefulness of it. "Oh my . . . How nasty things are going to get with an artifact of that magnitude present. At the very least, it should be quite fun to watch! Wouldn't you agree, Jalel? Speaking of which, I do wonder why you never told me about this. Didn't you once describe Riven as, and I quote, 'unimpressive in all regards'?"

The queen's glare caused her nephew to stiffen, and sweat was already beginning to trickle down his forehead from where he stood ahead of the two armored elites that'd escorted him here. They glared at his back with crimson eyes flaring, fists tightening around long obsidian swords.

When there was no response, Nephridi harrumphed with amusement and then turned back to eating fruits and watching Riven try to figure out what to do. Watching these two children had become a favorite pastime for the queen, and she'd forgone many of her responsibilities running the empire in order to do so. "I find it very hard to believe that you intentionally withheld such an interesting secret from me, Jalel. But although you are not my most competent nephew—you are not THAT incompetent. You would have known what Riven held. Jalel, you have two minutes to explain to me why you tried to hide this and why I should not execute you and your entire house for treason. You can begin explaining . . . now."

[Quest Dispensed: Find Your Succubus Princess—You have found and rescued your spider princess, Athela; now it's time to find and rescue Fay. Cultists have taken your minion from you by force with nefarious intent, and it is likely they will eventually kill her if you try to get her back.
Quests aside, you know you don't have a choice. Find and rescue Fay within twenty-one days, four hours, and five minutes to avoid catastrophe concerning Fay's well-being.]

Riven dismissed the notification almost as soon as it came, scoffing at the mere idea of having a quest for this kind of thing. He needed no quest to urge him to save her, and anger surged inside him as he thought about what was likely happening to her even now while he sat here attempting to solve the riddle of the ritual these cultists had used to escape.

Fuck the twenty-one days. He'd do it in two.

Beside him, Azmoth was contemplating Riven's recent display of hellfire, trying to gain insights from his master's use of it to integrate those concepts into a stamina-based martial art rather than Riven's own spell form. And hunched over in a corner of the stone puzzle-box room, still in a state of shock from the things he'd witnessed only two days ago, was Luke. The old man's red eyes blinked occasionally, but otherwise he remained as still as a statue while trying to compute the magnitude of violence unleashed by his master.

Luke obviously had far more misgivings about the event than Riven did, because the vampire had already tossed the guilt aside. He didn't have time to feel guilty, and he'd fucking do it again if given the choice.

Closing his eyes, Riven entered a meditative pose while letting his Shadow subpillar feel out the surrounding remnants of magic used to escape this place. That it was Shadow magic he was certain of, and that it was also similar to his own Riftwalk spell was also a certainty. He could feel just how the lock-and-key mechanisms these cultists used were similar in shape to his own fractals, the ones on his Shadow subpillar when he activated Riftwalk, only that here in the cube's alternate reality, the remnant ritual fractals had been brought out into the open with a few key modifications.

They'd been hard to detect at first, but he'd mostly pieced them back together by now.

Mostly.

He'd done a little bit of runecrafting in his attempts to learn totem making early on, but that was truly his only exposure up until now. This ritual used something similar, with figurines of ashy trails littering the air about him—invisible to the naked eye but present to his mana sense, which resonated with his Shadow subpillar. Riven rearranged the eighteen figurines in different patterns and reconnected the pieces to one another by manipulating the remnant mana—trying to form a convergence.

The visage of Gluttony's maw flashed in his mind, letting its presence be known and incorporating itself into his aura but otherwise leaving him be . . . interested in the proceedings as he struggled to grasp the secrets of Shadow.

"This ritual is . . . strange," Riven stated from his cross-legged position in the air, completely focused on the task at hand while sigils interchanged and the air about him shifted with passing Dao fields interlocking between them for every minuscule alteration he created. His fingers steepled together in thought, and

Riven pondered what he had wrong. "It is almost as if they created a wormhole without using a source of intent. My understanding of mana and spellcasting was that intent was a necessary piece, a fundamental part to any direction you wanted to take. Is this not the case?"

Riven curiously glanced over at the old elf thrall, and Luke blinked a couple of times to bring himself out of the stupor he'd been in.

"Sorry . . . Can you say that again?"

Riven frowned but repeated himself.

Luke thought for a bit, then shook his head. "You are correct in assuming that spellcasting needs intent. But for a ritual, they have none. Rituals are outside the realm of will and function on a more mechanical nature. An example of this would be an archer. The archer can initially direct the arrow by aiming it and imbuing it with power by drawing it back, but as soon as the arrow is loosed, it no longer contains the intent of the archer and can be manipulated by external forces like distance, wind, and gravity."

"You're essentially saying that this ritual was preset?"

"That's correct. All rituals are."

"Wouldn't that mean that they needed a predisclosed location to teleport to?"

"That would also be correct."

"I see." Riven's gaze shifted back to the black motes of mana he could feel in his mana field. He inspected every one of the sigils bit by bit, looking for the difference in mana signatures that would be a telltale sign.

And he found it.

One of the sigils had a mana signature that was older than the others'. Theoretically, this would be because the mana had been dispensed and cast at an earlier time than the newer signatures. When the opposite end of the ritual linked, some of that older mana would seep over to this side, depositing itself in a very small swap of space that was a signature requirement of his own Riftwalk. Prying the sigil open to expect it in more rigorous detail, Riven eventually grinned with a malicious sneer.

Perhaps Athela had been right. Perhaps he really was gifted with the magical arts after all.

"Get ready. I've found the way through."

Fay was utterly traumatized. Her wings had just been cut off and the stumps cauterized, and she let out another scream of agony as her back was branded with a hot iron amid the laughter of her new self-proclaimed owner.

"WAAAAAAAAHHHHHHHHHHH!!!"

As she struggled against the antidemon bindings, the left side of her face was slammed into the stone floor and pressed down.

Cackling, the robed blond man beside her continued to press the hot iron brand against her skin. His sweaty fingers pinched her cheek, and then began to pull that cheek back to expose her teeth like one would do a horse while she brayed. "This is great! You're a lot more responsive than all the others were! Oh, I do love my torture."

Fay didn't know what *others* this man was talking about, but she was in too much misery to ask as amid her choking sobs. "P-please, let me g-go!"

"HAAAAAA-HAHAHA!" The man crowed and repeatedly yanked her head back by the hair to slam her bruised face into the ground, causing her to grunt loudly with each impact—much to the irritation of the other three remaining cultists who'd escaped with him.

"UGH! UHH!! UGGGH!!"

Huffing, the old Japanese man, Kenji, folded his arms atop the table in the center of their underground hideout, where they were going over the loot. They'd been sorting through the stuff they'd taken off the two other Chalgathi participants in the cube—both of whom had each only had one artifact. But what they lacked in artifacts they had made up for in wealth, with tens of thousands of coins and some enchanted class-oriented gear for both archers and berserkers.

"Can you keep it down?" Kenji asked with a snarl, his posture rigid while he glared. "If you're going to continue playing with your new toy, take it out into the hallway so I don't have to hear it any longer. It's beginning to wear on my ears and this place is cramped."

"Agreed," the lone remaining woman cultist said from underneath a black cowl, watching with distaste as her accomplice manhandled the crying Succubus on the ground. "I've had enough of a show for one day."

The blond man glared back at them, yanking Fay's head back up by her white hair and standing, then beginning to drag her across the room. "You guys are buzzkills. Fine, I'll stop the torture. I was about to get to the good stuff anyways."

Kenji muttered under his breath, sharing a look with the woman across the table from him and then glancing over to where her minotaur was standing against the wall. "I truly dislike that man."

The woman nodded in agreement. "He was imprisoned before the integration set in—always talks about how many girls he buried and how he did it. I think he talks about it intentionally to make me uncomfortable, but I also believe every word he says. The things we've seen him do since we banded together have been very unpleasant to witness, even for me."

Kenji gave her a twisted smile, setting down one of the trinkets he was trying to inspect with a clink of metal. "Funny coming from you."

"Being a serial killer doesn't have anything to do with torture."

"Really now?"

"Yes. For me it is a compulsion, nothing more and nothing less. I kill because I need to. Do I enjoy it? Yes, but I do not take my time to draw it out. I am quick, methodical, and careful in my approach. Always have been—that's one of the reasons why I was never caught, like this imbecile."

Kenji furrowed his brows in thought, then nodded. "If he wasn't so skilled in spatial magics, I probably would have already killed him myself. I can do some of what he does, but not everything. Long-distance teleports are a lot harder to . . ."

He shifted in his seat, glancing over at the ritual area, where candles were still lit and the fourth cultist was kneeling in meditation. "Randin? Was that you?"

Randin, underneath another black cloak, was too engrossed in meditation to reply, head bowed and in a trance.

"Did you sense something?" the woman asked curiously, staring alongside Kenji with raised eyebrows. "I didn't—your Perception must be higher than mine. But if you did, it was like the spell Randin's working on. He continually experiments with the infernal arts and has even recently been trying to create an elemental from hellfire, believe it or not."

Kenji's frown did not leave his face. Standing up and ignoring the ruckus from the other side of the room, where the grunting Succubus had been taken, he walked over to the ritual circle and continued to stare.

There it was again. That very faint but distinctive aura of hungering dread, a cold, absolute desire to consume him ten thousand times over, an aura he'd only felt one time before.

Kenji's heart thudded in his chest, and he felt his blood run cold. Had he just imagined it? There were wards to seal this place off from outsiders both physically and through means of scrying. There was no—

There it was again. That brief flicker of black mana.

Somehow they'd been found. Somehow, the portal was being reopened.

How was that even possible?

Kenji took a slow step back. As calmly as he could, he put on a smile to ease the concerns of the woman at the table. "Ah, it was nothing after all. No need to worry, just Randin's experiments again."

Kenji's heart was hammering in his chest. He didn't have time to collect all his things, the artifacts, the money. His mind raced as he casually picked up his spatial sack with a fake yawn, beginning to put some of the artifacts inside—just enough for him. There was no reason to give the man further need to chase him, right?

No. He'd leave the other artifacts behind and just take a set for himself. Kenji hoped the vampire's attention would be diverted by his minion being abused on the other side of the room, and when he felt another pulse of that aura—stronger this time to his extremely high Perception—he began to move more swiftly.

"What are you doing?" the woman asked curiously and with a deep frown, crossing her arms along her chest. "Why are you putting those into a spatial sack?"

"Organization!" Kenji stated with a chuckle, trying not to sweat or shudder. "That's all! Just organization."

The woman across the table let out a short exhale through her nose. "You'd better not be trying to run off on us, Kenji. You know the deal—at least two of us get sets first to better our odds at the temple. We stick together, collect the pieces together, and work together until the end, where we will split the rewards. That's what we agreed on, and I won't hesitate to cut you down if you try anything."

Kenji only rolled his eyes, then hesitantly dropped the sack back onto the edge of the table. Aside from that idiot who was securing the succubus in tighter bindings near the corner, Kenji would be able to make the fastest getaway through the layers of bedrock overhead. That left at least two and perhaps even three of them to deal with the vampire when he forced his way through.

Those brief nudges had only been probing actions before, testing the veil they'd built here to prevent any riftwalkers from entering the hideout unannounced. But now they had something far more serious about to blast through, and Kenji's hands began to twitch—forming various motions as he muttered under his breath the chant needed to cast his teleportation spell.

It would be any moment now.

The cultist across the table from him became distracted for a moment when the Succubus they'd abducted began to sob even louder. "SHUT THAT DUMB BITCH UP! God! I'm so tired of hearing you two—"

Kenji felt the pulse and immediately teleported out, right after grabbing the sack as a blast of malicious hunger roared to life over the ritual circle's center. Then he teleported again, and again and again, before running out of mana and beginning to run as fast as he could from the terrifying presence he'd left miles behind.

Riven stepped through the black portal with Jackal in hand, streams of blood flowing all along the blade and shaft before burrowing into his own body as if the weapon was a part of his arm.

His footsteps seemed to echo as they touched down onto a stone floor, and time seemed to freeze as he took in his surroundings. A large minotaur to his right, a kneeling hooded man entranced in meditation directly in front of him, and a woman sitting with an expression of disbelieving shock at a round table in the middle of the room. A humanoid Cthulhu demon dressed in purple robes slowly rose from a sitting position on a dresser nearby, evaluating the turn of events with more curiosity than anything else—and then finally, to his left, he saw it.

Riven just stared, at a loss for words as the blond man standing near Fay with pliers in hand just gawked at him with mounting horror. Riven felt his facial muscles twitch with a flurry of emotions that were soon overcome by just one, and his aura blasted the room around them to flood the underground lair with a landslide of cold fury.

"We meet again so soon . . ."

Riven's body erupted with Blessing of the Crow—encompassing him in wisps of red speckled with black, and his armored foot kicked the meditating man straight in the jaw.

The man's head exploded from the impact, and his body was sent flying in a spray of blood.

The woman screamed in a panic, and both her minions moved to protect her—the minotaur charging with horns down and the Cthulhu man beginning to cast arcane spells of some kind that glowed a deep purple amid flourishing hand gestures.

Riven blurred, engaging with a stance Luke had taught him only two months ago, before cleaving right through the minotaur with a sidestep. Simultaneously, storm balls exploded from around him to crash into both the Cthulhu man and the woman, who'd begun to stagger back from the table.

All three were mutilated puddles of gore in seconds.

To his left, the blond man had tried to summon a portal to escape, but just as it began to open up, Riven's cold, gluttonous aura clamped down hard.

The portal only opened halfway, not nearly big enough for the cultist to run into, but he tried nevertheless. Screaming profanities and abandoning Fay entirely, he tried to force himself through the tiny rift without success.

Riven blipped forward, still clamping down and suppressing the other man's mana effortlessly. It was like an elephant stepping on a bumblebee when comparing the sheer quantities of power between the two casters, and Riven's armored gauntlet slammed onto the man's shoulder—yanking him out of the portal and flinging him like a comet into the opposite wall.

CRUNCH

The cultist screamed, the left side of his rib cage snapping like a series of twigs while his left shoulder and arm flattened against the stone. Bouncing off the wall with an obvious concussion, the man stumbled forward and began vomiting blood.

Only to be picked up and bodily slammed onto the large oak table face-first.

Conjuring needlelike black snares, Riven yanked the man's broken arm and fastened it to the thick wood. The cultist underneath him whimpered loudly and then screamed again with an unintelligible plea when Riven crushed his other wrist and fastened it to the table's opposite side.

Riven stared at the sobbing villain, hunkering down to a squatting position to be eye level with the broken, violently coughing cultist who was no doubt about to go into shock from blood loss. Yanking the target's chin up to look back at him, Riven snarled out the last words this man would ever hear. "Seems like you're dying too fast for me to keep my earlier promises on how you'd go, so this will have to do instead."

Smashing the man's bloodied face into the table again, Riven hoisted his spear up and came back around. Aiming directly for the man's backside, Riven drew back his weapon and speared the cultist directly through the rear.

The weapon easily cut all the way through the thick table's wood and into the stone floor below as the man shrieked like a hyena, but he was too weak to do anything other than lift his head in that garbled wail and tug weakly at the flesh-eating nets bindings his broken wrists to the wood.

Violently kicking the dying man for good measure, snapping one knee at a backward angle while the cultist went into shock, Riven ignored the various artifacts and expensive baubles around the room. He only cared for one thing.

And surprisingly, when he did pass the quest items by, the Chalgathi artifacts he wore detached themselves. They drifted off his body and floated over to intermix with the other set pieces—connecting with them and forming a chrysalis of mana that quickly created a ball of impenetrable, swirling multicolored light.

Riven continued in stride, his armor still mostly intact, and eventually came to settle down next to the weeping woman he'd come to know over the past months. Her eyes were swollen shut and her body was absolutely broken. Bruises covered her, a brand was burned into her right lower back, she was bleeding from numerous small cuts, and her wings had been cut off and cauterized.

He extended a hand, hesitating halfway to her when he heard her breathing pick up in fear.

". . . Ri . . . Riven . . . ?" Fay asked with a shaky voice, tears still dripping down her bruised sky-blue skin.

There was a long pause as he tried to figure out how to approach her. How could he face her like this? Would she hate him for not protecting her?

Tears welled up underneath his own eyes, and he nodded with a sniffle—but his voice remained strong. "Yeah. It's me. I'm so, so sorry—"

"WAAAAAAAAAAHHHHHHH!" Fay began to sob again as she almost threw herself off the bed trying to get to him—still hog-tied with metal chains and almost toppling onto the floor before he caught her.

She continued to bawl as he picked her up and held her, using strings of mana to get rid of the chains binding her, the antidemon metal snapping, crackling and popping as he angrily destroyed them with a lurch of mental power.

The chains dissolved, and she threw her trembling arms around him and buried her face in his chest, specifically in the pocket where the maw used to be, between the parts of metal breastplate that'd been modified for the amulet.

Azmoth and Luke had stepped through the portal as well, and they watched in silence as Fay cried, shook, and clung to Riven like a castaway holding on to a piece of driftwood.

Riven didn't know what to say, so he didn't say anything. Choking up and holding her tightly, he just let her sob for as long as she needed to—but motioned for Azmoth to bring over a healing potion in the meantime. Azmoth did as asked and set two of them down on the nightstand next to the small bed, then bent down with another motion from Riven.

"Take that man stapled to the table out into the hallway. Keep him on the edge of life and death with potions—make sure he feels pain," Riven whispered into Azmoth's ear, nodding to the cultist going into shock not far off as Fay sobbed loudly. "Don't worry if he dies accidentally—but I want his death to be drawn-out and agonizing."

Azmoth smiled wickedly, nodded, and then stepped away to pick the speared man and table alike. Carrying both out of the room and into an adjacent hallway with Luke to give Riven and Fay their privacy, he shut the door with a thud behind them.

Eventually, after many minutes, Fay calmed down somewhat, enough to whisper in a muffled croak, "You found me! I can't . . . I can't believe you found me . . ."

Her fingers curled around the back of his neck, and he took this moment of clarity to open her lips and pour a potion down her throat. After she drank the second one in quick succession, he saw her wounds slowly begin to heal.

"Yeah. I found you." Riven let out a wavering sigh of his own, settling down into a more comfortable position and knowing she wouldn't be letting go anytime soon. "I know that you're hurt, but things are going to be okay now. Take as much time as you need . . . and we'll talk when you're ready."

Still keeping her eyes closed, sniffling, and nodding with quivering lips, she curled into a ball beside him on the bed. Violently shaking, she stayed there for hours, neither of them saying a word, until she finally felt safe enough to let herself go. She passed out from sheer exhaustion after that, still clinging to Riven's body with a vise grip, and soon thereafter the traumatized Succubus's violent shaking slowed to a halt.

CHAPTER 49

Two days prior

It was her very first day of school, and Allie was excited.

Allie's living quarters were in one of many two-story barracks behind the arena—though she wouldn't have ever called this specific set of quarters a barracks herself, as the rooms were made for high-class lords and ladies of the court. She nevertheless was given one of the best available and was stationed on the top floor despite insisting to be treated like any other academy attendee.

Following Sherine—who was doing her best to act like it wasn't a struggle carrying Allie's five heavy books—she gave an amused smirk and stopped the handmaid. Taking them from her without saying a word, Allie bobbed her head for Sherine to continue leading.

"I'm—I'm sorry I'm so weak . . ." the girl stammered. She obviously was worried beyond what should be normal, and it showed, though Allie hadn't intentionally tried to make the girl feel worried.

The vampire—who now just looked like a very pale and extremely beautiful human girl—gave an encouraging smile and motioned for Sherine to lead on. "It isn't a problem at all. I'm naturally stronger—you shouldn't feel bothered at all."

After entering the Roman-style barracks building through a set of heavy double doors just like the ones she had walked through earlier to meet the archmage, Allie was immediately led up a spiral staircase to her front amid a lavish reception area filled with red velvet couches, paintings, and a card table. Carpeted hallways extended to her right and left with doors spaced out every twenty yards. Coming up the spiral staircase, she came immediately face-to-face with a door that had her own name inscribed on a golden nameplate in the system's generic language.

Sherine pushed her red locks to the side and fumbled with a key as she glanced up quickly. "Here, my lady, this is a copy of the key to your room. I will have the spare."

Allie took the long, delicate key and felt the cool brass against her skin. As the door opened and the maid shuffled to the side to let Allie through, a sweet aroma met her senses to match the decor.

It was a large, well-lit room with marble countertops and fine glass windows from ceiling to floor, with curtains opened wide for a view of the front walkways leading to the building. There was a door leading into the less splendid maid's quarters on her left and a built-in kitchen, too. Fine linens on a feather bed were laid out, velvet drapes hung from the ceiling around a king-size bed with a polished oak headboard.. The center of the room had a rectangular dining table, also of polished oak, big enough to fit eight people, with chairs to match.

"Mara will like this."

She walked over to a closet that slid open to reveal numerous sets of fine noble's clothes similar to those she had seen on the women in the classrooms. Frills, silk robes, dresses, and fur coats weren't her style, but she could certainly appreciate the quality of the finely made shirts and feminine pants that were in abundance in multiple colors. Vests along with well-made leather boots were also present, and she was quick to pick out a basic outfit and lay it on the bed.

Sherine was standing directly beside her, expectantly, and Allie looked down at the slightly shorter woman with a confused frown.

"Just give me a moment and I'll be ready."

The girl's eyebrows furrowed, and she nervously shuffled her feet. "You . . . don't want me to dress you?"

Allie's frown turned into a smirk when she began to chuckle. "No. I'm a grown adult. I can dress myself."

Again the girl seemed worried, but she nodded and stepped back. Minutes later Allie had finished changing, and she glanced at herself in the mirror— formfitting white shirt, blue vest, pants that clung to her skin, and high-top leather boots with heels.

She looked pretty good.

"Lady Wraithtide, you put your vest on upside down."

Allie paused and looked down. It appeared to be on correctly, at least in Allie's opinion. "Are you sure?"

"I'm certain."

Allie sighed, face-palmed, and took it off. She threw the vest onto the bed in irritation and picked up her five books next. "Okay. We can go now. What's my first class?"

"Are you not going to don something warmer?"

"I feel very little concerning the cold."

There was a pause, and the maid nodded after processing her words.

"Your first class for the day is already over, as morning classes start shortly after sunrise. Your second class is currently ongoing and will last another two hours. Here is a copy of your first-year schedule; I have it memorized, so feel free to keep this paper for your own knowledge. This said, the schedules are simple and you may choose which class to attend if they overlap. Sometimes they do, sometimes they don't. It depends on what the instructor decides to teach that day. Classes occur every day unless the instructor for that day decides to take time off."

YEAR 1 SCHEDULE:
Beginners' Magic Theory—Instructors, Kremsin Bots and Ori Orumi
- **Mornings**

Beginners' Battle Abilities 1: Applications of Magic, Miracles, and Martial Arts—
Instructors, Jaimest Vorvus and Thoi Jorsem
- **Afternoons**

Beginners' Battle Magic 2: Combined Warfare Tactics—Instructor, Mince Quarteple
- **Afternoons**

Combined Combat Class—Instructors, Nester Rose, Jokzofrie Belfast, and Jupis Astirith
- **Evenings**

Beginners' Healing and First Aid—Instructors, Nuthak Ororin and Jan Wetzle
- **Evenings**

Allie grimaced as she realized there was no organization to it. "When do we eat? And do we get any time off?"

To this, Sherine let on an amused smile. "You are the queen of the Thane Necropolis, my lady. You can do whatever you want."

"Yes, but that's not what I mean. Nobody knows I'm the queen except for you, the archmage Zefima, and the king. So pretend I'm not a queen and tell me like I'm a normal person."

Allie would be damned if she didn't get a true college experience out of this. It was all she'd ever wanted as a kid, and now that this opportunity had presented itself, she'd not be treated any differently.

Sherine opened her mouth to renounce the idea, but shifted uneasily upon Allie's intense gaze and nodded with a gulp. "You have time in between each class for meals; you'll be able to either eat in your private quarters or the academy's dining hall."

Sherine followed Allie out the door and locked the room behind them. Then she pocketed her own key and motioned for Allie to follow with a small bow, hands clasped in front of her. "As for time off, you'll be done with classes somewhere around an hour before sundown if you truly wish to keep the schedule. Most of the time each class is many hours long, taking up most of every day. You're free to do what you want with the time after classes and before you go to bed."

"What happens if we don't go to class?"

"You may attend class at your leisure, but if you fail any examination more than twice, you will be dismissed from the academy immediately. Or at least that's how it is for other people—not for you. For this reason, it is very rare for people to not attend class, as this school is very expensive. Even for nobility."

A beam of sunlight reflected off drifting snowflakes hit Allie full in the face and caused her to squint when she exited the building. Sighing to herself and bearing the light with a gritting of her teeth, she still couldn't help but feel excited and simultaneously nervous for the coming day.

Why was she, of all people, nervous?

She was a goddamned serial-killing bloodsucker mage badass!

Yet here she was, palms sweaty.

No spaghetti.

Allie gave an uneasy but unnaturally beautiful smile, tossing her brown hair to the side with a laugh. "Yeah . . . Well, let's go. I'm interested in seeing what this school has to offer me."

Unlike many of the other classes, which had been located in indoor amphitheaters, this one was actually outdoors, in the middle of a field with round tables set out at intervals and people occasionally lining up to practice casting spells. At the front of the class was a series of stacked shelves, boxes, and wardrobes, where a man enthusiastically lectured from a grimoire about the wonders of lightning when used in conjunction with water magic.

Allie was led across the snow-covered grasses, adding her boot prints to many others as the white field crunched underfoot. Oblivious to the cold, her hazel eyes scanned the class of perhaps forty or fifty people, not counting the servants who stood in wait.

However, as she followed Sherine closer and closer to the rows of tables and the lecturing old mage dressed in a burgundy robe, her classmates slowly began to focus on her. Eventually the lecturer noticed his students weren't paying attention to him anymore, and huffing in irritation, he homed in on the cause of the distraction while scratching his wrinkled chin.

Settling his eyes on Allie, the old man stopped and stared, eyes widening with mixed expressions flitting across his face.

But the old man was quick to recover from his apparent shock when Allie stopped in front of him beside her handmaid, Sherine, evaluating the staring, slack-jawed young men around her or the hatefully glaring young women.

"And who may you be?" Thoi Jorsem asked rather rudely when he'd finally gotten ahold of himself. The old mage was just starting to bald and was otherwise clean shaven, with a grimace that almost never left his face. "What makes you think barging in during my lecture would be tolerated? Why are you here? Surely you can see that I'm teaching my students. State your name, girl."

Allie's eyes silently shifted back to the old man as she stood with straight posture—all perceived nervousness gone. Instantly, the instructor was simultaneously overwhelmed by both her extreme beauty and a sense of eerie dread that he couldn't get a true hold on.

"Lady Allie Wraithtide. I'm of a noble house in the outlands. It is a pleasure to make your acquaintance."

Allie had known this would be the general reaction to her presence from strangers, which was why she recognized the conflicted signs immediately. According to Kathrine, it was a well-documented phenomenon among pure-blooded vampires when around humans—or even with the lesser vampires, to some extent.

But Sherine was quick to intercept the angry mage and handed him a sealed letter. "Master Thoi Jorsem, a letter from the archmage."

Thoi's eyebrows rose at the maid's words, and he ruffled his robes to glare at Allie again. "Funny accent you have, girl."

He took the letter, quickly unsealed it, and began to read. A look of surprise crossed the old man's face, and a minute passed as he reread the letter, and then he set down the parchment to quickly turn on Allie. "So she expects you to just walk in halfway through the year and be able to catch up to the others? What is Zefima thinking?! Ridiculous! I've never heard of something so stupid before! You're an ENTIRE SIX MONTHS behind them! Whose strings did you have to pull for me to put up with your horseshit?! I will have words with the head of your house for this!"

Allie was taken aback and recoiled slightly. "Listen . . . I don't know—"

"YOU LIKELY DON'T KNOW ANYTHING!" the old mage screamed, to the amusement and curiosity of many of the students. "DO YOU TRULY THINK YOU CAN KEEP UP?!"

Allie's features darkened, and with massive amounts of self-control, she quelled her rising aura with a vise grip. Quickly considering whether or not she should outright blast the man into hell right then and there, she closed her eyes, took in a deep breath, and calmed herself. "I don't know what I did to offend you, Teacher, but I do apologize for whatever mistake I made. If it appeases you, I'll just sit silently by and mind my own business while attending your classes."

Sherine was the only person there who knew Allie's true identity, and thus was the only one who'd gone absolutely rigid, with a pale-white face that almost matched Allie's own natural complexion. Stuttering a whisper of something unintelligible, she raised a hand to stop the mage before he did any real damage—but she was of a much lower caste than this old man and eventually got cold feet in her brief attempt.

Thoi sneered and crossed his arms, mimicking Allie's perfect posture and clasping his hands in front of himself like she was doing while holding her books. "Let you mind your own business? I am paid to teach you ingrates. Every one of you comes here with a big head, thinking that because Mommy and Daddy have money, you can get away with *murder*. Well, I have news for you, little girl! You're going to sit your ass down in the chair I assign you to and you're going to struggle like hell while trying to catch up! BECAUSE IT'S MY JOB TO TEACH YOU WHETHER I LIKE IT OR NOT!"

The wiry elderly man spun around and gathered some materials from a series of shelves at the front of the classroom. He walked back to the large desk at the front and placed it all on top of Allie's books. A series of vials and ingredients, none of which Allie was familiar with, were placed in a stone bowl, leaving her absolutely clueless.

"Which ability types do you have access to?" the old mage asked.

Allie frowned and shifted uncomfortably, side-eyeing the other students, who were whispering in low tones to one another and laughing quietly. "As in which pillars do I have an affinity for?"

"Yes, that."

Allie shook her head and then began to lie. If she was going to play the part of nobody important, she was going to play it well. "I haven't accepted any attribute for magic yet. I was hoping to do that when I get a feel for it and can decide which of the foundational pillars I like best. They're permanent, right?"

"DAMN IT, ZEFIMA!" Thoi screeched in rage as he shoved the ingredients over, off her books, onto the ground. The old man quivered in rage and was practically seething as he glared even harder at the stunning young woman in front of him. "IS THIS A BAD JOKE?! HOW AM I SUPPOSED TO WORK WITH YOU IF YOU HAVEN'T EVEN CHOSEN A SINGLE AFFINITY TO MASTER?! DO YOU EVEN HAVE A KNACK FOR MAGIC AT ALL?! WHAT ABOUT MIRACLES OR MARTIAL ARTS? I AM A GODS DAMNED MASTER OF OCEAN, STORM, AND VOLCANO AND WILL NOT WASTE MY TIME ON THE LIKES OF YOU!"

The mage spun around again in a rage now, to the open laughter of many of the onlookers, as he began to sort through his desk. Shortly afterward, he pulled out a glass cube and shoved it into Allie's hand. "If you don't get this cube to light up, I'm dismissing you from my class immediately. You'd better hope Daddy and Mommy thought this through when they assigned you to the academy. Without potential you're as good as dog shit and will be dismissed immediately, even if I have to go above the archmage to do it. Now, hold this cube and focus on it. Pour your soul energy into it like your very future here depends on it, girl. Because, believe me, it does."

Allie curiously turned the cube in her hands while Sherine glared hard at the ground with a gaunt look. Allie had to assume this item would indicate what affinities someone had. She was sure of it when she let tendrils of her mana feel the contraption, localizing certain spots that would churn out different colors based on what type of mana was naturally produced.

"FOCUS, GIRL! SHOW ME THAT YOU BELONG HERE!"

Rage boiled up inside her as the laughter of the onlookers became more pronounced and obvious. Why was this man such an asshole? Was he trying to piss Allie off or make her look like an idiot? She looked up, stared hard into the man's eyes, and gritted her teeth.

Should she do it?

Considering whether to let out an absolutely wrathful blast of death mana directly into the man's soul, Allie sighed and let the slight go. Pouring in just a teeny tiny bit of magic, she handed it over to the mage to inspect.

"Give it here," he instructed, brushing off snowflakes in irritation and while continuing to glare. He picked up the golf ball–size cube and set it on the table, muttering under his breath as the onlookers waited curiously for his assessment. "I'm going to assume you know how this works, girl. Say your prayers now, though I doubt they'll help you if you truly don't have the knack for it."

Allie just sighed, a bored expression painted across her visage, and waited.

The old man took it as a sign of resignation and sneered in disgust. "These goddamned nobles think they can send just any of their filthy children here to get—"

Thoi tapped the cube with his finger, and to his clear astonishment, it simply shattered, a wave of overwhelming death following immediately after. He gasped as the mana hit him, only a microfraction of an ounce of what Allie could really dish out, and stumbled forward to catch himself on the desk. Other students had gone wide-eyed at the display while Allie calmly looked on, and eventually the old man got ahold of himself and stood back up. Staring at the pieces of the shattered cube, he shook his head in disbelief. "These fucking things don't work like they used to. Hold on."

He turned around and quickly retrieved another cube.

The same thing happened a minute later.

And then again.

And again.

After the fourth time Thoi saw the cube shatter, he raised his eyes to Allie with both suspicion and curiosity. Muttering and low whispers enveloped them. "Are you . . . What are you doing to the cube, girl? Is this some sort of trick?"

Allie gave the older man an annoyed stare—her usual confidence and lack of empathy trickling into her words as her patience began to rapidly decay. "No, imbecile. Apparently your trinkets are nothing but garbage. At least the ones at the last school I attended worked."

Thoi sputtered something under his breath, not used to having students mouth off to him. "And WHERE is it that you attended, girl? If you haven't even chosen a pillar to follow, I find it hard to believe that you've—"

"Just give me a basic ritual from any of the affinities you or the students here witnessed and I'll recite it. You can see for yourself," Allie insisted with a shake of her head. She had had enough of this babbling fool and was very tempted to just head straight back to Brightsville to continue her own, much higher-level experiments while dabbling in the necromantic arts. "Stop wasting my time or I'll leave to find someone who can actually teach me something. I know for a fact that the most basic rituals will still react to people even if they don't have the attribute for a class acquired—as long as an affinity is present. Give me anything at a base level and I'll be able to perform it, and do it now."

A sneer crossed the mage's face. "Quite the arrogant bitch, aren't you? Fine. Repeat this one, brat. I'm no necromancer, but since there's an obvious death attunement in here somewhere, I'll give you one from the textbooks."

Allie's maid, Sherine, hid her face behind both hands and groaned in dismay.

The battle of wills was on. A parchment was set on the table, and the grumpy mage began writing furiously with a quill pen. The ink splotched twice with the man's sloppy handwriting, but Allie was still able to make it out easily enough.

"This is a base spell for conjuring soulflame, a common element used in low- and midtier battle necromancy. Go on, girl, show me that you're not just full of proud words." Thoi continued to sneer while Allie raised an eyebrow to glance down at the poorly worded ritual.

She looked back up. "You wrote it wrong."

"HA!" Thoi pointed and began to bark a deep, guttural laugh. "I THOUGHT SO! NOTHING BUT HAUGHTY ARROGANCE FROM THE LITTLE BITCH WHOSE PARENTS BOUGHT HER WAY IN! YOU CAN'T EVEN CAST THE MOST BASIC OF—"

His words caught in his throat when Allie's ritual spun runes of teal and black light in the air.

Swirling discs, one after the other, compounded on the original. The stack she'd made created the spell Thoi had drawn out for her in a bigger, better, and far more cinematic way that eventually resulted in a hovering ball of teal and black flames the size of a bowling ball.

It was essentially just a death ball, but a larger one stabilized in ritual form. It was a spell she'd mastered long, long ago.

Silence followed, and Allie could hear the mage's ragged breathing and see the shocked expressions of all the other students.

"You said you didn't have any affinities . . ." Thoi muttered, bewildered.

She condescendingly glared his way with a snort. "I lied. You not only drew the ritual wrong, which was either on purpose or you truly are an idiot, but you also didn't explain any of the fundamentals concerning basic spellcasting that would be needed even for a ritual like this. You purposely sabotaged me, thinking I didn't know about the initial intent requirement, even if rituals don't have a lasting intent later in the casting. Not only that, but you failed to mention vision, you didn't talk about any of the lock-and-key mechanisms, you failed to distinguish between any of the other affinities I had also incorporated into the cube, and you assumed that I'd mix them—resulting in a failure just by inherent lack of pillar separation. You are nothing but a miserable old man who is quickly nearing the end of his life in more ways than one—and I doubt I'll be back. It's very apparent that you're good for nothing but insults, and I don't have time for an old fool like you."

Then she turned heel to leave.

Turning over her words with a shocked expression, Thoi reached out a hand to clamp down on her shoulder. "You little witch! Did you just threaten me?!"

She stopped, glanced back at him, then gave an innocent smile. "You picked up on that? Good to know. Now remove your hand before I remove it for you."

The old man's mouth dropped open in disbelief, but he quickly removed his hand with a yelp when she sent a pulse of death energy through her shoulder that caused the top layers of his skin to quickly and painfully decay.

"But in the end, your drawn spell is most likely just a fraud. One made to make me look bad," Allie said confidently as the magic died down, staring coldly at the old man as he clutched at his hand. "Don't ever touch me again, Thoi Jorsem, or it'll be a lot more than the top layer of your hand that you lose next time."

Surprised mutters and whispers followed Allie out amid the embarrassed screeches and insults the old mage was flinging at her. But she didn't look back.

Her first day at school had not gone well.

CHAPTER 50

Present day

"Are you sure you don't want company? You haven't left your room since your first attempt," Mara stated with worry in her voice and furrowed brows. She looked like a schoolteacher with those glasses on. A lot more human and a lot less ghoulish, with brown hair and lavender eyes, thanks to another of the amulets the king had supplied for Allie and her subordinates. "I worry about you, Allie. It was bad when Riven left, but now it's even worse. Forget about that grouchy old man—if anything, just do what you always do and murder him."

Allie giggled slightly at the thought, finally giving her best friend a sideways grin from where she stood in the doorway to their shared room. Meanwhile Sherine, the handmaid, quietly brewed some tea in the kitchen.

"I just want some alone time," Allie replied with a brilliant smile, donning a slender fur coat and stuffing her hands into her pockets with a flip of her hair. A couple of young men a year above her whistled as they walked by, but she ignored them as Mara rolled her eyes, hard. "I'll be back in a bit. Talk to you soon."

She kept her head low while exiting the barracks dormitory. Snow crunched underfoot and flakes continued to fall from a gloom-ridden sky, with groups of students in their off time laughing to one another about various things on the sides of the road. There were even a few small coffee shops or cafeterias, which were social hubs of the campus. Despite what Sherine had said, a lot more students chose to take occasional days off despite the price of attending this academy.

Allie walked down the road for another hour, past the inner campus grounds and out into the miles of gardens. Flowers still peeked through the white in abundance, and large trees with looming, weighed-down branches cast shade along her path. She even saw two other girls her own age walking back the way she'd come from, and they exchanged polite smiles—but that was all.

She continued to walk until she came upon a bench overlooking one of the small ponds that wasn't completely covered in ice, where colorful fish drifted through crystal waters. It was a rather secluded spot, situated between gardens still running the length of the long, straight road in either direction, and knowing that she was finally and truly alone calmed her.

The old wood of the bench felt strong as she put all her weight on it and leaned back underneath the shade of a small tree. The breeze felt nice and cool on her skin. With only the occasional splash and churning of water, it was rather calming.

A spotted yellow fish jumped out of the water to catch some kind of ice-attuned insect gracefully in its mouth before landing with a splash, sending ripples across the pond. Allie put her chin in her hands, watched them radiate out to reach the shoreline, and took in a deep breath of the fresh air.

"Nice . . . isn't it?" a stranger's voice said from beside her. Allie looked up in surprise, not having heard a heartbeat, to see a scrawny young man in a wheelchair.

Her eyes narrowed at not having noticed him, but he looked harmless enough. If anything, it didn't look like he could harm someone even if he wanted to, and he wore a very innocent, sheepish smile while waving back at her with one good hand. His lower and upper left limbs were disfigured. Withered down into green-black husks of normal limbs, they looked like smoked meat—but he was able to clumsily manipulate them even if at great effort while adjusting his position in the wheelchair. He had soft blue eyes, curly brown hair, and looked rather boyish in the face despite obviously being a young man.

Allie cocked her head, intrigued. "How long have you been here?"

The young man gave a sheepish laugh, nervously tugging at his collar as her beauty and negative Charisma simultaneously afflicted him. "I've been watching you since you started walking down the road, over by the hill that way. Sorry if that's weird. You're just . . . very unique."

Allie leaned back on her bench, maintaining eye contact until the young man blushed and turned back to watching the pond in silence. They didn't say anything for a while after that, with the young man bashfully trying not to cast glances at her while she openly stared at him. Eventually he became very self-aware and tried to hide his shriveled limbs with a blanket.

Allie huffed after a bit, annoyed at finding nothing out of the ordinary about him other than the fact that his heartbeat was just oddly gone. "There's something strange about you."

The young man turned a bright red. Hanging his head low in shame, he silently turned his wheelchair around and started to attempt to push himself back toward the school grounds. "I'll see myself out. Sorry if I'm too hideous for you to look at."

"That's not what I meant," Allie stated with one raised eyebrow. "Don't jump to conclusions; I'm not talking about your arm and leg . . . It's something else. Do you have a bloodline of some sort?"

Pausing, still looking at the ground and not willing to meet her eyes, he grimaced in confusion. "I'm not sure what you mean."

Sighing and seeing that she'd obviously hurt this young man's feelings, probably having touched a sore spot concerning his looks and physical disabilities, Allie got up and walked over to him. Coming around to his front and standing in his path, she clicked her tongue. "Sorry. My name's Allie Wraithtide, what's yours?"

"Lahn Lucio," the man whispered, still staring at the ground.

. . .

. . .

. . .

"Are you just going to stare at my feet or what?"

Allie knelt down in front of the hesitant, shifting man and put a hand on one of his own—the shriveled one—and she forcefully pulled it so he'd look at her. Finally getting him to stare back, she put on her most genuine, sweetest smile. "Hey. I really am sorry. I didn't mean to come off like that. Can I make it up to you, Lahn?"

The young man's blush began to fade, and he stared at her in wonder—jaw becoming somewhat slack before he righted himself in his wheelchair and nodded awkwardly. "Um . . . Yeah, that'd be great, but you don't need to. I just . . ."

He trailed off, not knowing how to finish the sentence.

Allie grinned. "How about we just enjoy each other's company? It's obvious both of us have a lot of things on our minds. Tell you what . . . You tell me what's on your mind, and I'll tell you what's on mine. Is that a deal? We can work as each other's therapists."

Lahn hesitated, then glanced around—inspecting the area about them. "You're . . . this isn't some kind of prank again . . . Is it?"

"What are you talking about?" Allie asked curiously, still holding his shriveled hand between slender, pale fingers. "How would this be a prank?"

Lahn frowned slightly, then shrugged with a loud huff. "My brother and sister attend this academy, and they always have their friends do mean things to me for their own amusement. They call me names, tip my wheelchair over by 'accident,' steal my food . . . pretend to be my friend. That one is actually a favorite of theirs . . . so I'd very much appreciate it if you'd just leave me alone if this is a prank. But otherwise . . . yes, I could use someone to talk to."

Allie couldn't help but wonder what kind of siblings would do that to their own crippled brother. The shock must have shown on her face, because Lahn gave a loud, croaking laugh while shaking his head.

"It appears I'm already talking about it," Lahn said with a hopeless smile. He withdrew his shriveled hand from hers, then began to push himself back to the pond. Pausing halfway and bobbing his head toward the bench, he gave her a hopeful glance. "Do you want to join me, Lady Wraithtide? By the way, that's a very cool name. I wish mine was Wraithtide instead of Lucio."

When Allie stood up and returned to the bench to sit beside him, it must have caught Lahn off guard, though he tried to hide it as best he could, pulling out bread crumbs to throw at the fish.

Tossing one of the crumbs in and seeing it get snatched up, Lahn sighed. "Long story short, I don't feel like I belong here."

Allie snorted in amusement at that, then glanced over at him with a knowing look. "Yeah, I basically got in a fight with my instructor and was told to leave class two days ago. So I get it."

"Wait, that was you?!" Lahn gawked in obvious shock—and something close to admiration, if Allie was getting it right.

"Am I that famous?" Allie teased with a nudge.

Lahn only nodded avidly. "Yeah! It's the talk of the school! I'm in that class, but I was sick that day. I wish I would have been there to see it myself. Wait, we're classmates! The archmage is apparently furious, not at you but at the instructor, and he may even be sacked is what I heard. Don't know why—the instructors yell at and belittle students all the time, but apparently something about this is different than the rest. Who knows. Is that why you're upset?"

Allie opened her mouth to reply, slowly making patterns on the ground with the heel of her leather boot, then nodded. "Partly. I was really excited to come here, and now it feels like I don't belong . . . just like you, actually. That and I miss my brother."

"Where's your brother?"

"Home."

"Where's home?"

"The outlands."

"Ah." Lahn gave a sage nod. "I haven't been out there yet. I don't travel well . . . so I stick to the capital."

"Well, maybe you can show me around sometime, Mr. Native." Allie winked, taking Lahn's breath away, and giggled to herself when he nearly fell over in his chair. "Unless of course you think you're too popular for me. I understand if—"

"I'd love to!" Lahn said with delight, a little bit too excited for his own good—and another sheet of embarrassment fell over his features. He was obviously not very . . . self-confident. "Sorry . . . I just, honestly, I don't have many friends here."

Allie paused to consider this. After some time, she decided to believe that he was telling her the truth. "Well, I'd love to be your friend, Lahn. Maybe we can even sit together in class. I don't have many friends, either, so let's make a pact."

Allie threw out a pinkie for a pinkie promise, and Lahn curiously stared back at the hand she held in front of him before raising one eyebrow.

She laughed. "You're supposed to hook your finger around my own. It's called a pinkie promise, and this one is a promise that we'll be friends. That, and you've gotta show me to the best restaurant on campus. I've been dying to try them out and haven't had anyone to go with except Mara—and she's been busy with . . . administration stuff."

"Mara? Who's that? She works for the school?"

"Yes," Allie lied flatly. In reality, Mara was still running the Thane Necropolis from their shared bedroom using a laptop. "So how about it? Show me around?"

Lahn huffed, then beamed back at her and struggled to turn his withered body in the chair so he could hook his good fifth finger around her own. "It's a deal! When do you want to go?"

The pinkie promise was set, and Allie hummed as she let go and leaned back on the bench once more. Staring out across the gardens, she tilted her head back and forth. "How about now?"

[The Apocalypse Beasts, Chalgathi, Quest Updates:
- **Linda Hoffman has fallen in battle to Riven Thane.**
- **Birch Irkwood has fallen in battle to Riven Thane.**
- **Thade Trendinburg has been defeated in battle and captured by Riven Thane, with his Chalgathi artifact being taken from him.**
- **Riven Thane has acquired seven of five set pieces for Chalgathi's Inheritance. Redistribution has commenced: extra pieces have been redistributed to other newly appointed Chalgathi's chosen who do not have pieces. Riven Thane now has five of five set pieces.**
- **Riven Thane is the third person to acquire all five set pieces for Chalgathi's inheritance and the first noncultist to do so. Only two full sets remain to be claimed.**
- **New Chalgathi's chosen will be picked one hour from now as a replacement for Linda Hoffman and Birch Irkwood.]**

Allie's eyebrows rose in surprise at the abrupt notifications, and then her face widened into an outright smile of glee. She almost didn't hear Lahn's enthusiastic reply before he started wheeling himself down the garden path, but she managed to get up and walk alongside him at a leisurely pace while he excitedly huffed beside her. Moving the wheelchair out this far must have been quite a struggle for him, and she'd no doubt offer to help soon—but she needed to figure out just what the fuck was going on.

Damn it, why did her communication orbs not work at such a long range?!

And as if on cue, the universe came knocking at her door.

"By the way, what do you think about those forum posts with Riven Thane? Have you seen them yet?! Did you get a look at the world forums lately concerning the necropolis?" Lahn said, breaking Allie out of her stupor. "Other than your backtalk, it's been the talk of the school as well. People who orient themselves to the Unholy pillar are making crazy insights, just by watching his fight."

That definitely got her attention, and she nearly stumbled. "Huh?"

"The world forums just lit up again. Riven Thane—the king of the Thane Necropolis to our north—just wasted hundreds of thousands of people to save one of his demons. It's really scary to watch, kind of evil, even, but it's also kind of romantic. He must really care about that Athela person, or maybe he just doesn't value human life. Could be either."

Lahn hesitated, seemingly not sure whether or not he was boring her with the lack of reply, but then became outwardly more confident when he'd realized it'd drawn in Allie's attention like a magnet as she frantically scrolled through the feeds but then became a lot more confident when he realized it'd drawn in Allie's attention like a magnet and she was frantically scrolling through the feeds. "You haven't seen it yet, then?"

Allie didn't reply at first; she was too busy blowing through the world forums to find whatever it was Lahn was talking about—until she found it.

Video footage of Riven demolishing an entire city, and the events that'd led up to it.

It lasted over twenty minutes, with Allie and Lahn just standing entranced in the middle of the garden path. Occasionally Lahn would comment on the fight, but Allie kept silent. She felt a mixture of conflicting emotions about the entire thing, which would give her brother an even higher level of power than he'd had prior to the destruction of the city of canyons.

She closed the video footage and notifications, only to scroll back over to the world rankings again. Still somewhat disbelieving, she stared at the top ten list for quite a while. Whatever Riven had done concerning his core, and along with all the levels he'd acquired from massacring an entire city of weaklings, it'd shot him up from the sixties right to the top ten list. He was now considered an Apex ranker at power spot number five worldwide—and he'd somehow acquired a second class. The only other person on the list who had more than one class was Chitter Teh-Sneaker, a level-120 rat man who actually had three total classes.

[Twenty-seven billion current participants have been analyzed. The ranking categories are as follows: Apex rank (top 10), Paragon rank (top 1,000), S rank (top 0.0001%), A rank (top 1%), B rank (top 15%), C rank (top 30%), D rank (top 50%), E rank (Bottom 50%)]

[Current Top 10 Native Participants:
1. Judith Marcina, Level 149 Human, Apex rank, Angelic Fallcaller
2. Retesh Vorath, Level 170 Corpse Lord, Apex rank, Elder Lich
3. Aren Hrall, Level 141 Snow Giant, Apex rank, Frostmange Berserker
4. Chitter Teh-Sneaker, Level 120 Rat Man, Apex rank, Dark-Blade Assassin, Poison Master, Sneaky Sneak Sneaker
5. Riven Thane, Level 112 Pure-Blooded Vampire, Apex rank, Warlock Adept, Harbinger of Gluttony
6. Thorman Bame, Level 134 Human, Apex rank, Hammer of the Mountain
7. Sinthil Tuk'tuk, Level 136 Lizardian, Apex rank, Wind Storm
8. Nithkik Brutishvase, Level 105 Dark Elf, Apex rank, Depthdweller
9. Brock Longbeard, Level 105 Sundering Dwarf, Battlemaster
10. Cherish Lightcrown, Level 104 High Elf, Everlight Witch
Your Status: Allie Thane, Level 68 Pure-Blooded Vampire, Middle S rank, Swarm Necromancer Adept
Guild rankings currently not available. Guild functions are currently frozen.]

She could only wonder at what updated notifications Riven had obtained concerning Chalgathi's quest line. Allie had zero doubt he'd had updates about it, but he hadn't returned yet and she wasn't sure if he would, depending on what those quest notifications would say. She only hoped that she'd get to see him soon and wondered whether or not she'd be needed.

But maybe he really was going to come back home!

She could only hope.

Smiling giddily to herself and feeling a weight lifted off her shoulders, she let out a long sigh and got behind Lahn's wheelchair. Slowly walking forward and pushing him along, Allie got a startled look from the man ahead of her.

"You don't have to push me! I'm strong enough to do it myself!" Lahn protested with a growl. "Come on, you're embarrassing me! If my siblings see me being pushed around by a pretty girl like you, they're going to give me absolute hell—in a bad way. They'd tell Father about how much of a lacking man I am because . . . well, it just wouldn't be good. And why do you seem so happy all of a sudden?"

Allie just hummed to herself and smiled back at the man, who was shooting worried glances toward the campus grounds. "Don't worry about it. I'll let you take over the wheelchair again when we get closer—just let me help. And as for why I feel so happy all of a sudden? Let's just say . . . I didn't realize things were going so well. Not until just now."

ABOUT THE AUTHOR

Ranyhin1 is the pen name of Trent Boehm, author of Elysium's Multiverse, an apocalypse LitRPG he originally released on Royal Road. A lifelong lover of fantasy, Boehm is also a science nerd, Dallas Cowboys fan, and wannabe gym rat. He hopes one day to pursue writing full-time.

DISCOVER
STORIES UNBOUND

PodiumAudio.com